The Donkey's Millstone

Olgivy Stent

NIMAN'S WAY DIST., LLC

For my Aunt Lois

who always encouraged me to write

and for my Dad who gave me the genetic code to dream.

THE WARM UP

"Clarence, there's another one dead."

"Well, get rid of it."

"How?"

"Where you get rid of the garbage, stupid."

"You shouldn't call me that, Clarence. I work for Boss, too."

"Just get rid of it."

Jiggy picked up the small form; washed, dressed, then swaddled in a thin sheet.

"Don't know why you bitches do all this when a plastic bag's all you need."

He leered at the girl sitting in the corner working a needle back and forth along the edge of a rag.

He put the bundle in the trunk of the red car and drove away from the cabin. After several miles of winding roads, he impulsively changed direction. He was ordered to never go into the village but Waybird City was too far. In Deacon's Hollar he could score lunch. Clarence would never know. It was a long walk to dump the package, and the fat man needed food.

****

"Will that be everything, sir?" She smiled behind lenses thick as the bottom of glass soda bottles.

"Yes, thank you."

Jiggy paid in cash. He grabbed the bag and pulled out the first of three roast beef sandwiches before he got to the door.

Squeezing between the steering wheel and the seat wasn't easy but he made it. He didn't feel the gun dislodge from the waistband of his pants and tuck securely in the crease, not of his butt, but of the backrest and the seat.

Jiggy knew he should take the package deep into the woods, but after the rain, he couldn't make it over the soggy ground to the cliff edge. He would just dump it where he did the rest, catch his breath, and leave.

He grabbed the object, careful to keep the face covered, and tossed the bundle into the brush. The trail seemed harder to traverse than the last time he dumped trash. The soft boggish earth was hesitant to let go of his shoes–the muck pulled at his pant legs.

It startled him to see three white dogs blocking him so close to the car.

"Hey, there puppy, puppy, puppy." The first one growled at him. The other two stared, their eyes narrowing in the waning light.

"Oh, so you want a fight, eh?" Jiggy grabbed for the gun at the back of his pants. It wasn't there. He saw a thick branch on the ground. When he stood, brandishing his pointy weapon, the dogs were gone.

"Yeah, like I thought. Somebody's sissy pets."

A pale blue fog drifted from between the trees, thickening as it enveloped him. A figure leapt from behind, planting its paws in the center of his back and knocking him off balance. The side mirror broke in his hand as he struggled to stay on his feet.

"Damn stinking dogs. To hell with them stinking dogs," he said as he tried to stand.

He heard himself scream as the first set of teeth ripped the flesh from his leg, through to the calf muscle and down to the bone marrow. There would be no second cry for help.

In moments his vocal cords were torn from his throat and tossed among the stones. Food for the night creatures.

Copyright © 2023 by Olgivy Stent

P.O. Box 888, Coldwater, MI 49036

All rights reserved.

Library of Congress TXu 2-360-470 2/6/2023

ISBN 979-8-218-17409-5

No portion of this book may be reproduced in any form without written permission from the publisher or author, except as permitted by U.S. copyright law.

This is a work of fiction. Not a single word generated by AI. Any resemblance to any person living or dead is purely coincidental. No sensitivity editor was harmed in the writing of this novel because it wasn't written for pussies. Any and all mistakes in this manuscript are totally those of the author, who deeply apologizes for the flaws.

As It Happens

Preface

"And whoever misleads one of these little ones who believe in me,
it would be better for him that a donkey's millstone were hanged around his neck
and he be sunk in the depths of the Jordan." Matt. 18:6

"See to it that you do not despise one of these little ones: for I say to you,
their angels always see the face of my Father in heaven." Matt 18:10

The Lunch Crowd

"Well, Barbara Walker, will you take the job?"

"I'd love to, Gracie. It's my chance to start over."

"You did real well this mornin'. That's why I'm makin' you the offer of the job. Great things are comin' to the Hollar."

"I'll be glad to be part of it." Barbara smiled across the table at her new boss.

"My, you have such pretty eyes, Barbara. Do you like Barbara, Babs, Barbs, Barbette or what do you wanna be called?" Gracie patted her French twist updo at the back of her head.

"Barbara's fine. Your nails look real nice, Gracie."

"Thanks, honey. Francine did them and my hair before I came in. If you need a good hairdresser, Francine will do you just fine."

Gracie sipped her coffee. "Got any questions for me?"

"No, don't think so. I've got the basics from other jobs I've had. I'll learn where things are as I go along."

"Good. Take a menu home with you after shift an' study it. That'll help you when you take orders on your own. But, sugar, don't study it too hard because with the remodelin', it'll all change."

"You're going to remodel?"

"Oh, baby girl, you bet. I've worked with the village council for three years to get federal grant money. The whole main street'll have sewers and gutters, new facin' for some of the stores, an' there'll be loan money to renovate some of the businesses. Mine included."

"Are you going to have a theme for the diner?"

"Theme?"

"Yes, like Western, Mexican, Country."

"No, not really. Now, we'll have somethin' for everyone but since we're a West Virginia business, I'm featurin' local dishes. If you've got a favorite recipe, we can test it out, and maybe add it. Stuff like that makes our menu different, sure does."

Gracie watched Guy Bennett carry a tub of dirty dished from the counter into the back kitchen.

"Don't be droppin' that tub, Guy. Dishes cost money. That's right, honey, I'm watchin'."

Turning back to Barbara, Gracie said, "I want everyone to feel welcome here. I've a large room off the back hall, but I want it modernized as a banquet room for gatherin's, meetin's, receptions, an' that kind of thing."

Barbara checked her apron pockets for change.

"What you lookin' for, sweetie?"

"I thought I'd buy lunch before things get too busy."

"Oh, put that away, Bridgette. Want grilled cheese an' tomato soup? On me? I mean if I can't buy my staff a little lunch, what kind of employer am I? Just a sec. I'll get it be right back."

"It's Barbara."

"Okay. I'll remember. Be right back, Babs."

Barbara smiled. She read while she waited for Gracie to bring the soup and sandwiches. "Today's special is Seafood Platter. Lobster tail and specially import-ed deep fried butterfly shrimp, presented on a bed of fresh lettuce, with cocktail sauce, clarified butter, grilled asparagus beside an ear of corn on the cob. Comes with hush puppies, side salad, and one beverage."

Gracie returned with sandwiches and two bowls of tomato soup garnished with a pat of butter and a small sprig of parsley.

"Thanks, Gracie. It smells delicious."

"You're welcome, Beryl. I'm glad you put in your application. I need to get everyone trained an' ready for the grand openin' after the remodel."

Grinning, Barbara asked, "How long have you had the diner, Gracie?"

"Well, honey, my Daddy an' me worked it after Momma died, so him an' me ran it all through my high school. He told me, he said, 'Gracie, someday this'll be all yours.' Unha, he sure did. Dropped dead right in the parkin' lot two weeks after I graduated high school. Yep, right out there, just under the sign. I was eighteen years old an' alone."

Barbara stopped eating. "Oh, I'm so sorry. That must've been terrible for you."

"Well, not only me, it was a shock for the whole community. The diner was a meetin' place for Deacon's Hollar. But, and bless their hearts, the folks who supported Daddy turned right around an' helped me. Aunt Gem helped with taxes, paperwork, an' Daddy's estate. Birdie Spry started cookin' up a storm an' kept me supplied with breads, rolls, pies, an' cakes.

"After Daddy's services, I was determined I was goin' to reopen. I was workin' in here til midnight an' beyond every night. The Morris brothers found me tryin' to paint the bathrooms by myself so they just up an' took over. They worked for food cuz I didn't have the money to pay them."

"That was so kind."

"They wasn't the only ones. When the opportunity came around to talk about the federal fundin' for small community empowerment, I went to Waybird City to get the particulars an' organized a committee here in the Hollar. Deputy Johnson served on the board, Justine Lemon, Mr. an' Mrs. Cunningham, an' a bunch more got all the paperwork in on time. We got approved."

"This is exciting, Gracie. I'm grateful you want me to work here. I was hoping as much. I already rented an apartment and Mr. Crawford fixed my car at a price I could afford."

"Mr. Crawford? Oh, Bowtie. Nice man. He keeps the sheriff's cars runnin', same with the school bus an' the county trucks. Bea, you can always count on Bowtie to take care of things."

"He gave me a great deal on the muffler when I said I was trying to get a job with you. Your name opens a lot of doors."

"Well, I treat my staff as family cuz I don't have really any of my own. My Momma's folks are down in Georgia, but they considered her a traitor when she married my daddy an' moved to West Virginia."

"Really? I thought Civil War stuff was old history."

"Oh, hell no. Not with my Momma's folks. Oh, no. I stopped goin' down there to visit because they bring up the Battle of Droop Mountain every dang time, like we was goin' to fight that all over again but with the Confederates winnin'."

"So, I take it they lost?"

"The Confederacy? Didn't they teach you that in school?"

"I know that, Gracie. I mean Droop Mountain." Barbara laughed.

"Yes, they did. It was the final straw an' the Confederates got thrown out of West Virginia. Bloody battle, but West Virginia wasn't going to be a slave state. But I'll tell you what, there's folks around there who say they can hear the thunder of horse hooves and men cryin' in the night. Even to this day."

"You're joking, right?"

"Oh, no I'm not. All these mountains have stories to tell. You stay around here long enough and you'll learn for every wrong, there's retribution. Sometimes you gotta pay what's owed." Gracie brought a spoonful of soup to her lips.

"Better blow on that, darlin'. It's hot. But, anyway, better thoughts. Are you settled in your apartment?"

Barbara had just taken a bite out of her grilled cheese when Tilly bridged the silence with a delivery receipt to sign.

"Gracie, this is for the last of the lobster and shrimp. Just waiting for a check."

"Excuse me, honey. I've got to take care of this. Tilly, want to finish my sandwich? I didn't touch the other half."

"Nope. I've got one in the hot box for later."

"Suit yourself." Gracie took the rest of her sandwich and left for her office.

"Tilly, help me with the lunch time seating?"

"Sure. Finish your soup while I take care of the delivery and I'll meet you at the front desk."

****

Tilly spread the seating diagram along the counter.

"I know meeting all these customers the first time will be a little confusing, Barbara, but just hang in there. Don't get rattled with all the new faces. Amy and me will help you.

"This is how it's laid out and after you know that, you learn the people, too. The tables are "tops." A four top seats four, a two top seats two. But if we get a crowd, we can push tables together along the back. Had a group of eighteen once and that's how we did it.

"Learn the rows: stools are A1-10, two tops are B1-6, center rows are C1-12, and the booths are D row. Every seat closest to the cash register is number one. Count front to back."

"Are the booths numbered the same?" Barbara munched on the crust of her sandwich.

"Yep. Booths are D1-9 along the window. Seat the skinny people in number five because it's so much smaller. When Gracie's daddy laid out the booths, he didn't measure right so D-4's bigger. Four is Sheriff Harris and the crowd of mutts he brings in."

"He brings dogs?"

"No, it's just what I call them. It's folks from out of town like visiting sheriffs, attorneys, folks from the state. We put them there cuz of the room for their legs."

"I get it."

"Sheriff likes to keep an eye on the parking lot, too. We put Justine Lemon and her boy, Dodger, across from Sheriff Harris if they come for Friday lunch. Then John Seven Star and Running Deer like that center at the back. John's tall and can stretch his legs out better. Robby and Bobby Morris usually sit along the wall. If the Perkins come in, they go to the last four top cuz they got little kids still. Those are about the regulars but most folks will just sit where you tell them when we're busy."

"It's like assigned seating in school?" Barbara grinned.

"No, just that they like to sit in those spots if no one else is. There should be plenty of the locals coming in for the special. Once the tourist season starts after the remodel, the place will be hopping with customers. Bring in some big tips for us girls."

"Tilly, do we split our tips with the busboys?"

"Nope. The guys do other work for Gracie when she needs it so they get a bonus, and that covers them bussing tables so we keep our tips. Okay? Are you straight with it?"

"Straight like a plate of spaghetti. If I think of anything else..."

"You just ask me or Gracie. Amy's new also but she's been here about a month. She knows plenty and she'll help you out. We all will."

"Guess I'd better wash my hands. The lunch crowd will be here."
****

At 11:15 am, the customers started drifting in. Barbara brought Sheriff Harris, Hector Cobb, Dr. Andy Glassman, and Deputy Johnson to the fourth booth by the window. When John Seven Star and Running Deer arrived, she had their table set and ready for them. By eleven thirty, Justine Lemon and Dodger arrived, seated at C-3. Barbara looked over the room. It was good.

"You're doing great, Barbara," Tilly whispered. "We'll let them settle and then take the orders. I bet you they'll go for the seafood platter. Easy ordering today." Tilly winked as she took a tray of glasses for the tables. Amy followed with a pitcher of water to fill them.

"I think I'm going to like it here."

Barbara smiled at the next couple to arrive.
****

Tilly took out her order pad and pen, while Amy finished filling the water glasses.

"Hey, Sheriff, Dr. Glassman. How are you, Hector? Deputy Johnson. Need menus?"

"Not for me. I'm here for the seafood special. Guys?" Sheriff Harris got the affirmative he wanted from the men at the table. "Tilly, we'll need coffee all around."

"Is this on one or separate?"

"I guess it's on me since I asked these fine men to join me for lunch."

Now, Bill," Hector Cobb drawled, "let's celebrate."

"Hector, I ran unopposed."

"But you still won? Right?"

Dr. Glassman laughed.

Deputy Johnson checked his wallet. "I'll split it with you, Sheriff, just as long as Hector doesn't go for dessert."

"I got this, guys. Put it on mine, Tilly."

"Okay, Sheriff. Will be right back with the coffee."

Deputy Johnson looked beyond Hector and said softly, "Hector, here's Justine."

Hector slid out of the booth and stood, turning toward Justine Lemon and her son.

"Here, Mrs. Lemon, let me get that chair for you."

"Thank you, Hector. So nice to see manners still in the Hollar."

"There you go. Here, Dodger."

"Say, I meant to ask you how Alice is doing in college?" Justine placed her purse on the empty chair beside her.

"Fine. She studies a lot. Got her first grades. Done good."

"And the dogs? Dotty? She must be around ten years old, isn't she?"

"Yes, Dotty's good, too. All the dogs are good, Mrs. Lemon. Thinking about another litter of puppies soon."

"Well, if you get a beautiful female, you can name her 'Justine.'"

"That's a fine name, Mrs. Lemon. I'll do that. Enjoy your meal."

As Hector returned to his seat, Mrs. Lemon waved at Sheriff Harris.
****

Barbara tapped Tilly's shoulder. "Should I have pulled the chair out for Mrs. Lemon?"

"No, not with Hector and the other men here. They always do that for her. She's been around the Hollar forever. I think she taught Hector or Sheriff Harris when they were in school."

"What about her son, Dodger? What's wrong with him?"

"I don't know all the particulars but when he was a kid he was out riding his bike and somehow fell into a gully. Took days to locate him. Everyone from the Hollar was out looking. I think one of Hector's dogs found him finally. He was pretty beat up. Was never the same. Mrs. Lemon schooled him at home."

Tilly looked at the door. "Here's the Morris brothers. Yep, you got their table open. Have at it, girl."
****

Gracie watched the diner fill with customers. Her waitresses bustled in the dining room taking orders and delivering meals. The kitchen kept up with the meal tickets. She grabbed two menus to usher Howard and Elsie Perkins to the last four top in the center row.

"By yourselves today? Where're the boys?"

Mr. Perkins hung Elsie's jacket on the rack by the door as Elsie adjusted the waistband of her skirt.

"Howard left the twins chopping wood, Tater is grounded for today, and Luke doesn't have vacation until later."

"And where's my sugar girl?"

From behind Howard appeared a redheaded four year old. "Here's me, Miss Gracie!"

"And don't you look pretty." Gracie scooped the child up in her arms and planted a lipstick kiss on Magdelyn's cheek. "Pretty as a spring blossom on an apple tree."

"I got a kiss on my cheek, Daddy?"

"Yes, you do. Just like Gracie's." Howard took his daughter out of Gracie's arms so they could proceed to their table.

Gracie placed menus on the table along with a coloring book and crayons at the bumper seat.

"Good to see you again. Enjoy your meals." Gracie left but not before she kissed Maggie's opposite cheek. More customers were coming in.
****

"Andy, that's Howard and Elsie Perkins with little Maggie," Hector whispered. "They've got twins, Nathan and Tobias. The youngest boy is..." Hector looked at Deputy Johnson for help.

"Tater. Youngest boy is Tater." Donald filled in the blank as he bit into a shrimp.

"Yeah, thanks. Luke is the oldest one and sells cars in Virginia I think. Good kids, all of them."

Sheriff Harris corrected the narrative. "He's a researcher at the Library of Congress in D.C. He doesn't sell cars, Hector. Who told you that?"

"I don't remember. But, dang, I guess I don't have an in to get a new truck."

Deputy Johnson waved at a figure at the cash register. "Here's Bowtie. Must have heard about the lobster."

The man with shaggy hair wearing a grease stained denim jacket with a faded illegible motorcycle patch on the back, stood quietly waiting for his takeout order. His blue jean work pants were ragged. The left hip pocket was hanging; the seam of the it failed long ago.

Dr. Glassman couldn't see the man's face so he asked, "Who's that?"

"Bowtie Crawford, Agnes' brother-in-law. Agnes is sitting over in that back corner with her boy, Fishbone, and new live-in, Walter Venter."

"But why do they..." Before Dr. Glassman could articulate the question, the man turned toward the dining room, wearing a perfectly knotted bowtie at the collar of his blue work shirt.

"Well, I guess that answers that."

"You'll get the hang of it, Andy," Sheriff Harris assured him.
****

Bowtie scanned the dining room. He nodded at Deputy Johnson, but broke out into a big grin when a young boy ran across the dining room and leapt into his waiting arms. "Uncle Bowtie, I miss you."

"I miss you, too. How's my buddy? You're getting big. Those long legs of yours'll make you as tall as me some day."

"I got lobster and shrimp."

"Shrimp, eh?" Bowtie ran his fingers just under Fishbone's arm and tickled his ribs. "Yep, I can feel one right there...oh, over here's a lobster. Better chew your food better, boy." His smile faded when he saw Agnes, her head down, sitting beside Walter Venter.

"You get over to your Ma. It's your job to protect her."

"When're you coming over, Uncle Bowtie? We could go fishing."

Still staring at Venter, Bowtie said, "Soon, buddy. We'll go fishing soon."

Fishbone kissed his uncle's scratchy unshaven cheek, then wiggled down to the floor and ran back to the table with his mother.

Walter scowled. He grabbed the boy's arm, shaking it.

"You were not excused..." Venter stopped when he looked at Sheriff Bill. Fishbone ignored Walter by scrambling into the chair and eating a hushpuppy.

Sheriff Harris waved Bowtie over to the table. "Bowtie, good to see you."

"Yep, Sheriff."

"You know Donald and Hector, but I want you to meet Andy Glassman. He's built a clinic in the Hollar. Urgent care for us folks and a veterinary clinic for the other wildlife we have here." Harris looked at Venter.

"I heard. Nice to meet you, Dr. Glassman."

"Just call me Andy."

"Okay, Andy. Hector, Donald, nice to see you. How'd the fish turn out?"

"Real good." Hector said.

Bowtie adjusted his collar. He stared out the window for just a second but Dr. Glassman detected a hint of sadness on his face, the look Andy had seen on the faces of soldiers in the 'Stan.

"How's everything up on the mountain, Bowtie? Got that overgrown road cleaned up? I might want to send Deputy Johnson that way on patrol one of these days and get him out of my chair in the office."

Deputy Johnson snickered.

"It's good, Sheriff, maybe in a month or so. While I've got you here, I thought to tell you I had some trouble with feral hogs. There's a herd came up the mountain higher than I've seen before. Shot a couple thinking I could scare them away."

Bill folded his napkin and tucked it under the edge of his plate. "I don't see a problem. If they're up there causing havoc, and you get a couple tender ones, just invite me for the stuffed chops. Better yet, if you get a big one, we'll see if we can get Gracie to put on a hog roast for the village. I know a guy in Waybird City with a roaster."

"You don't care it's out of season?"

"Out of season to hunt, but you're not hunting. You're defending your homestead. Sounds constitutional to me." Bill grinned.

"Okay, Sheriff. Just thought I'd let you know."

Bowtie turned when Tilly said his name.

"Looks like my order's ready. I'd better get going. Gentlemen." Bowtie gave the customary nod of his head to the group and a curl of his lip to Walter Venter.

"See you, Uncle Bowtie." Fishbone waved goodbye.

"Remember what I told you, boy."
****

Glassman drank the last of his water and watched Bowtie leave the diner. "Think he'll come to the clinic?"

Hector dropped his fork on the carpet and on the way up from retrieving it, said, "He will. Got high blood pressure so he'll come to get it checked out. Won't come with a dog. Don't like them. He went with me to Waybird City. Sat in the front seat with a pup of mine. Bowtie just about come out of his skin when the dog got a little drool on his pant leg. All that grease under his nails but a little drool gave him fits."

Bill lowered his voice before he spoke.

"Crawford's lived at the north end of the mountain, sort of reclusive, but both the boys did well in school. He and his brother came out of the Hollar and made the big time. Bowtie went off to college and studied finance. His brother, Arthur, or Art as we called him, was a businessman in Detroit. That's where Art met Agnes.

"Things were going pretty well. The first son, Joseph, was born in Michigan. Right after Art died, she found out she was pregnant with the youngest boy. Agnes moves back to the Crawford homestead. Fishbone was born here, but Joseph took off shortly after. Haven't see hide nor hair of him in five, six years maybe."

"What did Arthur die of, if you don't mind me asking," Andy said.

"The reports called it suicide, but I think a broken heart would be more accurate." Bill glanced at Hector. They both knew the story.

"I've never seen that on an autopsy report," Glassman said.

"Bowtie was a hedge fund manager on Wall Street. He shorted stock driving companies into the ground, then reaped the profits. What he didn't know was that one of those companies belonged to his brother." Bill rolled the toothpick from one side of his mouth to the other.

"When the dust settled and Bowtie found out the damages, it was too late. Art hung himself in the garage."

"So what's a Wall Street hedge fund manager doing in the Hollar as a grease monkey in a garage?"

Hector was quiet as Amy made her rounds pouring more coffee, but spoke when she left.

"Well, I heard he threw bunches of money toward charities trying to do some good. Guilt maybe. Their daddy was good with vehicles and Bowtie inherited the shop. With the old stuff we have around here, he fixes all our cars and trucks."

Deputy Johnson ran a hushpuppy around the bottom of the clarified butter dish, capturing every last drop of the golden liquid. "He keeps an eye on Agnes and her son. Hasn't been easy with all the boyfriends hanging around. That's all I'm saying on that."

Glassman looked at Hector. "My truck isn't all that old, but I'll need oil changes and tires. I'm done scraping my knuckles."

"Yeah, he'll do that, Andy. But you need to call ahead because he might be out with the tow truck. He's come out and gotten me more than once," Hector said. "You can get ahold of him by CB radio in a pinch."

"What's his handle?"

"Er,...Bowtie."

"Okay, makes sense."

Bill smiled. "You'll get the hang of it, Andy."

****

Gracie stopped at John Seven Star's table.

"How'd ya'll like the seafood platter?"

"Great, Gracie. Best I've had since I was out in California. My compliments to the cook." John dipped a shrimp in sauce.

"I like the hushpuppies," Running Deer said. "They have a little bite to them that's interesting. What's the secret?"

"Honey, I had the cook add just a dash of jalapeno juice, just a little bit, to the whole batch of batter. Don't want to burn the skin off anyone's tongue, but I think it adds somethin' different. Like you said, interestin'."

"Nice touch, Gracie. I'm impressed. I look forward to having this again."

John looked at Gracie and smiled. "Now, what do you think, Gracie? If a beautiful woman like my wife wants to come back for lobster, how am I going to tell her no?"

"You won't, that's for sure. Say, how's Sam and Spencer? I was goin' to call you about them."

"Still at Walter Reed. Spencer is yet in a wheelchair. The doctors said they would bring Sam out of the coma in a few weeks. John and I'll be there." Running Deer sighed and stifled a sob.

"Oh, sugar, I didn't mean to make you cry." Gracie handed her a fresh napkin.

"You didn't. I'm just a little fragile. We went to see the boys last week. It's hard to walk out of the room when we want to load them up and bring them back."

"Tell you what, if you and John get the idea to kidnap them, I'm in. That wouldn't be the craziest thing I've done. Might as well add kidnappin' from Walter Reed Hospital to my resume. Maybe get Sheriff Harris along in on it. Yep, he'd give us cover."

Barbara and Tilly watched the customers at the back center tables explode in laughter.

"What's Gracie doing down there?" Barbara started to chuckle, watching their reactions.

"What she does best—making folks feel good about themselves."
****

Amy paused at Mrs. Lemon's table with more hot water and a fresh tea bag. She started to take Dodger's glass for a refill of soda, but Mrs. Lemon stopped her.

"Amy, he's a little particular about things. Here, if you bring another soda, I'll give you his empty glass."

"Sorry, Mrs. Lemon. I forgot. I'll be right back."

Justine looked at her son as he dipped a forkful of lobster into the butter. He licked the butter off before eating the lobster.

"I have to make some arrangements, Dodger. I need to organize our lives and make provisions for the future. After all, when the Lord calls, we can not hesitate."

Justine wondered how much time she would have before it was her turn to answer the call. And who would take care of her son in her absence?
****

Bill motioned Gracie to his table.

"What's up? How'd you guys like the special?"

Andy lifted his water glass in a toast. "I have to say, and I think I speak for every man here, it was delicious. Thank you."

Bill leaned back in his seat. "I hope you'll keep this on the menu. I really enjoyed it. But tell me how you got fresh seafood delivered to the Hollar?" He put the shrimp tail on the side of his plate.

"Actually it was an accident that turned into an opportunity. Delivery man from Virginia broke down on the 219 highway so I gave him a lift to Bowtie's garage. We got to talkin' on the way an' he's an independent distributor. He was kind enough to put me on his route so we'll be havin' this as a special from here on in."

"What did I say about picking up hitchhikers? Could have been a serial killer."

"Well, William Harris, Jr.," she said with her arms akimbo, "he had 'Larry's Fresh Fish' plastered all over his truck along with his phone number so if he's a serial killer, you can call him for his confession."

"Never know, Gracie. He could have a corpse under all those Alaskan crab legs."

"Rest assured, if he delivers me a dead man along with the shrimps, I'll cut off the toes an' deep fry them with the hush puppies just for you."

Andy grinned, "Would you really, Gracie?"

"Got to get to the register, so with that I'll just say we'll never know."

Bill watched Gracie walk to the front of the diner. "Andy, don't throw the gauntlet. I've known Gracie all my life. She just might." Bill laughed. "I'll tell you about the Fifty Yard Line sometime."

Eyeing the pie case, Bill said. "I'm sure those are some of Birdie Spry's work."

Hector gulped his coffee. "I saw the last cherry went to Robby Morris and a meringue for Bobby."

Bill growled. "Deputy Johnson, see if you can find Robby's truck double parked."

With her coat on one arm, Justine stepped over to Sheriff Harris's table. Hector rose and helped her with her sleeve.

"Sheriff, that's a shame. The last piece of cherry pie should go to an officer of the law." Her laugh was like soft music tickling the ear. "But, if you stop by the house tomorrow, about one o'clock, I'll have Dodger bring one out to you."

"It would be greatly appreciated." Harris turned to his companions, "Gentlemen, be at the sheriff's office tomorrow at 1:15 p.m." He called 'thank you' to Mrs. Lemon as she and Dodger left to pay for lunch.

Andy loosened his belt by one notch. "If Gracie serves this on Fridays, I'll have Tootsie clear my calendar."

"Well, I suppose there'll be talk with us four men meeting every week." Deputy Johnson dipped a hush puppy in the shrimp sauce.

"I don't care what they say," Hector injected. "I love my niece but she can't hold a candle to Gracie's cooking. Sure enough, I'll be here every Friday. Don't tell Alice I said that. She'll have me eating peanut butter for supper."

****

Justine handed Gracie a twenty dollar bill. "I want to thank you for such a nice meal. Dodger and I enjoyed it."

"You're quite welcome, Mrs. Lemon. I'm glad you both came." As Gracie made change, she noticed Dodger's high top sneakers. "Well, ain't you somethin', young man. I don't think I've seen them in lime green."

"Gracie, he loves them and I can't say no. I think he has every color they make but he does seem to find the new ones on the computer when they come out. I hope it's not shameful."

"We all have our secret indulgences, Mrs. Lemon. Dodger's just happens to be sneakers. Thanks ya'll for comin'."

Justine reached over and wiped the saliva from the corner of Dodger's face. "It was delicious."

"You both enjoy the walk home. It's a beautiful day."

Dodger flapped one hand in Gracie's direction.

****

The lunch crowd was thinning out. Gracie helped clear tables until the last customer paid and was gone. She motioned for everyone to sit for the staff meeting.

"I just want to tell ya'll what a great job you did. Amy and Tilly got Babs through her first day. Scott, and Jake, great job bussin' tables with Guy, who didn't dump a pan of dishes this week. Thank you for that, Guy. Angelo, Ricky and Mable, the food couldn't have been better. Every plate I saw was perfect. I couldn't be more proud of ya'll."

Gracie's staff was beaming. "Anyone got any questions for me? Any problems?"

Tilly and Amy cast nervous glances at each other. It was Tilly who spoke up.

"Well, Gracie, there was this one man who got a take out. And he was kind of mean about it."

"Really? Did you get a name?"

"Yes, ma'am. Franklin Wells."

SHERIFF BILL'S TUESDAY

Bill brushed the crumbs of a fresh donut from the front of his uniform.

"Dang it," he said aloud. "I've gotta pick Gracie up to go to dinner tonight and this is my last clean shirt. She's sure to see this grease spot. I can hear her now— *'Bill Harris, why are you eatin' on duty gettin' donut crumbs all over your uniform? Do you know how many calories you have to burn for that donut?'*"

Bill flexed his right bicep as he squirmed to see his shoulders in the squad car's rear view mirror.

"You'd think Gracie'd notice my shoulders getting broader. I can afford to eat a donut now and then after a workout." He ignored the few gray hairs and concentrated on flexing in the small mirror.

He was parked behind Franny Atkin's shrubbery; hidden from the diner, but seen by Fishbone as the boy waited for the school bus. If Fishbone was on time for the bus, the ritual continued, a legal win-win for them both as long as Gracie didn't find out.

****

When the Crawford boy started missing the bus the beginning of the school year, Bill figured how to make things work.

"Fishbone, I've a favor to ask of you."

"What's that, Sheriff Bill?" The seven year old sat up very straight in the seat.

"You've been late to the bus three times this month."

The boy nodded.

"You know driving from the Hollar to Waybird City costs the county in gas money for the squad car."

"That's correct, Sheriff Bill."

"The folks in the county pay taxes to buy the gas to put in the car that takes you to school."

"That's correct, Sheriff Bill." Fishbone Crawford studied the passing countryside before he spoke. "But what's the favor?"

"I need you to help me save the county money."

"How?"

"I'll even make it worth your while."

"Worth my while? What's that mean, Sheriff Bill?"

"If you're on time for the bus, I'll make sure you've extra lunch money if you do something for me."

"What's that, Sheriff Bill?"

"I'll give you four dollars every school morning for getting three donuts out of the bag Chum's Corners Bakery drops off at Mrs. Sykes store. You eat one, take one for snack, and bring me one. The extra dollar you use for your lunch at school."

"What if I don't want one for breakfast? I mean if my mom gets up and fixes me breakfast before school?"

"Then you bring me two, take one for snack, and you keep the rest of the money."

"You don't want Miss Gracie to know do you."

"Fish, men don't need to tell women everything they do. There's nothing illegal. It's...it's a gentlemen's agreement."

Fishbone picked up Bill's hat and put it on his own head. He was very serious as he peeked out from under the brim. "Do I have to tell Walter Venter about it? Or show him the money?"

"No, you don't have to tell Walter Venter. And don't even tell your Mom. If you're worried about the money, I've got a jar you can keep the extra in at my office."

"What do I do with the money, Sheriff Bill?"

"You save it so you go to trade school or college. Do something with it good for yourself and others. Make something of yourself outside of the Hollar." Bill signaled his merger on the highway. "This is special operations, Fishbone. Just keep it to yourself. Got it?"

"Got it. Hey, there's the bus, Sheriff Bill. Can we pass it with the lights on?"

"As long as we have a deal, Fishbone."

"Deal, Sheriff."

Bill hit the lights and passed the bus with Fishbone bouncing in the seat and waving at the kids from Deacon's Hollar.

****

This morning, as the yellow bus pulled away, Bill's attention was on the lone figure outside Ambrie Sykes' grocery. He saw Ivan Becker stumble up the steps to find the store still closed. Bill looked at his watch, then back at Ivan.

Ivan was in the DT's. His hair was sparse and uncut; a week of salt and pepper beard on his face, gaunt, pale, and scruffy looking.

The Becker's moved into the Hollar when Bill and Ivan were small kids, but after a while Mrs. Becker had had enough of the old man's drinking and carousing, so she took four of the kids, leaving Ivan with a father who didn't spare the belt or the bottle.

Abandoning his son on the steps of the grocery, Mr. Becker disappeared. Sheriff Harris, Sr. took the boy home to be raised with Bill Jr. and Carolyn.

Bill got out of the squad car. He walked over to the man shivering on the steps.

"Ivan." The man looked up at the sound of his name.

"Bill."

"How long you been back?"

"Couple of weeks."

"Where you been staying, Ivan?"

"Up in the caves."

"Devil's Rooms?"

"Yeah."

"Getting kinda chilly at night, isn't it?"

"Yeah. I hear voices up there, crying sometimes, so thought I'd come into town. Find a room for sweeping maybe.

"Rough night, Ivan?"

"Yeah. I've been tryin' to get a handle on this drinking, Bill. Just a little shaky today. I think I can detox myself if I have a pint. Waitin' for Ambrie to get here and open up. I think I can pay for a pint."

"How much you got, Ivan?"

"A–abb–ou–about three dollars." Ivan opened his fist. Four sweaty liberated quarters fell out of his trembling hand, clinking on the cement step. "I guess not."

"Ivan, get in my car. The heat's on. Let me see what I can do."

"Thanks, Bill. I'll pay you back. I will. You've done a lot for me. I'll get a job and pay you back."

****

Bill used his pass key and walked around the counter where Ambrie had liquor in alphabetical order.

"I suppose any port in a storm will do," he said aloud to the glass pint of Ol' Hills Sipping Whiskey. "I'd better leave a note...where's the paper?" He pawed around below the counter.

He wrote out: "Ambrie: this is for a pint. What's left over, put on Ivan's tab. Going over to Waybird City. I'd appreciate it if you'd let Deputy Johnson know when he comes in for donuts. Thanks, Sheriff Bill." He left a twenty dollar bill on the counter.

In the car, Ivan's goosebumps were gone. He was still shaking but not from the cold. Bill said, "Just take a sip, okay? We've done this before, Ivan. Just a sip when you really need it. I'll get you over to Waybird City Clinic."

"Do I have to, Bill? I think I can detox myself and I'll be okay. It'll be different this time. I'm sure I can do it myself. I won't let you down this time. I just got to control this shakin'."

"Just a second, Ivan. Give me the bottle. You're gonna get whiskey all over my squad car, then what'll Gracie say?"

Ivan started to laugh. "She'll know you was out with me and we was drinkin'." He wiped a small droplet of saliva that shot out of his mouth and hit the dashboard. "Sorry, Bill. I don't want to mess up your car."

"That's okay, Ivan. Here, take a sip. We'll just sit here for a few minutes until you get under control."

Ivan stared at his dirty hands while Bill stared out the window.
****

Bill started the car. "Ready?"

"Yeah, if you think I should go."

"I think you need to go. Here, munch on a donut."

"I seen you got the Crawford boy on the payroll. Good kid."

"Yeah, he is. Had a rough start, but he'll make it. Don't you go telling Gracie."

"Secret's safe with me, Bill. Good donut. Is this Ambrie's?"

"Nope. Chum's Corners. Ambrie makes them on the weekends."

They drove in silence until Ivan spoke first, "I'm sorry, Bill."

"Sorry for what?"

"Your dad was good to me. Fishing with you and him were some of the best times in my life. When he died, I felt like I should leave."

"No one ever thought you'd leave and go off into the woods. I put messages in plastic bags along every trail I thought you might take. Hell, maybe some of them are still out there. It was hard on us when you left. We lost Dad, and then we lost you."

Bill drove toward the bypass to the highway. "Where'd you go anyway?"

"Walked around, hitchhiked. Got a job in Michigan working at a golf course. I was good repairing mowers and took classes in taking care of the greens. Even had a hazmat license to spray weed killers. I had a whole mess of keys on my belt so I could get in the buildings. That was a great place."

"What happened?"

"The owner sold it for development. He said he'd help me out but he didn't."

"What'd you do after that?"

"Got other jobs working in factories. I always had a job of some sort. I can drive a forklift, work on the line making car parts and stuff. I was a supervisor in a window manufacturing plant. They didn't care I didn't have full high school, only if I could manage the lines and get along with the workers."

"Why'd you leave there?"

"Plant closed. I kept finding jobs in other factory places. I was a good worker so I always got references when I needed to go to the next job."

"Drinking didn't get in the way?"

"Well, yeah, it did. I'm a drunk. Got thrown in jail in Ohio a couple of times. I'll tell you, those dang sheriff's don't care if you're hallucinatin', crappin' in your boxers, or barfin' in the corner. Plus, they make you clean up your own mess."

"Didn't they take you to rehab or the hospital?"

"Well, I think we were headed that way but when I tried to kick out the side window, it changed the direction of things. The deputy said, 'Hey, asshole, knock that off' and I said a few things and he whipped that car around so fast I was thrown against the other side. I was stunned but he'd run out of sympathy a few miles back. I remember him saying, 'I know just the place for you.'"

Ivan took another sip from the bottle. "And before I know'd it, we're at the county jail and I am tossed in a cell on my head. I'll never do that again."

"I guess." Bill remembered a few drunks he'd dealt with in his career.

Ivan took a bite out of the donut and washed it down with another sip from the pint. Bill shuddered at the combination.

"But it got worse."

"Yeah?"

"I told them if they didn't clean me and my cell, I was going to commit suicide."

"You didn't."

"Oh, yes I did. Before you could say 'Pass the gin an' tonic,' there was four cops in my cell, ripping off my clothes, takin' my blankets, pillow, pants and shirt. They gave me a size 4x bam-bam suit. My cell was still a mess and I was a mess and they left me. So I said, 'Hey, assholes, you gotta watch me because I'm suicidal' and they shouted back, 'Hey, asshole, we got cameras.'

"I thought it was only for twenty-four hours but I forgot it was a Friday and the psychologist wouldn't be in until Monday. I was like that all weekend. Never tell 'em you're gonna commit suicide on a Friday. Them walleyes don't play."

"Walleyes?"

"Yeah, that's what they call folks from Ohio."

"Ivan, it's Buckeyes. People from Ohio are Buckeyes."

"Oh, yeah. Walleyes is fish."

Bill cleared his throat to stop from laughing out loud.

"It's okay, Bill. You can laugh. I can laugh about it now, but at the time, I was pretty miserable."

Gagging on a giggle, Bill said, "Did you give up drinking for a while after that?"

"Oh, hell no. I saddled up with a gal and her and I were drinkin' but she had the smarts to stop before she got in over her head. One night I told her to take her stuff and get out. I think I drank almost a fifth that day.

"While I was passed out, she had five of her friends help her pack and banging boxes up and down the stairs while I was out cold in the bedroom. In the morning she was gone and left me with a broken TV table and my dirty laundry. After that, I was what they call a dry drunk. I was sober because I avoided the booze, not because I was rehabbed about it."

"I'm sorry, Ivan. I didn't realize…"

"Nothing for you to be sorry about. I did it to myself. If I'd stayed after your dad died…"

"Our dad, Ivan." Bill accelerated as he merged onto the freeway.

Ivan took another sip from the pint. "Yeah, I know that now, but at the time I was just a screwed up kid."

"We all took it hard, especially Carolyn. I was a jerk to her but she always liked you and looked up to you."

"Yeah, she was my baby sister." A tear rolled down Ivan's cheek.

"It's okay. We'll get things turned around for you this time."

"You always say that, Bill. And then I go and mess things up again. I wish there wouldn't be a next time. I just gotta get this drinkin' under control."

"You will, Ivan."

The men fell silent as Bill drove the squad car through freeway traffic to Waybird City. After a short drive across town, he pulled into the drive of the rehab center next to the hospital.

"I guess this is it," Ivan said as he looked at the entrance. An orderly was holding the door for a lady in a wheelchair.

"I guess it is. I'll be hearing from you I know."

Ivan got out of the car. "I'll keep in touch."

"Oh, and Ivan," Bill added. "I'll stay here to make sure you get in safely and don't get turned around." He grinned as Ivan gave him the finger and walked up the sidewalk.

Only when Bill saw the orderly waving to him did he leave the parking lot.

He had time to think on the way back.

****

Bill sat at his sister's bedside the last week of her life. Not wanting to give her bad news, Bill avoided talking about Ivan's spiral into the bottle. But she knew.

"Bill, I want you to promise me something."

"Sure, Sis, anything."

Bill thought she was talking about taking his nephews for a summer but Carolyn surprised him.

"I know about Ivan. I have little birds in the Hollar who tell me the news you won't."

Bill looked at the ceiling. He hated these serious discussions, but Carolyn would have her way.

"Okay, what is it?"

"I have a small life insurance policy..."

"I don't need your money, Carolyn."

"It's not for you, Bozo. You took enough money out of my green piggy bank."

Bill insisted on his innocence. "Sis, I never..."

"You did too! Every Saturday afternoon you always had gum to chew and my green pig had your greasy fingerprints around the plug on its tummy. You aren't the only one who watched shows about forensic evidence."

"Maybe once...maybe twice, but that's all."

"A sheriff shouldn't lie, Bill."

When she coughed, the rattle was like a knife in his heart.

"Anyway, the money's for Ivan's care. I know he isn't doing well, and I know he wouldn't take anything from me, but he will from you. Use it to put him in a sleeping room at one of the motels along the freeway, or maybe pay someone in the Hollar to put him up, or pay his wages, but it's for him."

"You know he'll just drink it up."

"Not with you doling it out."

"Why, Sis?"

"He was shattered when Dad died. He could've had a good life with our family if he hadn't been fractured by his own. I think Dad dying was like Ivan being left by his father on the grocery store steps all over again. We just didn't try hard enough to reach him, to convince him to stay with us. That's why. Promise me."

"Okay, I got it, Sis. I'll take care of it."

"I've made arrangements for my ashes to be spread by my boys in the mountains. You remember the out cropping high up just west of that trout run Dad used to take you? Take my sons there and let my ashes run through the valley. Then take them fishing."

The lump in Bill's throat became rock hard. "Yeah." He barely got that out.

"Now get out of here. I can do this dying on my own. You need to get back to the Hollar."

Warm tears fell on her forehead when he kissed her goodbye. She smiled at her big brother and was at peace.

****

Bill wasn't surprised the day a large check arrived in the mail after Carolyn's estate was settled. The note attached to the sympathy letter from the lawyer stated, "Carolyn said you would know what to do."

Every time it was needed, he knew what to do. Today wasn't any different. In his office, Bill wrote a check to the Waybird City Clinic for thirteen thousand dollars. "Maybe this time, Carolyn, maybe this time."

Before he left for the day, Bill checked his wallet for Wednesday's donut run.

ESIN

She embroiders. Farsi letters dance along the four sides of the material. Each movement of the needle, each tug of the thread, each secured knot, gives life to her prayer. It is repeated over and over around the hemmed edge. No beginning, no end: *nejatam bedin*-rescue me.

Esin prays for the others she meets. She cares for them when they return, sometimes drugged, sometimes beaten, all horrified by what was done to them and what they have become. She dries their tears with the hem of her skirt. She applies ice to their swollen faces. She sings and holds them until they sleep. They do not understand her language but they understand her song. Suffering is universal.

The greasy haired man forces her to go with him to the market for supplies. From the vendors she takes bits of cloth, remnants like her. It is stealing. It is a sin but it is forgiven. She steals for a good purpose.

****

"Jose, get the olive skinned one ready. The one with green eyes and dark hair. There's a customer to see her."

The girls comb her hair. They dress her in clean clothes. They apply makeup to her face. Esin smiles. She endures. There is no other way.

The greasy one drives, not looking at her. From the waistband of her skirt, Esin releases the prayer cloth out the open window. The wind takes it to where God reads such things.

****

Esin returns. The girls gather around her. One dries Esin's tears; another tends to Esin's cuts and bruises; another applies ice to her cheek. Her face is swollen and ugly. She won't travel for a while. Esin cries over the horror of what was done to her and what she has become.

Esin embroiders.

She counts the stitches.
She counts the hours.
She waits. She knows.
God will unleash His warrior to save her.

GRACIE BOWERS

Gracie gazed at the empty parking lot. She skipped church because she was physically drained and emotionally beat up. Angelo, Ricky and Mable were going to quit to work at the factory in Waybird City. Now what?

Justine Lemon tapped on the window of the locked door, startling Gracie. The elderly woman shaded her eyes against the glare of the sun off the glass.

"Hello? Hello? Oh, Gracie, there you are."

Gracie moved the "Closed" sign and unlocked the door for Mrs. Lemon and her son.

"Bright mornin', isn't it. Dodger, don't you look all sharp in your suit and purple high tops."

Dodger proceeded past Gracie and into the diner.

"Justine, did you know we're windin' down for remodelin'? Closed on Sundays for a while."

"Yes, but I thought since there wasn't anyone around, maybe you and me could have a little chat. Oh, look at that. Dodger is inside already like this is where he belongs."

Confused, Gracie held the door. "The Morris boys are here paintin' so don't mind the smell."

"Oh, that won't bother us. Where would you like us to sit?"

Gracie led them to a four top table with a blue checkered tablecloth. She held the chair for Mrs. Lemon while Dodger swept crumbs from his seat only he could see. He sat, slowly rocking side to side.

"Can I get you a coffee, Justine?"

"That would be nice."

After serving, Gracie sat across from her guest.

"I'll get right to the point. It's time for me to make arrangements for Dodger's well being. What I mean is, I think it's time he gets out of the house more and interact with other people. It would be good to stimulate his intellect and growth.”

Mrs. Lemon seemed frail. Her face was drawn; a grayish hue hovered just below her skin where the blush used to be. Her hand shook slightly as she added a teaspoon of sugar to her cup. Justine smiled after tasting her coffee.

“Humm, just right. I heard you had some employees quit. I thought I would put in an application for Dodger to work for you.”

“Well, Mrs. Lemon...Justine, I don’t know.”

“He’s a very good cook, Gracie. And he cleans up as he goes so the kitchen will be spotless when he’s done. He’s quite conscientious.”

Gracie blurted out her misgivings. “But how will he cook if he can’t talk to the waitresses or read the table receipts when the orders come in?”

“If you’re willing to trust me, I think Dodger can answer that.”

It was Gracie’s turn to smile. “What do you want me to do?”

“Go over the menu with him, page by page and give him a tour of the kitchen.”

–Oh, good hell, it’s a Sunday and I am trying to feel sorry for myself– “Sure, Justine.”

Gracie pulled a menu out of the holding rack. She went through the pages as Dodger stood beside her glancing at the numbered items when Gracie read the headings. She showed him the layout of the menu.

“Now, Mr. Dodger, let’s go into the kitchen.”

Justine heard Gracie’s muffled voice catching a few words about the grill, gas oven, and fire extinguishers. As Gracie gave Dodger a tour of the coolers and inventory, Justine offered up a silent prayer.

When they came back into the dining room, Gracie was still talking. “I guess you might as well hear it all,” Gracie said as she delved into food prep sanitation, health codes pertaining to feeding the public, and what she expected from kitchen staff keeping their areas clean at all times. She wasn’t sure he heard anything she said.

Gracie noticed that for not looking where he was going, Dodger didn’t bump into a chair–*I wonder how he does it?*

Gracie glanced at Justine while Justine was looking at Gracie, smiling in anticipation. Bobby Morris broke the smiling deadlock.

“Hey, there Gracie, Missus Lemon. Me and Robby are going to Ambrie’s grocery for a sandwich. We’re gettin’ hungry.”

“Wait, guys, I’ll fix you lunch. Just hold one minute.”

“Gracie, let Dodger. He’d be happy to make something.”

“Oh...okay...”Gracie stammered as she handed Dodger a menu. “Honey, fix the Morris boys two number fives. Ring the bell when you’re done.” She watched him go into the kitchen wondering if she really screwed things up letting him go back there.

Robby and Bobby Morris sat at their customary table along the wall. Gracie served the coffee and creamer for their first round. "You boys know I got the last of Birdie's pies in the case? Save room for dessert."

"Yes, ma'am." They both nodded as Gracie returned to Justine.

"Gracie, I want to be perfectly frank with you. Since my husband died, I've thought about what would happen to Dodger in my absence. I've left the house to him and some insurance money that will provide for his needs, but the idea of him sitting in that house alone, well, it terrifies me."

"I understand, Justine, I really do, but I've got to have trained staff who are willin' to jump in with both feet to work in the new place. Yes, it was a setback when those three jaybirds took off, but I know I can get more help."

"Which is exactly why you need my son."

Gracie avoided the issue by serving pie to the Morris brothers, then topped off their coffee, along with her own. When she placed the coffee pot back on the warmer, the order up bell rang.

"Excuse me, Justine." Gracie forced a smile, fully prepared for a disaster in the kitchen. Instead, she found two small steaks, sided with green bean and almonds, mashed potato topped with butter and chives. Dodger had his arms folded across his chest, rocking back and forth.

Gracie took the silver tray to the Morris' boys and served the dishes.

When she returned to her table she asked, "Justine, how'd he do that?"

"He's what they call a 'savant.' After his injury some sections of his brain were damaged, but other sections took over. As you know, he has difficulty socializing and some of his behaviors are off putting at times, but I think we can help him work through some of the rough spots."

"Hey, there, Gracie. Nice job on the steaks."

She turned in her chair to respond. "Pretty good, eh?"

Robby Morris nodded and Bobby grinned with steak sauce dripping from the corner of his mouth, "Bestuckevahad!"

It was the squeak of the kitchen door announcing Dodger left the kitchen. He made his way around the far wall of the room to the ancient upright piano. He touched middle C, then quickly ran his fingers up and down to play a simple scale. It was when he sat at the creaky bench and performed, he captured the hearts of the people in the room.

Dodger's fingers danced across the board, first striking the ivory and black keys with gentleness, and then harder as the music dictated a firm but not defiant stroke. He moved his arms with confidence as his hands stretched to make individual notes into doubles, triples, and full cords.

"What's he playin'?" Gracie whispered.

"That was a Rachmaninoff prelude, and this is Pachebel."

"It's beautiful. I just had the piano tuned to sell but Dodger is makin' me think twice about it. Where'd he learn to play?"

"I taught him a little but most of it he heard off the radio and could play it after hearing it once."

"What's this next one?"

"Gershwin. He won't play the whole thing, but this is just a sample of what he can do."

The Morris boys were mesmerized–ranch dressing spilled over Robby's lip and down his coveralls.

Gracie was totally dumbfounded. Her mind when into overdrive with a resurgence of hope–*Okay, okay…Dodger cooks and provides entertainment which would quadruple the customer base–extend the back for a private area–liquor license would be a good thing, tourist are always asking for mixed drinks–Gracie's Bar and Supper Club–no, no, Gracie's Diner, Grill, and Supper Club–no, too long–*

"Gracie, does my son have a job?"

"Mrs. Lemon, when can he start?"

****

Gracie watched Dodger work his magic at the grill and ovens, learning the prep work and managing his inventory. He never spoke or made direct eye contact, however Gracie realized there was a genius hiding behind his brown eyes.

Dodger turned his head slightly to glance at the guest slips clipped on the order board as they moved in the air currents of the ventilation fan. All the spices he needed were on a shelf above his head and as the orders came in, he would add ingredients, taking a container then putting it back in the exact place without raising his eyes. He continually cleaned his work area, order after order. The kitchen was spotless when he was done for the day.

At his three month evaluation, Gracie told him "Dodger, you got 100%. After the remodelin's done, Mr. Lemon, you're gonna to be the First Chef. I'll even get you one of them puffy white hats."

For the first time since she knew him, Dodger reached out and patted her cheek.

At closing, Dodger stood by the front door rubbing himself on the arm. He broke into a crooked grin as he saw Justine entering the spotlight at the corner of the drive. Disappearing into the dark, they walked home.

****

"Franklin Wells, you got yourself thirty seconds to get out of my diner and twenty-eight of 'em are gone."

"Gracie, I got every right to complain to the management about the condition of the food I was served."

"I am the management and there ain't nothin' wrong with that seafood platter and you know it. Get out now and take your little buddy with you."

Gracie flipped Jeff Connor's ball cap off his head. "What'd I tell you about bringin' in that orange hat into my establishment? This ain't no Tennessee hot dog stand."

Jeff grabbed his cap before it landed in the monkey dish of half eaten creamed corn.

The room was silent. The last of the diners watched the interchange between Gracie and Frank Wells.

Gracie wasn't done with Frank. "You don't come into my establishment stinkin' like you've been out in the woods for three weeks, then abuse my staff, and make everyone here sorry they came."

Gracie tapped her red painted nails against her hostess apron as she stood with her hands on her slim hips.

Frank jumped up, knocking his coffee cup across the starched linen tablecloth. "You see here, Gracie, you've been giving my family bad food for years clear back when your Daddy was running the place."

"Well, if that's the case, why ya'll keep comin' back?"

Frank threw his napkin on the floor.

"I'll have the health department shut you down. I'll have the state of West Virginia's biohazard team in here inspect that filthy kitchen, I'll have that retard in the kitche..."

"Anything else ya'll have darlin'?" Gracie took a step closer, her honeyed words lost all their sweetness and morphed into caustic acid as they fell from her lips burning into Frank's ears and ego.

Frank stormed past the register. Jeff followed.

"Hey, Frank," Gracie called after him, "wipe that spittle offa your face. Makes you look like a hillbilly."

The sound of Frank kicking the front door echoed in the diner. Gracie turned to her customers. "I'm sorry ya'll had to see that."

Daniel Standing Elk turned on his stool at the counter. "Grace, I was ready to come defend your honor, but something told me you'd do a fine job on your own. However, rest assured, I'd been proud to be your backup."

"Thank you, Dan. You're a real sweetheart and I love you for it." Gracie apologized again to her guests. "I'll tell all ya'll to make up for that, what about pie ala mode all around? Got Birdie Spry's confections in the pie case. Take ya'll's pick."

Jake stopped bussing a table long enough to tap Gracie on the arm and whisper, "You be careful with Frank Wells. He ain't right in the head. He doesn't like it when you say stuff to him like that in front of folks."

"You're too serious." Gracie reached over and patted down his double cowlick. "There's nothin' about Franklin Wells I can't handle. If he gets mad enough to leave the Hollar, it'll be like takin' a stone out of the village shoe."

She smiled at her busboy. "Jake, don't you worry now. When that government grant money comes in, I'll make sure there's enough for an armed guard at the front door to keep Frank Wells and his like from ever comin' in here."

"Gracie, you wouldn't."

"Honey, you just don't know what this girl'll do with her dander flyin' around. Hey, there's a twenty dollar tip off that four top. Scoop it up for the girls, clear the dishes, and let's get this place closed for the night."

Gracie shook the thoughts of Frank out of her mind like a dog shakes water off its coat after a bath. Amy approached her with the stained table cloth.

"I think he ruined the tablecloth, Gracie."

"Not a worry about that stain, Amy. I'll take it over to Ida Mae. She can get rid of anything."

****

Jeff slammed the door of Frank's pickup truck. They were parked in a dark alley along Hammond's Hardware. The men watched Gracie close the diner, lock the door, and walk across the parking lot to her car.

"How many times I have to tell you don't slam that door, Jeff? You'll tip her off we're sitting here watching."

"Sorry, Frank. She sure caused a scene kicking us out tonight."

"Yeah, she'll get hers. You just wait til my brother Clarence gets here. Things'll change big time for the Hollar and it'll be the Wells brothers who rule. Ain't no doubt about that."

Jeff watched the cigarette smoke whirling out of Frank's mouth and nose. The dashboard lights cast a greenish glow across his face; a ghoulish monster-like complexion.

Frank inhaled deeply then released the smoke and filled the cab of the truck, trapping Jeff in a coughing spasm.

"You need to man up. You let a little smoke bother you?"

"I am a man, Frank. Just never picked up the habit. Burns my throat."

"Anyway," Frank said, "I've been working on a plan for Miss Gracie Bowers. It will come to fruit-it-tion."

Jeff didn't respond as he watched the taillights of Gracie's car disappear among the dust clouds of the dirt road.

****

Sitting in the fourth booth sipping his morning coffee, Sheriff Bill watched Gracie take orders, fill waters and coffee, then disappear into the kitchen. He asked Amy, "What's up? You and Gracie running the place?"

"Yep, and don't tell Gracie I said anything. The kitchen all left when the factory opened up in Waybird City. Said Gracie wasn't paying enough, so they quit. Wouldn't wait until we close for the remodel. We been crazy busy."

"I'd heard some grumbling but didn't know it was going to happen. Was it over Dodger, him being different?"

"No, I don't think so. Dodger is different but he's just as sweet as he can be. Him, me, Tilly, Barbara, and the bus boys are here, if Guy Bennett don't put her out of business replacing the dishware. Gracie is cleaning every night in addition to being here all day. And, please don't say anything about her hair. She ain't had time to get it done."

"Oh, I know better than that, Amy." Bill smiled.

"Elsie and Tater Perkins wrapped silverware last night so we're good for a couple of days. Aunt Gem took over the books."

"Is Gracie doing all the cooking?"

"No. Dodger does most of it but he needs time off, too. She's running around like a chicken with its head cut off with all the cleaning. She's determined to work right up to the day of closing. Birdie started cooking breakfast for the time being and brought more pies."

"What time you closing?"

"Hour early, 8 pm."

"Okay, tell Gracie I've got the cleaning crew lined up each night until the remodel. Deputy Hodding will be here at 8:15. Have supplies out so my jailbirds can do something to help. Judge Dietz will appreciate it when he goes to sentence them."

"Sheriff, that'd be great."

"Just doing my part. Now, did you say Birdie brought pie?"

****

Some days were warm and welcoming and others were cold and blowy, settling into the joints, running a chill up the spine while giving fair warning winter would come roaring down the blue-gray mountains of West Virginia. It was one of the in-between cooler days, one of the Appalachian warning days, that the community laid Mrs. Justine Lemon to rest beside her husband in the Deacon's Hollar Cemetery.

Bernese at the flower shop made the floral arrangements. The casket spray with "Mother" on the ribbon was paid for out of Dodger's own money. The staff bought a plant Dodger could take care of and then put outside in the Spring. Signed by the Morris boys was a gift certificate for new tennis shoes. Gracie felt Justine would approve.

Just as Pastor Bob called for the last prayers, Gracie caught a glimpse of Frank Wells and Jeff Connor lounging on the O'Deal's family marker.

"Look," she said to Amy, "that grease ball Wells and his little buddy's over there. Ya'll keep an eye on them while I go speak to pastor."

With the last 'amen' not cooled off, Gracie saw Frank approach Dodger and heard Frank say, "You need to stay home, little retard." Frank grabbed Dodger's arm.

"Yuah...yuah!" Dodger screamed as if struck by lightning. He hit his head with a closed fist and spun in tight circles like a kid lost in the House of Mirrors at a cheap carnival.

"Good hell, Franklin, what's wrong with you? Ya'll leave that boy alone." Gracie stepped between them.

"See that? A crazy retard. Look at him, beating himself in the head at his mama's funeral. Crazy like a beakless bird tryin' to crack open a nutshell."

Dodger trotted from the group of mourners, flapping his arms. A woman in black broke away from the crowd and blocked Dodger's way. She spoke to him in a whisper; Dodger stopped crying and put his hand under her elbow. They walked back to the gravesite; Dodger's face stained with tears.

When the lady removed her sunglasses, Gracie saw the most beautiful green eyes. "Hello," she said. "I'm Dodger's aunt from New York. I'm Amelia Lemon."

"Glad to meet you, honey. I'll be right back."

Gracie had a profound respect for the departed so she tiptoed around the headstones, but still managed to back Frank Wells up against the Parson's marker. She poked him in the chest with a burgundy colored fingernail.

"Frank Wells, you are a stinkin' pile of Satan's sin. You leave that boy alone, or by the good graces of God, I'll sock you in the jaw. You best be thankin' God I don't have a gun cuz I'd shoot ya'll right now."

Frank looked over Gracie's shoulder to see Sheriff Bill walking up behind her. "Sheriff, you heard her. She threatened me. Lock her up, I'm pressing charges."

"What's that? Got a cold and my ears are plugged."

"Sheriff, you'd better do your duty."

"Franklin, I know what my duty is. How about you be happy you've stirred enough up for one day and go home."

"I swear, Gracie..." Frank didn't finish his threat. The look on Bill's face told him to stop.

"Come on, Jeff. We got better things to do." The two men left in Frank's truck. Jeff waved his orange ball cap at the sheriff.

Bill offered his arm and Gracie laced her long fingers around his elbow. They picked their way around the markers toward the line of parked cars.

"Bill, those two are drivin' what staff I got left nuts. They've put toilet paper over the sign, waxed the girls car windows, and yesterday there was a dead cat on the steps when Tilly came to work. A dead cat, for God's sake."

"Gracie, you don't know for sure it was them. What you think and what I can prove are two different things."

Bill liked walking with Gracie on his arm. Always did.

"You know he's tryin' to get the whole Hollar for himself and build a strip mall."

"You don't know that, Gracie."

"Oh, yes I do. The walls have ears. With the grant money comin' in for the upgrade, he's got his eyes on drivin' the rest of us out and take it all for himself. There's devilment in him, Bill. You know that first hand. Talk to him, hon. Get him to back off."

"If you keep calling me hon, I'll have to ask you out on a date." Bill smiled as he took Gracie's face between his hands. "Okay, I'll talk to him, but that cuts two ways. You've got to stop antagonizing him. I mean, it's not very ladylike to keep flipping him off at the only stop sign we've got."

"Oh, Bill, I never…"

"Gracie, the walls have ears." He opened the car door for her and stole a kiss on her cheek.

***

Frank parked his truck just beyond the main street in an old logging two track.

"What now, Frank?" Jeff removed his ball cap and smoothed his hair.

"Yeah?"

"What now? I don't know what else there is to get Gracie scared off. Dead cats, trash on the cars, all of that didn't work to get her to pack up and leave. So, what now?"

Frank slowly exhaled smoke from his cigar. "There's one thing that will get Gracie out of here." He cast a slant eye at Jeff.

"How's that? She's even more determined to stay since we got back from north Georgia than when we left." Jeff scuffed a piece of mud off his boot and onto the floor mat. "I just don't know…wait a minute, you don't mean, Frank? You don't mean to kill the girl? I'm not in for that, Frank, no sir. Not for that."

"It's the only way to bring this to an end and put the main plan into effect. Once my brother Clarence gets here, there'll be no time to fuss over the late Gracie Bowers. We'll be too busy making tons of money."

"But I thought you wanted to put in a strip mall?"

"That's only part of the plan, Jeff. That's the cover for the real operation, the one that makes all the money. We bide our time and wait for the moment. Now's not the time to back out. I have to know I can trust you, or I'll have to terminate our agreement."

"Yeah, you can trust me, Frank. I'm good. We're partners." Jeff wiped his mouth and regretted ever knowing Frank Wells. He didn't want to die young.

****

"I have to say, Miss Amelia, I'm so glad you decided to stay. And I appreciate your help over the winter."

"Thank you, Gracie. Moving from New York to West Virginia was one of the best decisions I've made. I think Dodger would've been miserable in New York. He's loved and respected here. Taking him away from all this would've been the wrong thing to do."

Gracie sipped her tea then rested her chin on her hand and looked out the window at the construction crews putting the final work on the parking lot. The lead contractor and his army of sub-contractors descended on Deacon's Hollar, like a cloud of locusts, remodeling the community, but keeping it's quaintness and character.

"Amelia, will you look at those busy bees. They've just about got all the big stuff finished."

"They've done a spectacular job."

Barbara served a pot of hot water, a basket of flavored teas, and a dish of lemons to Gracie and Amelia. "Thanks, Blair," Gracie said. Barbara smiled.

"When's the diner due for the rest of your remodel?" Amelia opened a packet of Earl Grey.

"Tonight's our last night. We close for a month and I turn the Morris boys loose on this place. All the supplies and new equipment is stored in the back and in Daddy's old smokehouse across the street. Robby's got an industrial electrician friend who'll do the kitchen wirin'. Then they work on the extra shop to the north."

Amelia stared at Gracie. "An extra shop to the north? You don't mean?"

"Yep, I sure do, darlin'. You'll have your tea shop right here. Tourist ladies will love comin' in. I just know it."

"I...I...don't know what to say. My own shop. I saved for years to open one in New York and couldn't get it done."

"Well, I had to do somethin' after I heard what you went through."

"This is amazing. Thank you so much."

"My pleasure."

Barbara delivered two pieces of Dodger's "Apple Caramel Delight" warm from the oven with a dollop of vanilla ice cream. "This is with Dodger's regards...well, if he would speak I know it would be with his regards. He's got the entire staff spoiled with all the new dishes he makes. Enjoy, ladies."

"Babs, ya'll gettin' things around to close tonight? We'll be remodelin' startin' on Monday. Need to freeze what can be frozen and toss what can't. Gonna be six weeks before we open again."

"Already on it, Gracie," Barbara said as she walked away.

Gracie and Amelia finished their tea and dessert just as Dodger left the kitchen and went to stand by the register.

Amelia ran her finger over the last drizzle of caramel on her plate. "My escort is ready. Seems like it got dark awfully early tonight."

"That's because there's rain clouds comin' in. Everyone else has punched out, so you and Dodger should get goin' before it starts. I'll make my final rounds in the kitchen and grab the deposit bag. If you're goin' to be home Sunday afternoon, I'll give you a call."

"Great." Amelia put on her coat. "We can start making plans for the tea room. I'm so excited. Thank you, Gracie."

"You have a good night. Bye, Dodger."

****

She finished her walk-through putting the diner to bed for the night. Habits were habits and the kitchen would be clean before the Morris boys swung the first sledgehammer on Monday.

Gracie walked over the dim parking lot to her car. Before she keyed the door, a hand reached over her shoulder and clamped on her mouth. She felt her arms pinned behind her as someone was grabbing for her ankles.

"We're just taking a little trip up the mountain, Gracie."

She struggled against Frank Wells dragging her off balance and kicked out at Jeff Connor with her feet. Sensing she had an opening, she bit down hard on Frank's pinkie finger.

"Yeeahhhh," he screamed. "Damn it all to hell, Gracie. Get her, Jeff. Get them feet."

"Dang, Frank, iffin' she ain't wiggling like a two-dollar cup of fishing maggots."

"Get them feet. Might go easier if you be still, Gracie."

"Yeeahhh," Frank screamed again.

"Dang it, Frank, you keep your gol dang hand out of her mouth, she won't bite you."

"Shut up, Jeff. You ain't got the heavy end of her...justa...get...thea...feet."

Gracie landed a kick to Jeff's crotch with the toe of her pointed heels. Jeff fell to the ground in agony. He wheezed, "Frank, she got my balls."

Frank eased his hold on Gracie. She spun around and plummeted Frank with the night deposit bag, cash and change scattering on the asphalt.

"Help me, someone help me." It was Gracie's turn to scream. "You black hearted turd...you bastard...Help me, help me!"

The full glory of her rage was set free. Knowing she only had moments before Jeff would recover, Gracie used her fists, money bag, and tangerine painted nails to hit, dig, and gouge Frank's face. Frank was bent over trying to fend off her blows.

She paused long enough to remove a shoe and started beating Frank's head with the heel. Suddenly she found her arms confined; Jeff grabbed her from behind.

"You thought you got me, oh, yeah, it hurt but not as bad as this is going to hurt you…p-payback for my nutsack."

"Shut the hell up and get her to the truck." Frank's breath was ragged. He never knew a girl could be so strong, but he was determined to pulverize Gracie's guts with Jeff holding her. Just as he started to swing, Amelia Lemon jumped on his back and screamed in his ear.

"Heeeeeyaaaahhhh! Leave her alone!" She wrapped her arm around his neck at his Adam's apple, choking off his air.

"D…damn…et…t…hell…woman!"

Amelia bit his ear. Frank let out a roar as he backed up, slamming Amelia against Gracie's car. She fell breathless to the ground. Without mercy, Frank backhanded Amelia across her face.

"That'll teach you to come here and mess up all my plans. Should–*slap*–have–*slap*–stayed up–*slap*–north."

And then it all stopped. Jeff released her and as Gracie turned, she saw him crumple to the ground, blood flowing from his head like the first trickle of melting water off an icicle in the sun, then gushing from the wound that dented his skull.

Someone brushed past her. A rock came down on Frank's head, again and again, musically, rhythmically, bashing Frank's skull, his blood sparkling in the soft neon light of the door sign. Gracie saw all the sharp edges faded out; the action drifted from one frame to another like in an old black and white home movie that was caught on the reel. Amelia's voice jerked her out of the time warp.

"Stop, stop. Dodger."

"Ma bike." The hand came down again, pulverizing the back of Frank's head. Wells slumped to the asphalt.

"Dodger, stop." Gracie heard Amelia pleading. "It's okay. Please stop."

Gracie took in as much air as she could, her sides heaving from the effort.

"It was Frank, wasn't it Dodger," she said as she took the stone from his hand. "It wasn't no accident, was it. It was Frank Wells who ran into you and your bike. All these years it was bottled up inside you and you couldn't tell your story."

"Is…is…he dead? And the other one, is he dead, too?"

"Yeah, darlin', just like mountain trout outta the water for three days." Gracie's breathing was slowing. She felt pain in her shoulder.

"Sheriff Harris will arrest Dodger and he'll go to prison." Amelia moaned as she put her red and swollen face in her hands. She was collapsing as the adrenaline left her body.

Gracie had seen this before. She knew she had to act without hesitation.

"Amelia, get up, girl." Gracie grabbed her friend and held her against the car.

"Ain't no one goin' to jail, you got that? Just let me think a minute."

She patted Dodger on his shoulder. "Well, darlin', I guess cookin' ain't the only thing you know how to do. Just a second, ya'll, let me think."

Gracie straightened her blouse, surprised the rose on her lapel stayed pinned. She smoothed the free strands of blonde hair from her sweaty face and tucked them back into her twisted bun.

In control of herself, Gracie said, "There ain't no one goin' to jail, to no prison, to nowhere, except you're gonna take Dodger home and the both of you get cleaned up, an' wash them clothes in cold water a couple of times. You boil some tea, that calmin' kind, an' let Dodger play the piano for a while, so all ya'lls settle down. I'm gonna stay here an' catch my breath a little more."

Noticing her hands, a look of absolute disgust came across her face. "Dang if that bastard didn't break eight of my nails!"

"Gracie, what will you do?"

"Well, I'll have Francine fix 'em."

"Not your nails, Gracie. You'll have to call the law."

"Amelia, this ain't New York City. You're in West Virginia now. We take care of ourselves. Don't you worry."

"You'll call Sheriff Harris?"

"Oh, good hell, no, an' you tell no one about this. No one. Not ever. We'll talk on Sunday. I'll call Ida Mae."

"Ida Mae?"

"Yeah, she knows how to get rid of anything. Now, hush, go home."

Gracie's attention was distracted by three little clouds caught in the trees across the road. They receded as she watched them. "Well, I guess you boys do show up. But hey, I got this."

"Who are you talking to, Gracie? Were their witnesses?" Amelia started to hyperventilate.

"Witnesses? No one you have to worry about, girl. Steady yourself."

Dodger stood between the two women, rocking gently side to side. He reached over, patting Amelia's arm. The bloody granite rock glistened in the faint light at his feet.

SPENCER TUTTLE

"YOU BOYS DO GOOD in trainin' and listen to what they tell you," Miss Gracie said before we left.

She was cryin' as me and Sam White Owl got on the bus to Parris Island for our first weeks in Marine Corps boot camp. Our dad was a Marine back in the day and so he put Sam and me through his version of Marine boot camp to get us hardcore and ready. I was thinkin' at the time that Parris Island will be easier.

Sam's folks, Runnin' Deer and John Seven Star, raised me ever since my dad died savin' John in the Otter Creek Wilderness. I was eight years old when that happened. Judge Dietz finalized adoptin' me into the Seven Star family so I could stay in Deacon's Hollar and not be a ward of the state. Besides, Sam and me were best pals ever since we met as kids so it was no big deal except I missed my dad.

All the summer before we left we worked for Gracie at the diner. Kept it cleaned up by sealin' the parkin' lot, waterin' the flowers out front, weedin' the rock garden, and puttin' deliveries away. We did take a weekend off and went to Charleston to get USMC tats.

Mom and Dad were there to see us off along with Miss Sykes, Birdie, Aunt Gem and Sheriff Harris.

"Well, you boys work this hard for the Marines, you'll end up being commanders or captains, or somethin' big like that. Anyway, you'll do us all proud, I'm sure."

"We'll do our best, Miss Gracie," I told her. And we did.
****

When we landed at Parris Island, our drill sergeants were just like John Seven Star said they would be only louder. When Sam told our drill instructor that we were brothers, he made Sam drop for twenty push ups.

"There ain't no way in hell ya'll's brothers except when I tell you ya'll's brothers. Now give me another twenty."

Of course I had to open my big mouth and say, "But we are, Sergeant."

"I am your Drill Instructor, boy. You're in the Marine Corps, not the Army. Now drop."

And I got dropped for twenty, then dropped for twenty more because I didn't ask permission to speak. It wasn't until Sam and me got our interviews that first week that we explained how it worked with me bein' adopted by a tribal family.

We were a mismatched pair, just like socks found in the bottom of the drawer after all the rest are in the warsh. Sam was bigger than me with long black hair, dark eyes, and always tan. I'm Scotch-Irish so I got the short, stocky genes and red hair, blue eyes. I also got freckles across my nose, plus a gap between my teeth, and big ears standin' out away from my head. My skin's so white I never tan, just burn. Mom put herb paste on me when I was in the sun too long and bought sunscreen 70 by the case.

Sam's real first name is Onacona, but it's not somethin' I would say every day. You have to be careful with tribal names because they are powerful. You could get hurt. That's what Runnin' Deer's mother said and that's the truth.

****

We got our heads shaved before we left. Sam gave his hair to Dad for safekeepin'. I was gonna donate mine but it wasn't long enough and probably no cancer patient wanted red hair anyway. They'd look too much like a wild autumn carrot.

Marine boot camp was tough with the drill instructors sayin' I wouldn't make it, not good enough to be a Marine. Seemed like I was always messin' up. This one DI was watchin' me all the time. And dang if he was always there when I did somethin' wrong or he didn't like. I was on disciplinary action for my boots, or my shirt. He even had me drop for twenty cuz I didn't wash a sleeper out of my eye one mornin'. It was wearin' on me. Maybe I wasn't cut out to be a Marine? I would have to face Runnin' Deer and John Seven Star in shame.

Well, let me tell you, Sam wasn't havin' any of that. He said all they see is the outside and they can't see the inside where all my toughness is.

"Besides," he tells me, "we're in this together. We don't leave each other behind no matter what and we stay together no matter what. We're Deacon's Hollar Marines." He threw his head back an' howled like a wolf singin' to the moon and then I did, too, and then the head DI caught us and dropped us for twenty. But, it was worth it.

When the chips are down and you got yourself someone like Sam, it just don't get any better than that. But there were a couple others I learned to count on.

****

We had three tribal men in our unit, all named Sam. In addition to my brother, we had a guy who was Navajo and his name was Hashkeh Naabah Tso and a man from the Lakota in North Dakota and his name was Ohanzee Crow

Dog. Hashkeh Naabah Tso and Ohanzee Crow Dog said their full names was so powerful they could make a white boy's ears fall off if he heard them. I told them I already knew that and I'd be happy if they'd let me keep my ears.

"You're okay for a white guy. I like you," Ohanzee Crow Dog told me. "But don't think I'm going to introduce you to my sister. Maybe Hashkeh Naabah Tso would like you as a brother-in-law?"

Hashkeh Naabah Tso looked me up and down. "Nope. Doesn't fit in with the narrative of the native red man. I mean he gets red in the sun, for sure, but wrong shade. He'd fry to a crisp when he tried to herd sheep. Either that or the dogs would eat him." They laughed at me.

Sam White Owl came out of the unit head, so I know he heard the talk because he stood up for me.

"You guys know he's my brother? His father gave his life to save my dad. He's been a part of my family since he was eight."

The other two got real quiet. What were they going to say?

"When we're together," Sam White Owl said, "you call him Red Hawk. Our mom gave him that name."

Tso tapped me on the shoulder. "So why is your name Spencer Tuttle?"

"I kept the name to honor my dad what died. Runnin' Deer and John Seven Star said it'd be okay."

From that day forward, I got me two more brothers. The unit called them Cherokee Sam, Navajo Sam, and Lakota Sam to not have to handle their whole names. The unit called me "Shrimp," but I didn't care. I knew who had my back.

I didn't think they were serious about me bein' a part of their circle until those guys from Brooklyn tried to beat me up in the unit head. The three Sam's heard the scuffle and were there before I could get my second punch in. From then on, the four of us worked together like we were one family. I got through Basic Trainin' and the School of Infantry, or SOI, at Camp Geiger. I was the Red Hawk in a group of Warrior Eagles.

Then it was off to Afghanistan.

Lakota Sam and Navajo Sam were assigned to a forward operatin' base or FOB, about 300 klicks north of where White Owl and me would be. It was the last I thought I would ever see of them. I told Sam I was a little jittery losin' two brothers just up and goin' not sayin' goodbye and all, but he gave me some good advice.

He said, "Warrior brothers are always banded together by the physical world or by the spirit world. We'll meet again. For now, be a good warrior." So that's what I did.

****

Marines who were in-country longer than us were instructors. They taught us all the ways the Taliban move in the mountains and what're the best strategies to use on patrol. With all the trainin' I just hoped I'd be ready to do as good as everyone else.

The first firefight I was in was exhileratin'. All my shit was tight. Our FOB team beat back an assault because our basic and IOS trainin' and experience took over. I didn't even have to think. I took aim, practiced trigger control, breathin', and fired round after round. I was tight.

After the firefight was over, Sam sat across from me in the dark, grinnin'. We learned we were warriors and survivin' is a rush.

With a few months in-country, we were good at what we did. And just like them mismatched socks, thrown together to make a pair, Sam and me made a pair. Socks only cover your feet, but no matter what they look like, brothers will cover your life.

In seven months, we started trainin' the new Marines in-country. Then, the shit hit the *dang* fan.

The Taliban mounted an offensive comin' along from somewhere in the south Helmand Province. Sometimes I can understand the population welcomin' the Taliban because of all the corruption in the police and national forces, but corruption wasn't our mission. Our mission was to seek out high priority targets and take 'em out. Only it didn't turn out the way we thought.

Oh, we got the target alright, gathered intelligence, a laptop, and some documents, but what we didn't count on was that ol' Taliban guy with the vest loaded with C-4 followin' aways behind. We got too big headed and we didn't cover our tracks.

By the time Holtzlander heard the small avalanche of rocks behind us, that Taliban blew himself up. C-4 is pretty powerful stuff so you can imagine there was some serious damage to the area. The mountain got the worst of it, but that didn't mean we were in the clear. Even though we didn't take a direct hit, there was enough force to take us off our feet, and enough shrapnel from the explosion to do some damage. It knocked me plumb off the cliff edge. That's all I remember until Sam White Owl came to take me back.

There were some SEALs not too far away. When they heard the commotion, they routed over to give assistance. Once the area was secure, the SEAL leader ordered a dust off. Everyone got loaded on choppers, checked over, and they left. Sam was unconscious because of gettin' his leg almost blow'd off, three other guys were too banged up to talk, and Holtzlander and Schultz were dead. That's how they forgot me, but not really forgot me because they remembered me later, but that's how the headcount got so messed up. I didn't know any of this happened because I was cold cocked by the explosion and tucked under a boulder by the blast.

To this day I can't tell you how long I was out but I knew when I woke up, I was just so *dang* thirsty. I saw the sun, or I think it was the sun. Could've been the search light from a helicopter. I don't know. I'd blacked out again. I'd have dreams of wakin' up and blackin' out, wakin' up and blackin' out. What made me know I was alive was my arm and my leg hurt something fierce. So, it was like I got pain, so I know I'm alive, then I'd black out.

I woke up all disorientated until I seen Sam standin' there. I said, "Sam, where's your uniform, Marine? Your weapon?" He was bare chested but wore some deer skin leggings under his tribal breechcloth. He wore a bear claw necklace and had a huge knife sheathed at his side. Must have left his boots somewhere but he rustled up a pair of some kind of shoes with beadwork on the toes. I said, "Sam, you look like ah...ah...Indian ready for war." He knew I was jokin' but maybe I wasn't jokin' 'cuz that's how he looked.

Sam said, "I *am* Indian, and I *am* ready for war. The question is: Are you ready to go home?"

"Sure," I said, "but how?"

"You need to do exactly what I tell you, Red Hawk. I'm going to get you off this mountain, but you need to follow my instructions, what and when I say."

"Okay," I said. He wiggled me out from under the big rock like he was takin' a page out of a book.

He offered me water. I tried to drink the whole canteen, but he made me drink sips. Then he stuffed a little deerskin bag against my gum and cheek. I started to tell him I didn't think I could walk all the way back, but Sam didn't hear me because he just put his hand over my mouth and whispered, "Bite down on the medicine bag." So, I did.

Next thing I know, Sam picked me up and was carryin' me like a baby. But at that point, I was too dang tired to care.

After a little while I woke up. Sam was squattin' there just lookin' at me. I asked him if I was dead.

"No, just resting."

"Are we close, Sam?"

"Yeah, Red Hawk. We'll have to walk close to the Taliban, so you need to be quiet. The medicine bag only stops the pain, not your voice. You clear?"

"Crystal. Just a few more drops of water and I'll have enough juice in my mouth to chew the bag. Is this stuff Mom sent?"

"Yeah. Those are herbs from home. Should do you some good."

"I'll have to tell her thank you when we get back."

"Yeah, I'm sure she'd like that. Here's a little water to slosh around your mouth. Are you ready?"
****

Sam was a great hunter. In the mountains and hills, he always got the biggest buck and the heaviest doe. He knew the best spots for pheasant, grouse, woodcock, and got huge rabbits for the bunny pie cook-off at Miss Gracie's. Sam took me huntin' with him and said the hardest part of huntin' was learnin' to be part of the forest.

He didn't use the gimmicks they sell at the huntin' stores, no doe-in-estrus spray, or bait piles, no tourist hunter stuff. He said be part of the forest and the animals wouldn't see me. Once you learn you're related to everythin', it changes your perspective and you become part of the forest. You respect the forest and the forest respects you.

"This is going to be like hunting back home. Remember when I told you to be part of the forest? There's no forest here but you need to be part of the desert. You clear?"

Sam looked me dead in the eye.

"Crystal. Be quiet and blend in."

"Right."

He picked me up and started walkin' across the desert of Afghanistan. I mean, I always knew he was strong and determined and smart, but he was one special man to carry another man across the desert. I opened my eyes, just lookin' through the slits because I heard voices.

That's when I saw Hashkeh Naabah Tso walkin' beside us. He looked at me, reached out and stroked my head with the back of his hand like he was pettin' a bird. I started to say somethin' then Ohanzee Crow Dog touched my lips with his finger and made the sign to be quiet, like shushin' a little kid.

There we were walkin' right through the dang camp of the Taliban. I could hear the Taliban talkin', saw the glint of the fire off their weapons stacked close by them. I smelled the goat meat they were cookin'. Three Warrior Eagles and the Red Hawk, walkin' right through the enemy camp and they didn't know we was there.

I never felt so safe in my life. I was with my brothers and we could have taken out the enemy camp if we wanted to. But the mission was so I got back to the FOB and I wasn't left behind.

Yep, ahuh. They were makin' sure I got home. I loved them with all my heart.
****

Sam stopped because I must have been cryin' out. I opened my eyes with Sam's hand over my mouth. He took some herbs out of a bag at his waist and sprinkled them in the hole in my leg. He stood up as tall as he could, which was pretty tall, and opened his arms out wide. His head back, a soft whisper came from his lips. Crow Dog and Tso were not far behind, but they stopped and did like Sam. All three of them were prayin', I think.

Sam picked me up, and we started again with Crow Dog and Tso coverin' our six. I kept watchin' them, but after a few minutes I couldn't see them anymore. I waved a couple of times just in case they saw me through a rifle scope.

Sam told me we was almost back to the FOB.

"Where's the two Sam's?" I had to juice up the medicine bag in my mouth with a little water. I was startin' to hurt.

"Took us as far as they could."

"I guess their sergeant couldn't cover for them bein' away any more. I'll have to tell them thank you when I see them. Buy 'em a pizza an' a beer at Miss Gracie's in the Hollar."

In the moonlight, Sam was squattin' on the ground, grinnin' at me. "Yeah, they'd like that. Here, take the rest of the water. How's your leg?"

It hurt but not that bad so I said, "Mom's herbs are good. I'll have to thank her when I see her."

Sam kept grinning. "Yeah, Red Hawk, I'm sure she'd like that. We'll be home soon. Ready?"

He picked me up and walked, but now I noticed how long his hair was so maybe the sergeant let him grow it. I was a little confused to how it grew back so fast when mine was still high and tight. Didn't matter. We were together was all that did.

When he put me down, he gave me a flare gun. "Fire this off, and someone'll come. I'll see you when we get home."

"Okay, Sam. I'll buy you a beer and pizza at Miss Gracie's."

The last thing I remember I was looking up at the stars in Orion's belt.

WALTER REED

I WAS OUT OF pain pills and patience. No one would tell me when I could go home, but one thing was sure: I wasn't goin' until Sam White Owl was goin' with me. I don't like gettin' mad about stuff but there are some things worth gettin' mad about.

There was a guy out in the hall so I shouted to him. "Hey, you."

I didn't recognize him at first because he was in civilian clothes but it was Major Glassman who operated on me in Afghanistan and rode with me on the medical transport plane from Germany.

"Hey, Spence." He came into my ward and pulled up a chair beside my bed. "How you doing? I see they delivered your Purple Heart. Tough way to get a medal, but you're alive."

"Yeah, thanks for workin' on me." Once I started talkin' to Dr. Glassman, my anger shut down. He was a good guy in my book.

"You're welcome. I thought I'd stop by and see how some of my former patients are doing."

"You're not in the Army anymore?"

"No, I left. Went back to college and picked up classes in another degree."

"Didn't take you that long. 'Course I been here a while but you must be pretty smart. What in?"

"Veterinary. I had to get caught up on the animal species stuff."

"So you do people and animals? Should I call you Doctor Doctor?"

"Nope, Andy is good enough. It's no big deal."

"Where you practice?"

"Well, I've been to your old stomping grounds and set up there. Seems like a nice place to be."

"It is. Me and Sam was raised there."

"How's he doing?"

"They still got him in a coma. I sneak up to his room everyday. Our parents been here a lot but it's hard with Sam like that. Dad mostly stares out of his window at a big pine tree in the yard. Mom talks to him in her language. I never learned it but Sam did. I think she's healin' him."

"It must be tough on them."

"Yeah. I thought Mom was gonna build a small house out on the lawn and stay but Dad talked her out of it. I keep an eye on Sam and write no less than once a week so they know more of what's goin' on. The docs say he'll walk. They said you were the person what saved his leg. Heard them talkin' that you did a nice piece of work fixin' him up like you did."

"We aim to please." Andy pursed his lips, and it was like he was tryin' to think about what to say next.

****

I'll tell ya'll a little somethin' I learned about doctors at Walter Reed. When doctors start studyin' their fingernails and pursin' their lips, what comes next ain't goin' to be good. They may adjust their glasses, or comb their hair with their hand, but they all got somethin' nervous to do before they put the hammer down. I think they learn it in doctor school.

That's just what Andy did, true to form. He must've been a good bit nervous because he combed his hair with his hand *and* fiddled with his thumb nail. And sure enough, what came next wasn't pretty.

"Spence, you're a tough Marine. You had to be to go through what you did. I'm going to be straight with you. How you got across the desert no one knows, but when you fired off the flare and the patrol team found you, you were in pretty rough shape. You were shot up with shrapnel, dehydrated, and anemic from blood loss. When troops come into my operating room like that, they don't always come out. You know what I mean?"

I nodded and kept my look steady into his eyes just like Sam taught me to through a gun scope or down the shaft of an arrow durin' bow season.

"When the patrol found you they said you were waving your hand and arm, like signaling to someone, but there wasn't anyone there. You were covered in dust, bit up by sand fleas, and your leg had a hole in it."

"So?" I was wonderin' where this was goin' and which shrink Andy'd talked to.

"The nurses say you think Sam White Owl, Sam Crow Dog, and Sam Tso brought you back over the desert."

"Yep, ahuh. Sam White Owl came got me and the other two provided cover."

Andy squirmed in his seat. He had little beads of sweat on his upper lip and across his hairline.

"Doc, just say it."

"Spence, there's no way they found you and brought you back. Crow Dog and Tso were killed when their outpost was overrun. I operated on Sam White Owl and put him in a drug induced coma. He was shipped back to Walter Reed before you were found. I'm sorry, Spence, but it's just not possible. A lot of things can go through a soldier's mind when they…"

"Who put you up to this, Andy? Them psych docs?"

"No, Spence, I swear I haven't talked with any of them. You and me talked on the plane on the way back from Germany."

"Yeah, I remember now. You kept druggin' me."

"You wouldn't shut up."

"Not fair."

"Maybe not, but I needed some sleep on the flight, so it was nighty-night Corporal Tuttle."

"Okay, but still not fair."

"One of my past sins I'll have to atone for. Just a sec, I'll be right back."

Andy disappeared for a few minutes but came back in a white lab coat with a stethoscope around his neck and two cups of steaming coffee.

"You in camouflage, Andy?"

"What? Oh, yeah. Just in case anyone asks."

"I get it. You got the enemy looking for you so you come in my foxhole to take cover."

"Yeah."

"A woman?"

"Or two. Let's leave it at that."

You know, that was the best laugh I'd had in weeks. Hearin' he was hidin' from a couple of nurses at Walter Reed did me good. Them nurses are as tough as they come and could have broke him in half.

"So, Spence, tell me how you got back to the FOB?"

"I told you on the flight. Sam came and got me and Tso and Crow Dog provided cover. Sam gave me a flare and then I just waited until they got me."

Andy started to interrupt, but it's my story so I took the upper hand.

"Andy, you can scratch fleas and bay at the moon for a thirty day leave, but my story hasn't changed. I know'd what happened because I was there. No one figures that a backwoods boy from West Virginia could make it across the desert, but I did because I had my brothers holdin' me and takin' care of me. I'm only here because they gave their word and their word is sacred.

"I ain't sayin' it again until I talk to Sam. There's some things some people shouldn't be privy to. The fact is, I got back. When Sam wakes up, maybe he'll tell you and maybe he won't. But I'm done talkin' about it. Thanks for savin' me, but this is where it stops."

"I can respect that, Spence."

We sat in silence, me and Dr. Andy Glassman, until we finished our coffee. I told him about some of the best places to fish for brook trout and where to hunt deer. Then he left.

****

Mom sent another box of goodies so I went up to Sam's to open it and read him her letters.

Sam was layin' there so peaceful. He was in some sort of mechanical bunch of stuff taped and strapped to his chest and head. He was wrapped in bandages with wires and cables and stuff all over the dang place. A machine made his knee bend every so often. Both his hands were bandaged.

I didn't want to draw attention to the staff I was in his room, so I got as close as the wheelchair would let me and pulled the curtain around a little. Then I leaned over and whispered in his ear.

"Hey, it's me, Red Hawk. Just wanted to thank you again for bringin' me back." He didn't move but I know he could hear me because I was close and right up to his ear and Dad said owls hear really well.

"I got somethin'll help get you back on your feet. Mom sent a medicine bag just for you. She wrote that it was really strong, so I can only give you a little bit at a time. It's dried out, but I'll juice it up for you."

There was power in those herbs; I could tell when I put it in my cheek and started chewing. I thought better about the germs, so I put a straw full of Sam's water on it.

"I got this ready for you, brother."

I leaned over Sam and parted his lips. Then I squeezed some of the liquid from the deer skin pouch into Sam's mouth. Not much because I didn't want him to choke, but just enough it would run down his throat and into his stomach and start workin' to heal him.

"The doc who fixed us up stopped by my room. He wants to know how I got back to the FOB. None of those headshrinkers think I'm tellin' the truth y'all came back for me. They think I was around too many concussion grenades and breached too many doors. I stopped talkin' about it all together. Now, if you think I should say anythin', you let me know, but for now, I shut up. Maybe it's all tribal stuff anyway even though *I* know, *they* don't need to know."

It just about killed me to see him like this. It must have been really hard on him gettin' me down the mountain and back across the desert.

"I'll be back tomorrow to read you the letters Mom sent. There's one from Miss Gracie, a note from Sheriff Harris, and a card signed by everyone in the Hollar it looks like. I think it was hangin' in Ambrie Sykes grocery store. Got a lot of signatures on it.

"I'll bring the letters and your medicine bag tomorrow." I fumbled with the hem of the bathrobe they gave me in the hospital. It was my turn to be nervous. I didn't want to cry in front of Sam. I know'd he would hear me blubberin' like a baby.

"Guess I already said that."

It was so quiet in his room I could hear the red hand on the clock count off the seconds.

"Okay, I guess I'll go before that dang Spec-4 gets too much into my business. I don't want him nosin' around. After all, he's Army and you know what that means. So now you've got medicine from home, everythin'll be okay."

I didn't want to leave him so I had to force myself to push the wheelchair out the door.

"You sleep tight and I'll be here tomorrow for sure. I'll just head out so you get some rest. Oorah."

****

In the pine tree outside his window, the Snowy Owl adjusted herself in the boughs. She tucked a small stick back into the meticulous design of her nest. Once again comfortable for the evening watch, she hooted twice.

A smile danced over Onacona's lips; His eyes fluttered open as he whispered "Oorah."

Luke Perkins

He checked his watch against the horizon. He had a few moments to relax before sunset and movement to the target.

This is one of the easiest missions I've had. Diego Doc, Cobalt, and Zero supply cover while Scout places the AN/GSQ-187 and MAISINT sensors. A call to Langley's computer runs the diagnostics. The extraction is routine. Why are my guts tore up about it?

****

"You *will* take the extra two men as assigned and that's it. CIA case officers take orders, Luke. They don't give them and certainly not to me."

"I don't know anything about them."

"You don't know about the other four men but you're taking them."

"I selected those four based on their files. The two carnivores in your outer office are questionable resources. Do you throw them raw meat?"

"They have names. Smith and Jones."

"Yes, sir. The usual CIA names but I have the feeling they are not Agency employees."

"It's none of your business who signs their checks. That's it, Luke. They're assigned and before you ask, I do not give you permission to go above my head. It's a done deal. Dismissed."

Luke Perkins, code name "CB," turned on his heel and exited. An objectionable odor hit his nostrils as soon as he stepped into the outer office.

"Janice, would you give me the honor of dining with me at lunch?"

"Yea...yeah," she said.

Grabbing her handbag from a drawer, Janice was around the desk, with her hand on the door knob in seconds. Once in the hall, the administrative assistant grasped Luke's shoulder.

"Thank you so much. You don't have to take me to lunch, I'm just grateful you got me out of there. My God, where does the deputy get these people?"

A true West Virginia gentleman, Luke replaced her hand in the bend of his elbow. He felt her tremble. Janice Streeter was one of the few people in the Agency he could trust.

"I think we both could use a drink before lunch. My treat. I've got a taste for one of those Cobb salads you talk about. Where's the best place?"

Luke and Janice left the deputies' wing of the CIA. Taking an Agency car, Luke drove them into the city to get the calming effect of alcohol for not so dissimilar reasons.

****

During pre-mission training at Langley, he felt an unspoken bias hanging in the air like stale cigarette smoke. A young CIA case officer was placed in charge of a seasoned, cohesive Ranger Special Operations squad. Members of the elite 80th Regiment didn't need or want the CIA looking over their shoulders on any mission.

CB proved his slight, tough body could go the distance among the "barbarians" as he called them.

"Oh, hell," Scout shouted. "We were barbarians before we joined the Army. We only got civilized when they made us Rangers."

CB replied. "I was a Ranger for one year and the next, the CIA grabbed me. I was just getting warmed up and had to put my Ranger tab away."

Cobalt snickered. "Why didn't you say you were a Ranger? I might've been easier on you in hand-to-hand."

"Yeah. Right." CB rubbed the bruise on his shoulder from Cobalt's judo throw.

****

At five feet nine, Luke was a natural for covert operations. He easily disguised his appearance with wigs, makeup, and special skills taught at Langley. He was quick, wiry, and kept his mouth shut about assignments. In a den of liars and thieves, Luke knew who could be trusted. He was a natural leader and moved from one mission to the next, from one team to the next without issue. It was the career of a lifetime but one he didn't tell his parents. To them, he worked at the Library of Congress as a researcher.

****

With twenty-four hours to go before the drop in Afghanistan, the team met at Shorty's Grill. Around the table in the middle of the noisy barroom, Diego asked CB what he missed about being in a Ranger unit.

"The men, the camaraderie. Being a CIA case officer is not a team sport."

After downing the last ounce from his beer mug, CB continued. "I liked the rush, but it's when you're aching for the rush, that's bad. Has to be a balance, some normalcy."

Diego Doc threw his head back in laughter. "And you think the CIA is normal and balanced?"

"Well, you've got me on that," CB replied.

Diego was a short Latino rumored as the best Ranger combat medic the Army had to offer. His file indicated he was the best.

"I like the small, tight missions, saving my buddies from going to hell in a firefight."

After another round of beers, Diego explained, "My Dad's a brain surgeon in Boston. When he took a tumor out of the melon of some big shot at Harvard, he got me a hook-up to go there. I did a few years, but Dad and I both knew I wasn't Harvard material. I got cut loose from college, went Army 68Whiskey. Put in over 300 hours of advanced medical for my 18Delta."

"So you don't practice voodoo like I heard?"

"Nope, CB, that's all rumor. Besides, chickens scare me."

CB smiled. There wasn't anything that scared Diego Doc. "You married?" CB ordered a shot to go with his beer. "Make it a round, will you, honey?" he said to the waitress.

"Yeah. My wife hates every time I leave so I got her a dog. Boston Terrier. That's what she calls it. I call it a "Tuxedo Rat." She goes to dog shows. It takes her mind off me being *el pagano*."

Scout, brown-eyed blonde with a deep red beard, was the computer science and communications expert. CB noted in Scout's file he was a dissertation short of a PhD from MIT when he decided to quit and enlist.

When Doc and Cobalt took a bathroom break, Scout showed CB a photo of his family.

"My dad died shortly after my sister Leigh was born. My *dedushka* lived with us for a while, but he was a crazy Russian immigrant. Had all kinds of stories to scare us when we were small. I wasn't afraid of him, but Mom and Leigh were.

"I thought research was for me but I couldn't stand the politics of the universities or the socialism. Letting the Army payoff my school loans seemed like a good idea. My area of study was what the Army was looking for so they wrote the check and I signed on the dotted line."

"I bet your family misses you a lot." CB sipped his whiskey before the gulp.

Scout sat back and looked at the ceiling, then around the room. "Probably not. I have my grandfather's temper. I get along with family in small doses. They love me to death, but I know better than to hang around. I send them most of my pay so it makes up for it, I guess."

Diego returned to the table and caught the last part of the conversation. "Ask him what he's doing with all that MIT education."

CB shuffled his chair to let a wobbling Diego get seated before the medic knocked bottles and money off the table.

"I already know. He likes to spy on the Chinese and Russians."

"Also my family."

"You're kidding, right?"

"Nope. I knew the Ranger's were going to keep me away in God knows what parts of the world and I wanted to make sure the family was okay. I showed the Army I could get satellites to do certain things so they give me slack to go looking around the world...sort of." Scout threw back a shot of Leadslingers Napalm Cinnamon Whiskey. "Oh, that bites. I love it."

It was Cobalt's turn to order another round. He grabbed money from the center of the table to give to the waitress as he said, "Scout, tell CB about the car."

Scout snickered. "I'm scanning my mom's neighborhood, looking at the new deck the neighbors put on their house, and I see she's having trouble getting her car started. So I call a mechanic. He told her I sent him, so she's starts waving to my satellite."

The whack of a baseball bat against a large Chinese gong, startled everyone in the room except the Rangers.

"Last call, snake eaters." Shortstop placed his bat on the bar.

"Has he ever used that on anyone?" CB saw it was a Louisville Slugger.

Cobalt scratched his chin in drunken thought. "Not that I'm aware of but the old man scares me."

"Do you guys want another round?" CB checked his wallet. "I've got about enough for a pitcher but I don't think any of us need it."

"Nope, not me. I called Zero. He'll be here soon. It's not like any of us can drive." Cobalt gulped his last swallow of beer. "Well, speak of the devil, Daddy's here." Cobalt nodded at the figure who paused to speak to the bartender.

"Will he want a beer? I can cover him."

Nope," said Diego. "Zero doesn't drink. He doesn't want to get shaky. Explosives and all. You understand."

The wide shouldered, thick chested soldier called Zero, surveyed the scene.

"You knuckleheads ready to go? Take care of your business and your balls cuz there ain't no throwing up or pissing in my POV. This is the last time I'll be your designated driver. I should be in my rack right now instead of babysitting a squad of drunks."

He grabbed a leftover twenty dollar bill from the table.

"For gas and my inconvenience."

"Don't be fooled, CB. He loves us. It's a Ranger thing." Cobalt cupped his hand over his mouth and stumbled to the bathroom, lurching around two tables and another customer.

"I bet he wallpapers the head with puke." Diego gripped the table, laughing,

****

Zero pushed, shoved, and cajoled his brothers into the vehicle. He settled Scout and Diego in the second seat, then he stuffed Cobalt in the very back of the SUV by bending one leg over the spare tire. They were sleeping in minutes.

CB saw Zero tie a rope around Cobalt's chest and secure the end to the headrest above the snoring Scout.

"You're tying him up?"

"No, CB, tying him *in*. He fell out the back a couple of times so this is in the interest of national security...well, my security. Cobalt said if I let him fall out again, he'll beat me. He's a big boy. Scares me."

"Okay, I'm good with that. Let's tie this ankle to the other headrest. Looks a little floppy."

"CB, you fit right in. Welcome to the team."

Satisfied they would not lose Cobalt out the back, CB and Zero stood at the edge of the parking lot and urinated in the grass.

"I say this is the *last* time I'll ever come get them. Then, when they call, I come get them." He zipped his jeans. "Let's do one more security round."

Zero stood back to admire his work making the bodies all fit in the limited space. "Look at the little darlings. Everyone of them is a natural born killer."

CB checked the rope around Cobalt one last time before they left.

"Come on, CB. You can ride shotgun if you promise not to throw up."

****

"Always been in the Army, Zero?" CB snapped his seatbelt.

"No. Family business is fireworks." The the dash lights gave Zero's face a soft glow.

"Where?" CB swallowed a beer belch before it could explode in the truck.

"Started out Southern Ohio, some into Michigan, but now it's pretty much whoever has the money to pay. My great uncle Louis did the 4th of July over the Detroit River in 1996. He put his heart and soul into that display. Lasted for an hour, boom, bang, pop, whistles. It was his step up to international displays."

Zero drove for a few moments before he asked CB, "Where you from? I bet my uncles or cousins did some fireworks for you."

"West Virginia, deep in the mountains."

Zero tapped his finger on the steering wheel. "My cousin Dominic does Charleston, West Virginia every year using barges on that river and along Interstate 64. What's its name...I can't think of the name of the river."

"Kanawha River. I used to fish it with my dad."

CB's second beer belch wouldn't be held down and between subsequent burps he managed to ask, "So how'd your family get into the fireworks business?"

"My great great grandfather started selling sparklers and firecrackers out of his gas station in Kentucky. When he was away on business, a customer at the station lit off a sparkler while someone was pumping gas. Blew the whole station and three quarters of the village. That should've been the end of it, but the old man took the insurance money, paid for damages, two funerals, and went north to Ohio. He bought a warehouse and became a distributor.

"The family stayed in the business. I mastered the computerized stuff, using compressed air to control the height and timing of the shells. The old fashion method used gunpowder to shoot the shell up and out. Take gunpowder out of the equation and you drop the risk of somebody doing something stupid on the ground..."

"Like lighting a sparkler at a gas station?"

"Yeah, like that. You still get the shell up where you want it. The computer program gives you a phenomenal display."

"Why'd you leave? Probably pretty good money in fireworks."

"Yeah, but the Army has bigger booms. When I'm done, I may go back to that. My cousins'll make sure I get a paycheck."

The conversation ended just as Zero brought the truck in front of the apartments. CB had one more question. "Why do they call you Zero?"

"I tend to overload the target. Not much left.

"Don't they have formulas to figure that out?"

Zero nodded. "Well, those are actually guidelines."

****

Next morning, CB spotted Cobalt at the Lucky Star diner across the street from the apartment complex. It was time to talk to him alone.

From his file, CB knew Cobalt served as the team's interpreter, interrogator, and was fluent in Farsi, Arabic and French. He had black hair, deep violet blue eyes, and a permanent blue-black five o'clock shadow. The tats on his arms were his military service in pictures, although CB saw a couple Cyrillic letters in one of them. He was the silent intellectual; the academic, and whom one commander called an "apex predator."

CB slid into the seat across from Cobalt. "You're up bright and early. I struggled a little getting out of bed. Hair of the dog?"

"No," Cobalt replied, still reading the menu, "it all boils down to mind set. Designing a mental plan then making the body follow it. The most successful people in all of history mastered the mindset, not that they all used it for good.

Simple, really, just takes practice." Cobalt waived at the pretty waitress behind the counter. "I'm ready to order."

"Is this on one or separate...."

Cobalt said, "Separate. I'll have six eggs over hard, extra butter for whole wheat toast, and a double order of bacon."

"And I'll have the pecan waffles, toast, sausage links, hash browns extra crisp, and cream for the coffee."

CB watched the waitress walk away. Cobalt did not.

"Hey, how about those Tigers? I think Detroit might have a chance this year. It's been a while since they fielded a team with a decent offense." It was a weak conversation starter, but it was all CB had at the moment.

Cobalt picked up a book he had been reading and flipped through the pages. "I don't follow baseball."

CB asked him, "Aside from academics, what do you do for fun? Surfing? Handball? You look pretty cut so I imagine you work out a lot."

"Actually, I don't. I have good genes."

CB stared out the window at the parking lot. "There's a '57 Chevy, cherry red and white. Looks like it's right out of the show room."

Cobalt turned away from his book to watch the car drive away, as if it was the most beautiful woman in the world.

"You like old school cars?" CB asked.

"My uncle had a couple. They're interesting."

When the meal arrived, Cobalt wolfed down his food. He counted out money for his bill and a handsome tip on the table. He left.

"Well, that's a start. Not much of one, but a start." CB had a pre-mission meeting with the old man in two hours. He could eat slowly and think. Above all else, he needed to think.

****

The mission training was intense but in the end, CB knew Zero, Diego, and Scout better than he knew his brothers in Deacon's Hollar. Cobalt was the enigma. While packing, Zero stopped by CB's room.

"Getting all your silk shirts and Testoni's packed?"

"What's a Testoni?"

"Italian handmade men's shoes. About four grand per shoe."

"Yeah. They'll come in handy walking the Dolly Sods."

"What's a Dolly Sods?"

"It's a wild area not too far from where my folks live. Tourists like to hike there. You go from forest to open windswept plateau, then into wetland bogs. Beautiful scenery. You can see over the Allegheny Mountains."

"Sounds interesting. Maybe I'll go there sometime. My grandpa told me there'd come a time when I'd like peace and solitude. This Dolly Sods, they got land for sale?"

"The Sods is a protected wildlife area but there's land for purchase around there, I'm sure. Take a seat while I finish packing." CB moved a stack of t-shirts from the chair.

Zero helped himself to CB's fridge. "I see you've been trying to get to know Cobalt. You might want to save your breath."

"Why?"

"The unofficial version is he was the only one to walk out of the mountains when his unit went on a patrol. They went into an ambush. He's still looking for who set them up."

"What then? Do you think he'll kill him?"

"Oh, I know he will. Cobalt'll study him like he does those books he reads. He'll set up the day, the time, the circumstances. Dude will know why he's dying, too. My man will look right into his eyes so he understands Cobalt's taking him out. He'll do the deed, walk away, and go find a book to read."

Zero took a long pull from the water bottle, leaving it half empty.

"Cobalt is ice. Better believe it. If you're looking for someone to be your buddy, go look someplace else. He won't get close to people. Not after the ambush."

"Move your feet, Zero, my clean shorts are there."

"Sorry. Keep your shorts off the floor."

"With you around, I will. Tell me more about Cobalt."

"CB, he'll take a bullet for you. If there's only one parachute in a plane going down, he'll give it to you. Most honorable man I ever met. He'll do what needs to be done to make sure we all survive, but don't try to thank him afterwards. You won't find him because he avoids niceties. He'll get gone before the medals and the handshakes come out."

"He was talking at the bar."

"The Leadslingers loosened him a little. He doesn't let that happen often."

"Thanks for clearing it up."

CB rolled his last t-shirt and packed it into his ruck. "Before you leave, Zero, it's a dollar for the water. CIA has me on an expense account." He grinned.

****

Nightfall was coming. It reminded CB of home when he camped out on the mountain tops. The high country gave him a place where he could lose himself in the majesty of the Milky Way. Whether he was tracking hogs at dawn with Wink Decker and his boys, or tracking Taliban targets in the Helmand province, the blackness of the night hid him from his game until they spooked and he had them in his sights. When the time was right, he took the shot.

The team was tight, professional, and well rehearsed; CB was confident in their abilities. They'd been together long enough to develop a mental telepathy of their own. CB knew his men and how they performed. The mission came first for each of them.

This was his third landing in Afghanistan. CB wouldn't have time to make contact with interpreters he'd used previously. No time to find the woman who dressed him in her bright blue burqa to ride on the back of a motorcycle and escape when she couldn't. Moments like this, he wondered what happened to her.

In the dusk of a spectacular mountain sunset, CB looked at his men: Diego, Zero, Cobalt, Scout. CB admired and respected them. What bothered him were two he didn't select: Smith and Jones.

****

Cobalt dropped down beside CB.

"I always like the sunrises and sunsets in the mountains. It's beautiful. Peaceful."

"Until someone starts shooting," CB replied.

"Well, there's that, of course."

"Everything all set?"

"Affirmative. Scout is fine tuning his computer, Zero just rechecked his explosives and weapons, and Diego did a final check of his RATS."

"And you?"

"Don't worry. I'm good. Got my shit in one sock."

CB nodded, then leaned back and looked at the stars. "This reminds me of home."

"Where's that?"

"Deacon's Hollar, West Virginia. Small place, quiet. Not heavily populated but nice people. Some retirees live there rather than Florida or out West. I was raised there. A good place to grow up if you're a kid."

"What's there to do?"

"Fish, hunt, make money off the tourists when they come to ski or hike the mountains. John Denver wrote a song about the place. Pretty accurate."

Cobalt took out his pocket knife and proceeded to clean his nails. "Your family got a business there?"

"No. My dad works for the department of transportation on the roads. He was gone a lot when I was growing up, but he'll get a good retirement. My mom takes care of the farm with my siblings."

"You got schools there?"

"Not really. Some of the old ladies give the little kids a kindergarten through first grade education. In second grade level, they get bussed. Parents do a lot of teaching. Why'd you ask?"

"No reason. Just curious. I'm also a little curious about our uninvited guests."

"You mean the Smith and Jones duet?"

"Yeah, the men of few words but who can speak to *sus scrofa,* with or without the *domesticus,* on their own level."

"Excuse me?"

"Peccary, porkers, oinkers. Pigs, my man."

Luke stifled his laugh in the quiet of dusk.

"Zero has different names for them," Cobalt added.

"I'm sure he does. I don't know why they're on mission. I couldn't get a straight answer from the deputy director. Strange they were sitting in his outer office at the time I asked."

"Interesting. I thought you CIA spooks were all pretty close to one another."

"In a manner of speaking, we all have our secrets."

"That we do, CB. That we do."

Before CB could ask, Cobalt quickly found his way back down the hill to his place with the team.

****

Everything went according to plan. The landing was perfect, all the equipment at the rendezvous was exactly what was requested and supplies not disturbed. CB's contacts in the 'Stan were still on top of their game. He paid them enough US taxpayer's dollars to ensure they were.

The team mounted Christini 450 motorcycles and headed to the target. As they drove across the empty flat lands to the edge of the mountains, CB could almost taste the steak and fries he was going to order at Shorty's when he got back. CB glanced up at the skies ahead. No moon, but billions of stars; The perfect night for a bike ride.

Within two kilometers of the site, CB gave the signal. The team dismounted. According to Langley's surveillance, they were alone. They moved through the rising hills to get to the road, always on the lookout for what Langley said wasn't there. They had been fooled by technology before.

CIA HQ wanted to monitor all military traffic along the road into Afghanistan. Sensors implanted in designated areas would determine the size, weight, and an educated guess of the cargo, along with speed, and projected destination. It would all be digested and spit back at the computers at Langley. CB's men were to set the equipment and be gone. Easy assignment. Put the steaks on the grill.

****

"Crap," CB said under his breath as an earthquake shook the area. Within seconds, a voice in CB's earpiece came to life.

"We have registered a 6.5 earthquake, epicenter five kilometers from your location. Area will have aftershocks. No further information until seismic data received. Report on damage and topographical changes. Copy."

"Copy. We're still shaking. Over."

"Copy. Advise mission status. Over."

CB checked his men.

The faceless voice repeated, "Mission status. Over."

CB hated to talk to robotic voices. He knew there was a human being listening in the background, letting the soulless machine do the work. One day he was going to mess with the computer but today was not the day.

"Mission is a go. I repeat mission is a go. Rubber Ducky is in route to the targeted location. Out."

"CB."

"Yeah, Diego?"

"You know how I know this is a CIA operation?"

CB did not want to take the bait, but he did. "How?"

"Because of the bullshit code names. I mean 'Mother Goose' and 'Rubber Ducky?' Who even thinks of this stuff? Who you got working over there, Hans Christian Andersen?"

"That ain't nothing, Doc," Zero said. "When I was with the CIA spooks in Nepal, some nut job in Langley had us use 'Miss Muffett' and 'Spider Man.'" Zero was cut off by CB's order to leave.

"Mount up, barbarians. We're out of here."

The unit reformed. Sound and light discipline was immediate. The team crossed a dried riverbed and climbed around a pile of fallen stone. When Scout gave the nod, they stopped.

"Zero. Diego. Check out the north and south sides of the road. Cobalt to the east. Scout, set your video games and let's get out. Last one to Shorty's buys the first round."

"CB," Zero whispered, "what about those two?"

"They'll go up top. Keep your head on a swivel." CB signaled Smith and Jones to take the high ground.

"Bro, you sure you want them up there?"

"No. If they do anything that looks unusual, go full bore kinetic. I don't like them at our backs either. *Sabe?*"

"*Sabe* on Doom and Gloom." Zero disappeared into the darkness.

Working efficiently CB and Scout set the sensors and sound activated recording devices. CB waited patiently while Scout got his computer to make the connections and run diagnostics.

"Taking a little longer than I expected, CB."

Scout was whispering to the massive satellite, like talking to a scared child, urging it to connect and work with his receivers on the ground.

"Did you do an azimuth check?" CB presumed there would be an instantaneous hook up between sensors and satellites circling above.

"What? It's all digital. If you feel better, yes, I did an azimuth check. We're in the right spot."

"Maybe use a different computer. Earthquake might have fugazied it."

"It was an earthquake, not a solar storm, CB. Who's the 25Sierra here anyway? Go find Zik and Zak and leave me alone. There, see? I got it. Langley's on. Will take a few minutes to run the tests and we're good to go."

CB waved to Smith and Jones to come down from their post. He signaled to mount up.

****

"Someone is shouting in Russian. What are *they* doing here?" Cobalt asked.

"Probably the same thing we are." CB touched his throat mic. "Mother Goose, Mother Goose. Over."

"Copy. What is your status? Over."

"Mother Goose, uninvited guests have arrived. Over." Silence in CB's earpiece.

"Mother Goose, do you copy? Over."

"Copy. Investigate and report. Out."

"By the sound of it, someone is pissed," Cobalt said as he used his night vision binoculars scanning the forward area.

CB pulled the earpiece out of his ear and left it dangling. "They replaced everyone who had any common sense with a computer, now everything is a pile of hot steaming BS. Cobalt, you know Russian?"

"Nope, not my language. Ask Scout. His grandfather was Russian."

"I don't speak it well, but I can fumble around a little." Scout offered. "My Gramp's would swear at us kids when we were irritating him. Said he had more fun at the camps in Siberia than babysitting his daughter's spawn. Made us call him *praotez,* great ancestor. Wait, he's talking again. I know that one."

Zero nudged him on the shoulder. "What was it?"

"He said '*Ya vas perelovlu kishki. Trusi.*'"

"What's he say?"

"Well, it loses something in translation but I think he said 'I will catch you one by one and disembowel you. Cowards.'"

"I'm disappointed. I thought the Russians were more, you know, colorful."

"They are. I just don't know all he's saying. Could be some good ones in there, but I don't know them. He's caught under a rock...he's *krovotecheni ye*...bleeding. *Sukin sin* is son of a bitch."

Cobalt approached CB, Diego, and Zero. "What's up? What's Langley want us to do?"

"I don't know. I think someone poured coffee on their hard drive. To hell with them." CB didn't know how this was going to complicate the mission, but he was sure there would be wrinkles.

"Scout, scan the area. See what you can pick up. Diego, get ready to determine the extent of his injuries and if we can move him. Zero, get close enough to monitor anything that could take us out if we hit a trip wire. If we're clear, Cobalt and I'll pull him out. We'll leave before too many eyes pick us up. Don't want the NEIC giving away our position on their next update."

"What's the NEIC? Never heard of them." Zero took his weapons belt up a notch.

Cobalt placed his hand on Zero's helmet and shook the head under it. "That my friend, is the National Earthquake Information Center where every time you blow something up, their gauges and needles have spasms."

"Oh, so they heard about me, too?"

"What about Creep and Creepier?" Diego adjusted his medical pack.

"They'll cover our six." The feeling of unease which plagued him since acquiring those two came back on CB in full force. He wasn't going to break out in a sweat about it. There was time for that later.

Scout tapped Diego's shoulder. "He's calling for help. He's back cursing them at the moment. Used the word *'padlec'* which means something like, um, they did something dirty behind his back. *Padonak* is scum."

"I need to get to Moscow and teach those people how to swear with some class." Scout heard the disappointment in Zero's voice and smiled.

CB let the Russian curse for a few minutes longer. "Scout, are you sure he's not calling in air support?"

Scout adjusted the transmitter tape around his neck. "*Zmey* is snake and he's calling people *predateli* or traitors and *idi k chertu*, or maybe that's going to hell. He isn't saying any numbers, CB."

"How do you know *zmey* is snake?"

"That's what *proatez* called my aunt's husband."

CB looked over his shoulder. Smith and Jones were at the back, their fingers off the trigger. "Zero, you got eyes on him?"

"Yeah. He's trapped between boulders. Here, take a look."

CB peered through the scope. "Doesn't look like he's booby trapped. Moving his arms too much. He would set off his own explosives if he was. Scout, picking up anyone else in the area?"

"There's a vehicle heading away from our position, CB," Scout reported. "Don't know who they are but they are fast tracking to the border. Wonder how Langley missed *that*? And there are some SEALs lost in the desert a few clicks away."

Cobalt was startled by that. "How'd you know they're lost?"

"Because they ain't Rangers." They all grinned.

Rescanning to make sure the injured man was not wired with explosives, Zero gave the all clear to approach.

"CB," Cobalt whispered, "Look at his tats and his side arm. Russian all the way. What do you want to do with him?"

"I suppose a bullet would be the wise choice, but there's opportunity in every event. Diego, give him the once over. We'll have to take turns piggybacking him to the bikes."

CB sighed. "He doesn't smell too good. I'll take first turn. Load him up when ready, Diego. Transporting a smelly Russian in Afghanistan. The things I do for my country."

Smith and Jones were watching the area intently, grunting to each other. CB heard the squawk coming from his ear piece as Langley tried to get a response.

"Damn computers anyway." CB pulled on the wire to disconnect.
****

"So, you're awake. Do you speak English?"

"*Da*. My English better than your man speak Russian like *suka*. Get rid of him."

"I don't have him because he is or is not fluent in Russian. Why you are here and how I dispose of you are the real questions."

"If you give me drugs to make me talk you not know who I am."

"I'm not interested in who you are..."

"But maybe we make deal? I have feeling we are same. Maybe I can be of help to young CIA agent in areas of Afghanistan where he should not be?"

CB didn't show any indication he was surprised the Russian knew he was CIA. The slightest flinch would affirm the Russian had the right bait on the right hook for the right fish.

"Sorry, but I rescind the invite to your hallucination. Anyway, I need to figure out what to do with you. I got a hot date in Paris in twelve hours." CB glanced at the opening of the cave.

"You didn't divulge any state secrets, but you do ramble a lot when dehydrated. You ramble in French, Spanish, and German. You are Russian, but just how much Russian remains to be seen."

"Okay, Secret Agent Man. Let's stop with cossack and bandit games. You have something I want and I have something you want. Let us have *détente* and see what become."

CB was interested. "I'll ask the questions. You know, simple things like what are you doing here? Why did your men leave?"

"I hear things in delirium. In interest of getting what I want, which mean you get what you need, I answer. Your *ved'mak* has me restrained, in manner of speaking."

"My *ved'mak*?"

"Your witcher, CB, he is *ved'mak*."

"You need to answer my questions, without this being a class in linguistics."

"CB, may I call you CB?" The agent nodded.

The Russian continued after clearing his throat. "CB, I try make contact with American unit would be here. How do I know? Russia is not just land of ice and snow. We have technology, too. I was looking for *you.*"

He took a drink from the bottle at his side. "Ah, CB, you are good. Never even wink eye."

CB did not blink, but his heart was racing. "So you got up this morning, took a walk to Afghanistan, and came looking for me. Santa Claus is real, pigs can fly, and Elvis is working at the Piggly Wiggly in Memphis."

"Ah, I love Elvis. I'll have bluuuuueeee Christmas without you...."

"Doc," CB called to Diego, "how much juice did you give this guy?"

The combat medic hustled into the dark and checked the Russian's pulse. "Apparently not enough."

The Russian pulled his arm away. "Remove your *ved'mak*. You and me, CB, maybe we talk like turkey?"

"Talk like...You mean 'talk turkey,' not like a turkey."

"See? You know Russian idioms."

"I'm pretty sure that it originated in the US, like around colonial times."

"No, came from Comrade Lenin but, not matter, eh?"

CB nodded Diego away. "You were looking for me. You found me. Now what?"

The Russian straightened the collar of his shirt and said, "I am Mikhail Ivanovich Verkhovensky and Langley will not find me on rosters of the Russian Army, KGB, or FSB. My name and appearance have changed since the years. Old *komandir* don't know who I really. Sometimes I forget myself, but I know what I want, CB. I make offer, like in movie, offer you can't refuse."

"And that is?"

"I give you information about all Chinese and North Korean missile defenses along borders and those out in North China Sea."

"Nope. Sorry, friend. Those systems are old news. Why'd your team leave the area?"

"Because they are cows who go to hell."

"Because they are cows who go... you mean cowards?"

"What I say, *trusi.*"

"That doesn't make sense. You'd have three men who would've engaged in a firefight."

"No, CB, *my* mission was to find you. If I found you, I would shoot them in show of good faith."

"You would kill your own men in a show of good faith?"

"Not my men. It was *their* mission to kill *me.*

"Why didn't they kill you in Moscow?"

"For CIA spy, you not too smart, CB. They only caught me in Afghanistan. They think earthquake kill me, but they don't make sure. They thinking I dead in mountains, covered in boulders. Kremlin gets rid of spy who knows too much, case closed. They go back to Moscow have parade or free meal or something."

"What kind of commander kills his own men?"

"They *not* my men. You think zombies at your back are favorite uncles? If you fail, they have their mission. You're not smart like you think, CIA CB."

The Russian hit a nerve, but CB didn't flinch. He needed to show he wasn't the chicken in this game.

"Let's get back to our deal. You have something maybe I want, but I definitely have something you want. What is it?"

The Russian looked over CB's shoulder making sure he was not overheard.

"I want free of this. I want passage United States. I want place where no one will think look for me. Russia has very poor track record how they say goodbye. Retired friends have unfortunate accident fall out of window, drink poisoned cocktails in London restaurant. I don't want like that. I want watch sun rise as free man. I want peace, young friend, *peace.* You go now. Talk to Langley. Don't tell them there is leak. Your boss not like Russian spy find hole in his sock."

"A hole in his sock?"

"You disappoint me. Must be rich man's son. Never had hole in sock? Means toe is sticking out, the traitor is sticking out, like big toe from hole in sock. You find traitor and then find me nice place. Get me back to Moscow for little longer. I want pack my good shoes."

Diego and Cobalt were on post above the cave. CB nodded to his men as he walked thirty meters down the trail.

A breach? Wouldn't be the first time there was someone at HQ who couldn't keep their face or mouth off social media--someone in his chain, or a branch of the chain, knew his team's mission--and why are the two mummies trailing along?

The Russian called it a 'hole in sock' and CB was determined to discover to whom the toe belonged.

****

CB sat staring as the Russian snored through another dose of Diego's combat juice. "Who the hell are you?" he whispered.

"I am best friend," the Russian answered. "You need to walk softer. Not nice wake up old man."

"You're not as old as you would have me think, Mikhail. Can I call you Mikhail?"

"Certainly, CB. But old? Maybe. Maybe not."

"For me to risk my life and those of my men, you'll have to come up with something better than..."

"I know, I know, CB. Something better than missile sites already known."

"Yes."

"But method they use to change codes and passwords?" Mikhail smiled. "I thought not."

Thanks to training, CB opened the pack of energy bars from his cargo pocket without his hands shaking.

"Okay, so you get me that. We still have a problem." He offered the Russian a pack of peanuts, an energy bar, and bottled water.

"What is problem?"

"You need to get back to Moscow."

"Yes. Unfinished business."

"I need time to get you out of Afghanistan. It's not like I can book you first class on American Airlines."

"I don't fly American Airlines, CB. Ugly women. I fly Delta."

"What?"

"Am kidding. All beautiful. You need laugh more. Be like Russians. We laugh all the time. Is good for heart pressure."

"Blood pressure."

Grabbing a crumb of the energy bar that fell from the wrapper, Mikhail asked, "What day it? And hour?"

CB looked at his watch. "Today is the 18th, 0430. I've had my men take care of you for two days."

"CB, can I call you by your first name? Can I call you 'C'? Not funny, no, I guess not. You Americans have no sense of humor when humor on you. So, give pen and paper." Mikhail scrawled numbers across the notepad CB handed him.

"I want my pen and notebook back."

"*Da, da,* Yankee. Very cheaply made. Not like good Russian paper. But more important, can you get me coordinates I give you, by tomorrow at 2000 hour?"

CB looked at the paper. "To Termez? Uzbekistan? Seriously?"

"Of course seriously. You think I like country without vodka? I have friends there. Is not far. Can you get me?"

"I can get you close but we're not crossing the river. Can you walk?"

"*Da.* Maybe I walk on water, too, eh, Yankee? Maybe in couple hours, be better and with not so much of the *ved'mak* poison. I can see in his eyes your witcher wants to kill me."

"He won't kill you unless I tell him."

"I don't trust him, but I trust him more than the living dead you have with you. Look at team, CB. See what does not fit." He was hungry and took the last bite of the chocolate without chewing.

Mikhail sighed. "What would my comrade *komandir* say me teaching CIA? Get me close and someone cross Thalweg of Amu Darya River. Call your soldiers."

CB checked the coordinates again. "Scout, I got something for you. This number, this time, these coordinates."

"Are you serious?"

"Like a Russian buried under a rock in Afghanistan. Can we make it on the bikes?"

"Yeah, if we piggyback the Russian, load up on fuel cans, and leave the two Lords of Nine back here."

"No can do. They come, but load them with gas cans. When we come back, they ride in front." Scout mumbled something CB didn't want to hear so he chose to ignore it. Turning to Mikhail, he said, "Got it. My men will make it happen. I get you there, you owe me."

"Don't worry, CB, you have I promise."
****

At the river's edge, CB and Mikhail passed the time in silence. CB's men were positioned in the surrounding area; Scout and Zero covered the valley from the south, behind the trees and brush that lined the area close to the river. Smith and Jones were on the northside, while Cobalt and Diego covered them.

Mikhail stifled a groan moving to get off his hip. "Your *cherno knizhnik* is good. I can almost forget he is not Russian doctor."

CB pulled out an envelope from his pocket and offered Mikhail two white caplets. "Here. My *ved'mak* didn't want you to suffer...much."

"No, is fine. Am sure from his personal stash of strychnine. I don't like the way the big one looks at me...ah...like a Spaniard at the Inquisition, dark Moor beard with radioactive blue eyes. Very strange people you hang out with, CB. We don't have those kind in Russia."

"No pills, I get it. Just don't tell Putin I didn't offer. Here, take this." CB handed over his phone.

Mikhail dialed a series of numbers with his back turned to CB. "No peeking. Is secret."

CB slowly shook his head while Mikhail chatted in Russian to his contacts. "You charge me long distance rates on phone?"

"Only if you used up my minutes. You think you're funny."

"All Russians funny. We sing, dance, drink vodka, and tell jokes. But not at Lubyanka. No, they have no sense of humor there. I was for reeducation once. Called it Moscow Hilton. They make me stay thirty more days since I like so much."

The silence of the night was broken with the faint sound of a camouflaged watercraft approaching the bank. CB and Mikhail heard the motor of the launch cut out about the same time Cobalt radioed to CB, "Taxi stand is full. Cut and run."

CB replied, "Copy."

Mikhail smiled faintly. "CB, is only room for one. I know you want to go Mother Russia, but no extra seat. Here, you take phone. I already reverse charges so you pay. Ha, ha! Reverse charges." Mikhail chuckled as his eyes scanned the black waters.

"Mikhail, you're on your own. I don't want your friends to find me here."

"*Spasibo*. You watch those two *krovososushchiye vampyr*."

"Vampires?"

"I say blood sucking vampires. See? You learn Russian. Is good."

"Get out of here before I call in an air strike and burn your ass out of the water."

"I will miss you, CB."

"Don't tell me you're going to start crying?"

"Ha! I cry when I am in my new home with garden, dog, and cupboard of food and vodka." Mikhail flashed a red light. "Maybe I find round American woman to wash my clothes and warm my bed, eh, CB?" When he turned to say goodbye, there was no one there. Into the dark Mikhail spoke softly, *"Da blagoslovit vas vsekh bog*...God Bless you all...friend. I will not forget my debt."

Mikhail waved but CB and his men had disappeared into the shadow of the mountains, their retreat covered by the river's mist and the coming night.

LUKE PERKINS - MOSCOW

"Damn it, Perkins. You get your butt to Moscow on the next flight and don't come back until you have a flash drive in your hand. I made the mistake of filing a positive report with the Director and you have nothing."

"The team set the sensors as instructed so the mission was a success."

"Where's your head? Up your ass? Any other field officer would know the sensors were secondary to nuclear codes and passwords. I was against sending you to Afghanistan. You're too inexperienced, but I was out voted. So, now you know." The Deputy Director swallowed hard and began to sweat, but now he knew the sensors were set and functioning.

"Sir, I never said..."

"But you strongly indicated you had or could get the intel."

"Sir, what happened..."

"I could give a shit what you say happened but let me tell you what's going to happen, Luke. Unless you come up with the data, your next assignment will be in the Chilean Andes looking for alien love letters to Area 54. Get out of here before you piss me off anymore."

Luke made a mental note to remove the Deputy from his Christmas card list.

Closing the office door, Luke winked at Janice Streeter.

"I need you to notify transportation I'll be..."

"I heard. Too bad you'll be away for the Christmas holidays. Your family will miss you."

"Christmas in West Virginia is magical, but so is Moscow. I'll stock up on gifts at GUM."

"GUM?"

"Yeah. Huge department store, great bargains, and a fantastic toy collection. I've got younger brothers and a sister who benefit from my travels."

"Hey, as long as you're going, could you get me a set of the hand painted nesting dolls? I'd like to add those to my collection."

"Still playing with dolls, Janice?" Luke laughed. "I never thought you as a collector. But, sure, I'll get you the best I can find."

She reached for her purse.

"Nope. Wouldn't think of it. After that ass chewing, your dolls are on the Deputy."

"Thanks, Luke. I'll make sure your arrangements are first class."

"You have my eternal gratitude, Janice. Where're we going for lunch? I need a drink."

****

Luke loved Moscow during its New Year's celebrations in late December. The city holiday tree in Red Square was magnificent. Vendor stalls trimmed with boughs of pine, globes of green, gold, and red danced in a cold wind. Snow blanketed the city in a comforter of winter.

The *Ded Moroz* event was an attraction he did not want to miss. Hundreds of men dressed like Santa Claus, known as Grandfather Winter to the Russians, walking the streets to usher in the New Year. The beautiful young women dressed as *snegurochka,* the granddaughter of *Ded Moroz,* helped deliver presents to good children.

Luke adjusted his tie and zipped his coat to his neck. He was a cybersecurity representative selling data products to Russian companies doing business with US markets. He played the part of a tourist as he videoed ice skaters and costumed stilt performers amazing the children; mothers grabbing cups of hot chocolate before spilling on winter coats.

"Skol'ko stoyat kukly Bubushki?" He stopped at a vendor's booth. The old woman behind the counter, bundled in a coat and scarf to ward off the cold evening wind, smiled.

"Nyet." She reached under the counter and offered him a paper bag with some undisclosed article in it.

Ignoring the bag, Luke said in English, "The dolls. How much?"

"Nyet." She shoved the bag at him with increased force.

Luke slowly pronounced each word: "How. Much. Dolls?"

The vendor replied in broken English, "Misha say not smart. Wooden head, take bag. Following you."

"Misha? This is from Mikhail?"

"Da, da. Misha." She pushed the bag into his gut.

Turning away from the vendor with the bag stuffed under his coat, Luke dodged into a crowd of elderly adults. He made himself shorter in the crowd, bending his knees as he walked. From the bag he pulled out a red hat trimmed in white and an oversized jacket trimmed the same. Wearing his new garb, Luke moved into the passing group of Santa Claus men. The bulk of his jacket changed his silhouette, confusing whoever was tailing him.

Mixed in with the mass of celebrants, he passed the old woman's booth. She was being interrogated by three huge men, each wearing a white scarf.

"Nyet! Nyet! Nyet!" She pointed in the opposite direction Luke disappeared. The thugs ran where she pointed.

"Spasibo," Luke whispered under his breath.

He walked along Red Square waving to the crowds on the street.

St. Basil's was behind him and the Kremlin to his left. The GUM department store, on his right, was outlined in white lights which made the area easy to see. He looked for what didn't fit.

And what didn't fit were three men, all wearing white neck scarves, weaving through a throng of celebrants dancing to the music under the lights.

He felt a squeeze on his arm, "Psstttt, Luke. Sssttt."

He looked into the cloudy eyes of an grandmotherly woman, dressed in a heavy coat and a brightly colored headscarf, her face reddened by the cold.

"Psstttt, Luke.. Here, Misha, *da.*" She dropped her purse. Pulling his cap snugly over his forehead, he retrieved her handbag from the gutter. She pressed a flash drive into his hand. *"Spasibo, Spasibo,"* she whispered as she and her aluminum walker disappeared down the street.

He was lost to his followers in the mass of red and white. Luke broke from the crowd and slid down a side street, observing from the shadows. The subterfuge was over. Tearing off the Santa Claus disguise, it was CB who emerged from the alley.

CB transferred the flash drive into his left pocket as he scanned the city streets. He ducked down and reversed his coat, using the lining as camouflage. CB grabbed a green knitted cap and scarf from the counter of an unsuspecting vendor, and a hot drink from a distracted patron. He slipped back into the mass of people, blending in with the crowd walking past Lenin's tomb.

He cut across Red Square, and ambled toward Nikolskaya Street, hoping to be far enough ahead to turn and follow those who were looking for him. The hunted becomes the hunter.

There it was. The scarf. This time on the other side of the street and by itself. They split up. He had to get off the street, get to a different avenue, and maybe disappear in a cab. CB doubled back, re-crossing *Nikolskaya* and disappeared into the crowd at Kremlevskiy Proyezd.

His luck changed when he entered a bar packed with young Muscovites celebrating the New Year. CB discarded his coat and hat, ruffled his hair and started to bounce up and down like the other dancers. The CIA agent made his way toward the back, and hopefully, an exit.

One white scarf entered the bar; then the other two. The men entered like a caricature of hitmen from Hollywood. The DJ kept the music blaring, unaware of what was happening on the dance floor as shouts and screeches echoed off the walls from the dancers being pushed and shoved out of the way. Tempers flared as the thugs penetrated the crowd. It was but a few seconds until vodka induced bravery surfaced and bottles were broken for weapons.

CB ducked behind the end of the bar. Peeking between bar stools, he saw a foolish young man break the leg off a chair. A crowd of half drunk heroes were no match for professional fighters. His killers made their way across the floor, dancer by dancer.

Estimating the distance, in three strides he would be in the alley, but when shots rang out in the bar, the crowd fell to the floor in unison, exposing CB to his executioners.

Instantly he dropped, rolled, and took cover. Two more shots exploded and a new level of hysteria rose from the crowd.

One of the hitmen fired randomly. A bullet ricocheted off the door molding above CB's head, while the second round ripped through the sleeve of his sweater, grazing his arm.

He removed the Sig 365 from his leg holster and fired directly into the chest of the closest brute, who fell backwards, unharmed.

CB rose, pivoted, and fired as he made his exit. Out of a dark alcove, an arm jerked him into a hidden pantry between the kitchen and the back door. With alcohol infused breath, a familiar voice whispered,

"Welcome Moscow, my little CB. Now my turn save life. Shhhhh."

A quick blow to CB's peroneal nerve dropped him to the floor.

Mikhail Ivanovich stepped around CB. "Stay and let big dog take care of *schchenok*." The Russian brought his index finger to his lips as CB raised his head and tried to speak.

"Shhh, Yankee. Take nap."

CB saw two kitchen workers rush past the pantry, followed by the three assassins.

Like a cat on soft paws, Mikhail followed the trio who were unaware of their new status. Immobile, CB could only watch as Mikhail disappeared around the doorway.

CB heard three shots, causing another round of hysterics from students trying to flee the madness. Mikhail returned, reloading his magazine.

Not fully recovered from the paralyzing strike to his nervous system, CB pointed to his own face and then to Mikhail's. Looking in the glass, Mikhail wiped a smear of blood from his cheek. "Still handsome, da?"

"Women don't like a bloody face."

"Ah, we pick up. Now you think like Russian. Come. Get off floor. Make you look weak."

"You didn't have to take me down."

"Oh, and if say pretty please, you stay? I think not. Get up. I fill you with vodka on night of reconciliation."

"If you haven't noticed, the party's over." CB dusted off his sweater and examined the slight wound to his arm. "Maybe leaving would be appropriate? None of the women seem willing to sit and talk."

"Okay. We make go vodka."

"It's vodka to go."

"Americans, always so stubborn. Okay. Vodka to go." Mikhail grabbed a half filled bottle from one of the few standing tables as he fired two shots into the ceiling. The American grabbed his jacket from the floor.

CB and Mikhail picked their way between the two rows of terrified students crawling to the door. As the hysterical party goers flooded into the street, fear rippled into the crowd, who, like rings on the surface of a silent pond, transferred terror to others, only adding to the pandemonium of the once content shoppers.

With his arm around CB's shoulders, Mikhail whispered, "We old friends who celebrate New Year. I sing loudly and you laugh and we make our way down street everyone know we drunk. Here I sing for you.

Ey, yablochko
Kuda ty katish'sya?
ya ustal ot svoyey zheny
Davay bludit'.

"See? They ignore. Car two blocks around corner."

"What about...?"

"Three men, three shots, good, eh? My little Yankee CB, come with me. I like you. We talk."

"You mean you shot them and left?'

"What? I call priest? *Neyt!* They left me die under boulders, I leave them die behind trash cans. Debt paid. Must be first job, eh, CB? You get used over time. Is nothing."

As instructed, CB put his arm around Mikhail's shoulders and his laughter echoed between the buildings on the snowy Moscow night while the faint sounds of sirens signaled the arrival of the *politisya* and ambulances to the bar. The men slipped around the building and into a beat up Volga.

"How old is this car?"

"Oh, maybe 20, 30 years. Don't know. Borrowed from boyfriend of ex-wife."

"So if we have to dump the car and make a run for it?"

"No problem. Not my car. What I care? Here, shortly, we change again make sure not followed. You didn't do too well when you dressed even as *Ded Moroz*. So much to teach you. I lose respect for CIA. Look closely how I do tail ditch"

"It's ditch a tail." Ignoring the insult, CB said, "Those old women were from you?"

"You like, eh? You could not keep up. Survivors, all of them."

"Does the Kremlin know you're running an espionage ring using *babushkas*?"

"Shhhh, CB. Let them think they in charge."

Mikhail brought the car to an abrupt sliding stop, intentionally hitting two parked cars, making a long, deep scar on the side of the Volga.

"Don't worry. Is boyfriend of ex-wife. No problem. Did I say already?"

"Yes, you did."

"Must be getting forgetful in old age."

CB rubbed frost from the inside of the car window. "For a minute there, I thought it was because you're drunk."

Mikhail accelerated, along with his blood alcohol levels, and drove for a few more twisting, turning miles before slamming on the brakes in front of a dilapidated, gray apartment building. CB had no idea where he was. All the landmarks had disappeared behind the falling snow.

Mikhail sighed as he reached into his vest pocket. CB immediately pulled out his handgun.

"Stop, Yankee, only getting cigarettes. Do you smoke?"

"No, never picked up the habit."

"What is CB anyway? What name that is?" Mikhail lit a cigarette and slowly exhaled the smoke, filling the Volga.

"Stands for Chaw Bacon."

"Eh? What woman names child Chaw Bacon?"

"Where I come from it's a term for a hill person, an uncultured person. People who call other people that are rude, elitist, arrogant."

"Are people where you come from uncultured?"

"No, actually, they have a lot of culture."

"What is real name? I mean I steal state secrets and commit treason, I deserve knowing who for I commit treason, I mean on whose behalf."

"Luke. You can call me, Luke."

"Good. I hate Chaw Bacon. CB not bad. Is Luke. That good name. Luke the physician, writer, friend of Jesus. Come, Luke, we have more route we take."

He hated to admit it, but his trust in Mikhail was growing. This fast trip to Moscow was to retrieve the flash drive with the promised data. Would Mikhail deliver? Luke would hate to kill him.

****

He followed Mikhail into a dark, dreary apartment complex. Not even the sparkling flakes of snow could disguise the misery etched into its face between the windows.

Luke noticed none of the doors were numbered. Mikhail saw him pause.

"When questioned by police, if don't know number, how you know who lives there? First rule under Soviets, Luke, deny, deny, deny. Come, hurry, is cold."

They walked in silence through the hall and out the back door. There stood another dented red Volga. "Are all the cars you have red?"

"Why not? Is good color."

"Does the heater work in this one?"

"Maybe. Maybe not. Is second boyfriend of ex-wife car."

"Are you going to crash this one?"

"No." Mikhail reached under the seat and brought up a pint of vodka and a fat cigar. "See? I like guy. Now you quiet. I need think while I drive. You sleep."

Sleeping was the last thing Luke did. He was watching for signs to the major highways and thoroughfares he studied on the plane while in flight across the Atlantic. His cover was blown. He would have to rely on training and luck.

Luke was jostled out of his thoughts as Mikhail suddenly turned down a narrow street, drove the car through an opened garage door, and slammed on the brakes. The door dropped, plunging the men into darkness.

"Laser beam shut door. Like in America. Now we wait."

"Wait for what?"

"For while is what we wait. If we followed, they come soon enough. We wait. You too impatient, Special Agent Luke Chaw Bacon. Have you ever been hunting?" Mikhail took a hearty pull from the bottle.

"Yes."

"Me, too. Grandfather take me hunting long ago. Russian Boar hunting. You should understand spy game like hunting wild pig. Big boar, more skill hunter must have. Must have patience. Must be determined. Must have goal in mind before bullet leaves the barrel. Otherwise, *pftttt!*"

"Pfttt?"

"Hunter distracted and pig run away. But, pig run away smarter pig. Spy game is same. You learn from every spy you meet. Otherwise, they get away and hunt you. Understand?"

Luke nodded.

They sat in the darkness, the smell of Mikhail's vodka laced breath along with the stale aroma of his cheap cigar made Luke nauseated.

Mikhail opened his door and exited the car. In the dimness, he turned and stared at Luke through the dirty window.

"Well, Yankee Chaw Bacon, you want us talk, we talk." A massive belch punctuated Mikhail's remark.

Luke had to admire the Russian. As intoxicated as he was, he could still drive, stand, and walk.

Mikhail led Luke up a set of rusted stairs, missing a step only once, and through what looked like a supervisor's office. A tilted desk in front of an overturned chair, an ancient rotary dial phone, and torn pages of a calendar were the only evidence of a once bustling industry. Dirty windows, witnesses to the pain and suffering of workers long gone, concealed the visitors in the long forgotten warehouse.

Mikhail left footprints in the dust as he crossed the empty room. He pushed open a door to another staircase, the end of which Luke found himself on the roof of the structure. Pulling his gun, he scanned the area for an ambush.

"Yankee Chaw Bacon. Put away. If I want you dead, I kill you in club and be awarded Cross of Lenin. They make me national hero kill US spy. Please put gun away and listen what I say."

Luke holstered his gun. "What then?"

"What then? I need favor." Mikhail's words tumbled from his alcohol soaked brain. "I need favor."

"You just saved my life. We're even for Afghanistan."

"No. We not even until I say even. You could taken those three monkeys out yourself. They no brains. Never should been sent to kill you. You far too good, Chaw Bacon, little Yankee." Mikhail leaned against the railing, gazing over the city lights of Moscow. "We had deal in Afghanistan. Something for something."

The snow eased up and from the height, Luke saw the lights of Moscow bounce off low hanging clouds, casting the city in an eerie glow. Cars sped smoothly along the highways.

Mikhail turned and studied Luke's face. "I older than my time. I did voluntary things should burn in hell for, and did them gladly at request of superiors. My past keeps me up in nights. You never want to see scenes playing in my head over. Never worried me when young and thought was righteous thing I do. Convinced myself serving higher purpose, bigger good." Mikhail paused as he lit another cigarette. He slowly released the smoke, each curl and swirl reflected in the lights of the city, the blue haze hovering around his head.

"But comes moment in life, maybe is age, maybe is memory, but something starts stirring in brain and you understand. All things you thought were right..

.ah...they were never right, never good, never higher purpose. What you did," he coughed softly, "were someone else sin piled upon your own."

Mikhail took another drag off his poorly rolled cigarette, the cinders of which he flicked from his leather jacket. "No burn holes. I like jacket. Was gift from my *tovaris komandir* for job well done. Don't ask. Was job well done is all."

Mikhail spit over the edge of the roof. "So well done even many years later disgusts me."

The blue smoke poured from his mouth and nose as he exhaled; it was picked up by a slight wind and traveled to some unknown destination.

"Sin gets heavy, Luke, in mind and soul. I grow weary carrying someone else sins. Mine hard enough I carry."

"The deal was I have the flash drive, and you have a ticket to the US."

"Flash drive you picked up before bar is bullshit."

"So what is it?" Luke relaxed his shoulder ready to draw his weapon.

"Flash drive is not from Korean agents. Is copy of dry cleaner's bookkeeping records."

"What?"

"In Russian. I think you not notice about shirts and pants."

"I haven't looked at it yet. Things were a little hectic back there."

"Go ahead. Look now so you know I telling truth. Pull your gun out and point at me. Go ahead, Luke."

Taking a few steps back, Luke plugged the drive into his phone.

"What's written?"

"*6 par bryuk, 2 belye rubashki, 1 plato.* Six men pants, 2 shirts, 1 overcoat."

For a few moments, the only sound they heard was the soft exhale of smoke from Mikhail's lungs.

****

"You like Russia, eh, Special Agent Chaw Bacon?"

"Yes. My family owes a debt of gratitude to one of your fellow citizens."

"Really? Tell me."

"My great uncle's ship floundered in the North Atlantic in January 1975. It was an old Soviet fishing trawler, *Chechen,* that gave assistance."

"Did captain save your uncle?"

"No, the Canadian Coast Guard did the actual rescue, but the story is the trawler picked up pumps dropped in the sea and was able to get them aboard my uncle's ship. *Chechen* captain stayed through the night watching. Next morning a Canadian destroyer, *HMS Assiniboine,* came to the rescue with a helicopter. My uncle's ship, *Barma,* was afloat for about thirty days and then was lost in the shipping lanes."

"You say *Chechen?*"

"Yeah. Someday I'll come back here and maybe do some research. Look up the captain's name. Probably all dead by now."

"*Da*. Probably. Good Russian captain try help."

"You know I came here for the info you promised in Afghanistan. You got me all the way here for some Russian laundry list. What do you really want?"

"I love my country but want out. I want go US and not be found. The same request I made in cave but more urgent. That is favor I ask, speed things up, get out faster."

"What do I get for that? An original copy of *War and Peace*, signed by the author?"

"If you want, I get Putin's copy."

"Hell, no. You know what I want. Besides, what makes you think you can blend into America?"

"You hear me speak French and Spanish in cave. I understand dialects and spit back out words and accents so you never know I not from area. Besides, torture, am good with language."

"Do a West Texan, from El Paso."

"City or cowboy?"

"Cowboy."

"Yeah, sky's black over there. Big ole dang rain clouds comin'. Watch the cattle, Buck."

"Brooklyn, New York."

"Give second. Must adjust brain. Wait...'Hey, my little glass shoes, are melting away, It's all inside of me, New York New York, I want to wake up on top of the pile and never peep...'"

"Stop. Please stop."

"What? You no like Sinatra?"

"I do. My parents still dance to his music."

"Your parents are old?"

"No, just still in love. Don't sing anymore, please."

"I was joking, little Chaw Bacon. CIA will not invest money training me in American. Am international traveler. Know how to fit in."

"That was terrible. You still sound like a Russian. Where'd you learn that stuff?"

"American movies stolen from Russia."

Luke shook his head. "Okay, so let's say I can get you placed in the States. You still owe me a flash drive."

"Was test. I give you Chinese missile program, intellectual property stolen from your universities, and their new ten year program."

"Nothing from Russia?"

"No. Not I would object giving you information, but your people have most of it. Besides, since Gorbachev, you can not make war. Mother Russia very liberal. You stole generations of good communists with blue jeans and rock and roll."

Luke laughs. "I never expected to be standing on the roof of a warehouse on the outskirts of Moscow talking with a Russian operative who wants to quit the game and settle in the US." Luke shook his head. "I should kill you."

"But you won't. You know what I have is well worth inconvenience of helping me."

"You want to be in the witness protection program?"

"No. Too easy hack. I want you find me place. Place remote. I want home where no one think of looking for retired Russian spy. Beautiful with woods. Peaceful." Mikhail drew deeply from the stub of his cigarette. "Where I can fish, hunt, and watch sun disappear. I can sleep at night."

"I think I know just the place but it won't be El Paso or Brooklyn. Give me the hard drive and if it bears out, I'll be in contact."

Smiling, Mikhail took a small package from his inside jacket pocket. "Here, Chaw Bacon. Mr. Luke Chaw Bacon."

"What makes you think I'll make good on the exchange?"

"I saw in Afghanistan your men respond, how they look to you. You don't lead men into combat and death, if you not man of your word."

Mikhail used his cigarette to relight the cigar, flicking the ash remnant into the alley below.

"Good cigar. Maybe Cuban. Not get in US. I'll miss these." He gestured with the cigar, offering Luke a drag. Luke shook his head.

"Okay, but, here are keys to car below. You go to your drop and get out of Russia with drive. Make plans for my new life in US."

"If the drive checks out and has the information you say it has, I'll let you marry my girlfriend. If not, I'll find you and kill you."

"You Americans. So many threats. What makes you think I want to marry your girlfriend? Probably too skinny for a viral Russian as myself. I leave from Novorossiysk and make my way to New York City. There is Moscow Tea Room, very well known..."

"You'll be there?"

"No, too well known. I'll be at coney dog place across street. Here is phone. Only one number. When I call, in New York. I be there eating my face full of Coney Island dogs. Lots of hot mustard and vodka."

"It's 'stuffing my face' and coney dog places don't serve vodka."

"No problem. Will bring own."

"I'll have everything ready."

"Don't worry, Chaw Bacon. You not only man of his word."

****

On a darkened side street in Moscow, Luke wiped the inside of the Volga, removing his fingerprints. He stole a second car and made his way into Moscow's heart. The festivities were back in full swing but he avoided the establishments along Kremlevskiy Proyezd where the fight broke out. There were cameras along Red Square and he didn't want to give the authorities another photo session. Luke checked his phone map and found a perfect spot to dump the vehicle.

It would be a cold walk to the safe house, but he had a lot to think about along the way. Tossing the keys on the driver's seat, he took several deep breaths and stepped onto the snow covered walk.

–If Mikhail was to be believed, the flash drive contained the information Langley wanted. But if I hand it over at Langley, who's to say I wouldn't be giving it to the one who leaked the information about Afghanistan and this trip to Moscow?

The cold air cleared his mind.

–We placed sensors to monitor traffic–too simple–We found a Russian defector–The goons the deputy director forced me to take Smith and Jones—what was that all about? Better yet, who is directing this charade? Going back to the hotel is off the table.

The academy instructors emphasized there would be things in his career too far above his pay grade to concern himself. "Yeah, but maybe I'll concern myself anyway."

His whispered words fell to the ground with a fresh flurry of snow, lost among the sparkling flakes.

****

After emptying the locker at the drop location, collecting money, credit cards, and passport, Luke ducked into a fashionable men's clothing shop on Tverskaya Street. The male attendant was a former MI6 agent Luke met in Beijing. Now comfortably retired, he provided Moscow with a most discreet and upscale men's store, only dabbling in espionage upon invitation.

Winston was a professional. Luke was not inviting Winston to engage; it was attire he needed, not information.

At the counter, Winston stated, "The gentleman appears to have the same measurements as before. I believe we have everything the gentleman will need. Would the gentleman like to try on the leather three quarter overcoat? Also, suits, ties, and hats?" All this said without looking Luke in the eyes.

"Yes, sizes are the same. If you would put something together for me, I'd appreciate it."

"Very good, sir. Just to note, sir, I have an establishment in London if the need arises."

"Thank you. I'll keep that in mind. I'd like to shower and shave before trying on clothes."

"Certainly, sir. Come this way, please. Will the gentleman want his clothing washed and delivered to his hotel room?"

"No, that won't be necessary."

"And disposal of this attire?"

The acrid smell of cigarettes hanging on his sweater and the memory of Mikhail's horrible breath, Luke said: "Burn them."

The hot water and soap helped relax Luke. As he scrubbed the night's events away, he knew it was imperative he get back to Langley, and even more important, determine the leak. Ever since Afghanistan when Mikhail planted the seeds of doubt, Luke moved carefully not to arouse suspicion or tip off the traitor he, or she, had been exposed. Like a hunted wild boar, the traitor would make a wrong step. Luke was determined to be the one to pull the trigger. He planned as he watched the soapy water disappear down the drain.

****

In the US Embassy anteroom, Luke waited for the ambassador's secretary to return with his tickets to London. He accepted the offer of coffee, but refused any food. He would eat on the plane. First class food was excellent.

The secretary, Mr. Albertson, returned to the waiting room.

"The Ambassador has been called away to the Estonian Embassy and sent his regards. Here is your ticket and boarding pass, sir. Is there anything more I can do?"

"Yes, actually there is." Luke took a small padded envelope and a medium sized square box out of the shopping bag at his side. "I'd like the envelope sent to Langley, and the box to the address attached. Please put it in a shipping box and don't wrinkle the bow. Better yet, send it by courier then by US mail after it gets to D.C."

"By diplomatic courier?"

"Is there a problem with that?"

"No, no, not at all. The Ambassador said to give you anything you want."

"That's what I want. It's a gift for a special little girl."

****

The deputy buzzed Janice Streeter into his office.

"Janice, do you have the report from Moscow? The one Luke sent?"

"Yes."

"Please bring it in."

Seconds later, Janice entered the inner office of the Deputy Director.

"Go ahead and read me the summation while I check these figures."

"Yes, sir." She withdrew the cover sheet from the manila envelope.

"Just give me the conclusion, Janice."

"The flash drive given to this department translates as the bookkeeping files of a Moscow dry cleaning establishment. Nothing follows."

"What?"

"The beginning entry is six pairs of men's pants."

He slammed his fist on the desk. "Damn it, Perkins!"

CLARENCE WELLS

CLARENCE PAUSED SLIDING THE half empty bottle of whisky across the table to his companion, Jose Garza. Jose's twitching left eye fascinated Clarence from the first day they met. It was when Jose rubbed the lid, Clarence broke the line of sight and got back to what he intended to do in the first place, which was pass Jose the bottle.

"Last load up from Georgia." Clarence squinted to avoid the acrid smoke wafting around his head from the end of the cigarette. Out of boredom he twirled a quarter on the table. "Last load and we get paid."

Jose poured another shot of the cheap rotgut liquid into his own glass.

"Where're they coming from this time? Georgia was getting too hot. Too many *federales*."

"Yeah. I know. If that deputy outside of Adell had gotten a bit more nosy, he would've gotten his head blow'd off. My man Skull don't take to having the law interested in what he's hauling."

Clarence started to laugh but a dollop of brownish green phlegm caught in his throat, cutting off the scratchy cackle. His thinness, lethargy, and the sallow grayness seeping up from his innards to his skin, gave him a color akin to an old black and white movie demon. He lit another cigarette and sucked it between coughs.

"So what're we going to do? You got a plan? Where're we going to go? You know they're going to be looking for us up and down the coast."

"We ain't going up and down the coast."

"Well, then?" Jose hated playing these guessing games.

"Don't you worry, Jose. I've got it all figured out." Clarence was trapped in another coughing spasm.

Jose shuffled his chair away from the table.

"You know those things are going to kill you. You'll get lung cancer, or that disease where gradually you can't get any air, or your chest will blow up from a heart attack."

"Ain't nothing," Clarence replied as he spit dark brown sputum into his handkerchief. "Ain't nothing. My folks smoked. Whole family did. Used to steal smokes off my brother Franklin."

He coughed again from deep inside his lungs. "Never stole from my Pa. That would've gotten me a butt whipping."

Leaning back with two legs of his chair touching the floor, his boots propped against the table edge, Jose asked, "Think you'll quit before they kill you or they'll kill you then you'll quit?"

"None of your business. Once my plan goes into effect, I'll get the best doctors and everything. Money will take care of that."

"Did your folks drink, too?"

Clarence wondered for a brief moment why Jose was asking personal questions, but, in between sips of whiskey, he ignored it.

"Yeah, they all did. My Pa started us out young by giving us his shot glass to lick out or leaving a few drops of beer in the bottle. Franklin didn't like it, but he didn't like much of anything. Made my dad laugh so I got the hang of it." Staring out the window, Clarence was uncharacteristically wistful when he said, "The others died young. Just me and Franklin left. But we'll make do."

"Who were your folks?"

"Tony and Arvilla Wells. They died in Kansas prisons because of that black hearted cop, Bill Harris. His boy, Bill Junior, was an okay guy when I lived around here but Bill Senior was a bastard. He detained them until the Federal Marshals caught up to them. I'll make sure there's restitution for my Ma and Pa. You can be sure of that."

"So your brother, Franklin, he's okay with what you want to do?"

"Yeah. He's got plans, too, but he'll go along with me because there'll be more than enough money for the two of us."

"Three. The three of us."

That eye was twitching again. Jose's anger made the eye move faster, almost like a blink. The lid didn't twitch all the time, but often enough Clarence couldn't help but stare at it when it started its flurry of fury like it was doing now.

"Yep, don't worry, Jose. I misspoke because there's two of us Wells boys and one of you but you're not a Wells so that makes two Wells boys but three total partners. Hell, I couldn't pull this off without you. Three of us. Yep, three of us."

The smoker took another sip from his glass and turned his stare away from the twitching eye which did not deflect the dagger stare of Jose Garza.
****

"How'd you know the shipments will be safe here?"

"Jose, my man, because Franklin and me slept in the caves when we was kids after our folks was gone and there was no one to take us in. Franklin and me know the hills, trails, and the best hiding spots because we lived in them. Don't you spend any time worryin' about how we're going to hide out. We both know how pissed Boss will be when he finds out we took one of his shipments and got money he didn't, but Franklin and me got that covered. We move slow and steady, always checking out behind us. Franklin and me know'd how to lay low..." Clarence stood up quickly, reaching out and made a fist. "...and when we need to, grab the snake by the neck before he bites us."

Clarence's snake grabbing reaction time was hampered by the number of whiskey shots he consumed. Jose made a mental note to have a pistol with him because there were not only snakes to shoot.

"Boss is resourceful, Clarence. He has contacts in the military and when they go lookin' for you, they'll find you some way, *amigo*."

"Not this time." Clarence sank back down in his chair. "Ain't no one in the US Army knows the hills in West Virginia like the Wells boys do. Ain't no one. We'll keep the product stashed and when the heat cools off, make our way to Montreal using the same routes Boss uses but he won't be looking for us there."

"How's that?"

"Cuz I'm a lot smarter than what you think, my little MexiCali friend. I've already got a scent for Boss to follow that'll take him far away thinkin' we skedaddled where we ain't. Don't you worry none. Ol' Clarence and Franklin Wells got it all taken care of. That's for sure."

But Jose wasn't so sure. He'd seen what the cartels in Mexico do to traitors. Why wouldn't Boss do any different? The head of the organization may dress better, but Jose would put even money on him being just as ruthless, maybe even more, than the enforcers in Mexico. Rats and thieves were not liked in any part of the world.

Clarence poured another shot. Why not? It was free and Jose hadn't raised any objection. After all, they were partners.

Jose looked at Clarence with disgust as the tiny stream of whiskey, *his* whiskey, drizzled down the corner of Clarence's lip. He only looked away when Clarence looked at him. The message was sent; Clarence wiped his face with the sleeve of his shirt.

"Where's the next load from?"

"Why'd you care?"

"Just curious to what's coming."

"Ha! Well, they're coming from China like I said yesterday. So you want to tap into some of the chinky stuff? Ha! Soon's they get here, we get gathered up and go. Not too many this time. Draws too much attention."

Jose scratched his dirty ear and slicked his hair back, forehead to crown. He finished grooming by wiping his nose on the back of this hand as he looked around the room.

"What you looking for? Room's the same as it was when we got here. Whassa matta?" Clarence cackled again. "This is the same run, Miami to Montreal. I'll do all the driving until we get into a flatter area. I'll get us through the mountains."

"That ain't it, Clarence."

"What? You worried about the crew? Ain't no worry about them. For Christ's sake, Jiggy's so fat he he can barely run to the next sandwich. Jiggy does what he's told. Nothing to fret about there."

"Yeah, right, if you say so. But what about the others?"

"Racy? I can tell you right now he'll get taken out by the cops. He hates police. No cops done anything to that swarthy Cuban. He grew up ingesting all the poison his people told him to drink."

"I suppose he'll fly off the handle at the wrong time and place." Jose picked a drop of crusted mucus from his eyelash. "What about Skull? He'll mess things up for us when he gets wind of this."

"Jose, don't you know a thing about people? Skull's a degenerate. He got kicked out of Satan's Crawlers. I mean, how much of a degenerate do you have to be to get kicked out of a gang of degenerates? Those idiots he's got with him providing security? Ha! Take out Skull and the rest are too stupid to know how to breathe on their own. But, the one thing is degenerates like Skull have their weaknesses just like everybody else. I've got Skull figured out so he ain't gonna be a problem."

"And Allen? What about him, Clarence?"

"Allen's justa street punk from the Bronx. Allen can take a punch as well as throw one, but he's a hot head with more mouth than what he's big enough to handle. You don't worry about him. My brother Franklin can take of the likes of Allen."

"What about Boss, eh? W-what about him? You got some big plan to take his load, but you ain't worried about him?"

"Boss. I'll spit on him when I get my fair share of this last load. I ain't afraid of no pansy assed soldier boy–bastard always showing off like he was better than everyone. He'll be too busy tryin' to keep his diamond trimmed shoes out of the mud. Shit, Jose, he ain't nothing. Just keep to the plan and you'll go back to Mexico rich as a king. Just keep to the plan. Better believe it."

There was big money at stake. Cutting out Boss and his posse would take a lot of guts. Clarence needed the money from one load to cover overheads. All they had to do was to keep in the shadows, away from Boss and make it to Montreal.

He knew what was bothering Jose now. "You getting all antsy in your pantsy? You want one? There's plenty back there. That dusky one is Albanian, there's an Italian and the itty bitty one is from India. Don't be touching the one with white hair. There's a special customer for her. Otherwise, you take your pick. While you're back there, enjoy yourself, while I'll enjoy myself here."

Clarence poured another shot and smiled as it burnt its way slowly down his gullet and into his stomach. He ignored the whimpers of the women in the other room as Jose shut the door.

CLEVELAND COOP

Senior Special Forensic Agent Cleveland Coop sat outside Director Purdy's office door. The chair was comfortable, but nothing Coop could buy with his department's budget. He noticed the waiting room had been repainted since the last time he was summoned by the head man, but for the life of him, he couldn't remember what color it was. The current shade reminded Coop of his grandmother's ham and pea soup.

Across from him, a beautiful young woman sat typing with dedicated fury on her computer. Cleveland heard her nails hit the keys. Women loved false nails; a conclusion he formulated over the years looking at autopsy photos. He speculated on the color.

She was a brunette, probably with brown eyes. Her eye makeup extended beyond the zygomatic process, drawn up toward her temple. Rather ghoulish like that singer...Whitehorse or something.

She wore a lavender blouse, purple skirt, white pearl earrings, and a matching pearl necklace.

He was observing her but trying not to be seen observing her to avoid some misguided notion of offending her. He couldn't help it. He was a scientist. Paying attention to detail, noting the things that other people miss, and drawing accurate, evidence based conclusions had been his job for thirty-five years. He was published in professional journals several times during his career; some of his cases were in textbooks. After all his years with the West Virginia Forensic Lab, one would think he had more to show for it than three divorces (his third wife said his absentmindedness was cute), five grown offspring, and a twenty year old car. Women were complicated. Definitely, the dead ones were easier to figure out.

Coop decided to make a bet with himself–*Ummm, she's wearing purple nail polish to match her skirt and shoes.*

Her phone buzzed. "Yes, he's here. Yes, I'll send him in."

Without looking at Cleveland, she waved toward the door, flashing fire engine red nails. "You can go in now."

****

"Cleveland, come, come. Good to see you." The scarecrow thin man behind the chrome desk reached over to shake hands.

"Director Purdy, good to see you, too. How's the family?"

"Call me Kester, Cleveland. We've known each other long enough to end the formalities."

Kester smiled as he continued. "The family's good. My youngest is heading off to college. Don't know how long after he graduates I'll stay on, but that's a way off. And you?"

"Which family? I've had three of them." The agent settled in the chair. "They're good. Kids all grown, alimony and child support finished. I can start saving for my retirement."

"When's that?"

"Six months."

"I'd better help you rack up some overtime." Kester grinned. "Can I get you a coffee, Coop?"

"Sure. Double cream."

Director Purdy poured two coffees from the service on the wood credenza. "Fresh pot fifteen minutes ago. Made it myself. Women's lib stuff has really changed things."

"Yes, it has."

"Besides, my temp secretary out there is my daughter."

"She is..." Agent Coop could forget his own kids' names.

"Claudia. She's the middle girl. I got her this summer job but she can't, or won't, get her old man a coffee. She had no objection me paying her tuition, books, and off campus housing. Feminism only goes so far, you know."

"Yeah, I feel your pain."

Rustling through folders on his desk, Director Purdy pulled out a file. Scanning it's contents, he cleared his throat. "Well, Cleveland, I got something I want to offer you so let's get down to business."

Some things Cleveland knew for sure: one, the director never "offered" a subordinate anything, it was an *assignment*, and two, no matter what, refusing an assignment was not an option. Coop stared at the surface of his coffee waiting for the inevitable shoe to drop.

"Ever hear of a place called Deacon's Hollar?"

"Yes, sir. I was raised at Wild Goose Run. Deacon's Hollar is only a few mountains away. My dad used to take me there fishing. I haven't been there in years so I'm not up on current events.

"If I remember correctly they were part of Pocahontas County, but something about a clerical error when the territory became independent of Virginia and Deacon's county was on it's own."

The director smiled. "That's right. They operate more like their own *country* than county, but that's just speculation. I didn't know you were a history buff. It'll impress the locals when I assign you there for a few weeks."

"To Deacon's Hollar?" Cleveland examined the director over the lip of his cup as he sipped his coffee.

"They had an interesting crime in August 2017 against the person of Miss Daisy Foster. Older lady... ahh...briefly, her house was broken into, she got hurt defending her home, and was assaulted. The perps committed arson by burning her house down."

"Her in it?"

"No, that's the strange thing. As fragile as she was, she was found under some brush a safe distance from the burning home. No one knows how she made it with the condition she was in. She's in the care of her family currently. Not known if she will live independently again." Purdy flipped through more papers in the file.

"That sounds like something to really piss off those folks in the area. They don't like crimes against old people or kids. Did somebody in the community shoot the perp or perps? Isn't this a local issue? Maybe the State Fire Marshal's jurisdiction?"

"Too many questions, Coop. You're getting ahead of me. No one's gone vigilante yet. The locals are leaving this alone for some reason and staying pretty tight lipped about it. The Fire Marshal's report is in the file, along with witness statements, and a statement from Sheriff William Harris, Jr., he's the local authority. The issue, Cleveland, isn't the fire or the assault."

"What then?"

"The issue is the condition of the body or bodies of the perp or perps unknown. Here's a couple of photos. A little grisly, but you've seen worse."

Cleveland Coop had seen worse, but he was having trouble determining from the pile of goo in the photos if this was human to begin with. "Let me get my glasses on, Kester."

"Take your time, Cleveland," Kester sat back as he drank half his coffee in one gulp, then burped. "Sorry. Excuse me. Stomach's been terrible lately."

"You should be drinking peppermint tea. They've got it growing wild in the arbor downstairs."

"Think that'll help?"

"Sure. The hill people swear by it." Cleveland turned the photos one way, then the next. "Am I looking at the body of Miss Foster in this?"

"No, no. She's staying with a niece."

"Yep, that's right. Sorry. Kester, I'm not sure what you're asking me."

"First, would any cases you remember be similar to this where the body is in this condition after an assault by some kind of animal?"

"Like goo?"

"Yeah."

"No. From the photos, there's nothing really recognizable: no teeth, fingers, skull, or major body parts. No exposed bones. No animal would do this. Black bears could kill you, but they wouldn't pulverize you. There'd be claw marks which we could use to determine the size of the bear. They might take an arm or leg, but there'd be something left to study."

"What about a mountain lion?" Director Purdy loosened his tie. Never did like autopsy photos and the room was getting a little close at the moment.

"In West Virginia? They were driven out of here in the 19th century along with bison and elk. Besides, a mountain lion would take the body for eating later or if a female, sharing with cubs. There'd be a trail leading to a den or up a tree. You'd have something besides...besides small piles of goop. You know that it's human?"

"DNA doesn't match anyone."

"A lot of people not in the database. What's this really about?" Coop's suspicions were aroused.

"I want you to go there, blend in, see what you can find out. Sheriff Harris, here's his phone number, he'll take you trout fishing and help you make connections."

"Not season for trout."

"I'm not an outdoorsman."

"It shows."

Kester laughed. "I guess it does. Pick up your packet down at the lab. You'll have everything you need. I'm paying for a rental car so watch the miles. Got woodsman stuff?"

Cleveland looked at Kester Purdy and smiled. "Yes, sir. I got woodsman stuff."

"You might have to make some trips into Dolly Sods or Otter Creek Wilderness."

"Otter Creek? Are you kidding me? That's so thick and remote I don't think the Forest Service goes there."

Agent Coop rose, shook Director Purdy's hand, and went to the door.

"Oh, and one more thing. In your packet is a cell phone, just for your use. All evidence from this case will be sent directly to the FBI lab, but on our paperwork. You'll have a contact there, Ubell Gant. When you're settled in Deacon's, call him. You won't use names, but you'll need to know each other's voices."

Coop started to chuckle. "FBI, Kester? This is all you're going to give me, sending me out into the wilderness of Dolly Sod, and God knows where else, and not tell me what I'm getting into?" Coop paused and chuckled. "You do know that cell phones don't work much in the mountains, right?"

"You'll manage, I'm sure."

****

Coop sat in the back seat of his car, mumbling to himself while going through the forensic packet, laying out documents in the space beside him.

"Blend in? How am I going to blend when people know just by looking at me I'm a stranger in town? I'll go, be who I am, investigate and leave."

Cleveland was impressed. Whoever put this set together was a true professional. Forms WVSP 53 and 53A were original and not photocopies; he had duplicates of the file Kester gave him, along with the reports and documents having to do with the crime; Swabs, solutions, evidence bags, gloves, collection bottles, chemicals, extra batteries, LED flashlights, tape, pens, markers and more were neatly packaged in the case.

He fiddled with the phone.

Coop hit the auto dial feature and heard it ring.

"Ubell Gant, here."

"Mr. Gant..."

"Call me Ubell, Mr. Coop."

"How'd you know I'd call so soon?

"Curiosity got the cat."

"And you can call me Coop, or Cleveland, or whatever."

"Nice to meet you. I've studied some of your cases when I was in school. Your forensic work is legendary. Are you running the lab in Charleston?"

"No. In the field too much so I missed out on promotions."

"That's where I'm lacking for promotion, not enough field work."

"Well, you'll get your chance I'm sure. Keep at it." Cleveland looked at the rush hour traffic on the overpasses. The thought occurred to him to visit his cousin in Pocatalico sometime before the snow flies.

"Ubell, I'll call you again when I have something to send in."

"Got it, Coop. Later."

He gathered the packet and placed it in his briefcase. He took his keys out of his suit jacket pocket, and now sitting behind the wheel, started his ancient car. Deacon's Hollar was in the middle of nowhere and probably didn't show up on many maps or GPS. Had great fishing as he remembered.

Director Purdy knew he was going to retire in six months. Director Purdy was also a cautious, deliberate man who had the talent for placing the correct agent on the correct assignment. What was the bee in Purdy's bonnet about sending a tired, worn out agent into the tangled backwoods of West Virginia?

As he merged with traffic on the I-84 heading home to pack, Cleveland couldn't shake the feeling this last case would be the most important of his career, or the one that did him in.

Mike Green

Mikhail Ivanovich Verkhovensky was alive only because Dimitri Abramov was dead. In the depths of the cargo hold, Mikhail began the metamorphosis into Mike Green. Soon he would be reborn. He needed to be ready with his lies.

Dimitri activated the escape route, sacrificing himself as a gift to Mikhail.

"I will never leave Russia. My health no good. I'm too sick to leave. But you, my Misha," Dimitri lowered his voice, "you are young enough to make the trip. You go. Everything ready."

Dimitri was as good as his word. The preparations went unnoticed by the authorities. Mikhail, as Dimitri, was just another warm body on the big ship. The crew was used to the lazy relatives of party officials skipping out on work.

Mikhail stayed out of sight for long hours after the ship left Novorossiysk. It crossed the Black Sea for the Bosporus. The ship would sail to the Mediterranean and the Atlantic. After docking in Stockholm, he would lay over for a few days on the waterfront in a nondescript seedy hotel, then catch a flight to London under a second identification. Further changes would take him to Montreal, Seattle, then finally New York City. Dimitri knew his craft.

Alone in a womb-like crate hidden in the hold, Mikhail practiced his accent. "Portland, party, washing, mountain, zebra, willow." He repeated the "w" sound over and over. It had to be authentic.

He used the small recorder to refine his accent. He accessed the internet on an encrypted IP address to research his cover story: retired art dealer leaving the art world to enjoy clean air and slower life. The art dealer angle was a good identity; if he slipped in his accent it would be easy to blame living in different parts of the world due to the nature of his business.

Mike Green was a widower (lie). Mike Green had a dog named Spot as a kid (lie). Mike Green lived in Michigan after leaving the art world (lie). The falsehoods had to be anchored in a truth, making them comfortable for him to tell. He liked western style omelets, wore blue jeans, flannel shirts, and hiking boots; he read books, and loved cooking. The last vestiges of Mikhail would hook up a satellite link to monitor anyone looking for him.

Lie upon lie, building a history and saying it over and over until the lies became the truth. With each falsehood he pushed Mikhail into the dark past and diligently brought Mike into the light.

Every moment at sea created Mike Green. What didn't Mike like? Pineapple on pizza, cooked spinach, and warm beer. What history should he know? Basics of the Revolutionary War, Civil War, America's role in both world wars, Vietnam, divisions between the East and West Coast from the Midwest, the best oranges are from Florida, movies, music, basketball, college football, and the list went on.

When ignorant, his defense was "I'm not aware of that....of course, you're right." Believe in the backstory, wear the new identity until it's permanent, and have an exit strategy if boxed into a corner.

****

When the plane landed at Heathrow, Mike hailed a taxi to the city. He changed cabs twice, used two buses, and then another cab to insure he wasn't followed.

He discreetly changed his appearance using small items he kept in his pocket: eyebrows, glasses, a cap. Simple things gave him multiple options.

The last cab took him to the place where his transformation was complete.

"Good afternoon, sir. Welcome to our new location in London."

"Thank you, Winston. The cabbie was versed in the addresses of Savile Row, but not your shop."

"Yes, sir. That's to our advantage. We don't make bespoke suits for general patrons of the Row. Will the gentleman be traveling?"

"Yes, Winston. I'll be leaving in a few weeks. I'll need a variety of clothing for abroad."

"Cosmopolitan?"

"No."

"Maybe four seasons attire? Something warm but comfortable, durable but not standing out?"

"Exactly. Blue jeans, flannel shirts, work gloves and boots. Casual and comfortable."

"Yes, sir. The gentleman's room is ready for your convenience. Please follow me. I believe we have the gentleman's sizes on file. Any changes?"

"No changes, but a black suit with ample pockets."

"Yes, sir. Multiples?"

"Just one extra in a carry on bag."

"Certainly, sir. And the attire you have on? Would you like it washed and sent to your hotel?"

Mike Green looked at his reflection in the full length mirror. Hiding out in a cargo hold for several weeks didn't help his personal hygiene, and he was sure Winston was mentally holding his nose as did all the people on the plane from Stockholm.

"No, I won't be needing them."

"And the disposition of the gentleman's clothes?"

"Burn them."

****

The trail was well laid for the authorities in Moscow. Posing as Mikhail Ivanovich, Dimitri left by train for vacation to the Black Sea. He boarded a plane to Rostov-on-Don, then rented a car under his assumed name and drove along the A280/E58 to Taganrog where he spent the next day sightseeing by tourist bus and walking. People remembered the very kind man who treated strangers to lunch.

He traveled along the coast of the Sea of Azov, stopping for dinner, then retiring at a small hotel. Dimitri drove to Melitopol where he took a plane to Simferopol on the Crimean Peninsula. He rented another car, arriving at the sea port of Sevastopol. After a few days, Dimitri hired a small boat from which to go fishing.

Just out of the harbor, there was an explosion. The boat and the passenger were destroyed in the fireball. The captain was thrown into the ocean but rescued by a yacht in the vicinity.

The explosion was witnessed, the Captain determined to be telling the truth, and whatever was left of Mikhail Ivanovich Verkhovensky was cremated and put back in the sea.

Dimitri had two weeks to live due to an aggressive cancer but provided one last service for his friend by going down with the ship. Eight thousand miles away, Mike Green walked along the Avenue of the Americas. A secret between two people remains a secret only if one of them is dead.

****

New York City wasn't always exciting to Mike. He thought it was the height of decadence, a traitor to the simple design by the Founding Fathers of America, a Jezebel to the ideals of morality, humanity, and equality. The new Mr. Green would not be so judgmental of New York. After all, even Stalin had his indulgences.

Mike took his time walking. In the huge glass windows, he watched the foot traffic across the street. Old habits die hard; He doubled back making sure no familiar faces behind him.

At the men's clothing store Mike bought a shirt, cap, a plain duffle bag, and a backpack, "For my son," he told the clerk.

Slowly he strolled down the busy street, avoiding other shoppers, then ducked into a ladies' lingerie shop.

"Can I help you, sir?"

"I'm shopping for a special lady."

"Your wife, girlfriend, or other?"

"Ah...girlfriend."

"Do you know her size?"

"About your size but not as attractive."

She blushed. "Thank you, sir. We have new boudoir sets from Paris."

He glanced out the front window while the saleslady continued her pitch. He smiled at her.

"Thank you. She'll like them. I'll take one in each color."

"Wonderful. Would you like them gift wrapped?"

"No, not necessary."

"What credit card, sir?"

"Cash. I'll pay cash."

She rang the order, then wrapped the garments in a bag.

"Excuse me, but do you have a back door? I think my wife's having me followed."

"Oh, of course, sir. Just go down the hallway and take the half stairs down. The door will lock behind you. Thank you, sir."

"No, thank *you*." He pressed a fifty dollar bill in her hand.

Mike consolidated his purchases as he walked out into the alley. He put all the lingerie in one bag and tossed it into the dumpster. His "son's" clothing he rolled, and stuffed all of it into the duffle bag along with the backpack. He ruffled his hair, put on sunglasses, and became just another traveler trying to hail a cab.
****

Chewing on one of three Coney dogs slathered with hot mustard, Mike watched the entrance to the Moscow Tea Room. He observed several of his old contacts enter the establishment, one of whom was supposed to have been eliminated after he was caught leaving the Ritz-Carlton on Tverskyaya Street with the wife of his old *komandir*.

—Ilya lives. Interesting–I wonder how he got out of that one–Ramadani, the Albanian bastard, what's he doing here?--and his partners, Misters Dervishi and Marku–devils from the bowels of hell.

"Refill on the soda, mister?"

"Sure, thanks." Mike pulled the phone out of his pocket and pressed talk. After a few moments a familiar voice answered.

"Yes."

"I'm on my second Coney dog. Everything was as expected?"

"Y-yes, it was."

"You hesitate, my little Chaw Bacon. I wonder why. But not my business."

"This means you are..." He was cut off.

"This means I'm here. That's all it means. Now, I expect you to live up to your part of the bargain."

"You sound very good. The accent is..."

"Gone. Don't worry about it. I'm a quick learner. Now, about arrangements?"

"Take a cab to 600 3rd Ave. There's a coffee shop there. A waitress wearing the name tag 'Vivian' will take your order. Pay her with a twenty dollar bill. As you leave, she will follow you out the door telling you that you dropped your wallet. Thank her and..."

"Thank her? You don't think I have manners?"

"...before I was so rudely interrupted, there's a key in the wallet to a lock box in Grand Central Station. You can call me when you get to your destination."

"No. Three seconds after the last voice modulation, your phone will dissolve the network inside. I'll be too busy with my new life to worry about a Chaw Bacon, but if maybe we run into each other, you can buy me vodka."

"I just might do that." Luke was going to add a 'goodbye' but he paused too long. There was a puff of smoke in his ear as the phone fizzled itself into oblivion.

At Langley, Luke Perkins packed the remnants of the phone, along with a classified stamped folder in a burn bag. He dropped the bag down the incinerator door and was out of the building three minutes later.

****

In New York, Mike Green paid his bill,

"Sir, you've got mustard on your chin," the waitress said.

"Oh, thank you." He smiled warmly. "Here's a little extra tip. I've got a meeting and can't go looking like that. Where is your men's room, honey?"

After drowning his broken phone in the toilet and flushing it several times, Mike opened the stall door to see a man disguised as a woman smiling at him. "Not interested. Step aside."

"You'll regret saying that."

"Step aside."

"I've got something you want." The drag queen reached behind his back.

At that, Mike grabbed the lapels of the interloper's coat, driving his forehead into the man's nose. Mike pivoted around so that the heavily made up and bleeding face was backed into the stall. Mike removed the gun from a feathered leather jacket.

"Hey, what the..."

"I said I wasn't interested." Mike delivered one quick punch to the eye, dropped the queen on the toilet seat, and shoved the gun into his own belt while shutting the stall door. He checked his appearance in the mirror, and exited the back door as a man with a limp, round glasses, and hairy eyebrows. "Imagine that—a mugging on my first day in New York."

****

Mike arrived at the coffee shop on 3rd Ave. He ordered a muffin with his tea. "Blueberry, Miss Vivian. I would like blueberry."

"Blueberry. Yes, sir." She delivered his order then proceeded to clean the counter and take care of the other customers.

As instructed, he gave Vivian a twenty dollar tip and left. She followed, right on time, to hand him his wallet. Mike smiled and thought--*young lady, in a different time and a different place.*

****

He was in Chicago after nineteen hours by train. Mike made the Amtrak connection from Union Station to Indianapolis. A car was reserved under the name Rhett Butler-*yes, funny Chaw Bacon, Gone with the Wind, da, funny, I get.*

When Mike arrived in Charleston, West Virginia, he transferred his bags into another vehicle at a downtown parking garage. He back tracked to Sutton, where he picked up the keys to an older model four wheel drive truck. Instructions were in the glove compartment.

"Ah, Deacon's Hollar. A cabin on the side of a mountain, fully stocked, a bio of the area and people. I even get a puppy."

Mike decided to keep the leather satchel from New York and stuffed Luke's notes in it. He needed to get food, gas, and a few hours of sleep. He had time and it had been an exhausting few days.

****

There was one stop Mike needed to make. The GPS led him to a winding backwater road, more like a two track for deer. The area was thick with vegetation in shades of green, yellow, and red. The young forest trees bent over the path, almost caressing the vehicle as it passed. When the brush cleared, Mike knew he was near. He parked the truck and made the rest of the way on foot.

Pausing twenty feet from the rustic cabin, Mike put his leather jacket over his arm and took off his shirt. He stood waiting to be noticed. A priest in a long black *ryasa* and a pectoral cross appeared on the porch.

"So, you've come. Mikhail Ivanovich Verkhovensky. Talk. Let me hear your confession, Mikhail."

"The name's Mike."

"And the last name?"

"Doesn't matter."

"Then why are you here, Mike? A nice visit perhaps?"

"You can stop the bullshit."

"You come looking for forgiveness?"

Turning, Mike showed the priest his back, a labyrinth of scars like a spider's web but unlike the work of a spider, the scars were evidence of the chaos of hate. They played out over the entirety of Mike's shoulders, thoracic spine, and lower back, long tails of scars that left wisps along his sides from his waist to his armpits.

"Does this look like I need forgiveness?"

"No."

As Mike put his shirt on, he looked around the area. "Nice place you've got here. Peaceful. Remote."

"Yes. The locals think I'm a hermit priest praying for the sins of the world."

"I bet they do."

"Why did you come? Time to forget the past, Mikhail."

"The name's Mike."

"Okay, Mike, then. What do you want?"

"Just to share my scars with you, Lev Nikolayevich Drozdov."

"I don't remember that name."

"In a dark cell at Lubyanka, I remember."

"There was nothing I could do, Mikhail. I tried, but–"

"I disagree, Lev Nikolayevich. There was much you could've done but didn't."

Lev looked to the woods but he knew he wouldn't make it. Getting back into the cabin and arming himself was his only option.

"Mike, Misha, please come in. We'll have tea and talk."

"You're right, Lev...Leva, we can talk."

"Agreed. Enjoy my hospitality, Mike. What else can you do?"

While he buttoned his shirt, Mike said, "I can do exactly what you taught me to do."

Mike pulled his gun from the jacket and fired once, twice, three times. The thick Russian accent slipped from his lips, "Enjoy next life, *tovaris komandir*."

In the sparse cabin, Mike found weapons, ammunition, and money under the creaky floorboards.

"Ah, Leva. See? I find. Just like you teach."

Mike spent the next hour stripping the house, and Leva, of any priestly garments, religious medals, and documents. He went through the cupboards finding a flash drive in the sugar, another in a loose tea container, and grabbed the laptop from between the mattress and box springs.

"Nice bed, Leva. Was good for bad back. *Da?* No back worry now."

Confident he had everything he came for, Mike dragged the naked body into the cabin and positioned it at the table. Using a filet knife, he removed three bullets from his mentor's chest.

"Tight grouping, *da?* Lev Nikolayevich, you teach me well."

Mike draped his leather jacket over Lev's shoulders. "Time to give back, Lev. Keep you warm, *da?*"

He placed a delicate Russian bone china tea cup set in front of his old boss.

"Leva, this gift from Lubyanka when you turn me in? Fit for *Tsarina*. Very expensive. But, alas, time say *do svidaniya*."

Mike shorted out the electrical box setting the cabin ablaze, staying only long enough to watch the fuel oil tank explode.

****

He pulled an envelope from the glove compartment when he stopped under a shade tree to eat a hamburger. The vanilla ice cream shake and fries satisfied his hunger after working at Leva's cabin the day before.

"If you're reading this, welcome to Deacon's Hollar. Most folks go by first names except the children who are raised to use Mr., Miss, or Mrs., and a last name. The people are friendly and maybe a little nosy at times. The sheriff is Bill Harris. The general store keeper is Ambrie Sykes (She has your puppy). There's a diner, gas station and mechanic, and a post office that's run out of Livisia Stanton's home. Her husband, Edgar, is your mail carrier. He has a bad back so don't get packages that are too heavy. DH has a doctor/veterinarian who was a combat ortho doc, Andy Glassman. He'll take care of you and the dog. Lots of hunting and fishing. Any questions about the best places to hunt, you'll need to find Wink Decker. John Seven Star and his son Sam White Owl, are the best for deer. They'll help you get the big bucks on your side of the mountain. Spencer Tuttle is your man for rabbits. There's a radio, landline phone, and a phone book in the cabin.

"You'll like the brook trout from the stream at the edge of the property.

"Just down from your place is an outcropping of stone that has the best sunsets in West Virginia. More cash in the back room in small bills. Save the big bills when you go into the cities.

P.S. There is a bottle of Zyr in the back cupboard. Save a shot for me. CB."

****

Mike busied himself investigating the two bedroom cabin. He noticed the propane tank down the driveway and rummaged around until he found the latest bill hanging by the chalkboard in the kitchen. Delivery was made to "New customer's place, up from Aunt Gem's." No address numbers or road name. At least he knew he had a neighbor down the hill. It must have been her cabin that was barely visible on his way up. He made a mental note to have someone introduce him to her. No time like the present to become part of the community.

The original cabin looked handmade with rough hewn lumber visible in the ceiling. He walked through the living room and kitchen, then down a short hall where it split off into east and west wings.

The westside would be for his computers and satellite hookups. The view from the window was clear and unobstructed by trees. The east room was larger and he took that for his bedroom and weapons. An addition on the cabin was sheet rocked. He could hide things between the studs. He didn't plan on having much company, but an extra gun or two behind a false wall is always a nice touch.

He turned the knobs on the stove to make sure they worked, then put over a kettle of water for tea which he found in the pantry. Mike went from cupboard to cupboard looking at the kitchen utensils, dishes, and pots and pans. The refrigerator was stocked, top and bottom. He smiled when he heard the hum of the deep freezer.

Mike was not disappointed with the assortment of meats, vegetables, frozen fruits, and ice cream.

The bathroom was well stocked with necessary supplies: soap, razors, towels, and a loofah brush. Mike took a quick shower.

After hanging up his shirts, folding his jeans and underwear in the dresser drawers, he fried eggs, bacon, and made toast in his new home.

The dirty dishes could wait until tomorrow. Lying back on the bed, Mike fell into a deep and untroubled sleep. The transformation was complete. He even dreamt in English.

Cliffer Jennings

Florence watched Sheriff Harris and the silver haired man get out of the dark blue sedan. She wiped her hands on her apron and scurried to the back door.

"Cliffer?' she called out across the yard. "Bill's here." Florence scanned the garden until she saw her husband by the garage door.

"Comin' Florence. Just make 'em'ta home while I clean up."

She returned to the front door. A soft knock bounced the screen door a quarter of an inch.

"Hello, Bill." Her warm smile welcomed them.

Bill removed his head gear before entering.

"Coop, I'm happy to introduce Mrs. Jennings. Florence, this is Special Agent Cleveland Coop from the state forensic lab. I hope we didn't interrupt you or Cliffer coming out so soon after the call. I don't mean to rush you."

"Oh, not at all, Bill. Hello, Mr. Coop, nice to meet you. Won't you please come in?"

Cleveland, out of old school etiquette, did not offer his hand. He smiled and nodded. "Nice to meet you, Mrs. Jennings. It's certainly a picturesque drive up the mountain. Must be beautiful in the fall."

"Why, yes, it is, Mr. Coop."

As she led them through the house, Florence spoke over her shoulder, "I hope you didn't have too much trouble coming up that old sigogglin' road full of potholes."

Cleveland smoothed his hair with his hand, flattening the stubborn cowlick he inherited from his father. He followed Sheriff Harris through the alcove and into the main house. The living room was immaculately clean. Coop saw crocheted doilies on the table tops, displaying tintype photographs of family members and several group photos in front of a white church.

"You've a lovely home, Mrs. Jennings."

"Why, thank you, Mr. Coop. My grandfather built this older part. Him and grandma raised six kids here. When Cliffer and I married, we added a new kitchen, Cliffer's workshop and the garage. I was determined not to live as hard as my grandparents. No, sir, I'm a modern woman and I want my water heater and gas stove."

Her laugh was infectious. She brought the hem of her apron up to her mouth and giggled like a schoolgirl. She was a warm and uncomplicated spirit. Cleveland couldn't help but see the similarities between his mother and Mrs. Jennings.

"Would you gentlemen please have a seat here in the kitchen? I've got short-bread and it won't take just a minute to make a pot of coffee to go with it."

"Thank you, Florence. I thought I smelled something tasty."

As Florence chattered about the recipe for shortbread passed to her from her Scottish ancestors, the men smiled and nodded as polite men do when they have absolutely no interest in the conversation.

"Let me get the coffee while you settle at the table. Cliffer'll be here in a minute."

Cleveland stared at the black oak china cabinet which stood guard over the Jennings kitchen from the south corner of the room. The trim was a bias-relief carving of wildlife in the mountains. Centered at the top was a small waterfall, everything cascaded from that point down each side: deer in a meadow, rabbits profiled under a bush, brook trout, fox, and three wolves walking down a trail. The woodworking was an excellent example of the craftsmanship older generations were known for and which modern manufacturing killed.

Florence chattered pleasantly as she set the table with matching mugs, cream and sugar, and a dish of shortbread cookies, all on the embroidered tablecloth. After she added a well polished silver spoon and cloth napkin beside each cup, she stood back to admire the setting.

She noticed Coop's intense fascination with the carvings on the cupboard.

"Isn't that amazing? My granddaddy did that. He was illiterate but he sure could express himself when he held a knife to carve. This is the story of our family. That little church at the top was the first church built in Deacon's Hollar. Then, there's the fence, which is how grandpa made his living, making split rail fences and selling to a buyer from Charleston. Oh, he did other lumber work, but fence was the easiest. Look real close and you can see the second cabin built on our homestead. There at the edge of the woods.

"There's the bear he killed. Such greasy meat. I never cared for it, but any-thing's good when you're hungry, don't you think? We had chickens, of course, but granddaddy never liked chickens so he didn't cut them into the pattern.

"See the birds? There's a crane, cinnamon teal, white winged dove, and anhurgia." Florence lovingly ran her fingers over the carvings.

"I thought some of those birds were mythical, never in West Virginia," Coop commented. He was fascinated by the detail of the three wolves.

"Well, my granddaddy couldn't read or write but he carved what he saw, so I guess they're not so mythical, are they?" Florence smiled. "Oh, here's Cliffer."

Mr. Jennings walked into his wife's kitchen, wiping his hands on a clean white towel. He stood about five foot ten with muscled forearms, solid from splitting wood, drawing shaker shingles, and working the earth. He was so physically fit, it was hard to age him. He nodded to the standing visitors and said, "Gentlemen."

Sheriff Harris made the introductions. "Cliffer, this is Special Agent Cleveland Coop. Mr. Coop, this is Cliffer Jennings."

"Coop, you say? Any relation to Wicker Coop from Wild Goose over by the plateau? Real good reputation for hunting that Wicker Coop."

"Yes, sir. Wicker Coop was an uncle. Most of the Coop's are gone and away from the run, but that's where we're from."

"You hunt, Special Agent Coop?"

"No, that was my uncle's thing. I like to fish."

"That's alright. Plenty of hunters around here if you need meat. When's the last time you were at Wild Goose?"

"More than a while ago. I'm getting ready to retire and thought about going back to see if there's a spot for me."

"I'm sure they'll welcome you. West Virginia folks are like that."

"Yes, I'm sure they will." Cleveland started to relax with the formalities out of the way. There was always ice to break.

Florence served coffee. "You gentlemen can have a seat and enjoy your coffee and shortbread. Cliffer, I'm going to Ida Mae's to work on a quilt. Mr. Coop, it was nice meeting you. Bill, always nice to see you." She kissed Cliffer on the cheek. On her way out, the front screen door banged twice.

"Cliffer," she called, "tighten up the hinges today, please."

"Yes, dear."

Cleveland started to speak, but was cut off by his host.

"Just a second. I want to make sure she's gone. Florence has been known to double back on me. Caught me dippin' into Harland's white lightening once. Almost lost her mind. Her folks got a lot of alca-halics in their blood. Mine don't, but you know women. One little sip and they think ya'll's gonna worship at the altar of Satan."

When Cliffer could no longer hear his wife's car, he settled back in his chair. "If I ever fix that muffler, I'm screwed. So, gentlemen, what can I do for you?"

"Mr. Jennings, I'm investigating evidence surrounding the assault on Miss Foster. Her statement was a little confusing, but I hoped I could get clarification by interviewing people in the community. I was directed to you as one of the people to interview about what happened."

"Well, seeing as I wasn't there, I know you're not asking me *what* happened, but clarification on *what might have* happened, cuz y'all don't know."

Coop regretted his phrasing.

Cliffer, biting into a shortbread, signaled the other men to do so. After a few chews, and a couple of crumbs among the flowers embroidered on the tablecloth, he said, "Probably her nephew, Charlie Foster, suggested you come here. He runs his mouth more than his brain. For someone who doesn't live around here, he seems to know everything goes on and what he don't know, he'll make up."

"Mr. Jennings…" Cleveland began as he opened his case of equipment.

"Call me Cliffer."

"Okay, Cliffer. I'll be recording your statement. This computer will identify your voice and turn your statement into text. When you're done, sign the screen with a special pen which verifies this is your sworn statement."

"Okay."

"First, I want you to read this text so the computer recognizes your voice and identifies your speech patterns. Second, I'll have some questions to ask." Cleveland Coop hesitated. He offered the mic and the text to Cliffer, glancing at Sheriff Harris.

Understanding the look, Cliffer said, "Don't worry. I can read. Been reading since I was four years old. Aunt Gem taught me. I read to my blind grandmother. Shakespeare, Hemingway, Wolf, Faulkner, all o' them. Graduated from high school with honors in math and science, and I still keep up with what's new. Don't let the accent fool you."

Cliffer signed the release papers and was sworn to tell the truth on Florence's family Bible.

"My name is Cliffer Jennings. Not Clif*ford*, just Clif*fer* Jennings. Ya'll came to ask me about the incident at Miss Foster's last August. Someone told you I might know somethin' which I do.

"The story started back in Civil War times. It's kind of long, but you need the history. I'll make it short as I can.

"The counties that would be West Virginia wasn't slave territory, but Virginia was. There were problems for decades between the western counties, that'd be us on this side of the mountains, and the tidewater counties, which would be those toward the Atlantic.

"There were hard feelings between each side regarding taxation, representation, and the issue of slavery. It was pretty much two different states anyway, just no one had done the paperwork on it until the Wheeling Convention of 1861. At that meeting, Waitman T. Willey called it "triple treason": Virginia leaving the United States, the western counties leaving Virginia, and the issue of treason against the Confederacy.

"Well, they had a vote and the western counties decided to be their own state and side with the Union. President Lincoln signed the paperwork. That's it in a nutshell so to speak."

Coop wiped his mouth with the napkin by his plate. "I don't know how this pertains to the Foster case."

"I'll get there, Mr. Coop."

Sheriff Harris winked at the forensics agent and smiled. "Special Agent Coop, on this side of the mountains, we put things in context. Makes understanding easier."

"Sorry I interrupted."

"That's fine. Now, in the situation we've been discussing, there were three brothers who sided with the North from a farm up on the ridge. And in the area also lived a Confederate sympathizer. After the boys went off to war, the Confederate wiped out the family."

Cliff left the table and went into the pantry. He came back with a bottle of single malt.

"Gentlemen?" He offered a shot to the men at the table.

"No, Cliffer, I'm on duty. Maybe Mr. Coop?"

"No, thank you. I'm on the clock, too."

"Then you won't mind if I do. This next part of the story is always hard for me to tell." There was no need for decorum. Cliffer took a long pull from the bottle.

"Well, when the boys finally came home, they were scarred in heart and mind over what war could do. They figured it was over and they could leave it down South. They didn't know the war would reach its ugly hand back and touch them.

"They had to jump the creek as the bridge was burnt down. The woods was silent an' nobody called back when they shouted. When they rounded the bend, there was nothing. The stone work of the hearth and chimney of the cabin was there, but the framework had all burnt up. The barn was ashes. Livestock was gone.

"Soldiers go through death fields so often they get immune to it, but this was family dead, not strangers. One of the boys found his daddy's wedding ring on a hand still wrapped around the rifle stock. There wasn't much to the rest of him. The other boy found the mother and sister resting up against a section of the fence as if they were runnin' away an' got shot, and fell right there. The girl still had her sun bonnet on what was left of her head, holdin' her doll in her little skeleton arms. Story is the third boy clutched that doll so tight an imprint of his heart was left on the doll's dress. They found jacket buttons off a Confederate uniform so they put two and two together.

"While they was still in shock, a soldier come out of the woods wearin' a Confederate coat. They was on him an' *tore* him limb to limb. When the three was spent, they realized under the Confederate long coat was a shirt from the Union.

"The dead man's papers were an honorable discharge from the Ohio Militia. He was just tryin' to get home."

Cliffer coughed and wiped his eyes.

"Imagine that. He was just trying to get home. Well, they got what they could to dig. Buried their kin an' that Union soldier. The boys made crosses for each of the graves. Then they knelt in a circle an' held hands and cried.

"They cried for their family, for all the dead soldiers on both sides. They cried for the families split by the war and for the hungry people with hollow eyes, for the dead rotting by the roads, an' for the sin of the country in the first place. But mostly they cried because they just killed an innocent man.

"The Bible says thou shalt not kill, but do you know what was originally written?"

Bill and Special Agent Coop glanced at each other. Neither knew scripture well, so they shook their heads.

"Well, I'll tell you what was written, 'Thou shalt not *murder*.' God knew there were times when someone was going to get killed as a believer defended themselves. But, to up and *murder* someone? That makes God *wrathful*. Murder is what those boys did to that soldier."

Cliffer looked at his quiet audience. "Okay, let me explain it a little differently. Have shortbread while I talk." The plate was empty.

"No more? Gentlemen, I can fix that. Excuse me for a moment."

Cliffer returned from the pantry with a pie in each hand. "A is for apple so let's examine this one first, then we'll cut the cherry. Florence didn't make a blueberry so we'll skip that letter for today. Can't have apple without a sharp cheddar alongside, can we." Cliffer cut and served.

****

"Now, the thing about murder, take King David for example. King David saw Bathsheba bathing and he desired her. David sent Bathsheba's husband to the frontlines, knowing full well he'd be killed. David made his move on the woman. David should have walked up to the fella's house and said, 'Hey, I'm taking your wife, house, and servants because I'm King David and I can. Here's a spear through your heart for the trouble.' But he didn't. He lied about his sin.

"God turned his back on the king because pride led to murder. It took a holy man to set things right. Psalm 50's the one Nathan wrote to get David out of trouble: 'Thou shalt wash me, and I shall be made whiter than snow.'

"Getting back to the Union brothers, there was a full moon and under the light, those boys were changed. They were changed because of their pride and their sin. They were changed into beings like nothing they were before.

"The three of them, always together, havin' to pay for their action. Like they're waitin' for their Nathan come to get them clean enough for God.

"We call them snow dogs not to frighten the children who heard the stories, but I think they're some kind of wolf hybrid or something else. Maybe warrior angels. Maybe not."

Cleveland glanced at the battery level on his computer. It was still recording.

Cliffer refilled the cups with black coffee. He sliced venison summer sausage and set it the table. "Please, use your fingers, gentlemen. Protein will balance all the sugar we ate."

Satisfied with his hosting duties, he sat and continued his story.

"Like I said, I know science, but I live in these hills, and I know things in the mountains don't always agree with science. So, when I tell ya'll what happened next, remember it's coming from a man who believes in science, but a man who understands Deacon's Hollar. You can believe me or not, but it would be wise if you put aside your scientific bias."

"Do they make sounds, Cliffer?" Coop jotted a few notes on his yellow pad.

"Well, of course they make sounds. Depending on how quiet the mountains are, folks say you can hear them on misty nights. The experienced dog men around here say it isn't anything like they've heard before. Wolfish but dog-like. Eerie it is, when they put their heads back and howl at the sky. Still asking for forgiveness, I guess."

Coop interrupted. "What makes you think they're not wolves?"

"Well, Mr. Coop, you've forgotten your country roots, no offense intended."

"None taken."

"There's a sayin' about wolves, 'A howl in the night, a track in the snow.' A wolf can blend into the underbrush and ya'll *never* see him. A wolf can be sittin' on a stump in the woods, in a clearing no less, and ya'll can walk right by him and never notice him. Masters of camouflage. They blend with their environment. You get the howl and a track, but that's all you get.

"Difference between wolves and snow dogs is that the dogs let you see them because they don't blend, they *control*. They get visible to remind us they're there. Besides, wolves don't have a blue eye, gentlemen, and they certainly don't have any loyalty to mankind. Dogs do."

Cliffer poured the men another cup of coffee.

"Gentlemen, looks like the apple is done for. We can cut into the cherry now."

Coop knew his blood sugar was through the roof at the moment but he didn't refuse the red tart pie placed on his plate.

"So," Cliffer said as he studied the sweetness on his fork, "down through the generations there've been sightings. I won't go into all of them but a few are worth noting for your files, Coop.

"There was the train wreck over Shyline Creek. Railroad company said someone pulled the spikes out along the track. The conductor survived and said he saw white dogs among the wreckage, licking the faces of people, wakin' them up so the rescue people knew they're alive, but nobody else reported seeing them.

"Then there were those kids who were missin' from a campsite, but found two days later deep in the woods, jibber-jabbin' about dogs keeping them warm and led 'em to the berry bushes to eat.

"The late Doug Flatwater took a girl into the woods to rape her. Doug started screaming and he rolled off her and that's when she saw the snow dogs. They were *tearin'* at Doug's legs an' his back. The girl hid behind a tree and watched the snow dogs *butcher* him to pieces til he was dead. The dogs looked at her with those ice-blue eyes; She said the eyes looked right through her.

"When she told Sheriff Bill about what happened, she swore on the Bible that the dogs did not have a spot of blood on them. She's a hill woman and she knows what wolves can do. There's always blood—but not on them. They turned an' walked into the woods."

Coop asked Sheriff Harris, "Any way to interview her?"

"No. She was killed in a car accident in Ohio several years ago. I'll get you her original statement at the office."

Coop made more notes while Cliffer continued.

"Now, about what brings you gentlemen to my door is about Miss Foster. I don't know who broke into her house, and then set it on fire. But, if she says the snow dogs pulled her out, it's the honest to God truth.

"Listen an' write this down as I tell you, Coop.

"That night Flo's cat was scratchin' at the window. I opened the screen door an' let it in. When I looked up the hill, I saw three mists moving in and around the black trees in the woods. They floated down along the mountain, on Heartbreak Ridge, due south toward Berryton Cross. If you draw on a map, it'll take you directly to Miss Foster's. That's where the mist was headed, an' that's what I saw."

"Cliffer, was it foggy?"

"What? No. Sky was clear as a bell, and the mountain was dry. Now, about the white hair that was found at the scene–Yes, I heard about that already. I told ya'll I believe in science but there's something I know, and that's the dogs can be like a liquid, a gas, or a solid. The night I watched them walk down the mountain, they were gaseous, all floatin', but when they were at Miss Foster's, the dogs were solid. That's how they dragged her to safety.

"The science people in Charleston are going to test your samples ten ways to Sunday an' it won't test as bear, elk, deer, or rabbit. It won't test like a dog, either. They'll sit on their ten-thousand-dollar stools and scratch their heads. I'll tell you right now it was those snow white dogs or what have you. They delivered retribution on behalf of Miss Foster."

"Are there others who will support what you say about the snow dogs?"

"Mr. Coop, things couldn't be so different in Wild Goose. You understand not a lot of people'll talk to you. Some'll laugh you off and some'll shut the door in your face, especially you being a government man, with Bill Harris or not.

"How can I be sure? Just you wait until ya'll run your science."

I swear the above statement is true and accurate to the best of my knowledge and belief.

(signed)

Cliffer Jennings

(signed electronically) SFA Cleveland Coop, West Virginia Forensic Lab

(signed electronically) Sheriff William Jefferson Harris, Jr.

*****END OF STATEMENT. NOTHING FOLLOWS.********

****

Cliffer rose from his chair and put the dishes in the sink. He stared out the kitchen window as the sun came from behind the clouds. The light filled the room; a narrow beam fell across the three dogs carved into Florence Jennings' cupboard.

"Coop, you got a camera with you?"

"Yes, I do. Here...."

"Move slow and stay down. Bring it over here, but no quick movements. I want a picture of this for Florence."

"Cliffer," Bill whispered. "I can see them from here."

"Then don't move, Bill, because they can probably see you. Coop, come along my side and hand me the camera. Stay low and stand behind me."

Coop did as instructed. When he peeked over Cliffer's shoulder, he was stunned: "*Aquila chrysaetos* and at least fifty *corvus brachyrhynchos*. I've never seen...."

"Shhh, Coop." Cliffer snapped off photo after photo of a fully grown Golden Eagle perched on the sugar maple tree, surrounded by a murder of American Crow. "Neither have I. They're mortal enemies. Maybe Running Deer or John Seven Star will know."

"Who are they?" Coop whispered, still mesmerized by the sight of the birds.

"Tribal family over on the other side of the mountain. John's ancestors took refuge here when the southern tribes left the Carolinas around 1838 and before. The ones who came here weren't Cherokee, but they saw the writing on the wall. Locals took them in and hid them in the caves until things quieted down. Descendants have been here ever since."

The men watched the eagle depart first, heading south, then the crows flew to the north. Cliffer and Coop returned to the table.

"Now, who wants the last slice of cherry pie?"

Coop saw the recording was still going; his proof it was Cliffer's idea to eat the second pie.

"I can see ya'll will be wanting to come back for more of Florence's cooking. Yeah, I can see it on your faces."

"If I keep eating here, you'll be seeing more on my waistline than on my face," Sheriff Harris added.

"That's no mind to me and Florence. She loves to cook and ya'll be welcome."

They split the last slice to avoid talking about what they didn't understand.
****

Cliffer walked his guests to the driveway.

"Gentlemen, about those birds. I'd ask Running Deer and see if she'll explain anything. Birdie Spry might talk, or shoot, but I don't know which. Aunt Gem won't talk, that I know. Something's out of balance. I can feel it. We just don't see that kind of stuff, I mean, golden eagles and crows? I wouldn't make this public, if you know what I mean, for the Hollar's own good."

Cliffer tapped on the roof of the car. Coop slowly accelerated down the drive to the paved road as Sheriff Bill waved goodbye.

Fishbone Crawford

Aunt Gem set aside her cross-stitch project. She couldn't ignore the second series of soft taps on the glass. Her home was quiet except for the tap, tap, tap at her door.

She stood from the comfort of the hickory rocker, touching the arm to steady herself. Gem gimped the short distance from one side of her living room to the door. Through the lace curtains she didn't see anyone at eye level. Then she saw the ball cap. Gem gave it to Agnes Crawford's boy the first time she took him fishing.

"Well, what're you doing on my front porch?" she said as she opened the door.

"Here's from my mom, Aunt Gem." He gave her the wrinkled note from his pocket.

"You've been crying?"

"Yes, Ma'am."

"What for?" She slipped the note in her apron pocket as she watched the child's lower lip quiver. "There isn't to be any crying on my front porch. You come in the house. I don't want you scaring the wildlife."

Aunt Gem put one hand on the boy's shoulder and ushered him in as she shut the door with the other. She pulled back a double armed wooden chair and motioned for the child to sit at the walnut table covered by a red checkered table cloth.

****

"Sit. Tell me why you're here."

Fishbone's shoulders started to shake.

"Ah, ah, tell me. Don't cry."

"I'm under pressure, Aunt Gem," he said. "The teacher said once she gets the government to pay off'er loans she can get out of the back'ater hillbilly schools."

"What's that got to do with you?"

"She said I was one of the back'ater hillbilly kids who don't learn letters and words. I told her I was not and then she said she was going to call my mom. The kids laughed at me. My mom said never you mind about some teacher from Waybird City, an' she said she'd get me the best teacher that ever was in the Hollar an' she gimme the note an' said to get up the mountain to you." He bowed his head and cried.

Aunt Gem pursed her lips for a second, looked out the kitchen window, then back at the boy. Humiliation is a heavy coat to wear. It burdens the shoulders of the strongest men but certainly has no place on the back of a seven year old boy. She gave him a tissue.

"Okay, Fishbone. Crying time is over. Dry your eyes, blow your nose and tell me what else."

"Then that man said he was going to spank me and if I didn't behave he'd make me disappear cuz he knows magic."

"What man?"

"Walter Venter. He lives in my house. I hate him."

"Hate's a pretty strong emotion. Takes up too much room when you need to be having fun and learning about the world. Don't hate, child."

Fishbone studied the table cloth as he swung his feet.

"Don't worry about that teacher. Some of the folks aren't smart enough to get cat food out of a can."

Fishbone giggled.

****

"How'd you get up all the way here without getting into trouble?'

"Jackson Latcher gave me a ride to the road in his truck, then I rode my bike up."

"You not afraid of a bear or painter getting you?"

"Nope. Gotta have faith, Aunt Gem."

"Yes, I suppose. God protects children and fools. So which are you?"

"Too young to be a fool, so I guess I'm a children."

"I guess you are. Well, then, do you want something to eat?"

"Mom said I could eat when I got home."

"That wasn't my question."

"Well, I ain't lyin' if I said I could use a sandwich or somethin'."

"Here," Gem said as she scooted a step stool to the sink. "Wash that streaked face and those dirty hands. Soap's on the ledge and you can use the towel to dry off."

Gem busied herself in the larder getting bread, a dish of butter, sliced ham, pickles, and a pint glass jar of peaches. Pausing, she read the note--"Pluz tech my boy ta red. Agnes Crawford"-- she stifled a sob and wiped her eyes. She returned to the table to see Fishbone back at his place, his face relatively clean with a few drops of water on the back of his hands. Effort counts at Gem's.

"Half or whole?"

"Whole, Aunt Gem, but I'll split it and them peaches with you."

"Okay." Gem took a knife from the counter and cut the sandwich in two.

Fishbone said nothing until his fourth bite. "Good sandwich, Aunt Gem. Bread's nice and fresh. My mom used to make bread. Gave me the heels just loaded with butter."

Between chews Gem asked him, "Do you know your letters, boy?"

"Yes, Aunt Gem."

"Do you know some of the words the letters make?"

"Yes, Aunt Gem."

"Then why did the teacher say you can't read?"

"I stand up to read I hear the kids start to giggle and I forget what to say. The teacher gets mad at me an' the kids keep laughin'. The Kirk kid calls me a dumb chaw bacon."

"A chaw bacon? I haven't heard that for a while. Say, are you kidding me?"

Fishbone leaned forward with emphasis: "No, ma'am. I are *not* kidding." He picked up his dish and licked the peach juice out of the bottom of the bowl.

They finished their simple meal in silence.

"Aunt Gem?"

"Yes?"

"I need to go outside."

"Okay, You know where the outhouse is. Take the roll of paper with you and hook it on the hanger."

"Yes, Aunt Gem."

"And boy?" The child paused, his hand on the door knob. "That lower hook, by the door, there."

After a few seconds Fishbone nodded at the hook as he put his finger on it.

"Yes, boy. That one's for your cap to hang when you come back to the house."

"Yes, ma'am."

****

Agnes Crawford's son lacked confidence. Gem was sure at lot of negative things went on in the Crawford house. Agnes, in her mental confusion, brought men into the home who used the strap on Agnes and her son. Neither would discuss the details.

The scrape of the chair on the floor brought her thoughts back to her new student.

"Here, take these plates and mind you don't break any putting them in the sink." The boy did as instructed.

"Now, I'm going to teach you just like I do all the kids who come to me to learn. Same books, same words, so if they all can read so can you. Besides, you just might be a little smarter than most of them, I'm thinking."

Fishbone watched Gem wipe the top of the china hutch, releasing a cobweb's death grip on the ceiling. Reaching above the cabinet's bias relief carving, she put her hand on a thick book with a thin and ratty red worn leather cover. She used the corner of her apron to wipe the dust from the binding. In all, she took three more books from the top of an adjacent matching curio case, behind whose streaked glass peeked the china cups and saucers brought by her great great grandmother from England.

"You'll learn a lot from this book. It was my favorite when I was growing up. This one and the Bible, of course. Sit here on these books so you can reach the table. Books are not just for reading, Fishbone. You can sit on them when the need arises. Can't do that with a fancy computer."

Gem opened the red book and placed it before him.

"You remember Joshua? My middle boy?"

Fishbone shook his head no.

"He's been off the mountain for a little while. Sometimes I forget how long it's been, but he was the same way, scrawny, like you, but wiry, like you."

"Did you learn him to read, Aunt Gem?"

"Yes, I taught him to read. Same way I'm going to teach you." Licking her thumb to turn the pages she said "Let's see now if I can find the exact place Joshua started on...um...here, here it is.

"Fishbone, look at this word. Not all of it. Just the first letter. Now tell me what it is and all you know about it."

"Aunt Gem, there's the letter 'n.' Mom says it's like nuts."

"What do you know about nuts, Fishbone?"

"The squirrels eat walnuts and Mom puts them in cookies. So's there's walnuts, an' peanuts, an' cashew nuts, those are the expensive ones. Then there's the acorn nuts the deer like. The North Star starts with 'n' an' when I sleep out in the back I can find it."

"What's the second letter?"

"That's easy. 'O' like the Orion's Belt. He's got three stars on his belt." Fishbone grinned.

"And what else?"

"Like the owl that's in the pines on Baker's Ridge. Sam White Owl called a hooty owl and made it call back to him at night across the valley cuz that's his spirit animal. Sam go'd "Ooooo--oo--oooo. an' the owl go'd "ooooo-ooooo-oooo" an' Sam called that old hooty owl into his backyard. It see'd Sam for a minute then flew right off into the moon. Sam and his mom can talk to animals."

"What else?"

"An' 'o' is for the octopus who lives on the bottom of the ocean an' shoots ink to disguise hisself when something comes from the dark tries to eat him. And it's for o-rings Uncle Bowtie puts around the rim of fittings on the tractor when he changes fluids so nothin' leaks out on the ground wastin' money."

"You know how to do that?"

"Yes, ma'am. ' O' is for Obadiah, a prophet in the Old Testament; 'o' is for October when Jackson Latcher takes me rabbit hunting in the fields over by Grass Mountain. We got six rabbits last fall and Jackson showed me how to dress them out for the cook pot."

Gem pointed Fishbone to the next letter. "What's this last one?"

"W."

"Tell me about 'w'."

"That's the water letter, wind letter, winter wishing letter, the whisper Christmas secrets letter, the washing clothes letter, the wasp sting letter."

Aunt Gem sat back in her chair. "You're amazing. Do you realize you not only spelled a word, but you demonstrated your knowledge about tree nuts, the deep diving octopus, and the fifteenth letter of the alphabet. I'm proud of you."

"You are?"

"Yes, I am. You can't let those kids worry you."

"But they get under my skin."

"Some folks are so uncomfortable in their own skin, they're not happy unless they get under someone else's."

"I guess, Aunt Gem."

"A lot of people you meet in life will get under your skin. But, the most important thing is *you* are *Fishbone Crawford*. There isn't anyone in the world like you. The teacher from Waybird City and the Kirk boy don't know how to shoot a rabbit and dress it out, but you do. They don't see Sam White Owl talk to the animals, but you do."

Gem tapped the open book in front of the boy. "Reading is like following a map. Start with the first page, on the first word, on the first letter. Once you get that first letter, then you put the second and the third until you have them all together, then you go 'til you get to the little white space. Then you hop over it to the next letter and the next word. You keep going until you've got a map of words in your brain."

"What's on the map, Aunt Gem?"

"The world."

He stared at the page before him. All the letters, lines and spaces.

"Boy, the words are ideas, plans, and dreams about everything up and out of this valley. The more you read the more you dream. You can make those dreams come true. You can fly off this mountain and swoop down the valley like Sam's hooty owl. You can sit on Orion's Belt and get a job counting stars.

"With words you travel the oceans and swim with whales or look for pirate gold off the coast of Florida. Words show you things you'd never see on this mountain. Words help you grow up to be a man."

Fishbone looked over the page with a single illustration. He cleared his throat and asked the first of what would be many questions arising from his new relationship with Aunt Gem.

"What if I don't know what the new words mean?"

"I'll help you with that. Meaning will come later. For now, just read the words."

"Can I use my finger to point?"

"Yes, you can point."

****

Fishbone pushed his chair back, then walked to the kitchen sink, and back up on the step stool. He scrubbed his hands with lye soap and used a wooden toothpick from the counter, cleaning under his nails.

"I wanted my hands clean for the words."

"That's very respectful, Fishbone. Start at the first word, please."

The young Crawford boy cleared his throat and pointed.

"Now is the w-winter of our d-dis...discon...tent."

From memory Gem recited along with her new student,

"Made glorious summer by this sun of York; And all the clouds that lour'd upon our house, In the deep bosom of the ocean buried."

"Aunt Gem?"

"Yes?"

"I bet there was an octopus in the deep bosom of the ocean buried."

"I guess you'd win that bet, Fishbone. And by the way, do you know who wrote those words?"

"Nope."

"William Shakespeare. He was an English playwright and poet." Gem took a book from her mantle. "Here's one we'll read this summer, too. Maybe this one is more important to talk about than Shakespeare."

"Who's that one?"

"Wait...that's not the one...here, move your butt, boy, you're sitting on Aristotle."

Fishbone raised his hip allowing Gem to retrieve *Nicomachean Ethics* from his chair.

"He wrote about bravery, endurance and integrity. These are all things a young Hollar man should learn."

"I want to be brave and interg..."

"Integrity. We *have* integrity is how you say it."

"What's it mean?"

"It means doing the right thing when no one is watching. It means doing something because it is good, even when you don't get paid, don't get any awards, and accepting that you might die doing what is right."

"Like when Spencer's dad saved Mr. Seven Star?"

"Exactly like that, Fishbone. Mr. Tuttle was willing to give his life to save Sam's dad. See? You already know what Aristotle was telling the Greeks."

She welcomed him into her arms for a hug.

****

"Someone's here, Aunt Gem. I heard the stone crunch."

Gem looked out her kitchen window. Sheriff Harris and another man got out of a car and walked to her porch.

"Stay here." She shut the door behind her.

"Coop, I'd like to present Aunt Gem McKenny to you. Gem, this is Cleveland Coop of the West Virginia..."

"I know who he is."

"Miss McKenny, I'd like to talk about the..."

"I don't know nothing about it. And you can tell Cliffer Jennings to mind his own business."

Coop had heard that tone of voice coming from his grandmother when he was a kid. There would be no interview.

"Sheriff Harris, the Crawford boy is at my table learning to read. He's had a long day so I'd appreciate you giving him a ride home. His bike is at the side of the railing. Thank you, and good day, gentlemen."

She turned on her heel and went inside. Fishbone came out with a bag of baked goods.

"Mr. Coop and me are going to give you a ride home."

"Sheriff Bill, you tell my mom that Gem gave me this bag so Walter Venter knows I didn't steal it."

"Don't worry, I will. Walter thinks you steal?"

"Yeah, and lie. He says he can make me disappear if he wants to. He knows magic."

Sheriff Harris squatted and looked Fishbone in the face. "Are you kidding?"

"Nope, Sheriff Bill. He knows magic."

"I'll take care of it. Let's get your bike in the trunk of the car and get you home before dusk."

Bill and Coop exchanged glances as they sat for a few seconds in the car, thinking the same thing–*what kind of man threatens to make a seven year old kid disappear?*

TATER PERKINS

AGENT COOP MOVED THE microphone closer to the young boy sitting across from him, letting out a soft, almost inaudible breath of air to relax himself. Interviews with children were not his specialty.

"Take a deep breath and speak into the microphone, Elias."

The boy leaned forward, his lips brushing across the protective mesh. Taking a deep breath as instructed, the child shouted: "Minesnames Tater Elias Perkins."

He sat back in his chair and ate another bite of apple he took from the bowl on the table. Pleased with himself, he swung his legs back and forth, rhythmically bumping against his chair, his toes not touching the floor.

Agent Coop said, "That's a little too loud, Elias. Try again but softer and slower this time, okay?" He smiled as the last few decibels beat against his ear drums. Sheriff Harris tipped his head gear over his face as he cleared his throat to stifle a laugh.

Barely breathing, the youngest son of Howard and Elsie Perkins whispered into the mic: "Minnes nameesss Taaaaaater Eeeliiiaas Perrkins."

Howard Perkins crossed the room in two steps and clipped his son on the head with a middle finger swept across his thumb. "Tater, Agent Coop didn't come all this way for your nonsense. Straighten up. Stop wasting the man's time."

"Dad, that hurt." Tater rubbed the side of his head. "You gave me a skill fricture."

"That's a skull fracture and if I'd of clipped you that hard, you would've known it. Sit up in the chair. Give me the apple and stop trying to talk with your mouth full."

"But, Dad..."

"Are you sure?"

"We don't argue with our dad."

Howard Perkins apologized. "He's usually pretty good, gentlemen, but about this time of year when I've been away on construction jobs for half the summer, my boys tend to get a little head strong. Now I'm home, they'll have their minds right soon."

The six foot one, lean but muscular, Howard Perkins took the apple and finished it in a couple bites before leaving. He paused when he opened the screen door. "Tater, your Ma will be listening in so behave yourself."

"Where're you going, Dad?"

"Going to work with your brothers." The screen door slammed shut.

Tater rolled his eyes at the grown men across from him and whispered, "Ya'll know what that means?"

Sheriff Harris and Special Agent Coop slightly shook their heads side to side.

"Well, I'll tell you what it means," Tater put his chin on the table and spoke softly. "It means Dad found out that Tobias and Nathan didn't help like they was supposed to with firewood cut up and they didn't help take down laundry. Dad's got them one at a time behind the barn. Nathan says it's just talking, but I think they each get a lickin' on the butt."

Tater started to grin as Mrs. Perkins turned from the kitchen sink.

"Tater, do you know spreading gossip and idle talk is a sin? Would you like to speak to your father behind the barn?"

"Yes, Ma'am and no, Ma'am."

"You answer Mr. Coop's questions and don't forget I'm right here." Looking at her guests, she said, "You gentlemen are welcome to stay for dinner. Always room at the table."

Sheriff Harris smiled warmly. "Thank you, Elsie, but we'll be heading down the mountain before the sun sets. I hope you and Howard'll offer a rain check on that?"

"You know we will. And you can bring Mr. Coop if he's still here in the Hollar."

"I would be honored, Mrs. Perkins." Coop smiled at Tater.
****

"Shall we start again, Elias? Talk in a normal voice, and tell me what you know about those white dogs. Start at the beginning."

"The beginning? Okay. I have three big brothers and one little sister. We all got Bible names because Grandma Perkins named them except for me and my sister Maggie cuz she was dead."

"Your sister died? I'm sorry for your loss." Coop looked at Mrs. Perkins who gave out a sigh.

"No, Coop." Tater interjected. "Grandma died. She got herself old and died. She wasn't around to name the last two of us. You can't name someone if you're dead. Sheesh, I thought everybody know'd that. Maggie ain't dead, but sometimes..."

"*Tater!*" Elsie tapped the back of Tater's chair with her cooking spoon.

"Just kidding, Mom."

Interviewing children was as confusing as talking to his ex-wives. "Go ahead, Tater."

"Luke is first and then there's Nathan and Tobias. They're twins. Maggie's the only one can tell them apart but I think she cheats and marks them with a pen or something."

"Tater." Another tap at the back of his chair.

"And then there's me, and then Magdelyn. My sister's name is Magdelyn. She's the youngest but she had a twin that died when it was born and we buried her in the cemetery along with all the other people that we know'd like my grandma and....."

"Tater, attention." Elsie spoke as she peeled a potato.

Fearing he would get every scrap of information lodged between the ears of the boy with a summer tan and sun streaked hair, Agent Coop asked, "What about the dogs, Tater?"

"Oh, yeah, but you said to start at the beginning and I started at the beginning."

Coop felt the sweat running down his back. His whole interview was going off the rails. Everything the kid said was a long winding road of spiderwebs unrelated to anything except other spiderwebs in the six year old's brain. The agent would have to piece together a narrative acceptable as a report if needed.

"Sorry to interrupt. Go ahead and tell me however you want."

Tater sneezed and scooted off his chair, grabbing a paper napkin from the pantry counter to wipe his nose. Looking at his mucus, then holding the napkin up to the men, "Boy, that was a big one!"

"*Tater!* Throw that away. Sheriff Harris isn't interested in your boogers and neither's Mr. Coop. Go wash your hands before you come back to the table."

Special Agent Coop grinned as he watched Sheriff Harris turn in his chair to hide his smile but there was no hiding the law enforcement officer's shaking shoulders. The boy returned shortly with wet handprints on the legs of his jeans.

Tater adjusted the shoulder straps on his coveralls as he saddled back on the kitchen chair. One look from his mother, Tater knew he'd run out of all the second chances he was going to get.

"When it was my turn to be born, my Dad thought Juda was a good name but Momma said it sounded too much like "Judas" and just like this she said, 'It'll be a cold day on the Devil's doorstep before a child of mine is named Judas or anything like that. Kids at school would make his life unbearable.'" Tater dropped the falsetto voice.

"Tater, that's not the way I talk."

"That's how Dad does you when he talks."

"Really? Your Dad talks like that when he imitates me?"

Switching to a voice coming from the bottom of his chest, Tater spoke as he thought was close to his father's: "Don't forget, Tater, imitation is the highest form of flattening. I was just flattening your Ma."

"It's flattery. Get on with your story, Tater. I'm sure Mr. Coop and the Sheriff would like to go home sometime this decade." Elsie shook her head and started cutting spuds.

"So before I was born my Mom was thinking about a name for me so they named me Elias after the Prophet Elias. My Dad says he cooked potatoes for my Mom all day long cuz that's all she would eat. She ate potatoes fried, baked, sliced, raw, scalloped with cheese, and hashed browned. He said, 'Honey, you eat all those taters and that baby's gonna look like a tater root' and I did. Mom says I was pale, and dome headed just like a peeled potato ready for the pot, so that's how I got my name, Tater Elias Perkins.

"You got a cool name, Coop. Coop. Special Agent Coop–Cooper--Copper. That's a pretty cool name, Coop." The boy wiggled in his chair.

Cleveland tried a different approach with the boy. "I'm an investigator with a science lab and I'm investigating the case..."

"Where Miz Foster got beat up and her house burnt?"

"Yes, Tater, I am. How'd you..."

"Must not be from around here, Coop, cuz you know'd bout them already. Dad said you wanted to know what happened at church when the preacher felled."

"Yes."

"Okay. I'll tell you. The church on Davis Ridge. That's where we go and that's where this happened."

****

"Pastor Bob hops up and down when he talks on the Scripture. Every Sunday he casts off the Devil. He was hollarin' an' walking back and forth from one pew to the next and any minute I thought the Devil would pop out. Pastor Bob keeps looking at Mrs. Brubaker's hat so I know'd they was a devil or something in all the flowers she glued on it.

"Magdelyn and me started giggling because Nathan and Tobias was jiggling in the seats like they was the preacher. We forgot Dad was sitting behind us and he clipped us on the back of the head. Dad never clips Maggie on the head, just us boys.

"The hairs on the top of Pastor Bob's head was standin' right up straight, liked he put his finger in an 'lectrical shock and got blasted with 'lectrical juice. My dad calls it 'lectical juice but it's not the kind you drink like orange juice. Dad says enough of 'lectrical juice will kill you if you get poked with it. Like lightning in the mountains during a storm. That kind.

"Pastor Bob loost up his tie so he wasn't chokin'. He's charging back and forth.

"Tobias said, 'Ain't he gettin' all worked up?' and my dad whispers that it takes a lot of work to move the Devil out from here to somewhere else--just keep listening to the Word or something like that which means to turn around or you'll get clipped.

"Mr. and Mrs. Cummins was nodding their heads and I see Mrs. Cummins lips moving. Maybe I'd see a devil pop out of her if Pastor Bob would keep it up cuz I didn't see nothing come out of Mrs. Brubaker's straw hat." The boy paused. "Can I get a drink of water, Coop? I'm gettin' dry."

Mrs. Perkins anticipated her son's diversion and placed a glass of water on the table.

"Thanks, Ma."

"Welcome, Tater."

****

"The preacher got louder and louder and then he stopped and fell right in front of everyone. Right on the new carpet what came from Waybird City. New carpet and now there's the preacher falled on it with spit coming from his mouth.

"Everyone said 'Ahh.' Then the Sunday School teachers all rounded up the kids to get them out of church. I hid under the pew cuz I wanted to see what was going on. Maybe if he was dead, I see my first dead person.

"Mrs. Clellonds, Mrs. Butterfield, and Mrs. Hayes all started a prayer circle and held hands. A man in the back shouted, 'Reverend, get up, Reverend, get up!'

"Mr. Davis is a volunteer fireman and so Mr. Davis jumps up and says call the Sheriff and Dr. Glassman. Then Mr. Davis started blowing into the Reverend's face.

"I never saw a man kiss another man on the lips but Mr. Davis kissed the Reverend on the mouth. *Right on his mouth.* I started to giggle when I saw that. My dad was there pushing up and down on the Reverend's chest, so my Mom clipped me. She didn't clip as hard as Dad but she meant it. Then she said, 'Boy, you sit up and pray for the Reverend.'"

"I was looking up at the cross asking Jesus to save Preacher Bob when a wave went over the cross. Like when you open your eyes underwater and you come up and there's little bits of water on your eyes. I looked over to my dad an' he wasn't moving. My Mom wasn't moving. My brothers was sitting still.

"I look at Mrs. Hayes and everybody on her side of the church all froze up. All froze up like it was winter and they got caught in the lake water like the fish do waiting all winter long for the spring so they can unfreeze and swim away. But not me.

"Just me an' this lady could move and she was standing outside the circle of frozen people around the preacher on the new carpet from Waybird City. That's were they got the carpet. Over in Waybird City, West Virginia."

Tater paused as he twisted his hair above his ear.

"Her eyes had all blue in them like little lights. But the blue bits just moved around like water paints in a glass.

"'Now, don't be afraid,' she said. 'You're a witness, Tater Perkins.' I wondered how she know'd my name because I never saw her before.

"She put her hand out and it glowed. The Reverend's chest started to glow and then the two glowing parts met in the middle between them. Then she took her hand and slammed it on the Reverend's chest one, two, three.

"I looked at the cross again and saw that same dang ripple then everyone there got unfrozen.

"Sheriff Harris comes in wearing blue gloves, and Miss Gracie is talking on her phone and my Mom says, 'Please save him, Sweet Jesus' and Tobias says, 'Dang, he puts a lot into a sermon.'

"When I look there's Sheriff Harris with Mr. Davis and my dad. Mr. Davis kissing into the Reverend's mouth while the Sheriff pumps up and down on his chest and my dad sits back all out of breath.

"The Reverend starts coughing and sits upright. He was smiling, and thanking all the people around him.

"I ran over to the window Peterson's donated to the church. One of them glass windows, the kind with all the little colored pieces in it to make a Bible picture. When the men set the window of Jesus, one of the glass bits cracked. Me and Fishbone found it and keeps it a secret.

"I looked out that tiny crack and I saw her walking away in the fog but she wasn't by herself. Two snow dogs was walking with her. She and the dogs was getting smaller and smaller and then she looked back at the church. I had to rub my eyes twice to see what I was seeing but when I peeked back through the crack they was three snow dogs disappearing into the mist what comes down the mountains."

A tear fell from his eye. He moved to touch it; the moment was broken.

Agent Coop asked, "Tater, are you sure what you're telling me is what happened? Just like you say it did?"

"I know the difference between a lie and the truth and I wasn't sleeping in church so it warn't no dream and it warn't no lie. That's what happened."

Tater slid out of the chair. "Mom, can I have some bread 'n butter? I'm hungry."

****

Elsie kissed her son's hair as he took the bread, not correcting him when the kitchen screen door slammed. She sat in the vacated chair and placed a half peeled cucumber on the table beside the knife.

"Agent Coop, Tater's story hasn't changed. I've heard him repeat it three times and it's always the same. He told the same story to me as he did to you."

"Who saw the incident, Mrs. Perkins?"

"About the dogs? Only Tater. None of the rest of us saw anything. His sister and brothers have never mentioned it to me or Howard, so I believe just him and he keeps it to himself.

"You won't use my son's name. If you have to transcribe it, I understand that, but I don't want anyone recognizing his voice. We don't want people from outside traipsing up the mountain to harass my family. He was witness to an amazing event, but Tater deserves a childhood. Many of the folks around here have felt protected by whatever those dogs represent, and we don't want that to change for the sensationalism it would bring. My son's life will not be based on clicks, likes, or shares. The world is a nasty dangerous place, Mr. Coop. Howard and I have only so much time to raise children to know how to deal with it and stay true to themselves. Do we understand each other, Mr. Coop?"

"Yes, Mrs. Perkins." Agent Coop turned to Sheriff Harris. "Bill, do you think there's enough daylight to go up to the church and look around?"

"Sure."

"Just a quick look. Won't take long." Turning back to Elsie, "Thank you, Mrs. Perkins for your help and for letting me speak to your son."

"You're welcome. I want all of us to remember the agreement."

Both men replied, "Yes, ma'am." They left.

****

Howard came into the kitchen as Elsie finished setting the table, placing serving dishes and spoons on the sideboard. "Smells good. I see they headed down the mountain."

"I invited them to stay, but Bill said they'll take a raincheck."

Howard gazed at his wife's profile, still thinking she was the most beautiful woman in the world. "Any regrets?"

"Regrets? Regrets about what?"

"About us. About getting married so young and having babies. About never getting off this mountain, about not having a career like the girls you graduated with, about our life here in the Hollar."

"Now what brought this on? Remember the high school trip to Charleston? You remember what I said?"

"'I'll never leave my mountains for this, ever.' I took you at your word. Besides, I had to make my move on you before Bill Harris did."
****

At the church, Harris used his pass key.

"Bill, no lights, please. I can see better just using my flashlight."

"Sure." He turned the sanctuary over to the darkness, standing quietly while Coop methodically walked around the church, focusing his attention on the spot from his flashlight.

Coop went to the stained glass window. He squatted down to examine the lower corner. There was a cracked piece. The forensic agent continued along the wall, examining the carpet, occasionally flashing his light along the pews until he came to the front of the church.

"Where exactly did the Perkins boy say they were sitting?"

"He didn't, Coop, but the third pew back is where I always see them."

"Okay, one, two, three. Which means the pastor was about there," pointing to just beyond the first pew, "when he went down. So you'd have the pastor flat on his back, Mr. Perkins giving CPR about here, then Davis about here, and where were you?"

"I was on this side, giving chest compressions. I relieved Howard when I arrived."

Cleveland examined the areas where the carpet met the end of the pew. The agent suddenly dropped to the floor.

"Find anything?"

"Yeah. I think I have. Would you please bring my briefcase from your car?"

Cleveland heard the door shut. He found the minute piece of evidence he was looking for: a few white hairs trapped between the edge of the carpet and the support brace of the first pew.

ALICE COBB

"Alice."

"Uncle Hector."

"I'm leaving."

Alice walked into the kitchen with an arm full of textbooks. "Where're you going, how're you going to get there, and who's going with you?"

"Well, Miss Nosy, I'm going to Gray Hawk, Kentucky. They got a kid missing in Flat Lick Falls."

"And?" Alice poured a mug of freshly brewed coffee to balance her late night study session.

"I'm taking Rip, the Feds are sending a helicopter, and we'll be picked up in the church parking lot at Davis Ridge."

"The Feds?" Alice blew across the surface of the coffee before downing the pre-breakfast gulp.

"Vacationing senator's son got lost in the woods. I don't know much about it at this point. They wanted the best so they called me."

Looking over the top of her reading glasses and arching an eyebrow, Alice said, "The Feds specifically asked for you? I mean, someone in D.C. knows your name? Specifically, they asked for you? By name?"

"Well, yes...and no. I've made my mark. Don't look like you don't know." Hector squirmed as he met her gaze. "Well, yeah, they asked...a lot of the men in the FBI know me, er, well, they know of me...some of them know me." Still avoiding his niece's stare, Hector continued, "Actually they asked for Dotty."

"That's what I thought," she said. Her cup hid her smile. "You sure Rip can handle a trail like that? Flat Lick area is pretty wild."

Alice took peanut butter and cherry jelly from the kitchen cupboard by the sink, then two slices of bread from the loaf next to the toaster. Before rewrapping the fresh bread from Birdie Spry's kitchen, she nodded at Hector. "Want some?"

"No time. But to answer your question, Rip's good as Dotty, just younger's all. Don't tell her I said that."

"Believe me I won't. Know when you'll be back?" She slathered peanut butter and jelly on the toast.

"Nope. I imagine they got the scene all contaminated but we'll give it our best shot."

"How long the kid's been missing?" Alice could feel her salivary glands let loose as the aroma of the peanut butter hit her nose.

"Maybe eighteen hours. I'm guessing they called the state boys in first and the shepherds lost the trail in an hour, as usual. Deputy Taylor is my back up. My contact is a...wait, there's the paper by the phone. Special Agent Hector. Now, that's a good name. Full of character and manliness. Strong, dependable–"

Alice snatched the paper. "His name is Alfred Barns. At least one of us can read. But before you break your arm patting yourself on the back, know I won't hold supper for you tonight. You're on your own."

He looked at her with suspicion. "That my shirt you're wearing?"

"No, it's my shirt."

"Alice, it sure looks like my shirt."

"You're the only one who has a red flannel shirt with black stripes on it?"

"No, but I'm the only one who has a red flannel shirt with black stripes and a button missing off the left pocket."

He reached over the kitchen sink.

"Here's the button on the window sill so I wouldn't forget to sew it back on." Hector held the button inches from Alice's nose. "You, young lady, are *busted.*"

"Okay, so I borrowed one of your shirts. I think it looks better on me anyway."

"Huh. Guess I'll have to raise your allowance so you can buy your own shirts."

"Uncle Hector, you don't give me an allowance."

"Like I said, I'll have to raise it."

The bloodhound handler sloshed what coffee was left in his cup down the sink, rinsed it, and placed it in the dish drainer. He paused to look out the kitchen window at his dogs, lolling in their exercise pens as the sun came over the mountain. He was happy.

Removing his ball cap from its hook by the door, Hector gave Alice a quick kiss on her forehead as he grabbed the toasted bread out of her hand.

"Will you look at the clock? Taylor'll be sittin' on the porch waitin'." Taking a bite, Hector mumbled, "Tanks oo, weetie," and was out the door.

Alice watched him throw his trailing bags in the bed of the truck, then open the dog lot gate. He slipped a collar over the head of a sleek black and tan male. Hector touched the heads of a couple within reach, then tossed what remained of the peanut butter toast to the far end of the lot. Hector made a clear run out the gate as the pack of flapping ears followed the smell of food.

Hector opened the driver's door and Rip jumped into the cab. The dog knocked Hector's ball cap off with one fling of his tail, and with the next, flipped the driver's visor. A cascade of maps, receipts, and papers, everything ricocheted off the steering wheel, cluttering up the seat and the floorboards. Hector looked at his massive dog and shook his head.

"There you sit, just waitin' to ride in the truck like I owed it to you. Dang it, Rip, you gotta start lookin' where you're flingin' your tail. That's one of my best caps and you got it all dirty."

Hector grabbed the loose papers, stuffing them behind the bench seat of the truck. "I'll have to clean that out one of these days."

Rip ran his nose along the gap between the seat and the truck cab window, searching for a renegade crumb among the fallen papers .

"There ain't nothin' behind that seat for you. You ate hours ago, so don't get any ideas of droolin' all over the place. Just turn around and sit pretty." The dog flopped on the seat, down for a nap.

From the front porch rocking chair, Alice watched the show: her toast tossed to the pack, Rip bouncing in the truck, and Hector spraying gravel on her flowers lining the drive as he drove away. She went back in the house to fix breakfast.

She loved her uncle but sometimes she wondered if the chips were down, who would he pick: her or the dogs?

Before she could shut it up, her left brain interrupted.

"No, the dogs are not always first and you know better to think like that."

"Who asked for your opinion?

"You did. Just now."

"I did not. Go away, I've got to study."

"But you know I'm correct."

Alice was worried she wasn't normal when she told Uncle Hector that she had conversations with herself. All he said was, "Cobb's are like that. It means you always have someone intelligent to talk to. Just think of it like a girlfriend you can't get rid of."

****

As she ate her second toast and looked over the economics syllabus, the sound of the dogs baying caught her attention. Alice saw a marked cruiser make the sharp curve at the bottom of the hill, maneuver the crooked driveway, and park out front. The early morning was getting warm and a touch humid as Alice stepped off the wooden planked porch, nodding to the deputy getting out of the squad car.

"Mornin', Alice."

"Good morning, Deputy Johnson. What can I do for you?" If she kept the conversation professional, she might keep the scab intact.

"Is a year long enough?"

"Nope. It was pretty nasty and not all his fault."

"Shut up."

"Hector here? Foster care had a walk away this morning. We need your uncle and a search dog."

"He's gone not fifteen minutes ago. Left for Gray Hawk, and took Rip. Sheriff Harris has Cricket and Hank at Nevada Mills for a tourist who's been missing for a month."

"Well, if he's been missing that long, they won't find much."

"Cricket and Hank are cadaver dogs."

"Sorry. I don't know all the dogs."

"The torso popped up after the flood, so that's why Sheriff Harris took the cadaver dogs. If there are parts, Cricket and Hank will find them."

Deputy Johnson frowned a little. "What about you and a search dog?""

"It's been a while since I ran a dog. Besides, I have tests to study for."

Deputy Johnson looked at the flowerbed and shifted his weight. Alice hadn't seen him this uncomfortable for a long time.

A worried look crossed his face when he said, "There's a cold front coming in this afternoon. Aunt Gem mentioned a blue mist from the hills tonight. Gem told Amelia Lemon yesterday."

"So you're hanging out with Amelia Lemon now?"

"No. I just heard that Gem was at the tea room and said that. I'm not hanging with anyone, Alice."

An awkward pause stagnated the fragrance of the miniature lilac bush at the foot of the steps.

"Deputy Donald Johnson, please don't tell me you buy into all the hillbilly story stuff? Those old folks have been spouting tales of blue mists, white dogs or wolves or what have you, and the shadow of a fourth moon for generations." Alice sat down on the rocking chair, after unceremoniously removing the cat.

"You grew up around here and you know the Hollar has a history, Alice."

"Every town has a history, but there is no scientific proof of all that mumbo jumbo witchery stuff. It's all a bunch of old stories changed every time they're passed."

"Okay, okay. You've been to college and know all about it. I ain't here to squabble with you, Alice. I'm here because we got an old man lost in the woods and need a team to find him."

Donald took a deep breath before he continued, thinking that flattery might work better than legends at this point.

"Remember the kid you found over at Turtle Pond? People still talk about how you ran that trail. What dogs did Hector leave behind?"

Without thinking, the truth tumbled from her mouth. "Dotty's in her kennel."

"OK," replied the Deputy. "Dotty it is. I'll help you get the equipment."

Alice and Donald walked to the kennel behind the house. Alice regretted her words with every step.

****

She paused, her hand frozen over the gate latch. Could she handle Dotty as well as Donald thought?

Taking a deep breath, Alice slowly opened the kennel door and peered into the darkness. A beam of sunlight sliced across the cement floor, illuminating the deep red copper fur of the snoring dog curled up on her rugs.

Dotty was legend. Her searches were the stuff houndsmen talked about when gathered around campfires late at night. Was Alice up to handling a legend?

"Dotty?" Alice whispered. She held her breath hoping the bloodhound had died in the night and wouldn't respond.

"Remember what Hector told you? Say it firmly with authority but not meanness'."

Alice nudged the self correcting voice out of her head.

"Dotty. Come."

Awaken from her nap, the eighty pound dog extended her front feet. The stretch traveled through her neck and shoulders, then along her back and flanks, to her hips, down her legs and all the way to her metatarsals. She pointed her toenails to the wall. She brought her hocks under herself and rolled onto her belly. The bloodhound stood and stared at Alice, a low rumble coming from her throat.

The vibrations got louder as the dog came closer. Alice kept repeating "That's not a growl. That's the way they talk. That's not a growl."

The dimness did nothing to hide the size of the hound, who now stretched and standing, reminded Alice of a National Geographic lioness.

"When did she get so big? What should I do next?"

"What? You woke her up. You're supposed to know what to do next."

With shaking hands, Alice held the open choke chain in front of her in the shape of a downward "p". Dotty knew what to do; She put her head through the circle of the chain.

Dotty's trailing backpack hung on a nail by the door. In her bag was a collection of essential items needed by a team on a search and rescue mission. Alice grabbed the harness pack under Dotty's nameplate while Dotty pushed the door open with her nose.

****

As expected, people were milling around the search area when Alice arrived. She announced, "Would everyone not directly involved, leave the area? Please stay back while we evaluate what can be done. Thank you."

She kept Dotty in the truck as she gathered information from the staff.

"Alice." Donald spoke from behind her. "If there's anything I can do to help, please ask."

"Thanks, Deputy."

"Alice, I think you can call me Donald, okay? I mean we dated." He smiled.

"Yeah, but not any more."

The remark flew out of her mouth before her brain had an opportunity to apply the brakes. The air thickened like instant potatoes without enough milk.

"I'm sorry. I didn't mean it the way it came out."

She watched his smile fade like daylight over the mountains.

Donald looked around. "It's okay, Alice. It's okay."

She let the terrible aura she created float in the air for a few seconds before resuming her role as handler. Concentrating on the present might help clear the past.

"I need a scent article. Something only the missing man has touched, like socks, underwear, or a t-shirt. Put it in this bag without touching the item." Still embarrassed, she avoided saying his name.

"It's Donald, or Don. Okay?" He flashed a forgiving grin as he was excused to complete his task.

He had worked with Hector before and the instructions were always the same. Alice even sounded a little like her uncle but gratefully, she was better looking. The khaki dressed officer returned with a scent article in the bag.

Alice thought to start Dotty at the sun room where the man was last seen. She mentally reviewed the protocol as she went to get the dog, confident she had everything under control

She gasped when she opened the truck. Her pulse raced as she looked around the vehicle and the area. No Dotty. Then she saw the familiar slab-sided head above the driver's headrest.

"How did you get out of your crate? Get back here." The bloodhound hopped across the seats to her waiting handler, sweet and obedient.

****

From the sun peeking through the leaves of the over hanging tree, burnished highlights flashed across Dotty's coat. The copper color in her fur danced like flames of a campfire. Her black nose was moist in the humid air; hazel eyes hidden by her furrowed brow.

Dotty examined the air around her. She drew air in and out of her nostrils across the olfactory tissue high up in her snout, trying to identify her surroundings. Her head moved slightly, recognizing a multitude of smells: last night's trash cans tipped over by racoons, engine exhaust, perfumes, human body odor, and the acrid smell of permanent solution from the waste cans behind Francine's Cut and Curl.

Dotty sneezed three times in rapid succession. As Alice stepped back, she caught her heel on a stone. She went down with mucus in her hair.

"If anyone saw that–"

"So what? You tripped. Pick up your big feet and pay attention."

"Okay, okay, I've got it. Back to business."

Red faced, she dusted off while Dotty stretched on the tailgate then walked to the side door, and waited.

****

From a short distance away, Donald whispered to Deputy Crenshaw, "Watch this," as Alice opened the side door of the truck.

A massive front paw with hard, dark black nails, reached out almost touching the gravel parking lot. One paw down, exposing the foreleg, and then the other paw followed. The men saw her nose working as she gaged the distance to the ground.

Dotty's ears move gracefully as a breeze rustled leaves under the truck. The edges were lacey with the scars of trauma maintaining her place in the pack hierarchy; Dotty gave as good as she got.

"Crenshaw, look at her unfold herself. She goes on forever." Donald nudged his partner to make sure he was paying attention. "This is something you don't get to see every day."

Dotty stretched her neck. The skin folds of her head fell back when she raised her nose. She saw the two men watching her. Her tail thumped against the seat.

Taking delight in the grins of her audience, Dotty flexed her shoulders, hard and muscled, transferring her weight from her haunches, still on the floorboard of the truck, to her front feet and proceeded to expose her body, inch at a time. Donald was correct; it was like she went on forever showing rib after rib of her lean loin and back.

"Hey, Dotty," Donald whispered.

The dog opened her mouth, her long pink tongue cascading from between her jaws as she turned her head in his direction. She liked Donald. He gave her treats.

Dotty moved her front feet away to make room for the rest of her body. Her strong rear quarters cleared the door; her first and second thigh rippled drive and power. Her tail was thick at the base and arched like a scimitar, narrowing to a pointed tip. To finish her exit, Dotty kicked up gravel against the side of the vehicle.

As many times as Donald watched it, he was always impressed with the way Dotty got out of a truck.

"Crenshaw, see that notch, that dipped part on her hind leg? Up just above her knee?"

"Yeah, what's that from?"

"That's where some ol' boy tried to kill her with an arrow to get her off his trail."

"Oh, yeah?"

"Yeah. Dotty had part of that arrow hanging out of her muscle for quarter of a mile, still trailing him before Sheriff Harris shot the guy. Dude fell out of the tree like a drunk racoon at midnight. Hit a couple of branches on the way down, I guess. Didn't kill him because he took a swipe at Hector before we got the cuffs on him. Hector came back with a fist to his guts. Hector boxed in college, ya'know. Still throws a wicked right hand. Anyway, the guy sued the county but Judge Dietz threw it out. Gave him additional three years for assaulting an officer of the law."

"For swinging at Hector?"

"Nope, for the arrow what hit Dotty. She's the prettiest thing around here, outside of Alice."

"You still carrying a torch for Alice?"

"Yeah, I messed that up. I'll make amends when I figure she's cooled off."

"Well, Don, if she's anything like her uncle, you might want to lay in supplies because it could take a while."

"Yeah, I suppose. But, that Dotty, whew, what a dog."

Dotty glanced at the deputies watching her. She knew.

****

"Donald, if you keep staring at her, she'll want to play instead of work." Alice bent over the dog adjusting the buckles as she fitted the harness.

Dotty started walking, pulling Alice to the command center. The closer they got to the cluster of law enforcement and witnesses, the higher Dotty held her tail. Dotty trotted, springing off her hocks and elbows. She looked five years younger, agile, and athletic. Her entrance made it clear she was the star of the operation.

Donald walked Alice around the building. "I'll be close behind, but not too close. I put a radio and flashlight in the trailing pack with extra water, energy bars, and a heat blanket."

"No wonder it weighs a ton, but thanks."

She thought he looked a little worried, but when he said, "I know you can do this, Alice," she was even more ashamed of her unkind words but it didn't stop her from screwing up again.

"It's OK, Donald. I'd better get started before it gets too cold, and your blue mist fills the valley." For the third time Alice regretted the words tumbling out of her mouth.

Alice glanced at the sky and changed the subject.

"It was warm enough earlier." She leaned down and presented the scent article in the plastic bag to Dotty. The hound stuck her nose in. After a few whiffs, Alice gave Dotty the command: "Dotty, seek!"

The dog put everything she had into the harness and hit the first fifteen feet of the trail hard, catching Alice off guard.

"EASYDOT! EASYDOT!"

The handler dropped her weight into her heels, however Dotty already slowed. Alice fell backwards and landed on the soft ground. She jumped to her feet, gathering in the loose line.

Donald was wise enough to stifle his laugh with the back of his hand. He wasn't going to add fuel to the fire.

Alice adjusted the backpack and watched Dotty work.

Going across the field was easy. The thick red tail moved side to side like a metronome, regularly ticking off a canine beat. Dotty was relaxed, going about her business.

Alice glanced behind. It was reassuring to see Donald and Crenshaw. They seemed a little far back but she knew they weren't supposed to crowd the handler.

As Dotty entered the wooded area, the terrain dramatically shifted from short grass to damp underbrush, fallen trees and the base of an incline.

"Easy up, Dotty. I just lost my cap on a branch…not too fast, girl. It's getting steeper here."

The trail was taking them higher and demanding more physical resources. Alice was intent on watching the bloodhound, ignoring the exhaustion starting to creep into her muscles. Handling the line was more of a challenge as her fingers became colder.

Dotty slowed. "Do you need another whiff?"

The canine looked back at Alice from under one hooded eye, then continued her search.

"I seem to offend everyone today." Alice pulled her boot out of a muddy spot and trudged on.

Dotty ambled into the bushes. She dug at angry chirping frogs from the fetid water around a log. She inspected the rotten timber. Tucked in among a billion other molecules, was the scent she was looking for.

She raised her head casting on the wind, flaring her nostrils to collect molecules of scent floating in the air. With eyes closed, she inhaled the delicate aroma like a sommelier inspecting a fine wine.

****

Dotty leaned over her front legs as she stretched forward, again moving her head back and forth searching the unseen currents of air.

"Whatcha looking for, girl?"

Alice studied the sienna bloodhound run her nose along the bottom of the rotten log, then put both front feet up on the bark. Dotty dropped down to the ground, walking to the end of the log, then back.

"He sat here for a while, didn't he." Alice was making the mental movie of the lost man, writing the script of his actions from the data Dotty gave her.

"Then, he walked to the log butt and back."

Pointing her nose to the sky, Dotty gave out a voluminous howl. She threw her full weight into her harness and was running again. She went fifty feet and paused, sniffing the trunk of a tree before taking off. The copper canine diva continued working her way over twigs and around giant pine trees. Alice visualized the old man leaning against the tree to rest, trying to understand his dilemma.

Without her watch, Alice had no idea how long she'd been on the trail; Looking over her shoulder, she didn't see her back up.

Dotty strained to pull Alice along, like a prisoner dragging a ball and chain. The scent molecules of the man filled her nose and brain. She didn't feel the branch poke her armpit, the laceration from a sharp stone on her carpus, or the razor-like thorns tearing her lip and underbelly. One smell drove her on; the odor was getting stronger and stronger.

Dotty's brain was on fire with the knowledge her prey was just ahead. Her long red tongue dropped to the side of her jaw as she inhaled copious amounts of cool air. Long strings of saliva fell from her flews, sticking to the vegetation as she ran. Dotty accelerated in the thinning woods. Her muscles strained to be free of Alice dragging behind. In an instant, Dotty was running as hard as she could over the ground, the thirty foot line trailing behind her.

"What? You let go of the line?"

"I fell. I didn't mean to."

"You let go of Hector's prized man trailer?"

"But it was an accident!"

"Dotty, wait. Dotty, come back. Crap, Dotty, slow the hell down." Alice ran and tumbled through the woods fighting for air as she shouted commands.

With her hands on her knees, Alice bent over taking in gulps of the damp forest air. The muscle in her side cramped with pain no matter how hard she pressed.

She put her hands on her hips, stretching her shoulders up, trying to expand her lungs. She saw movement through the trees as stabbing pain from her ankle raced to her brain.

"Oh, no. Ahaah." The adrenaline that kept her running had abandoned her.

Standing on one foot, Alice scanned the area. Dotty was leaning against the guy like she was a long, lost friend. Her big, fat paw over his knee, her chin resting on his shoulder. He had his arm around her, hugging the dog to his side. Dotty raised her head, licking the rough whiskers of the man's cheek as Alice hobbled to them.

****

"Mister, Mister," Alice paused to remember the old man's name. "Terrance, I'm Alice."

"I got lost. Would you take me to my wife? I'd like to go home now."

"Terrance, let's put this special blanket around you so you get warmed up."

Alice looked around but didn't see Donald or the deputies. The acid taste of panic rose in her throat, burning her tonsils.

She gave Terrance her jacket. "Take this till you warm up. Here, I've got a pair of fleece pants in my bag for those skinny legs. Lucky we're about the same size."

He eagerly drank from the bottle as Alice helped him into the survival clothes.

"Careful, Terrance. Don't drink so fast you choke on the water."

"Thanks for finding me. I can't pay you anything. I was just trying to go fishing."

Alice looked into the filmy green eyes.

"You don't owe me anything and this ain't the place to fish. We need to get you out of the woods before nightfall."

"Yeah. There'll be a blue mist coming down from the mountain tonight."

"What?"

"Got anything more to eat, lady?"

****

"K9 to Johnson. K9 to Johnson. I've got him. Do you copy? Over. K9 to Command. K9 to Command. I've got him. Do you copy? Over." No response.

"The stupid batteries are dead. He gave me a dead radio! What an idiot!"

"Idiot? Are you talking about us or Donald?"

"Donald, of course."

"And checking the batteries before you went out was not your responsibility?"

Alice calmed herself.

"You're right. It was my responsibility to ensure I could maintain radio communications and I should have checked before I left."

"So, what are you going to do to get Terrance out of here? Start thinking, Alice."

"I just don't want to die out in the woods with a crazy old man."

"Don't worry, you won't. Now, what did Hector teach us about backtracking?"

****

Alice knew Dotty could do such a thing, but the question was could Alice get Dotty to do it? Of all the bloodhounds, this one was the most temperamental.

Alice made sure Terrance could stand and walk. She checked his fingernails and lips, and was satisfied he wasn't showing signs of hypothermia. His pulse was regular and strong.

"You seem to be in pretty good shape. What kind of work did you do?"

"In the coal mines at first, then was a logger."

"You're in better shape than I am."

"Probably so," he replied as he worked a raisin between his gums.

Alice wrapped the end of the trailing line around his waist and made him take it in both hands. She switched on the cap's small revolving red light. Snugging the reflective vest across his chest, she then tucked the survival blanket in the top of the fleece pants. He looked like a traffic director on a construction zone.

"Terrance, if you hang on to this line, the dog will take you home. Listen to me. Hang onto this line and tell the dog: 'Take me home, Dotty.' Say it. 'Take me home.'"

"I think you should come with me."

"Can't, Terrance. I hurt my ankle, so you send help back to me, okay?"

"Are you sure I can go?"

"Look," Alice replied, "You walked all the way here, buddy, you can walk out. Now say it: Dotty, home."

The old man repeated it several times. He looked at Alice. "You're the girl in the sparkle shoes."

"The girl in the sparkle shoes? Um...Yes. You tap the red dog three times and she'll take you home." Dotty was tired and so was Terrance; they would be evenly matched.

Alice spoke in Dotty's ear: "Get him out of here."

Dotty snorted. Something welled up in Alice and she pushed Dotty's head skin backward. Alice looked into the hazel brown eyes: "I am not afraid of you any more. DO IT!"

Connect! Alice felt it and Dotty felt it. Handler and dog were one.

A tired Dotty began the slow process of retracing her path.

****

Alice watched the pair until she could no longer see the flashing light on his cap. She hoped they would meet Donald in the open field.

Sitting on the fallen tree trunk, she shuddered as the cold traveled up her spine and rattled her teeth. She should hear shouting any minute.

Her ankle started to throb. Unlacing the boot went well, but trying to remove it was agonizing. She noted the broken blood vessels and the pin point pattern of blood under the skin. Putting the boot back on almost made her pass out.

"Dumb move, Alice. Should have left the boot on."
"Agreed. Probably should elevate it?"
"Right. Brace it on the dead branch sticking out."
"Good idea."
"Get into position—raise my leg and..."
The intense pain of moving her ankle made her scream.
"If I scream in the woods, and there is no one around to hear it, did it really happen?"
"I heard it."
"Okay, we're good. Thanks."
"You're welcome."
She saw the blood on the moss.
"What? I checked him over. He was okay."
"Did you check the dog, genius?"
****

Alice lowered herself to the ground. The palms of her hands grated against the bark as she lost control and dropped. She screamed again. Her hands were bleeding and her ankle was unbearable.

She wrapped her palms in gauze from the first aid kit. Holding her hands between her thighs kept her hands warm but did nothing for the rest of her. She started to shiver a little at first and then uncontrollably. The chill went deeper. She started to nod off.

"Don't fall asleep, Alice. It's dangerous."
"Okay, I won't."
****

The cold crept through her skin, into her muscles, centering in her core. In her light sleep, the events of her life unfolded before her eyes like a movie.

She was at a big table, bouncing her heels against the braces of the chair; the six year-old witness to her parent's ugly divorce. The judge looked like Santa Claus–custody was granted to Uncle Hector and Aunt Mae. Alice laid her head along Uncle Hector's neck as he carried her out of the courtroom.

Her first piano recital, dressed in a pink ruffled dress–Alice heard Hector snore from the front row.

Something fluffy brushed her nose. Alice waved her hand, but was too tired to wake up. She shuddered and fell back into her dream.

She was sixteen joy riding, shooting mailboxes and stop signs with her friends, her first drink of stolen white lightning, caught spraying graffiti on the side of Hammond's Hardware. They had to work the entire summer cleaning dog runs, and general yard maintenance for every senior citizen in the Hollar who signed on as ordered by Judge Dietz.

"Alice! Wake up!"

A noise echoed in the trees. Looking around to see who spoke to her, Alice slapped her arms and blew into her hands. She found the key chain compass/thermometer: 49 degrees.

"No one can get hypothermia at 49 degrees."

"Yes, they can."

"I'm not going to listen to you."

She rummaged around in the trailing pack and found a box of chocolate covered peanuts. As she nibbled, a gray squirrel in the maple tree saw her chin drop to her chest.

"Wake up!"

Alice shook so hard she cut her head on a sharp branch projecting from the tree. A small stream of blood dribbled down the side of her face. The squirrel started a noisy, angry chortle, alerting the woods something was wrong.

"Squirrel, I'll leave as soon as I can, but I have to wait for the...who's the coming others."

Alice rubbed her temples trying to clear her mind. She massaged a sore spot on her spine and she felt the indentations the tree bark made in her skin. Her thoughts felt thick. How did she get in the woods?

She turned the trailing pack upside down, spilling the contents on the ground: a bag of tuna, a candy bar and powdered soft drink. She ate the candy bar and stuck her finger into the redness: cherry.

Sugar fueled, she had enough energy to balance herself along the top of the log. Stretched out, she propped her leg up on a protruding branch. In two breaths she was sleeping.

The watchful squirrel made his move to abscond with a candy on the ground.

****

After Aunt Mae's funeral, she found Uncle Hector in the kennel, lighting a pipe bowl of cherry tobacco, Mae's favorite aroma. Alice watched Hector whisper to the dog, his hand patting Dotty's head.

A warning bellowed in her brain:

"Wake Up! For all that's holy, Wake Up!"

Alice rolled off the log onto the ground, the smell of the bear filled her nostrils. She opened her eyes. Fear made her want to look away, but fear also forced her to see the animal standing not fifty yards away, sniffing the winds.

"Don't make eye contact. Don't challenge it. Just play dead."

She never realized how big bears were until one stood on its hind paws opposite her. But was it real? Was she sleeping? She wiped her eyes to clear the smoke that permeated the air; her fingertips were tinted a pale periwinkle blue.

The bear roared. She knew it could close the distance in seconds. The bear roared again. Its foul breath carried on the wind.

Alice hunkered down further, hoping to melt into the log, hiding in the tree rings. She squeezed her eyes shut, waiting for the pain.

A flurry of yips and growls, barks and snarls came from behind her. Glancing up she saw the under belly of three wolves jump the log, their speed a blur over her head in the air, charging the bear as it was charging her.

The pack sank their teeth into the fur and flesh of the bear. The power of their drive thrust the bear back and down, tumbling into the depths of the woods, the thrashing bundle of black and white fell over the edge of the berm. Fighting for its life, the death call of the bear reverberated off the canopy of trees setting up an echo chamber roar that shook the hills.

****

"Hurry, Alice. Use the stick as a crutch. You have to get out of here. They'll be back to kill you. If they can take down a bear, you are dessert. Get out!"

She pushed against the tree bark behind her, tearing the gauze and reopening the lacerations on her palms. The adrenaline coursing in the veins of her body propelled her into action. As she rose, her heels slipped against the dampness of the moss and wet debris on the forest floor. She fell back against the log.

"Don't give up. Get the stick under your arm and get out of here. Hurry Alice. They'll be back."

"I can't make it. I just can't make it."

"Alice, use your meditation breath. Slow down and think. Get out of here, stand up, damn it, stand up."

Alice took a few jagged and jerky steps to a massive oak tree, its girth the size that made lumbermen salivate, but for Alice, it would be her last stand.

She didn't know how long her death would take, but she was going to face it. A calm came over her. The hammering pulse in her ears began to slow.

"If I'm gonna die, I need to see it. If you're gonna kill me, let's get it over with but I ain't going down without a fight."

She rubbed her bloody hands along the ragged bark of the tree. The hounds would pick up her scent. Cricket would find her body for a funeral.

She turned to face the danger which would tear her to shreds, dine on her innards, and drag her mutilated corpse across the Appalachian Plateau. A tear slipped from between her eyelids and trickled down her cheek as she imagined the grisliness of her body when the bloodhounds found her. Her hands were clenched on the stick as her last defense.

Alice struggled for a deep breath, possibly her last. Nothing happened. The thundering roars were gone; the sounds of snapping branches and twigs were gone; the snarling growls and barks were gone.

From the depth of the gorge came the saddest and most plaintive howl Alice had ever heard. Three animal voices joined as one, sending a unified song to the skies.

She slid part way down the trunk of the oak, no longer strong enough to hold her weight on one leg.

"Let come what may, God. Thy will not..." Silence in the woods.

Opening her eyes, Alice watched the tips of the upright ears, the heads, and the blue eyes appear over the mound. Keeping their distance, the three sat with their fluffy tails covering their front paws. They watched Alice as she watched them.

She could breathe, her heart rate recovered to normal. The pain in her ankle returned, and she felt the burning in her palms. She relaxed against the tree, the old oak supporting her, comforting her. The sun filtered through the canopy of the trees, dancing across the leaves and moss surrounding her, filling her with awe.

Alice was mesmerized by the multitude of colors in the iris of their eyes, twisting and turning, making a kaleidoscope of calm. The dogs were pure white as if they just fell out of a cloud.

Should she try to touch one? As Alice reached out, one leaned toward her, the softness of its fur and whiskers so very close and inviting. Its breath warmed her fingertips. The vapor from its mouth turned into sparkling crystals, like diamond dust floating in the air. Just to touch the downy silk of its ears, to be caressed by its velvety muzzle, and to fall into the serenity of those blue orbs was intoxicating.

In a feeling of exhaustive peace, Alice closed her eyes. She slid to the ground, received into a soft bed of pine needles and leaves.

HECTOR COBB

From his seat behind the pilot, Hector craned his neck to see the church parking lot enlarge as the pilot zeroed in on the landing marks. The search and rescue at Flat Lick Falls was wasted effort. Hector was disgusted. The doped up kid stumbled back into the command center while Hector and Rip where thigh deep in brambles and muck looking for him. Rip followed the trail to the doper on his cot in the medical tent.

Hector felt a nudge on his arm. Deputy Taylor pointed to the sleeping dog at Hector's feet. Shouting into his headset mic, Taylor said, "I guess flying in a helicopter doesn't stress him out too much."

Hector shook his head. "Nope. I get each one of my man trailers up at least once when they're pups."

"He don't mind the noise?"

Hector lifted one of Rip's ears. "Cotton plugs." He pointed to the ground. "We're home, Taylor."

The thud of the landing woke Rip and he responded accordingly, "Baaarooo." Hector kissed the dog on its head, then gave the command to exit the craft. Taylor gathered the duffel bag of equipment.

Deputy Taylor saw the flashing lights of a cruiser making its way up the winding mountain road.

"Looks like we got an escort."

"You want to ride back with them or in my truck?" Hector asked.

"I'll take the squad car back. Rip takes up too much of the seat. And he farts."

"Not as bad as his sisters." Hector laughed.

"Looks like Deputy Johnson driving." Taylor waved as the driver applied the squeaking brakes just short of Hector's truck.

"Hector, I need you. Alice went out on a search and we lost her...I mean I lost her."

"What was she doing out on a search? She has school."

"If Taylor will drive your truck, you can ride with me and I'll explain everything what happened to her and Dotty."

"Dotty? If you lost Alice, what in dang hell happened to Dotty?"

"Dotty's okay. I've got her at the command center."

"Command center?" Hector tossed his truck keys to Deputy Taylor. "Donald, whatever have you done?"

"Come on, Hector. Rip can ride in the back."

****

By the time they arrived at the command center, the bloodhound handler knew exactly what he was going to do, starting with Deputy Johnson's demise.

"Hector, I'm..."

"Don't say it. I need to focus on Alice rather than how I'm going to kill you if I don't find her alive and in good shape."

"Yes, sir."

"Where's her truck?"

"Over here."

"Okay. Now ya'll get the hell out of my way."

****

The first responders watched from a distance as Hector and the dog started the search. Rip ran his nose over the seat, frantically wagging his tail.

"Yep, that's Alice. So, big man, let's go get our girl."

Hector let the lead line out. He gave Rip the length needed to determine which way Alice left the area from the foster care. Deputy Johnson briefed him, but Hector wanted verification from the dog.

The radio crackled with static. "Command Center to K9. Over."

Hector hit the mic button attached to his shirt. "K9. Go."

"Sheriff Harris is on his way back from Nevada Mills with two of your dogs. Do you want him to give assistance here? Over."

"Negative. Drop the dogs off at my kennel. He knows where they go. Over."

"Copy. Standby. Over."

"Copy. Tell Johnson to cover my six. EMT behind him. Over."

There was a pause.

"Copy. Johnson and backup at your six. Command Out."

"Copy. K9 Out."

Hector patted Rip's sides and ruffled the dog's ears. "Let's show them what a real search engine can do."

The big dog rubbed his drooling mouth along Hector's pant leg and nudged the lead line with his nose.

"Seek, Rippy. Seek." Hector's voice to the dog was like two old friends gossiping on a sunny day.

Even though hours old, Rip picked up the trail immediately. Hector played the thirty foot line out for Rip to study the ground, then gathered the slack, always keeping contact with the D ring on the harness.

"That's it, Rippy." In fifteen minutes the dog led Hector over the grassy field and into the wood line. Rip ran his nose over the branch of a bush, then let the leaves from a low hanging limb tickle his muzzle. He sneezed on occasion like the reboot of a computer to clean the data.

Rip leapt five feet from the ground and grabbed a knit cap from a branch. The dog tossed it up in the air for Hector to catch. The handler smiled.

Hector knew this was the last stretch of the search when Rip stopped, twenty feet out, and looked back at his handler. The bloodhound wagged the tip of his tail; then pranced in place, a canine version of the elegant Lipizzaner *piaff* but without the elegance.

"You know where she is. Okay, I'm ready. Hit it."

Rip stopped his dance and lowered his body. On the command "hit it" he burst into a run.

Hector's ectomorphic long legs allowed him to keep up, although his breathing wasn't coming as easy as it once did.

He followed Rip up and over a log. Hector threw the lead line in the air, side vaulted over the butt end of the fallen tree, and grabbed the leather handle before it was out of his reach. Rip was hot on the track, his tongue lolling out of his mouth, his deep chest pulling in massive amounts of air as his streamlined body dodged and darted along the trail.

When Rip shifted gears by reducing his speed, Hector knew they were close. Finally, Rip used his hind legs and wide paws to slow his speed dramatically. He braked with such force that all four feet left long skid marks in the mossy damp earth. He brought himself to a full stop between Alice's outstretched legs and landed with his chin on her belt buckle, his eyes locked on her face. Hector was seconds behind.

The plop of the dog's head on her stomach woke her. "R..R..Rippy?" She looked up to see Hector. "I'm okay." She grasped his arm.

Hector keyed his mic. "K9 to Command. I've got her. She's alive."

"Command copy. Units 3, 7, 10, and 12 report your location. Over."

"Units 3, 7, 10, and 12. We have eyes on K9. Over."

"Command to K9. Medical personnel standing by. Will you need helicopter to Waybird? Over."

"K9 to Command. Negative. She's responding. Negative chopper. Dr. Glassman at the ready. Copy. Over."

"Command to K9. Loud and clear. Glassman notified. Over."

"K9 to Command. Standby."

****

"Alice, honey, are you okay? Where does it hurt?"

Rip extricated himself from Alice and sniffed the caked blood on her forehead. He excitedly lapped the wound with his hot wet tongue.

"Rippy, don't," Hector said. "Just sit right there and pant yourself down. She's fine. I got her. Good boy."

"H..how long did it take him to find me?"

"Once he scented the truck, maybe fifty minutes all told. Rip was on your trail from the get go." Hector checked her pupils, fingernails, and the wound on her head. "Backup will be here in just a second, honey."

"Uncle Hector, I saw them."

"Them?"

"The snow dogs. They saved me from a bear."

"Okay, sweetie, let's not worry about that stuff now. You took quite a blow there."

"No, really. I'm not imagining it."

"Okay. We'll talk later." Hector turned to the sound of footsteps crashing through the undergrowth. The flashlights were bobbing in the dusk.

Deputies Johnson, Taylor, Hodding and Kirkpatrick brought the first aid kit and stretcher. EMT Granger dropped to her knees, opening her bag.

"Hey, Alice. Let me give you the once over." Granger conducted a field physical looking for signs of serious trauma.

"You got a nice sprain going for you, honey. I'm going to cut this boot so I can put an air cast on you just to make you more comfortable."

Alice cried into Rip's neck when Granger pulled the boot.

"It's okay, Alice. Sorry it hurt so much, darlin'."

****

The men gathered in a small circle away from Alice and Granger.

Hector directed, "You four, man the stretcher and get Alice to the field for transport to Glassman's. I'm going to look around a little before I head back. Keep your radios on and the squelch low. Copy?"

"Copy, Hector." Deputies Taylor and Hodding prepared the folding stretcher for the transport as EMT Granger finished and gave the okay to move Alice.

The relief Deputy Johnson felt was palpable. "Whew, I'm sure glad we found her." He rested his hands on his equipment belt.

"I bet you are," Hector said. "I guess I can toss the plans I made to kill you."

At that moment, Donald was sure Hector was serious.

****

Hector walked around the immediate area once Alice and the rescue squad were out of sight. Using a stick, he moved moss and leaves. He found footprints, one complete and one a partial, where Alice limped from the log over to the tree. The bear prints weren't too deep, indicating maybe a young boar, 275 to 350 pounds, still quite an adversary for a woman without a gun.

Rip nosed the scattered papers and the opened backpack. When Hector called, he raised his head with a strap caught behind his head and another over his long nose.

"Dang, if you don't get into everything there is, Rip. This is embarrassing." Hector stopped when he saw a tuft of white hair caught in the bark of the log.

"Well, I'll be." He put the hair in the palm of his opened hand. A burst of air picked up the hairs. He watched them float skyward until they disappeared among needles of a nearby hickory pine.

"Won't find them, Rip. The evidence is gone." Hoping the wind would take his words, he called, "Thank you."

With the backpack on his arm and Rip's lead attached to a clip on Hector's belt, they left the woods and its mysteries.

****

Alice was sitting in a chair with her ankle elevated and encircled with an ice pack, when Hector arrived at the clinic. Deputies Hodding and Johnson were on either side of her. He looked into the exam room where Dr. Glassman and his assistant, Tootsie, were giving Dotty a physical. Hector looked at Alice, then looked at Dotty, then back at Alice. He walked to the exam room.

"How's my dog, Andy?"

Alice whispered to Deputy Johnson, "I knew he'd say that."

"Well, the ear needs stitching, then there's a puncture wound on the left center pad. She's got a vertical tear on her dewlap here—we won't ask how you got that, eh, Dotty?" he said as he patted the bloodhound on the head. "Some razor sharp thorns tore up her chest and belly. But all fixable."

"What's the swelling on her wrist?"

"I'm going to x-ray that, and around this knee. Humm, I don't like it at all, but she may have just hyper flexed it. I'm sure there's nothing broken. It's all soft tissue damage I believe. Look over here...hum...on the inside of the rear left leg. This laceration on her stifle. Appears as she may have got it caught and then pulled it out. Who was with her?"

"Well, Dr. Glassman," Alice paused trying to gather her thoughts before sinking herself in the truth of the matter. "Umm...no one was with her. She was backtracking."

"Poor, Dotty. Out in the woods by herself." Glassman patted her head. "Tootsie, let's start some fluids, electrolytes and a shot of antibiotics...say eighty five pounds of dog here. Dotty's had a rough day."

Alice looked surprised. "How'd you know?"

"I've got a shortwave radio and citizen's band so I can call Bowtie if I get stuck somewhere. Also a police scanner to pick up the local news. And guess what? You're on it. I know Deputy Johnson lost you in the woods."

"Oh, crap. I suppose it's all over the state."

Dr. Glassman shrugged his shoulders. "Probably. There are more important things to worry about."

He turned to Hector, "I'm going to register Dotty for a few days in the Glassman Spa and Mineral Bath Clinic. I think she's had enough of human beings. Ha!" He was the only one laughing.

"Okay, well, humm, Tootsie, let's get a cage ready for Dotty."

"All done, Dr. Glassman."

"Deputy Hodding, help me get her off the table and settled. Alice, I'll be right back to look at that ankle."

Tootsie finished wiping the x-ray table. She called for Alice to come into the room. Deputy Johnson started to pick Alice up, however, Hector nudged him out and picked her up himself, the ice bag falling to the floor.

"Still mad, Hector?" Deputy Johnson said.

Hector curled his lip and growled.

"Okay, I deserve that."

****

"There you go, sweetie." Hector gently placed Alice on the table.

Dr. Glassman centered her ankle under the tube head and light collimator. "Okay, everyone out while I take the pictures. State law." He started to step behind a lead shield.

"Hey, wait a minute. Shouldn't I be on the human side of the clinic?" Alice asked.

"Nope. I use one machine for all species. Cheaper that way. Besides, you and Dotty look like you've been in close proximity. Both you girls are dressed in dried leaves and blood. Let me look at these and I'll have an idea how to treat you. Hold still and say 'cheese'."

****

In the lobby, Hector replaced the ice bags around her ankle while Alice sat back and closed her eyes.

"Alice," Dr. Glassman slid into the empty chair beside her. "Nothing's broken so I think you got lucky with just the sprain. Hector can take you home now. Ice for twenty to thirty minutes every two hours, elevate it higher than your heart for forty-eight hours, and use the crutches for up to the bathroom only.”

“Ah, Alice, the chance of a lifetime; I cook for you.” Hector grinned.

“Maybe I should check into Dr. Glassman’s spa with Dotty.”

“Call me if you’ve got any questions.”

“What about my hands and the cut on my head?”

Andy looked at the wounds. “Hector’s got some antibiotic cream for the hands. Same stuff we use on the dogs so there’s no sense in buying any more. Wash them, then wrap them with gauze bandage. Just going to tough that out. As for the head, don’t worry about that. It’s superficial and doesn’t need any stitches. Looks like EMT Granger cleaned it off.”

“No, that was Rip.”

“Well,” Dr. Glassman looked at the cut again. “He did a pretty good job. Maybe I should make him an associate.” Dr. Glassman looked around the room at all the tired faces. No one was laughing. “Okay, you folks look like you need some food and a rest.”

“Thanks, Doc.” Hector picked Alice up from the chair and carried her through the lobby. “Let’s get you home.”

Tootsie held the door. “I’ll make sure he calls you when he has more information about Dotty.”

“Thanks, Toots.” He adjusted Alice in his arms. “Better lay off those pasta salads, sweetie. You’re gettin’ heavy.”

Alice just shook her head.

****

They drove in silence the last few miles. Hector turned into the drive, careful to avoid the ruts and potholes. It took a little maneuvering to get her out of the truck, up the steps, and into the house, but before Hector went to the kennel to do the chores, he made sure Alice was set up in the bathroom to wash and change clothes. By the time he got back in the house, she had hobbled to the recliner chair in the living room.

“Everything okay with the dogs?”

“Yeah. Hodding brought Rip back. Sheriff Bill’s been here and fed. I washed dishes, cleaned the lots, and put the radio on for them. I’d say they’re settled.”

Alice smiled. “Did you kiss them goodnight?”

“Just Rip. Now, I’m going to fix you something to eat. Better take those pain pills cuz I figure that ankle’ll be singing its own tune pretty quick.”

He returned shortly with a bowl of steaming venison chili, warm buttered bread from Birdie Spry, and a glass of milk. He watched Alice take her pills. “There’s more chili if you want it. Can I get you anything else?”

“No, this is fine, Uncle Hector.”

"Now, blow on that chili cuz it was almost boiling." He sat in the rocker across from Alice. He lit his pipe and inhaled until the tobacco glowed in the bowl. "You want to tell me what happened? How Deputy Johnson hoodwinked you into taking Dotty out?"

"It wasn't hoodwinking. There was a lost old man and I made the decision that maybe I could help."

"With Dotty? A dog you've hated most of your life?"

"She was the only one here that could do the job. And she did."

"Yep, she did."

"I'm so sorry she got hurt. I'll pay the vet bills."

"Nope, not necessary. The county'll pay for a lawful search. She'll be alright. So, how'd she do?"

Alice beamed. "She was great. All the lessons I took from you and Aunt Mae, honestly some of that stuff went over my head, but when I saw Dotty work, it all fell into place. It was remarkable working with Dotty until…"

"Until she got away from you?"

"Yes."

"Don't feel bad. She's done that to other handlers. When Dotty takes a notion in that pea-sized brain of hers, it gets done."

"I found that out."

Hector set a small TV table beside his chair. "Just a sec," he said as he went into the kitchen.

Alice dunked her bread in the chili, capturing a couple of kidney beans on the crust. "If they serve this in Hell, I'm going."

"What say?"

"Chili's good."

Hector returned with two mugs of steaming water. "Here's tea with herbs Running Deer and Birdie Spry put together. Your Aunt Mae swore by those concoctions an' elixirs to heal things. I mean, it ain't gonna hurt."

Alice nodded and caught the chili sauce from her lips with the back of her hand.

Hector was cautious when he asked, "Anything else happen when you were workin' Dotty?" He slowly rocked in his chair.

"Well, I don't know for sure. EMT Granger said I had hypothermia so, maybe I was in some kind of dreaming state."

"What'd you dream, sweetie?"

Alice set her empty bowl aside and picked up the tea. She blew the steam across the top of the mug.

Hector relit his pipe.

"Well, I was on the ground. I was cold but I could feel a warm breath on my face, like something was smelling me. Then this gray squirrel started screaming at me. Then I remember being in the courtroom with you and Aunt Mae...and my piano recital when I wore a pink dress and you snored during *Clair de lune*...and I flashed on the summer when I got in trouble."

"Yep. I remember. You kids did a good job painting the kennels for me."

"That was the easy part. When you and Judge Dietz made us work at the rendering plant, I have to admit I hated both of you."

"Yep, but you got straight A's in school after that. It was an interesting summer for sure."

"Uncle Hector, there was something else. This is where things get hazy."

"Cobb's can get hazy." A single thread of smoke from his pipe curled up toward the ceiling, dancing to currents of air from the furnace. "I'm listening."

"Well, I was dreaming, and then I was fully awake because I saw a black bear...he was sniffing around...I couldn't run...then I could smell it...the wind changed and it could smell me...and I thought I was going to die...and..."

"Slow down, Alice. I'm not going anywhere. Just tell me."

"Then it stood. I never knew how big they were until it stood up...and it roared...God, it roared like a lion...so loud I could feel my eardrums vibrate...and it saw me...and I prayed to die quick...but then...

"The wolves appeared from behind me. I was on the ground with my back to the log, and these wolves jumped over from behind me and they attacked the bear. They were yipping and growling...this ball of black and white rolled down the berm. I grabbed a stick for a crutch and got as far away as I could...but I had to stop. I knew the wolves would come back to me. I...I...left a blood mark on the tree so Cricket could find me...I used my stick as a spear...I wasn't going down without a fight."

Hector watched the anxiety attack take over. First, her toes, then her feet began to tremble. He saw the pain on her face as the injured ankle was affected and her other foot spastically tapped the floor. Hector pulled the ottoman to her chair, scattering the newspapers to the floor.

"Look at me, honey. Look at me." Hector placed his hands before her, palms up. "Alice, remember what we did when you were a little girl and were scared? Look at me, sweetie."

In spite of the slow jerking of her head, Alice turned her gaze to her uncle's face. "Yeah...yeah..." She placed her bandaged hands over his, her bruised fingers on top of his wrists.

Hector said, "My power to your hands, my strength becomes yours."

Her breathing slowed and the trembling stopped as she gained control over her body, mind, and spirit.

Not releasing herself from his touch, Alice fixed on his eyes.

"I saw them come, three of them. They had these eyes, blue like outer space, then they'd change and be like turquoise with silver running through it. They kept changing the more I looked at them. Two of them sat back, but one came toward me. When it panted, the moisture in its breath was like diamond slivers floating on the air.

"I reached forward to touch it but something stopped me.

"I couldn't get over how peaceful I felt looking into it's eyes. I wasn't afraid anymore. Then, Rip was in my lap and I saw you."

Satisfied that Alice had returned to normal, Hector pushed the ottoman back to its place and gathered the newspapers. He sucked on his pipe a few times, noting it was out.

"Still hungry, sweetie?"

"Maybe a little. I'll take more of that venison chili if you've got it. Is that Aunt Mae's recipe?"

"Yep. Give me just a second." He took her bowl and tea mug.

"Am I crazy, Uncle Hector?" Alice called after him as he ducked into the kitchen.

"All Cobbs are a little crazy. That's why our friends are never bored."

Coming back into the room with hot chili and tea, he used his toe to push the tv table closer to Alice.

"No, you're not crazy." Hector returned to his rocker and relit his pipe. The slow comforting squeak of the rocking chair was interrupted only by the methodical ticking of the mantel clock.

Alice looked at him staring at the oval rag rug his wife made the year before she died.

"Well?" Alice spooned another bite of venison chili into her mouth, scooping a dropped bean off her shirt.

"Well what?"

"Was it true? It felt like it was, even now. I thought I was with angels or warriors. Something was protecting me."

"How do you prove it?"

"How what? How do I prove it?"

"Yep. How do you know it isn't some old hillbilly folk story?" He knocked a few ashes into the tray beside him.

"Because you didn't tell me I was confused...you didn't interrupt to deflect me off in another direction. I could never make sense about all those stories I heard growing up, just bits and pieces...all the whispers from Aunt Mae, and the adults go all quiet when kids came in the room. It's all true. All of it."

"What makes you think that?"

"Because you never said it wasn't."

****

Hector watched Alice succumb to the pain medicine. He took her dishes to the sink then returned to carefully lift her out of the chair. She mumbled something in his ear.

"You're going to sleep down stairs for a couple of nights."

He placed her on the bed, put pillows under her leg, then kissed her forehead. "Good night, sweetie."

The mantel clock struck two a.m. before Hector emptied his pipe and covered himself with two of Mae's crocheted blankets.

Tomorrow he'd go back into the woods to look for the remains of a bear he was sure wasn't there.

<h1 style="text-align:center">SPY MASTERS</h1>

"Tater, what's he doing now?"

"He's walking around the house with an ax."

"You think he seen us?"

"Dang. He got us, Fishbone. He's waving."

Mike Green shouted to the boys, "You might as well come for a snack. I'm sure watching me works up an appetite."

The boys grabbed their field glasses and slung their homemade bows over their shoulders. They picked their way down from their hiding spot, careful not to let the ground vines trip them.

"How long did it take this time, Mr. Green?"

"Not long. The sun glinted off your binoculars. It gave away your position."

"They never find the spies that quick in the movies." Tater was dejected. "I just don't know how they do it."

"Because, Tater, the movie isn't real life. It's all fake. Movies are just to make money. Be something different than a spy. It's never like in the movies–nothing is ever like the movies."

"They don't have movie spies work construction like my dad does. There ain't no heroes driving front loaders, Mr. Green. Spies have way more fun. They never come home dirty or too tired to play."

"You might be surprised, Tater. Heroes come in all shapes and sizes, from all walks of life. You don't have to drive a sports car to be a hero."

"You ever meet a real hero, Mr. Green?"

"I did. On a rooftop in a snowstorm, far away." Mike looked across the valley and thought about Moscow.

Fishbone pulled a comic book from his backpack and waved it in the air.

"Tater and me been trying to get our master spy buttons from *Secret Heroes Comics* but we gotta finish our log of activities to get certificates."

"How're we going to get a master spy button if you keep finding us?" Tater shifted his bow on his shoulder. "Dang thing cuts into my skin."

"Tell you boys what. Next time you come for a visit, how about you bring the instructions and we'll see what we can do so you get your master spy buttons."

"That'd be great." Tater grinned. "This spy stuff gets complicated."

"I should say for starters, you are not at all quiet when you walk through the woods. You should probably speak in whispers if you're going to spy or use hand signals."

"Probably right," Tater said.

"You know any spy stuff, Mr. Green?"

"Sorry, guys. I don't know any spy stuff. Could you use something to eat?"

The trio entered the coolness of Mike's redecorated cabin.

"You spymasters take a seat at the table while I check something." Mike made sure the radios were off and all the doors to the back rooms were shut.

"What'll it be this time, guys? I got cherry soda, cola, and orange."

"No lime, Mr. Green?"

"Nope. Miss Sykes was out when I shopped. Sorry."

"You can call her Ambrie but us kids calls her Miss Sykes. It's politer that way."

"I'll remember that. Thanks for the tip."

"You're welcome. Tater'll have cherry and I'll have the cola then we can split it and both have cherry cola."

"Absolute genius." Mike brought two bottles, two plastic glasses, and a bowl of chips. "BBQ okay, fellas?"

"Thanks, Mr. Green." Tater grabbed a handful.

"Mr. Green, wha'd ya do before you come to Deacon's Hollar?" Fishbone asked.

"I was an art dealer. Traveled all over the world selling paintings."

"Paintings of what?"

"Buildings, people, landscape."

"What's landscapes?"

Fishbone ripped off a belch sending the three of them into a fit of giggles. "Excuse me. My mom says to say that, but I don't mean it."

"I won't tell her," Mike grinned. "Now getting back to your question, look, this is a landscape." Mike removed a drape from the canvas on an easel in the corner of his living room.

"Oh, wow. That's down the valley where all the flowers grow. I know that place," Tater said. "We play down there. It looks just like it does in the spring."

"Whatcha gonna do with it?" Fishbone grabbed another mouthful of chips.

"Maybe sell it when the tourists come. Maybe hang it in Gracie's Place. I haven't decided yet."

"What's that one over there?" Tater went to the covered painting.

"Don't pull on the drape. It isn't ready and you'll smear the paint."

"Sorry, Mr. Green."

"Sun's starting to set. How about I give you guys a ride home?"

"Okay. My mom said to be home before dark."

"You can finish the soda on the way down."

Mike put their bows and arrows in the back of his truck and opened the cab door for the boys to crawl in.

"You boys get anything with your weapons?"

"Just target practice. Running Deer told us not to shoot the birds or squirrels." Fishbone thought for a minute. "Tate hit a trout in the creek but it got away."

"Yeah, and we almost got a rabbit but Fishbone bumped my elbow and I missed."

Mike tapped the horn as they passed Aunt Gem's place. Everyone waved. "How's the reading lessons going, Fishbone?"

"Pretty good. I read Shakespeare and we talk about it. She's teaching me Latin like the Romans talked."

"Really? Say something in Latin."

"Yeah, Fishbone, show Mr. Green some Latin."

"Remember, I'm just learning. But...ummm...*Aqua fridgia est. Aqua bono est.*"

"Fish just said the water is cold and the water is good. He shows me what Aunt Gem shows him. We write Latin for spy code."

"Has Aunt Gem sent up you any cookies? She makes the best sugar cookies in all the Hollar. She puts a big fat walnut right on the top."

"As a matter of fact, on my way back I'm going to stop in and have supper with her. She promised a surprise."

"That's nice. All us Perkins but Luke went to her house when Maggie had her fourth birthday. Aunt Gem made a cake with cream frosting. Never had that before but it was good."

"What's she making for you, Mr. Green?" A few drops of cola splattered on Tater's blue jeans.

"I don't know. It's a surprise."

"Well, let us know'd when we come to spy again."

"Sure will. I'll make a note on my corkboard to remind myself of it. How's my dog doing at your place, Fishbone?"

"Had to keep it at Tater's house. Walter Venter don't like dogs."

"Who's Walter Venter?"

"He's that man what stays at my house. I hate him."

Mike decided it wasn't a topic he should explore now. There would be time for them to talk man to man.

He made the last turn of the gravel before it connected to the main asphalt road, driving into a thick mist.

"Stop, Mr. Green. Stop now!" Tater was frantic. "Stop now."

"Okay, okay. I'm stopped. But calm down, Tater. It's just a little evening fog."

"Stay stop, Mr. Green."

The boys scooted to the front of the seat with their hands on the dashboard and stared at the cloudy mist. Gradually it dissipated from the west woods, across the road, and vanished into the forest on the east side.

"You can go now, Mr. Green," Fishbone cautioned. "If you ever see that again, you stop your truck and just sit there like we just did. Promise." It was not a question but a command.

After a few minutes of silence, Mike asked, "Care to tell me what that was about?"

Tater and Fishbone looked at each other, then at Mike.

"Nope," they said in unison.

APOLOGIES

Wednesday night. Shorty's was empty except for a couple of dedicated alcoholics trying to play pool and the four burly men sitting in the corner eating massive buffalo burgers, fries, and bowls of coleslaw served by the bartender, Shortstop.

"Where's that pretty waitress you had here? She quit on your moldy ass?"

"Actually, she's in my office. When she saw you jerks pull into the parking lot, she begged to do the payroll. Last time you guys were here, you puked all over the bathroom. She helped me clean it up. Took us six hours to get your beer vomit off the walls."

The Rangers looked at each other. Zero spoke first. "Shortstop, I don't think it was the beer alone, but maybe the Leadslingers Napalm Cinnamon combo."

"Could be just the cinnamon," Scout added. "But then again, it's a natural substance."

"If it isn't organic, who knows what the consequences could be? I think more the beer. Speaking from a medical viewpoint," Diego Doc said.

"I don't care what it was. You were the last ones out and so it's on you. Sometimes you Rangers are more trouble than you're worth." Shortstop took money from the center of the table to cover the burgers and beer.

"Guys," Scout said, "we need to make this right."

Diego added, "Scout's on point. We screwed up. Gotta make it right."

"Shortstop," Cobalt shouted, "tell your girl you whipped us into shape and we're sorry. You're closed on Sundays from 0100 to 1300 hours, right?"

"Yeah, what's it to you?"

"We'll meet you in the lot at 0130 and make it up to you and your girl. Deal?"

"Okay, Cobalt. Deal. But you guys better show up, and show up sober."
****

Shortstop arrived at 2330 Saturday to prep the bar's kitchen for the Sunday afternoon crowd. As agreed, he let the Rangers in at 0130 with their equipment.

"Behave yourselves. And stay out of the way of the staff trying to close up."

At 0230 he then locked them in so he could go home and sleep.

****

Exactly at 1200 hours on Sunday, one hour before opening, Shortstop keyed open the door. He saw Diego, Scout, and Cobalt playing Go Fish at their usual table. Zero came out of the bathroom hall covered in paint, the smell of which had almost dissipated from the bar.

"What the good hell…"

"Hey," Zero said, "come see what we done. Check it out."

"Holy cow," Shortstop wheezed.

Cobalt left the last hand of cards and joined Zero and Shortstop in the hall.

"Cleaning up was the least we could do. Once we got into it, repainting didn't seem enough. In the men's room, you've got new walls, flooring, highly washable I might add, and we pulled the sinks and urinals to drywall and caulk all along there. In your honor, Shorty, we used a baseball theme with the posters, historical memorabilia, and stuff. Even got white and black wallpaper with logos."

Scout tapped the bartender on the shoulder. "Come look at the ladies' room."

"Guys," Shortstop was touched. "Oh, wow! How'd you come up with all this?"

"The associate at the paint store showed us a couple of designs so we bought the stuff that looked more girly," Zero said. "I got this. Sprays lavender mist. All you gotta do is hang the new signs on the doors."

****

The soldiers gathered the equipment, empty paint cans, tarps, and ladders into the back of Zero's pick up truck.

"Guys, I'm speechless."

"Shorty," Cobalt said from the back seat, "We've been pretty messed up lately, so this was one way we could make things good. We took up a collection to give to the waitress to say we're sorry for us being such…"

"Assholes?" Shortstop offered.

"Well, I wasn't going to say it, but…"

"Shortstop's right. We've been that and more," Diego said.

The bar owner shook his head. "Sometimes I wonder about you boys, keeping the country safe, but then there's other times I know you're the right men for the job. Thanks."

"Not at all," shouted Zero. "We were happy to change things around."

"Where are you boys headed next?"

"Somebody signed up to build a church in Honduras," Cobalt said as he picked a dried paint droplet off his arm.

"Oh, man, that's great. Have a good trip. Thanks again, guys. You're welcome any time." Shortstop waved as the truck pulled onto the highway.

****

"Cobalt, bro, you lied to him. We're not going to Honduras."

"Diego, my spotted Latino Sun God, you insult my honor. I didn't say *we* were going to Honduras, I said *somebody*. I'm sure *somebody* is, it just ain't us. You know all our missions are classified. You expect me to commit treason and tell him? After all we've been through?" He lightly cuffed Diego's ball cap.

"What a logical human being you are, Cobalt. A man of the times gone by." Diego chuckled.

"Gentlemen, I have laid in a course to paradise for our sixty day accrued leave vacation." Scout pushed a few keys on his mobile computer. "Get your kit together and meet at my place. I borrowed one of those heavy duty black Excursion trucks for our trip. We can haul a trailer so pack what you think you'll need."

Scout smiled to himself as he fed information into his keyboard.

Diego stretched his legs out and laced his hands behind his head. "This is gonna be great. I'll call this my "Divorce Rehabilitation.""

Scout asked, "Did she keep all the dogs?"

"I got one, the best show dog of the bunch, and gave it to my mom to keep her company."

"What about your retirement and savings? Did she get all of it? I mean, you're still gonna make beer nights?" Zero was genuinely concerned.

"I can pay for rounds, don't worry. My dad bought her and her attorney off. Pops said it was part of my inheritance anyway." Diego asked Scout, "Can you be away that long from your Mom and sister?"

"I have my own satellite, dude. I can..."

"What? You commandeered a government satellite for your own use? Are you serious?"

"I didn't commandeer it. I just made it ignore their computer so it would listen to mine. Even got it to talk." Scout smiled in the green glow of the screen.

"No shit?" Zero held his chest.

"Here, listen. Constance, what's the weather like at Daytona Beach right now?"

A soft and delicate voice came over Scout's device. "Well, Daddy, the weather in Daytona Beach is seventy-five degrees, balmy, and sunny all day. Do you want to go for a swim?"

"Daddy? You got a military satellite that calls you Daddy?" Diego dropped his hands and arms in a sign of adoration. "You, dude, are legend."

Cobalt scratched his chin. "Scout, have you've weakened our national defense?"

"Negative. I just created overtime for a shitload of PhD's and other contract brainiacs as they try to figure out what went wrong. I set it up to keep bouncing the signal. The country's still safe."

"Can you put it back?"

"Oh, yeah."

"Have you tested that?"

"Tested what?"

"Giving the government control of their own satellite when you're done messing with it."

"Well, not yet, but in due time."

"Maybe I should call ahead for our accommodations at Leavenworth?"

"It ain't illegal until you get caught."

Zero pulled up in front of the apartment complex. "Guys, have your kit and crap ready to load at 0700 hours tomorrow. I'll get the trailer first so we know how much room we have for the coolers then meet you at Scout's to load."

Still picking paint off his arm, Cobalt said, "Beer doesn't have to travel cold."

"Hey, dude, I ain't a Brit. I get thirsty on long rucks. Cold keeps the vitamins fresh. Medical fact. Ask Diego."

Cobalt got out of the truck and stretched. "Scout, where'd you get the truck and trailer from? How much do we each owe on the rental?"

"Nothing. It was a gift."

"Oh, shit. From the same resource you got the satellite?" Zero whistled. "I'm truly in the presence of greatness."

"Where're we going for the next two months anyway?" Diego asked.

"Men, we're gonna get fresh air, clean water, brook trout, and shit faced drunk under the stars. I've laid in a course for Deacon's Hollar. We'll look up ol' country boy while we're there."

****

At exactly 0700 Monday morning, the Rangers gathered at Scout's driveway. The trailer and Excursion were waiting for loading. Cobalt passed the coffee and donuts.

"Zero, what's in the metal containers?" Diego tried to look in the boxes.

"Stuff."

"What stuff? Let me see. Holy crap, why'd you bring grenades on vacation?"

"Hell, you never know when you need one. Didn't you listen to anything in Basic Training?"

"Scout, Zero brought explosives."

"Well, how else do you expect him to fish? They're coming out of the water one way or another."

"I'm glad someone's on my side. What'd you bring, Cobalt?"

"Just what I need."

"Yeah, yeah, what you need." Zero pulled the cover back from the heavy case. "Shakespeare, Brooks, Asminov, four Tanto K-bars, six pistols, ammo, looks like the stock of an M4, MK16 SCAR, three barrels each, with EO Tech 553, M3X tactical light, and a LA-5 infrared laser. What gives, dude?"

"I brought enough for everyone."

"Well, that's okay then. We're good."

UBELL GANT

"Coop? Can you hear me? You're breaking up."

"Just a sec.....mo...ca...different....plac..."

"Coop?"

Ubell pressed the phone to his ear, pacing around his desk.

"Come on, this is important. Every time I have something to say, the call gets dropped or there isn't a signal. 5G was supposed to be so great."

Second time around his desk, Ubell fumbled his coffee cup off the edge, making the catch but sloshing the liquid on the floor. He put the phone down to clean up the spill with a paper towel.

"Ubell, are you there? Can you hear me?"

At the sound of Coop's voice, Ubell's anxiety level spiked and he jostled the mug again reaching for the phone. He did not make the catch a second time.

"Gant? Gant?"

"I'm here. I dropped my coffee mug–*twice.* I think my record is four times in eight minutes but that was an hour before I had to testify in federal court the first time and I was a little nervous."

"Nothing is worth spilling lab coffee over. Take a breath and tell me what's up."

Ubell tossed the saturated paper towel into the trash can from the lab's three point line, then straightened his white coat, tie, and belt, as if he was going into a job interview rather than talking on the phone.

"Phew, Coop, let me get my thoughts in order."

"That's okay," came the reassuring voice of the senior agent. "Take your time. I've got Alice Cobb with me showing me around. Her uncle has..."

"Can you hear me okay?" Ubell was so shaky he didn't realize he interrupted his colleague.

"Gotcha, Ubell. Had to get to this turn off. The valley is beautiful. Did you get the specimens?"

"If it was anyone other than you, I'd ask if you're joking or drunk."

"Huh?" Coop laughed but Ubell began to sweat.

"Hum, no...no...Mr. Cleveland...I mean Coop."

"I'm kidding, Gant. Just kidding.

"The specimens of hair you sent, um, you said it was from wolves or like wild dogs."

"Yes, I did. What's the problem?"

"I don't know how to say this because I didn't record the results. I'm sure of my results so I could have put them on the forms, but I haven't finalized anything with the forms because if I put this on the forms then..."

"Ubell, slow down. Take a deep breath. And another. Okay? Now, what's the problem?"

"The problem is the samples are...p... panguite. It's made up of titanium, scandium, aluminum, magnesium, zirconium, calcium, and oxygen." Ubell let the words out all at once like water released from an newly unfrozen pipe.

"Okay, Gant. Good job." Coop took a bite out of his breakfast sandwich and munched slowly, hoping Gant wouldn't hear. These were liberal times but some things are still considered rude.

"Are you eating, Coop?"

"Sorry. What has you excited about some dog hairs? The paglue-nuite..." Coop picked at the bacon and a bit of cheese protruding from the biscuit crust.

"Panguite, Coop. *Pan--gu--ite.*"

"Okay. Panguite. What's the problem?"

"The *only* problem, Coop, is that it's *NOT* dog or wolf fur." Gant was trembling again. "Y-You don't find panguite in dog hair for Pete's sake because you can't find it on *Earth*. It was discovered in the Allende meteorite that fell in Cancun. *It predates our solar system.* That's the problem, Coop, that's the problem, because the problem is it predates our solar system...older than the Sun and Pluto."

"Sit down, Ubell, sit down. Probably more tests to run before you get your Nobel Prize in Science."

"Coop, you need to take this a little more seriously."

"A sample you say predates the solar system is a pretty big leap from the dog hairs I sent in. Are you sure? Did you have anyone in the lab check your data?" Coop laughed. "Better question is did you turn on the ventilation hood fan?"

"Coop, I just threw a scientific landmine in your lap."

"I'm sorry, Gant. Just teasing. With that said, keep this under your hat. Don't show..."

Alone in the lab, Ubell dropped his voice to a whisper. "Coop, do you know how crazy it would sound if it got out you're sending in dog hair samples from dogs who are from another planet somewhere? Keep it under my hat? I won't mention this to my *priest*, for Pete's sake."

Gant swallowed hard as he coughed into the phone before continuing.

"Excuse me. I'm a little excited. My mouth is dry. I spilled my coffee. Coop, sorry, but my hands are shaking. Wait, someone just came in so hold on...I want you to.."

Gant's voice changed to a steady, reassuring professional. "Yes, sir. Dickens is in charge of that report and will have the results for you by this afternoon. Okay, nice talking to you, Director. Yes, thank you, sir. Good afternoon, sir."

Ubell took the phone out of his pocket. "He's gone. That was close. Still there, Coop?"

"Okay, Gant. Got it. Catch up with you next week."

"Okay...wait, not next week. This is Friday and I'm officially on vacation at five p.m. for thirty days."

"Where're you going?" Coop took a bite of his sandwich and held the phone away from his mouth. If this was the bombshell Gant thought it would be, why would he be going on vacation with the discovery of the century before him?

Ubell stuttered, hemmed and hawed, then blurted out, "Nowhere really. Just going to hang around my apartment and catch up on journals, you know, that kind of thing."

"I've got a better idea. Pack a bag, bring the equipment you think you'll need, and come to Deacon's Hollar. I have a feeling it will be more exciting than sitting around reading other peoples' work. Bring the results of the dog hair with you and we'll go over it."

"Do you mean that? I'll get to work with you in the field?"

"I'll text you the addresses and phone numbers, and reserve a room for you where I'm staying."

"That's great, Coop. I can't thank you enough. I'll pack a bag and be there as soon as I can. This is great, Coop. Thanks so much. I'll have to call my mom."

"I wouldn't tell her about the plangutite..."

"*Panguite.* It's panguite and I won't tell her. She'll have to see her famous son on the six o'clock news like everyone else."

Coop hung up and continued his breakfast biscuit meditation on the mountain side.

Four hundred miles away in Knoxville, Tennessee, a frantic Ubell Gant punched out of the lab early, and made his way to the parking structure. His thoughts were in hyperdrive and it took him a few minutes of searching until he located his SUV. He was ecstatic about the month with Senior Special Forensics Agent Cleveland Coop, but worried about what to tell his mother.

****

"But, Ma, I'll come and visit you next vacation."

"You come now. I be dead next time."

"Ma, you're in perfect health. You said so the last time we talked. This is really important."

"Ma not important. I call Dad."

"Are you talking to him again?"

"No, I no talk. He like you. He no come visit."

"Ma, you've been divorced for ten years. Why should he come to visit?"

"He you father. Should come visit mother of his child and bring money help with expenses." The woman spewed out a large ration of Chinese words over the phone.

"Ma, I swear I'll come see you next vacation. I promise...wait, Ma, you know I don't know Chinese. English, *please*."

Mrs. Gant caught her breath, switched from Mandarin to her style of English.

"I try...I try hard teach you Chinese. You be sorry you not learn. China take over world and you not know nothing. You go jail."

"Ma, China isn't going to take over the world and besides, I've got you to explain I'm a good Chinese man."

"Only half Chinese, but I try save you. Just wait. Then you see you should come and see Ma."

"Ma, I'll be there soon. Just let me do this, okay? Wǒ ài nǐ, māmā."

"So you know maybe little Chinese. Not so stupid son. Yeah, yeah. You go and make a lot of money. Then come see Ma. I wait. Why you not doctor like Bin? Bye."

****

His phone rang. "Hello?"

"Coop here, Ubell. I just texted you an address and instructions."

"This isn't from your phone."

"Don't worry. I've got a techno-savvy friend and I'm using her phone. Alice is giving a tour of the area. I'm sending the corrected directions. She figures you are about...how far, Alice?"

Ubell could hear the pleasant feminine voice reply, "Six hours, fifty-six minutes over four hundred forty point five two miles, not allowing for fuel or rest stops. Weather forecast is clear, thus far."

Taking the last gulp of his coffee, Coop said to Ubell, "The weather looks good at this point, but things can deteriorate rapidly in the mountains and passes. Don't take any chances. You check into a hotel if things get rough. I'll cover the cost."

"Sure, Coop. Five-star within the budget?"

"If need be, but look for a Motel 6 before you have your valet parking ticket punched."

"Got it, Coop. See you in a bit."

"Hey, did you call your mom?"

"Yes. She's happy I am taking a vacation and going someplace."

"Good. See you when you get here. I'll arrange with my tour guide to take you around the valley."

****

After packing his bags and programming his GPS, Ubell was mentally exhausted when he finally hit the freeway. His OCD was in full swing. Ubell pulled over twice to check his briefcase, matching the documents and supplies with his list, repacking his socks, shoes, underwear and refolding his blue jeans, examining the pockets as he did so. The first time he stopped for fuel, he repeated the whole process.

Bent over the trunk, Ubell said out loud, "You'd think I'd be over all that obsessive behavior, that I'd have enough confidence in myself and my education that I could function like everyone else does, that I could be normal and have friends who I didn't drive nuts, that I'm a grown man who should have a wife and a family, if not a wife, at least a girlfriend. She doesn't even have to be a scientist, just someone I could care for and..."

A teenager came walking between the two cars. "Dude, bad day?"

Ubell realized he had been talking louder than he thought. He smiled. "Maybe a little."

"Here's a gift card for that ice cream place over there. Take it. I've got more. Maybe brighten up your day."

"Thanks, but I..."

The teen disappeared in the parking lot just as quickly as he appeared.

"Hey, thank you."

****

Coop dropped Alice off at the farm. He talked more than he had to anyone in a long time. The Hollar relaxed him.

"How's the ankle, Alice? Hope it didn't swell with the length of our drive."

"No, it's fine, Coop. But don't tell Uncle Hector. I'm still getting him to do my chores and cook."

"Well played, young lady. Again, thanks for the tour."

"If you need any help getting around, just call the farm. I'd be happy to assist you and your helper when he gets here. The area is pretty wild and can get confusing if you don't know the land marks."

"Thank you. I appreciate that."

Coop saw Alice wave when he glanced in the rearview mirror. It saddened him a little that he didn't have the relationship with his kids Hector had with Alice.

He stuck his hand out the window and waved back.

Birdie Spry

Special Agent Coop repositioned himself in the chair across from Sheriff Bill's desk.

Bill poured coffee from an aluminum percolator into three unmatched ceramic mugs.

"I thought about getting one of those single serve coffee machines but they want over a hundred dollars for one over in Waybird City. Besides, the coffee is so dang expensive and you gotta throw out the little plastic cup. I toss these grounds out along the wood line.

"This percolator was my mom's. The freshest coffee in the state right here in my jail. Anything in it, gentlemen? Do you want cream and sugar, Coop?"

"Double cream for me, but no sugar," Coop replied.

Sheriff Harris turned slightly and addressed the thin man in blue jeans and a flannel shirt. "Hector, I know you take enough sugar to make the spoon stand up."

"Yep."

Sheriff Harris served the coffee without spilling a drop.

"Guess I'd better make introductions. Special Agent Coop, this is Hector Cobb. Hector, this is Special Agent Coop."

"Call me Cleveland, or just Coop."

"Just Hector here."

"I'm grateful to your niece for helping me find my way around and giving me a tour of the area. I hope she's recovered."

"Yeah. She's a good girl. Just waiting for that ankle to heal before I get her whipped back into shape."

Coop smiled. The aroma of the coffee made his mouth water, but he wasn't foolish enough to drink it right away.

"She mentioned your family has bloodhounds. I keep hearing your name tossed around like a folk hero."

"Yep. Money vacuums. You'd think I'd understand there are easier ways of going broke than dogs. I should've invested in the stock market or bought me a mountain or two of land. Would've been further ahead."

The agent smiled at the self effacing comments. He knew Hector held a Master's Degree in Economics and one in Animal Behavior from Purdue University. Coop did his research. "So you've had this breed for a long time?"

"Yes, pretty long time. Five generations. My mother's people were the houndsmen, so you could say my father married into dogs. Dad was a writer but learned to hold a pup while he wrote or read a book. Mom handled all the training and breeding."

Sheriff Bill interrupted before Hector started talking about his dogs through all five generations.

"I've asked you here because Coop will need a friendly face with him when he goes to visit Birdie. Coop is investigating some things and he'll want to interview her. We washed out with Aunt Gem."

"Interview?"

It was Bill's turn to adjust himself in his chair. "I can't go. Birdie's still mad at me for having her truck towed."

Hector grinned.

"Miss Spry isn't a gentle senior citizen?" Coop blew on his coffee. The stuff was still boiling hot.

"Well, Coop, yes and no. Birdie will do anything she can to help someone in need, but if she thinks you've done some dirt, well, she's got her own sense of justice."

Coop took a chance on the coffee, burning his tongue. "Dang, that's still hot. You think she'll shoot first and let me ask questions later?"

Hector let his mug sit a bit longer. "No, well, yes. All the women here over the age of ten can shoot, but if Birdie taught them marksmanship, they can pepper the ass out of a fly at 300 yards before kindergarten."

Bill laughed outright while Coop chuckled.

"Gem McKenny can charm the wings off an angel with her education," Bill stated, "but when Gem says no, as Coop found out, it's final. I mean Gem can shoot, but she'd rather slam the door in your face given a choice. Can't tell with Birdie. She fluctuates too much."

"Okay, I'll play the role of the peacemaker." Hector watched Bill wiggle in his chair and Coop sink a little lower in his.

"She likes you because Beatrix found her cat in a dry well one year."

"Beatrix is?" Coop asked.

"A hound. Dog didn't like looking for a cat, but Beatrix found what she was set on. Ever since, Birdie's taken a liking to me. Drops off fresh bread when she comes into the village. Don't worry. Birdie won't shoot *you*. Bill here's another story. Shouldn't have towed her truck. I'm surprised Bowtie Crawford even put a hook on it."

Sheriff Bill smiled. "Well, he didn't want to. Said he was worried about retribution or some other nonsense. But that's all in the past. I'd still take a puppy with me if I was you. I'd hate to investigate a double murder."

"Dang, Bill, you'd hate to have to arrest Birdie!"

****

The winding road made Coop think he was being taken in a circle. Each grove of hard timber, generational gathering of stately pines, or outcropping of rocks and exposed cliff looked like the one he just passed. He knew he was going up but that was about all. The sleeping bloodhound puppy in his lap snorted.

"Do they all sleep like this?"

"Yeah. But I brought this one cuz she doesn't fart like the others."

"Well, I'm grateful for that."

"Thought you'd be." Hector flashed a big, toothy grin.

"I don't mean to pry about the woman's history but if you could tell me a little about her, it might help me focus my questions for the interview."

"Sure. I won't say nothin' in front of Bill, but she scares me. She's got her own ways, if you know what I mean."

Coop petted the silky ears of the puppy. The sun highlighted the red copper hues of her fur. He absentmindedly stroked her head as he absorbed the beauty of the West Virginia mountains.

"Birdie's people were German from the Pennsylvania-Virginia area. By the time West Virginia split from Virginia, Spry's had homesteaded around Deacon's Hollar for decades."

"Were they one of the first families here?"

"Not sure, Coop, but they could've been."

Across the valley, a gray pick up truck kicked up dust taking the curves at a high rate of speed.

"Hector, look over there."

"Yeah, I see. If he doesn't slow down, he won't make the next bend."

The dust formed angry clouds behind the truck as the driver fishtailed from one side of the narrow road to the other. Barely hanging onto the shoulder, the truck collided with a mountain bush, overcorrected, and headed for the open valley below.

Hector and Coop saw the back of the pickup dip. The driver hit the gas and the remaining three wheels pulled the vehicle up and onto the road. In the gravel, the truck lunged forward like a bull digging in for a charge,

"He's driving a Ford, I see." Hector said.

"You can see that from here?"

"Nope, Coop. A Chevy wouldn't get back on the road." He winked and grinned. "Fall right down into the gully. But, you'd better hang on. Might want to fasten your seatbelt."

Coop held the sleeping puppy on his arm and managed to get his seatbelt clicked just as Hector dropped into second gear and made a sharp turn into a sandy shade covered two-track. He downshifted to first gear, then back to second, as they climbed up and through over hanging branches and thick brush. Hector drove until he reached bare stone at the top. Coop looked out the cab rear window--the trees and brush had swallowed all evidence of their quick exit--but he was jerked around when Hector hit the brakes to avoid going over the edge.

"How'd you know the trail was there?" Coop was breathless.

"Well, me and Mae used to come up here. Look."

From the cab of Hector's orange beater truck, Coop had a stunning view of the valley. He was humbled at the beauty of the gentle slopes rising to steep walls of rock. He had the perfect vantage point to see the truck—it was a Ford.

"Watch the idiot come the last quarter mile. No way with him driving like that we both would've stayed on the road."

"But you're driving a Ford, too."

"We're good," Hector scoffed, "my truck has more experience."

Hector backed into a narrow turn around, then headed to the road.

As they crossed on a culvert over a stream, then went south, a red car sped toward them, almost side swiping them as the vehicles passed.

"Must be a convention someplace, Coop. We've had two vehicles on the same road in one day."

"Hector, did you catch the plates?"

"Nope. Didn't recognize them but the guy in the silver truck was pretty hefty, like he ate a lot of meat. The red car had a little guy in it. I'll mention it to Bill and Bowtie. Maybe they'd know."

Hector drove over a paved road and a two-track bisecting an open field. He made a sharp turn through over hanging boughs of tall brush to reveal a stone drive. Looking ahead, Coop saw the water crossing.

Hector steered his truck on the bridge and stopped. Coop looked out his window into the tiny trickle of a stream below. "Pretty sturdy bridge for such a little stream."

"Ha. Let me tell you about this little bit of water. When I was a kid, we had a hundred year flood. Washed out the old bridge to Birdie's. A bunch of folks came up and put this bridge in.

"Hauled the materials up for the abutments, handmade all the wooden forms, mixed the cement in wheelbarrows and poured it. Gracie Bower's uncle had horses at the time and they pulled the wagon with the I-beams and all the treated wood for the stringers. Had to get it high enough so the next flood won't take it out. Yeah, all done by hand."

"Sounds like a lot of work for just one household."

"Well, it was a good investment. Birdie can get down the mountain without getting her feet wet."

"Why'd you stop?"

"Self defense."

"What?"

"In case Birdie's outside with a gun, she'll see it's me if I stop here for a minute."

"You that scared?"

"Good hell, yeah." Hector drove the truck over the decking of the bridge, up another twenty five or thirty feet, then gunned the truck a little to get through the sandy part of the drive.

Still holding the sleeping bloodhound, undisturbed by the movement of the truck over bumpy gravel roads and potholes, Coop remarked how close to the driveway all of the flowers were planted. Hector smiled.

"Yeah, she does that so she knows if a stranger came up this drive. If you know Birdie Spry, you know to come up her drive and not let even an eighth of an inch of your tire touch one speck of her flowers. It's like a silent alarm system."

"Sounds like you've had some experience with her booby trap driveway."

"Oh, yeah, Coop. When I was in high school my dad had me deliver a pickup load and a trailer of cut firewood to Birdie's place. At the time to tell you the truth, I didn't even notice the trailer tires had squashed the periwinkle to death and ground her Forget-Me-Nots. I just beat the daylights out of those. Then, up there on the hill, I took out half of her rock garden, strawberries, and sweet peas when I tried to back up, thinking that I knew how much distance there was between that and her house.

"Whoosh. My dad was mad at me. My mom was even madder because her and Birdie were in the garden club down in the Hollar. There's this sorta religious connection between those ladies and their flower pots. Took me all summer and into the fall to replant, replace, and recant everything."

"Did she hold a grudge?"

"Nope. Well, maybe she did for a while. Birdie was younger then and I suppose she could have taken me if I stepped out of line, but I didn't want to test the waters. I did everything Birdie asked me and more. And I kept my mouth shut, too."

Hector smiled and nodded.

"Any one of these mountain women could've cleaned my clock in their day. Half of them probably still can." Hector leaned forward to see over the dented hood of his orange truck.

****

As they came closer to the cabin, Coop was impressed with the arrangement of plantings used to landscape the yard. He recognized many of them from classes in botany: *malaxis unifolia, medicago lupulina,* and *anemone quinquefolia* came to mind as he examined the separate grouping of fauna. He must have been mumbling aloud because Hector spoke up, "So you know all the science names for that stuff?"

"Some of it. The important thing is that I know where to look for the information. Sometimes we get forensic cases where vegetation is on bodies and I have to identify everything. You know what all this is?"

"Not all. She's got Adder's Mouth, Black Medic, Nightcaps and there's Crimson Bee Balm.

"Her and Running Deer make medicine from what they grow and gather on the hills. I think my mom had some of those blue ones. Mouse Ears is what they call them. Invasive species but pretty."

"I'm impressed with your knowledge, Hector. Is Running Deer someone I should interview? Her name was mentioned at Cliffer's place."

"Probably so but maybe not." Hector didn't take his eyes off the crushed stone path of the driveway. Making the last curve, he brought his truck to a stop and got out.

"Be sure you hold the pup. She'll put her gun away when she sees the hound. She'll know it's me."

Coop sat in Hector's dented, rusted out, faded orange truck. "You mean there's another truck like yours around here?"

"Well, come to think of it, probably not. But let's just wait until she comes out." Hector used his elbow to clean the dust off the side mirror.

Cleveland slowly opened the truck door, and as instructed, held the bloodhound puppy in front of him. Suddenly awake with the pressure of a full bladder, she threw back her head and howled.

From behind the truck a voice said, "If Hector told you that puppy was a bullet proof shield, he's wrong. Better put her down on the grass so she can pee."

Cleveland never saw the woman approach but there was Miss Birdie Spry, all four foot eight of her with wiry gray hair pulled back in a bun at the nape of her neck; her gnarly arthritic hands toughened by tilling the soil. A stained faded floral apron, covering her dress from collarbone to hem, wrapped around her slight figure and tied at the waist. Long cotton socks bagged at her calves and the toes of her boots were caked with mud. She held a small ax in one hand.

"I said you'd better put that pup down unless you want it to pee all over."

"Yes, ma'am."

As soon as the dog felt the grass, she squatted. Then she wandered around the garden beds, sniffing the flowers, grass, and gravel.

"Hector, watch that pup she don't go to pooping in my rose garden. I just turned all that soil."

"Yes, ma'am. I'll watch her close."

"And keep her away from that new plant bed over there."

"Yes, Ma'am."

Turning back to Coop, Birdie squinted one eye, raised the opposite eyebrow, and looked over the top of her round wire framed glasses.

"What will you be doing on my mountain, Special Agent Coop?" She tossed her head back and cackled at the look on Coop's face.

"You don't think you were going to come up here and I didn't know afore-hand about it? That's why I didn't meet you from the porch with a shotgun."

Cleveland understood word traveled quickly in rural communities, but he didn't think it was this fast. He didn't see any telephone poles or wires leading up to the house, nor was there a satellite dish in the side yard or attached to the roof. He didn't presume she had a cell phone or even knew how to use one. His general impression was she was born and raised on this mountain. While the rest of the world progressed, she was caught in a time warp. That was Coop's first mistake.

"You come in. And bring the pup. I've got fresh bread and hot soup. Never knew a Cobb to turn down a free meal. You're a lot like your father, Hector." The men followed Birdie up the wooden steps, across her weathered porch into her cabin.

****

"Looks like you've made some changes, Birdie." Hector noticed a small greenhouse off the west end of the living room, a deep freeze in the corner beside her refrigerator, and what looked like new facing on her cabinets. "I see you got a flat screen TV. How're you getting reception on this side of the mountain?"

"Antenna's on the other side. I had the Morris boys up a few years ago and made some changes for me. They added the greenhouse so I can keep my plants in winter. Put the cable for the antenna underground through the woods so none of you folks in the Hollar could look up the mountain and see what I got. Didn't want you all traipsing up here to watch those disgusting Hollywood movies when I can watch them just fine by myself."

She gave Hector a sideways glance around the fingerprinted lens of her glasses and chuckled at him. Birdie sliced warm bread at the table.

Coop remembered his own grandmother cutting off the heel and slathering it with fresh butter. He swallowed hard as he watched Birdie prepare the meal, overwhelmed with the blended aromas of the bread and soup. Being a gentleman, he needed a distraction to overcome his personal flaw of impulsivity with food.

Coop walked to a southern facing window and looked at the rock gardens. Birds were dancing branch to branch, collecting berries and seeds as butterflies paused delicately on the anthers and filaments, gathering pollen, liquids, and nectar to sustain them in this last period of their life cycle.

Monarchs, Hackberry Emperors, Silvery Checkerspot, and Painted Lady nibbled on apples, oranges, and pears, all cut up into small, precise pieces--*She could have been a surgeon--or a serial killer.*

"Hector, Mr. Coop, wash your hands at the sink."

Birdie saw the leaves of a potted plant move. "Did you touch that plant?"

"I...I..don't know," Coop stuttered.

"That plant is poisonous. Get over here and wash your hands."

He didn't feel any tingling or itching so he was sure he didn't touch the plant, but Coop hurried to the sink, turned on the water full, and used the bar of soap to thoroughly wash his hands and wrists.

"The leaves, berries, even the pollen is poison."

"Why do you have it in your house?"

"Because I like the plant and the plant likes me. Now, take a seat, please."
****

The hunger pangs rattled Coop's stomach right up to behind his eyeballs. It took all of his reserve not to cram the delicious crispy crusted bread in his mouth, pour the steaming soup down his throat, or pick up the bowl and lick the golden liquid from the dish like a dog.

"I have to say, Miss Spry, it's been a long time since I've had such a delicious meal." Coop politely placed his soup spoon on the plate.

"Have you eaten at Gracie Bowers' place?"

"Yes, I have."

"Her daddy stole my recipes."

Not knowing how to respond, Coop decided the punt was better than the pass and replied, "Well, I think you make it better."

"Thank you, Mr. Coop." She watched Hector across the table. "Hector, I haven't seen you eat so fast since you were a kid. Isn't Alice feeding you?"

"She's still laid up, but no one makes bread and soup like you do, Birdie."

"You'll have to fight who gets the leftovers. I've baked goods for Gracie and Alice when you leave. Help yourself to the rest of the bread and honey. Go ahead, Hector. If you act shy, I know you're lying."

"Yes, ma'am."

****

Birdie served two cups of peppermint tea to her guests, then placed a third on the table for herself. "Now you're full, let's get down to business. What do you want, Mr. Coop?"

"I've been sent by the State of West Virginia to investigate the unusual evidence recovered from the assault which took place on…"

"I know that."

"Oh, um, Miss Spry…"

"You can call me Birdie or Birdie Spry but not ever Miss Spry."

"Okay, then, Birdie. I've interviewed Cliffer Jennings…"

"I know that."

"…and Tater Perkins…"

"I know that."

"I was assigned the case due to the nature of the evidence collected at the scene…"

"You said that already."

"…I was wondering if you could enlighten me about the a-assault and the a-arson."

"Now, how am I going to do that? How am I going to enlighten you when I wasn't there? What kind of a question is that?"

Coop realized she took control of his interview. "Well, there was evidence…not about you…but…"

"What kind of evidence?"

"Well, ma'am, there were some white hairs found at the scene. And I collected what appears to be similar hairs at the church."

"And what is it you want from me? You've talked to just about everyone in the Hollar about your hairs. What's so special about it anyway?"

"I can't say as this is an ongoing investigation. I've never seen similar evidence at a crime scene, or a narrative about dogs or wolves that can turn into misty clouds and float down a mountain. Facts need to be separated from fantasy."

"And what is it you want to prove, Mr. Coop? Prove the fact or the fantasy?"

"Miss Spry…er…Birdie, I'm a scientist looking for facts. "

"A scientist looking for facts." Birdie picked up the plates and carefully laid them in the sink. The men heard the pump kick on when she turned the faucet handle to draw water to rinse off the crumbs.

"And what is science, Mr. Coop? What is science to you?"

"Science explains events, the environment, and our understanding of the world around us. It gives us a foundation to explore, to explain what we see and know to advance humanity, to progress."

"And what about faith, Mr. Coop?"

"I was raised in the church but I'm either in the lab or out on an investigation on Sundays."

"Let me interrupt you right there. I'm not talking about how often you have your butt planted on a hard pew, or how many times you've sung 'We Shall Gather by the River.' I want to know what stirs your spirit. What gives you direction? What causes your heart to leap with happiness? What brings you up from the depths of despair? What, Special Agent Coop, do you believe: science or faith?"

Coop was beginning to dislike Birdie. "I look for facts to help me...to....support the science of what I know to be true."

"So you already know what is true and you use science to buttress what you thought up rather than looking for facts?"

"I didn't say that, Birdie, I..."

"I know what you said. All your lab equipment serve the same purpose. The books and the seminars, the meetings around the world to pat yourselves on the back for your "discoveries" and all the hoopla, but you're still missing the point.

"Science comes after the faith. Science is the explanation of miracles around us. That's all. It's a matter of perspective, Coop, and a matter of understanding. You won't run out of science because the world will not run out of miracles. You do know faith and science are not mutually exclusive?

"Hector brought you up here because there's something in that bloodhound soaked mind of his and Sheriff Harris—who, by the way, illegally towed my truck. Hector, you can remind him permission to hunt my land is *revoked* until further notice."

The old woman dried her hands on a checked hand towel as she took a deep breath.

"Mr. Coop, you've been told plenty by Cliffer and the Perkins boy, not everything but enough to whet your whistle. Piques your interest, does it, Cleveland? So, before I answer any questions of yours, you answer mine."

Birdie was putting him on the spot. He had underestimated her. That was Coop's second mistake.

"If you have a choice between science and miracles, which do you pick?"

"I...I..don't know...I..." Coop stammered and glanced at Hector.

"Don't be looking at Hector. He can't help you. Which is it?"

"I suppose it would depend upon the circumstances, the evidence, and the investigation."

"Okay. That's the science part of you. Now, what if you stumbled on something that your science couldn't explain. Would you take what you see, even if it contradicted your science, would you take that on faith?"

"I suppose I could, but I still look to science to explain what I was seeing. I still look for facts."

"Fair enough. And when you found those facts, would you be under an obligation to divulge those facts?"

"I don't understand this line of questioning. I was sent here because of an unusual case."

"Coop, you interviewed Cliffer Jennings and he told you about some boys who came home from fighting for the Union to find their parents and little sister had been murdered. Cliffer also told you those boys beat another man to death. From those horrible crimes arose a narrative that has been passed down in Deacon's Hollar for more than one hundred and fifty years, generation after generation."

"Yes. As I understand Cliffer, the union soldiers transformed into some kind of spiritual beings that the locals call "snow dogs" who can change forms, and act as guardians in this area."

Birdie opened the curio cabinet in the corner of her living room. She placed before Coop a gold ring, the chard stock of a rifle, and three buttons off a Confederate officer's coat. When she laid a doll on the table, Coop saw the faint print of a human heart on the apron.

"Mr. Coop, you're at the farm where that story took place. At the edge of the new growth woods stands the hearth and chimney of the original house. Cliffer told you to come talk to me because this is where it started. Right here on this ground.

"This is what's left of the family butchered during a war that tore this country apart. So, here are your facts. As far as the snow dogs are concerned, I'll neither admit or deny I know anything about them. But, whatever you think about the stories of Deacon's Hollar, I will say this: just because you can do something, doesn't mean you should. Sometimes minding your own business is the best course of action."

Slowly, Coop raised his cup to his lips and took a sip. Looking up to meet her eyes, he responded, "Yes. My dad told me the same thing."

"Well, then, you need to understand something. The people who live here are not dumb or backwoods. We are close knit. Do you understand? We are our own tribe.

"When times are bad you don't rely on a person's skin, or hair or eye color. You rely on their heart and what's in it. There'll come a time when you need to weigh those facts, Mr. Coop, and do what is right. Maybe not what you want to do, but what is right."

An orchestra of night time insects began their serenade with the waning light. The same eeriness descended upon Birdie's cabin as it did in Florence Jennings' kitchen.

"Well, you boys had better get going. You've taken up enough of my time. Take your dog and head out before the light's gone."

Hector gathered the puppy from its place of slumber at the hearth, the last coals of the day warming its pudgy tummy.

"Thank you for the meal, Birdie. Coop, if you'd grab the sacks of goodies to go, we'll be on our way. Thanks, again, Birdie."

"Oh, before I forget, Hector, here's the bilberry syrup for Alice's cramps. She knows how to take it." The men looked at the jar as if it were a viper.

"Oh, for pity sake, Hector, take the jar and skedaddle out of here."

"Thank you, Birdie. I'll think about our discussion." Coop nodded.

"Nice meeting you, Mr. Coop. And Hector, mind the way you back that truck."

"Yes, ma'am."

The door was firmly shut behind them; Birdie was done talking for the day.

**** .

His hand on the truck handle, Coop glanced back at the cabin. In the window the *actaea pachypoda* plant was looking at him, nodding in approval as if it knew something, as if there were a deep secret it held close to its plant soul. He could swear he saw it move back behind the curtain.

The truck headlights scanned the property as Hector turned to head out the drive. At the edge of the new growth woods stood the hearth and chimney of the original house, its form in the shadows testifying to the events of the past.

"Was she too hard on you, Coop?"

"No. Just that I was testifying at my own murder trial."

"Yeah, Birdie can be like that."

"Hector, what about the plant bed at the back? The one she told you to keep the dog away from?"

"She has special plants back there."

"Special?"

"Yeah. They're all poison."

SAVING BENTLEY

"Okay, where'd she hide it?"

Dr. Glassman searched each cooler in the clinic. He rumbled around the refrigerator in the kitchen, inspected the deep freeze in the storage room, and then finally found the pitcher in the small OR cooler hidden behind stacked boxed of rabies vaccines.

"Ah, ha! Success!" He thumped his chest like a Klingon Commander.

The plastic pitcher was three quarters full. Andy put a few cubes of ice in his tall glass and added a shot from a bottle hidden in his desk. He poured the slushy lemon mix, then sampled it.

"A bit more won't hurt." He added a touch more Leadslingers. It was a slow afternoon and a bracer was warranted.

On the porch, he balanced his cigar and enriched lemonade on the railing as he opened a folding chair.

"Yes, Dr. Glassman, you hit the sweet spot." He couldn't remember the words to the song about West Virginia, so he la-la-la'd it until he saw Elsie Perkin's car kick up dust from the road and spin into his driveway, slamming on the brakes a few feet from where he was sitting. He could hear little Maggie screaming in the back seat.

"Dr. Glassman, Dr. Glassman, I need your help."

Andy stood and held the door for Elsie and her hysterical child.

"Elsie, what is it?"

"Maggie's dog got tore up by a coyote."

Andy looked at the two of them, not seeing any blood. "You've got the dog in the car? Give me a sec..."

"No," Elsie said. "here."

Andy saw a bundle of white fluffy stuffing and brown and black material gripped in the arms of Maggie Perkins. The child's grief knew no bounds. Her voice was pitch perfect and reverberated off the walls.

"She insisted I bring it here. She wouldn't let me fix it."

"Okay, Maggie, okay...let me see."

"I want my Daddy!"

"I know, honey, I know, but let's get you and Bentley into the operating room."

He winked at Elsie. If there ever was a mother who could use a drink, it was Mrs. Perkins. He handed the frazzled mom his spiked slush.

"What's this?"

"Tootsie made it and I made it better."

Elsie took half the glass in three gulps.

"Give it a few minutes."

Carrying Maggie in his arms, he touched her forehead with the back of his hand. "Boy, she's hot."

"Yeah. Redhead. Goes with the territory."

"I'll need some help." He flicked on the OR lights with one hand, then headed to the stainless steel double sink–*will I ever hear out of my left ear again?*

Elsie was behind him, holding an empty glass. "Got any more of this?" she asked, more stable than when she arrived.

Above the noise of the water filling the sink, he said, "Sure, help yourself. I put it in the freezer in the other room."

"And the medicine part?"

"It's on my desk. Help yourself to that, too." He laughed in spite of Maggie's cries against his tympanic membranes.

"Maggie, Maggie, settle down. I want you to listen to me. Let me have your dog."

"Ben...Ben...Bentley is his n...a...me. I want my Daddy!"

"Maggie, let me take Bentley. Your momma's going to give you a little bath in this sink, okay?"

He called for Elsie. "We need to get her cooled off. Check her over for scratches or bite wounds...anything."

Dr. Glassman let Elsie take Maggie.

"See, Maggie? Dr. Glassman will make Bentley okay."

"Bentley not dead, Momma?"

"No, Bentley's not dead. Dr. Glassman can fix him." Elsie used a cloth to sponge the water on her daughter's back and chest. The sobbing slowly subsided.

"Just give me a minute to get things around and I'll have Bentley fixed in no time."

Andy started piecing the stuffed animal together on the OR table. In two of the paws he found encased SIM cards; a small plastic container was glued over the heart squeaker. It contained a thumb drive. He worked deftly making the repairs saying nothing about the suspicious electronics.

"Maggie, where did you find such a nice canine specimen?"

"What that mean, Mommy?"

"Can you tell Dr. Glassman your brother Luke sent it?"

"Luke did."

Andy turned to the child and smiled. "You look much happier, Maggie. Not so red faced. Find any scratches or wounds on her? Any small bites or abrasions?"

"None, Dr. Glassman. She's clean as a whistle, just like the day she was born." Elsie, who was feeling much much better also, gave her daughter a kiss on the cheek.

Dr. Glassman pulled a paper drape out of a drawer. Folded in half, he judged where to make his first cut.

"Not only am I a world famous veterinary surgeon, I am also a dress designer. This is for her head, and here's a roll of gauze so you can make a belt."

"Thanks. Where's a towel?"

"In that cabinet to your right."

Out of the Epsom Salt bath and dressed in her blue surgical drape, Maggie stood on an inverted milk crate across from Dr. Glassman.

"Now, if you're going to be my assistant, you'll need to do exactly what I say. This is delicate surgery."

With the seriousness of a nun at confession, Maggie nodded.

"Okay, we can proceed." He laid out scissors, needle holder, hemostats, black suture threads, and a gauze wrapping bandage. He placed a small face mask over the toy's muzzle to administer the anesthetic as he explained, "This makes sure Bentley is not hurt during the procedure." He dramatically cleared his throat.

"So, Maggie, your brother shot a coyote?"

"Yes."

"Which one?"

"The one what got Bentley."

"No, I mean which brother shot the coyote?"

"Nathan did. Tobias throw'd stone. Then they others ran away."

"That was very brave of them."

"Wasn't brave to get Bentley with Nathan around."

"I mean your brothers are brave."

Maggie listened but never took her eyes off Dr. Glassman's hands.

Elsie sat on the corner stool. "You're really going all out."

"Anything for Maggie." Andy smiled at the little girl with big blue eyes.

He nodded at Elsie. "Mom," he said. "I think someone's ready to sleep on your lap."

Without an argument from her daughter, Elsie scooped Maggie into her arms. In seconds, the child was sleeping, totally limp, with her crown of red hair and face snuggled into her mother's neck.

"I turned the legs inside out when I stitched them so in reversing them, the tears won't show. We'll under stuff them a little so there won't be any stress on the suture line...er...I guess you'd call it a seam in the sewing world. But I'm missing an eye."

"Here," Elsie handed him a button off her blouse. "It was hanging by a thread anyway. Maggie was more upset about Bentley than she was the coyote. When she saw what a mess the toy was, she went into a crying rage. She's my only redhead. Howard told me when she was born it was a warning label."

"So a coyote came into the yard where Maggie was playing, grabbed the toy, then your son Nathan shot the coyote?"

"Yes."

"With Maggie hanging on to it?"

"Yes."

"Your son must be a pretty good shot with a gun."

"Both are. They tied in the gun competition at Waybird City. Sponsors had to buy a second trophy. Howard got back home in time to see his boys get their Golden Boy and plaques."

"Golden Boy?"

"Made by Henry. It's a repeating rifle. Highest quality. USA made," Elsie said.

"I bet he was proud."

"Sure was. It was nice for the family to be together except for Luke."

Andy fiddled with dressing the limbs. "What does Luke do?"

"He works for the Library of Congress. The job has him traveling for research. He was never a bookworm in school although he did get good grades. He went into the Army for a little while and then got the job at the library. Interesting career path, but it's his life. Luke always wanted to travel. He never liked caves like the twins do. They've been in all the caves around these mountains. Howard got them interested in that."

"Spelunkers? They're not scared of the dark caves?"

"Nope. Howard took them caving as kids. Bought them headlights, ropes, and all that stuff. With Maggie on the way, Howard decided to take a fall vacation and was gone for two weeks with the twins."

"He was gone for two weeks with a baby on the way?"

"No big deal, Dr. Glassman. Running Deer stayed with me and Aunt Gem wasn't far. The boys needed to be with their dad. We're old pros. Maggie was baby number five."

"Caving sounds interesting."

"If you ever want to go, the twins can take you."

"Thanks, Elsie. I might take them up on that."

****

A young male voice called from the lobby, "Mom, you here?"

"Yes. Just follow that hall."

Andy looked up to see Tobias and Nathan enter his OR.

"Boys, stop right there. This is Dr. Glassman's operating room and you both are dirty. Where's the coyote?"

"In the back of the truck."

"Ok, that's fine. Wait in the lobby until we're ready to go."

"How's Maggs?"

"She's fine. Here, one of you take her and put her in her car seat. I'll be out in a minute."

"Yes, ma'am." Andy couldn't tell which twin, but one of them took the child and the other followed.

"How do you tell them apart?"

"I'm their mother, but Howard can't. Maggie can, even at a distance."

He stepped back and examined his work. "Well, Mrs. Perkins, Bentley is all stitched, stuffed, and bandaged. Wait, a sec...I forgot the antibiotics."

He came back from his office and handed Elsie a small white envelope. "We might as well do this right. Tell Miss Perkins she's to give Bentley one red one daily and the green ones are for his pain."

"She'll want to know all about the bandages."

"Come around anytime and I'll take them off so she can see."

"I can't thank you enough."

"Not necessary."

"Tell you what, I've got a great recipe for whiskey slush. I'll make some up and bring it when we come back. Resupply your inventory."

"Sounds fair enough. Much appreciated. Thank you."

Tobias and Nathan stood when their mother came into the lobby with Dr. Glassman. "Maggs is still sleeping."

"Thank you, Nathan. I'll go ahead and get supper fixed while you boys tend to business. Thanks again, Dr. Glassman." Elsie carried Bentley in the crook of her arm like she would carry a sleeping baby. Tobias held the door for his mother as she left.

****

"Hey, guys, you got a minute?"

The boys looked at each other then nodded, "Sure."

"I'm kind of curious how all this happened."

"You mean about the coyote and Maggie?" The boy in the gray sweatshirt spoke.

"Who are you?"

"I'm Tobias."

"I'm Nathan."

"Okay, I got it. Tobias in gray, and Nathan in green. So what happened?"

"You tell him, Nathan."

"No, you can."

"But you shot it."

"But you chased the other ones away."

Andy interrupted the twins. "Guys, guys, I can't keep up with it. Who did what first?"

"Okay, I'll tell."

"You're Nathan, right?"

"Yes, Dr. Glassman."

"So what happened?"

"Tobias and I went out hunting. We got a couple of rabbits because Mom wanted to make bunny pie for Friday because Dad will be home and he likes that."

"We got three rabbits, Nathan. A couple is two." Tobias amended the story with fact.

"So, we got three rabbits and when we got close to the house we heard Maggs and Mom screaming. We came in the back door and right through the house to the front, and saw Maggie pulling Bentley with a young coyote on the other end."

Tobias cut in at this point. "Mom was on the porch with the Henry rifle Dad got her for her last birthday."

"Yeah, that was something to see." Nathan hitched up his blue jeans and continued. "She's not got the aim us boys have so I grabbed the rifle and took the shot. Dropped the coyote. Maggs fell on her butt, screaming."

"Your mother said you were pretty good with a rifle." Dr. Glassman was amazed. "Nathan, you responded really fast in a dangerous situation."

"When there's a life at stake, Dr. Glassman, you just got to evaluate and react. My Dad taught us that."

"Did you hit it in the head?"

The twins looked at each other.

"I didn't hit it in the head because you need to cut off the head and send it intact into the state lab to test for rabies."

"Yes, I knew that."

"Why'd you ask, Dr. Glassman?"

"I was testing your knowledge."

"Hit it in the chest with a .17 HMR round. The angle was so I got a clear shot and not my sister."

"You guys are incredible. Will you take me hunting with you sometime and give me some pointers?"

"Hell, yes, Dr. Glassman."

Tobias elbowed Nathan in the ribs. "You ain't supposed to swear."

"Sorry. We'll take you sometime. But first, where do you want the coyote?"

"Where is it?"

"In the back of the truck."

"You boys drove down the mountain?"

"Yes, sir."

"How old are you two?"

"Turned twelve in February."

"And you drive?"

"Dad said we could in emergencies. And with Mom taking off, we got the animal in the truck, and came here. That's what Dad would want us to do. That's our job when he's gone."

"To shoot coyotes?"

"Well, yeah, I suppose," said Tobias, "but we're supposed to protect Mom and Maggs when he's gone. That's what men do."

****

Andy watched the twins drive off in the old pickup truck. He went back into the clinic to remove the coyote's head, pack it in dry ice, and arrange for a pick up to send it to the state lab. When the clean up was completed, he refilled his glass with lemonade and Leadslingers. He found his cigar on the floorboards of the porch.

Rocking back in the chair, he put his feet up on the railing. "Protecting women and children because that's what men do."

After relighting his cigar, he sipped on the sour drink. A retailed hawk screeched as it flew passed the clinic.

"I love it here."

The bell mounted on the head jamb tinkled as Sheriff Harris keyed the door and called out, "Miss Ambrie? You up yet?"

"Oh, Bill, of course I'm up. It's almost time to open."

"I didn't want to catch you in a compromised situation."

"Good Lord, Bill, it's been years since I was in a compromised situation. Oh, you are a dear. That's a compliment at my age. A compromised situation. That's funny." Ambrie took her glasses off and wiped both lenses with the edge of her blouse.

"I brought your donuts off the porch."

"Fishbone not to school this morning?"

Taking out his wallet, Bill said, "No. His mom called the office and said he had a fever and she was keeping him home."

"Sorry to hear that. He's such a nice boy." Ambrie rang up the cash. "I often wish his dad was alive to see him growing up. It was such a sad end to Arthur."

"Yes, it was."

"Before we get too maudlin, let me ask you about coffee? You got time?"

Sheriff Harris smiled at the old woman looking at him in anticipation of a morning guest.

"Sure, Ambrie. I got time. I put Deputy Johnson in charge while I patrol today."

"Is Hector talking to him yet over losing Alice on that search?"

"I don't think so, but Hector's not plotting to kill him either, so that's good."

"I tell you what, Bill, Hector holds a grudge just like his mother. It's not good to talk about the dead, but Ollie Cobb could hold out longer than anyone I ever knew. God rest her soul."

"I didn't know her that well."

"I did. We went to school together." Ambrie poured two cups from her coffee station.

"Ollie went off to college and married but she came back to the Hollar. She never liked leaving the dogs. Too ingrained in her. That's why Hector is the way he is."

"Yes, he's quite the houndsman."

"Say, Bill, have you heard from Ivan?"

"Got a postcard from him last week. He's still in rehab but doing well."

"Sure hope so. I've prayed for him every day since his dad up and left. What a thing to do to a child. It still grinds me right in my craw."

"I think he'll make it this time. He's older now, more mature. He's getting sick of being drunk."

"I hope so. I'd give him a job but I don't want him to be around the liquor in the store and relapse. I'd feel terrible to think helping him was the harm of him."

Bill stretched to look out the side window of the grocery store, past the collection of 1940's pinup girl's thumb tacked to the frame and past the racks of cigarettes, to the main street. Hector Cobb parks his orange beater truck beside the cruiser.

"Don't worry, Ambrie. I've got Ivan lined up to work with the Morris brothers and Bowtie at the garage. Something tells me he'll be the man we all knew."

"I hope you're right, Bill."

The bell announced Hector's arrival. "Miss Ambrie, Bill. Am I in time for coffee and donuts?"

"Yes, yes, pull up one of those stools. Just had them reupholstered in Waybird City. I like that red, don't you?"

"Yes, ma'am, I do." Hector plopped down on the stool. He fished a cinnamon sugar donut from the bag.

"Ambrie, better get them in the display case before Hector decides to fill up on donuts this morning. He looks like he could eat three or four. Isn't Alice cooking for you?"

"Well yes and no, Bill. Once that ankle heals up, she's to get back to her chores." Between mouthfuls he added, "I had to crack the whip a couple of times but I got her in order."

"Hector Cobb, you are such a *liar!*" Ambrie giggled. "I think it is more like Alice to crack the whip with you." She stacked the donuts in the glass case. "You boys excuse me. I've got inventory to check off."

"Yes, ma'am. We'll be here for a little bit. Say, before you go, where's that lost and found board you put up?"

"It's on the wall behind the door, Hector."

"Thanks, Ambrie."

Bill poured himself another cup from the coffee station. He put a five dollar bill on the counter. "You lost something Hector or you found something?"

Hector pulled a pin off the board and stuck it through the silver link of a bracelet with a tiger's eye stone at the center.

"You're supposed to give bracelets to the pretty girls, not post them in Ambrie's lost and found."

"Well, it ain't mine to give, Bill. One of the hounds brought it back from her foray into the woods."

"You got a dog getting out?"

"Penni. She started digging and taking off on me. This isn't the first time."

"Why?"

"I don't know. Never had a dog that wanted to take off like that."

"Does she come back?"

"Yep. And she brings things with her. She found this bracelet yesterday. Last week she brought a kid's shoe."

"How long does she stay gone?"

"Few hours, half a day. Always comes back."

"Interesting."

"I think she's found a campsite someplace and is scrounging around stuff left by campers. I don't have a clue why she started doing it."

"Which one is she?"

"Sister to Rip. Looks just like him only smaller."

"Oh, yeah. I know the one you're talking about. She's long and lean, a real pretty head, but not as meaty."

"Yep. I have to figure something out before she gets the rest of them doing it. See monkey, do monkey."

"Hate to leave you and your dog trouble but I've got to go out on patrol."

"Bill, hear from Ivan? How's he doing?"

"Told Ambrie I got a postcard. He seems to be doing well."

"If he needs some work, I've got stuff I need help with in the kennel. It isn't much but will keep his hands busy."

"Good. I'll write him and let him know."

Ambrie came out of the back room. "You leaving, Bill?"

"Gotta earn what the county is paying me, young lady."

"I'm gone, too, Ambrie. Money's on the counter."

"You boys have a good day. Stop around about lunch time. Fresh roast beef sandwiches."

"That's tempting, Ambrie." Bill tipped his hat in respect. "Maybe I will. Have to see what today holds."

****

She dusted the shelves along the back wall after Bill and Hector left. There were few customers the rest of the morning. Bill didn't come back for roast beef sandwiches, nor did Hector, but she sold out to one of the construction crews working on the upgrades. Business was good.

As Ambrie straightened boxes of cereal, instant coffee, and tea, she saw the silver truck pull in and a stranger exit.

Jose Garza walked up the steps and was startled by the tinkle of the bell.

"Hello, can I help you?"

"Ah, yes ma'am. Do you have diapers? Baby food?"

"Why, yes I do. Over here along that back wall. You visiting the area with your family?"

"Yes, ma'am. Just for a few days. Do you have candy, mac and cheese?"

"Right along that other wall…over there…mac and cheese is by the soups. I've got crackers below the soups. Help yourself. When you're ready to check out, just ring the bell and I'll be right out."

"Thank you, ma'am." Jose watched her disappear between two curtains to the grocery's back room.

"Trusting old bat," he muttered. He stuffed a candy bar in the depth of his shirt pocket. "She won't miss this."

Jose made several trips down the aisles. He took all the diapers off the shelves along with the baby wipes. Next aisle over he grabbed oatmeal and cereal; from the cooler he took eight gallons of milk and stacked it on the counter.

"Suppose I should get these for the *las putas and la bruja.*" He swept an arm load of feminine hygiene products off the shelf. "Bitches. Always want something."

Ambrie watched from the crack between the curtains–*some family he's got–this ain't right–never had a tourist shop like that and take so much–he's got diapers but no baby oil or powder–with all those tampons, I wonder how many women are in his family and why they'd send a man to get those.*

In the candy and gum aisle, Jose took handfuls of gum, suckers, and sweets. Rather than get soda, he took boxes of powdered fruit drinks to mix with water. He circled round to get baby formula. The single pint of chocolate ice cream was for himself.

He stood at the counter and rang the bell. "Ma'am, hey, I'm ready to check out."

"Be right there. Need some boxes to get your order to the truck?" Ambrie stuck her head between the curtains and smiled.

"Sure. That'd be really nice."

With boxes stacked inside of boxes, Ambrie made her way to the register.

"I don't think I've got any plastic bags big enough or strong enough for all this. Mighty grateful you decided to shop at my store."

"You're welcome, ma'am."

Ambrie smiled while she rang up the order. She handed Jose each item for boxing.

"Hope you're enjoying your stay in Deacon's Hollar. Sorry for all the mess but we're getting an upgrade. Federal money comes in as a grant to help increase the tourist trade."

"That's nice, ma'am. "

"Yes, it is. We'll get new store fronts, paving and gutter on the main streets in the village." Ambrie flashed one of her sweetest smiles.

"You got a nice little place here. Ever thought of putting in a strip mall, some dollar stores, maybe some attractions?"

"No, no, we can't do that. The grant specifically says we keep the quality and nature of the community. We want folks to come enjoy what we have, not for them to bring what they have here. I mean, when you're on vacation, you need to see and experience something different, don't you think?"

Ambrie kept ringing up the order. She glanced out the window and saw Sheriff Harris's squad car stop below. Faking a sneeze, Ambrie paused only long enough to grab a tissue and flip a red card up in the window. That was the signal to Bill something was wrong.

"Well, that just about settles it. Your total is $456.78."

Jose pulled out a roll of cash and handed over $500. "Keep the change, lady. It was nice doing business with you."

"That's a tip?"

"Yeah, it's a tip."

"Well, young man, if that's a tip, how are you going to pay for the candy bars you got in your shirt pocket?"

"What?" His eye started to twitch.

"The three candy bars you thought you could shoplift from my store."

"*Puta*, I ain't got no candy from your store. I paid for everything and gave you more."

"That was my tip. Where's the money for the candy?"

"You got paid, old lady. Be glad I don't..." The door bell tinkled.

From behind him, a deep masculine voice said, "Be glad you don't what?"

Jose turned around and found himself eye level with the brightly polished gold badge of William Harris, Jr. Jose saw the 'serve and protect' on the bottom half of the badge.

Jose turned to Ambrie.

"I...I...well, nothing. Sorry, lady. I didn't mean to be rude. I got all these screaming babies. My wife had triplets and it's nothing but bottles and diapers. See how many boxes I bought? Yeah, I'm just tired and stressed. I am so sorry. Please accept my apology."

"Yes, I accept your apology and I fully understand. I've had children myself and they can be a handful. That being said, it's three dollars and sixty cents for the candy bars." Ambrie was no longer smiling.

Jose pulled out a twenty dollar bill and put it on the counter as he smiled.

"Let me help you with those boxes, young man."

"Sheriff, that won't be..."

"I insist."

"Okay, thanks, Sheriff."

Loading the truck was the excuse Bill needed to examine the front, cab, and note the license plate number. After the last box was in the passenger seat and Jose was behind the wheel, Bill said, "Glad you came to do business in the Hollar. Be sure to come back." His body cam caught Jose's smile, the tattoo on his neck, the scar in front of his ear, and the twitching eye.

"Thanks for shopping here, young man," Bill said.

"*De nada. Adios.*"

Jose put the car in reverse and eased out of the parking space like he was two days away from graduating from driving school. He was miles down the road before he gained any speed.

****

"What are you thinking, Ambrie?" Bill took a soda out of the ice cooler and sat at his favorite spot along the counter. He could see the road and his car.

"There's something up with him. He's a thief and a liar."

"Those two virtues usually go together. How so?"

"Diapers."

"Diapers? I know he tried to steal the candy bars, but I don't get the connection with the diapers."

"He said he had triplets, right?"

"Correct."

"Well, why did he buy all the ones on the shelf? They're seven different sizes. Those three babies would wear the same size. And no powder for their little butts? That's unheard of."

Bill was quiet for a few moments before taking another pull on the soda bottle.

"Ambrie Sykes, I'm gonna have to deputize you."

****

Jose arrived at the cabin and started to unload the vehicle.

"Hey," Clarence called. "Get the women to do that. That's what we got them for."

Jose heard Clarence call someone. Three of the older girls came out, heads down, and barefooted. They wore loose fitting skirts and dirty blouses.

"*Aquí, perras.*"

Jose opened the truck and shoved one of the girls to pick up a box. "Get it inside and put it away before I come back."

Clarence was into another bottle of whiskey. The place stunk like cheap tobacco.

"You got back awful soon. Should've taken you longer to Waybird City and back."

"I got the stuff. There's everything on the list."

"You didn't go into Deacon's Hollar, did you?" Clarence coughed up phlegm and spit it into a cup.

"No, I didn't. I did just what you said, got what you said, and I'm back."

"No one's the wiser?"

"Damn it, Clarence, no one's the wiser."

"Just making sure you didn't bring no one back here following you."

"No one followed me."

"Alright. I'm going to take me a nap. Need to get some energy. Been awful tired lately."

"Go to bed, man. I'll make sure all the supplies are brought in. We can take stuff up to the cave tomorrow."

"Haven't been there for two days. Suppose they run out of food?"

"Naw. I left them plenty."

Clarence ambled off to a back room. The squeak of the bed springs echoed in the kitchen as Jose watched the girls unpack the boxes of food and supplies. He was trying to decide which one he would have.

"Hey, you. India, come here."

The deeply brown skinned girl turned. There was nothing she could do.

Jose pointed to her, then to his crotch.

Together Again

"I gotta pull over for gas. You guys need to take a leak?"

"Yeah and I'm hungry," Cobalt said from the back of the truck.

"Good idea." Zero rubbed his eyes and yawned. "Are we there yet, Dad?"

Diego flipped the turn signal and drove the truck off the interstate. He slowed on the exit ramp then crossed to a service island, pulling alongside a gas pump.

"Diego and me will fill up, check the oil."

"Zero, you know you don't have to do that. There's an on board computer that'll tell you all that stuff with sensors and warning lights," Scout said as he checked for messages on his laptop.

"Well, what if your motherboard takes a crap and forgets to say the motor needs oil, like way out in the middle of nowhere? How about that, Scout?"

"Suit yourself. Check the oil. I'm on vacation."

Diego put the nozzle in the neck of the fuel tank. "It's beautiful country. How far out are we?"

"About four hours as the crow flies, but you wanted the scenic route so I figured to add another two to three hours because of all the mountains."

"I didn't think it would take this long. Nothing was faster?"

"Yeah, but dropping in from a C-130 might be a bit pretentious."

****

"Miss, miss," Diego called to the waitress. "This is on my check. I don't know what these guys want, but I'll have the farmer's omelet, whole wheat toast, orange juice, coffee with cream, biscuits and sausage gravy on the side."

She wrote on her order pad. "Okay, what about the rest of you?"

Zero, Scout, and Cobalt placed their orders, but Scout added, "And a big plate of bacon right in the middle of this table."

"That'll be extra, sir."

"It's okay. My buddy's paying for it."

"Oh, and Miss, he'll take decaf coffee," Scout pointed to Zero. "Caffeine makes him shakey."

"Well, we can't have that, can we gentlemen? I'll be right back with your water and coffee. My name's Clara. If you need anything, just wave. I'll keep an eye out."

"Thanks, Clara."

Zero sat back in his chair. "Did anyone tell CB we were coming?"

"Oops," Scout said. "I've got his number somewhere."

"Here, use my phone. I've got the number pulled up." Diego handed Zero his phone.

"Wait a sec, that's not it. The last four of his number is 0455."

Scout checked his phone. "No, you've got it wrong. The last four are 6132."

"Hold it, guys." Cobalt looked up CB's number on his phone. "It's 8643 with a 915 area code."

"Well, that little CIA puke," Scout said. "He gave us all different numbers. Gentlemen, we've been played like kindergarteners at recess."

"I bet he's got a secret decoder ring, too," added Diego as he scanned the area for exits and customers.

"Here, I'll call him." Zero rose from the table to go outside. He grabbed a piece of hot bacon from the plate. "I feel my protein levels dropping." He stepped out into the sunshine.

****

"Hey, CB. Zero here. Hooha, bro."

"Hooha, bro. Glad to hear from you. Where're you now? Syria?"

"No, we're in West Virginia, about six hours out from your place."

"What?"

"Yeah. We got a couple months of leave. The old man ordered us to go on a vacation so we figured we'd hit your place for the fishing. Maybe go to Dolly Sods. Check out property."

"We?"

"Yeah, I got the gang together. Scout, Cobalt, Diego and me."

"Er...okay. Good. It's all good."

"Got any motels there?"

"There's an old fashioned boarding house that can put you up. If you prefer a motel, there are some along the 219 highway, about eight miles out."

"Places to eat?"

"Gracie's Place serves the best food. As a matter of fact, I'm taking my parents there for a late lunch. When you get into town, call me."

"Well, buddy, seeing you gave us four different phone numbers, which would you prefer?"

"Doesn't matter. It's a CIA thing." CB paused. "Tell the guys to use Luke Perkins when you check into town. And I work for the Library of Congress."

"Got it. Luke and the Library of Congress. And what are we? Assistant librarians?"

"No. Keep the lie simple. You're military. I did research for you prior to a new duty station. Easy and kind of true."

"Got it. Our waitress just brought another platter of bacon and I see Scout digging into it. Later."

"Okay." Luke bit his lower lip. He glanced across the yard, watching Tater and Maggie play pirates in the sandbox. He would have to find things for the barbarians to do. They were not the kind of men to have time on their hands.

****

"Jose, where'd you get supplies?"

"Waybird City like you said,"

"Then why is the receipt from Sykes Grocery?"

"I don't know. I went to Waybird City."

"Don't you lie to me." Clarence was furious. The beet red color rose to his neck, unshaven face, and forehead. The stub of a cigarette stuck to his lower lip and jiggled hot ash off onto the floor as he spoke.

"It ain't nothing, Clarence. No one knows me around here. So what if I did?"

"So what if you did? You could blow the whole thing if anyone sees you with the truck. We got to keep a low profile. What's wrong with you? If you can't follow instructions, I can always terminate our relationship."

"Clarence, don't get stupid. Ain't nothing wrong. No one saw me."

"So you did go into Deacon's Hollar. What the..."

"You got my word. Ain't nothing going to ruin anything. We got a plan, Clarence. We're partners. We'll hook up with your brother, ditch Boss and his crew, and be in the clear. We got this."

Jose saw Clarence's eye dart to the booze bottle on the table.

"Settle down, man, you'll give yourself a heart attack. Let me pour you a shot and I'll have one and we can discuss this. Ain't no sense in getting upset."

Clarence tried to take a deep breath but was cut short by a spasm of coughs and choking. He grabbed the back of the chair as he bent over, spitting green phlegm on the floor.

Jose poured half a glass from the bottle and helped Clarence sit in the chair. Once he stopped gagging, Clarence lit another cigarette.

"This better not all go to hell. Boss will kill both of us if he finds out. I told you the things aren't all in place yet. I gotta get Franklin and put the two parts together to make a whole."

"And you will, you will. Ain't nothing going to happen. Just you wait and see. We got this, Clarence. The three of us. Here, take another drink. Let's have a toast to the future. We're gonna be rich."

"Maybe you're right, Jose. The Wells boys have been in tight places before. I just gotta get ahold of Franklin."

****

The large Humvee drove to the gas station from the highway. The driver stopped at the furthest set of pumps from the entrance to the service center. A second identical vehicle went to auxiliary pumps behind the station.

Cobalt saw a man from the first vehicle, dressed in an expensive suit, exit and walk toward the building. The diamonds on his shoes caught the sunlight, sparkling with each step. Cobalt suddenly was out of his chair and around the corner of the dining room behind the artificial plants.

"What's up with him?" Scout asked.

Diego and Zero shrugged their shoulders as they munched on the last of the bacon. Cobalt signaled for Diego.

"Dude, you see that guy with the Humvee at pump one?"

"Yeah."

"Go talk to him and put these sensors on the wheel well of the truck. There's another Hummer at the back. Do the same thing."

"I got it. You staying hid in the jungle?"

"Yeah. Don't ask, don't tell."

Diego, distracting the driver by using a Puerto Rican accent he learned from his buddies in high school, bumped against the Humvee.

"Hey, man, get off the truck. You drunk or what?"

"No, dude, jest gotts my stomach so bad." Deigo coughed into the waste receptacle. He placed the sensor as he stumbled away.

Cutting back through the service station, he grabbed a ballcap and bottle of window cleaner. At pump six, he said to the driver, "Hey, man. Let me get those windows for you," as he proceeded to work his way around the vehicle, peering through to the interior. He planted the sensors just as he did the first.

When the truck drove away, Diego shouted, "*Vaya con Dios*." One of the passengers rolled down a back window and flipped off the Latino service attendant.

****

Diego parted the leaves of the bushy plant. "You can come out now. I chased the big bad wolf away."

Zero and Scout joined Cobalt at the door.

"Zero, did you leave her a tip?"

"Of course I left her a tip."

"How much?"

"Ten per cent."

"You cheap bastard. It's at least twenty-five percent now."

"I don't know how to figure twenty-five percent."

"Freaking scrolled Ranger can't figure out a tip but you can calculate the explosives you need to blast the top off a mountain?"

"Well, yeah. That's my job."

"Here, put this extra twenty-five on the table by my plate. She'll know I'm not the tight ass you are."

"Ladies, ladies," Scout said, "when you girls are done arguing, let's get back on the road."

"Just one thing, Cobalt. Those boys are carrying some serious firepower," Diego said.

"Yeah. I figured."

Scout and Cobalt sat in the back looking at Scout's computer while Diego drove and Zero took a nap with his headphones on.

****

Inside the black Humvee, an assistant answered the phone, then handed it to Boss.

"Sir, it's the Albanians. Ramadani."

Boss took the phone but paused for effect before answering. He absentmindedly watched the sparkle of his diamonded shoes in the dim interior of the truck.

"Yes?"

The others heard Ramadani shouting while Boss remained calm.

"I assured you the product would arrive, as ordered, and would not be damaged. I gave you my word."

After a few minutes he replied, "I've sent two men ahead. Believe me, they are the best and can handle any situation that arises. They're in position now and ready. Let's get this done and over with. They don't like to wait. What time? Maybe six hours. Will contact you then."

Boss spoke to his assistant. "I hate these small towns. The accommodations are inferior, the food makes me sick, and the people smell. Once the product is examined, we leave for Charleston, then fly to Montreal. I trust you have the arrangements made?"

"Yes, sir."

"Good. This will be a profitable trip."

THE HOG HUNT

Amy Porter walked to Sheriff Harris' booth with the coffee pot in one hand and her order book in the other.

"Want it topped off, Sheriff? Chef Dodger's about ready to get your breakfast order started."

"Sure, Amy. You call him Chef Dodger now?"

"Yeah. Gracie got him one of those big puffy cook hats. He thinks he's Godzilla of the Grill. I don't mind long as he keeps making the cherry cobbler on Friday's."

Bill smiled as he slid his coffee cup toward the end of the table. He nodded to Gracie who was behind the counter setting up glasses.

"I'll have my usual. Ask Dodger to make the eggs over hard and the hash browns crispy."

"Right away." Amy then filled a cup in the next booth for Mike Green.

"You doin' alright, Sheriff Harris?" Gracie asked from behind the counter.

"Yes, ma'am, I am. With breakfast, I'll be even better." He winked at Gracie.

The noise from the muffler of the old Chevy made Bill turn in his seat. He waved and nodded to the two men in the cab, but only one came into the diner.

"Mr. Decker, good morning. Haven't seen you in a while. Have a seat. How're you?"

"Congratulations on your reelection, Bill." Wink looked around the room as he sat in the booth.

Bill waved to Amy. "I'll take care of Wink's coffee."

"Appreciate that, Bill." Wink smiled at the waitress. "Thanks, Amy."

"I see you brought Garl with you. He coming in?" Bill pushed the cream and sugar towards Wink.

"N-no. H-e'll stay in the truck."

"You want something to eat?"

"Nope, Bill. Thanks. Just need to talk."

Bill waved to the waitress, "Amy, hold that breakfast for a bit, would you please?"

"Sure, Sheriff." Amy disappeared in the kitchen.

"What's up?"

"Hunted all my life. Everything's legal, you know that, Bill. I got all my licenses with the DNR and the Feds."

"Yeah, I know."

Wink stirred three teaspoons of sugar and added a dab of cream to his cup. "I returned a call to an agency in Charleston a couple weeks ago. They had two men who wanted to book a hunt. So I told the price. The lady says that's fair, but these guys got money so if you raise it a little, they won't crab about it. So's, I says no, I'm not out to cheat anyone or treat anyone differently.

"I gave her all the particulars to pass aIong to the clients. I wasn't there when they arrived b-but they knew to get the key from under the flowerpot at Cabin 5. Left them a note I'd pick them up the next morning about f-five a.m. I got extra guns and ammo because I figure these guys are new to hog hunting and I want to have the firepower we need.

"I'd gotten a hold of Garl and set the day aforehand so he could bring his hounds and catch dog. All Garl's hounds are good hunting dogs.

"I'm a businessman like anyone else, but I also have my ethics when it comes to hunting. There are s-some things I won't do and things that just ain't right."

Wink's hand shook slightly as he raised his cup to drink. It shook even more when he set the cup down on the saucer. He nervously licked his lips. Controlling his stutter was hard work.

The hunter's brown eyes patrolled the tree line across the road and the parking lot. He nodded at the person in his truck, as he drew his napkin across his lips.

"Wink, did they want you to poach? Set up a still?"

"No, Bill, nothing like that. Worse than that, I'm thinkin'."

"Okay, fill me in."

"Well, they're ready at f-five a.m. On the drive up the mountain, I'm making small talk but these two just stare out the window, don't m-make eye contact with me in the rearview mirror. They're fair sized boys and take up the back seat. They don't mind the close quarters, but they ain't b-boyfriends if you know what I mean. Ain't sex that binds these two, it's something else."

Wink glanced out at his truck again. Garl was sitting in the same position he was when they arrived.

"Only thing they said in all that time was on the way out their employer would be there in a few days. The one says, 'Boss will be here soon' or something like that."

"Not very talkative, eh?"

"No, Bill, not at all. So we get up to Crow F-Foot Fork because there's a group of sounders and a..."

Bill shook his head. "You're going to have to explain what a sounder is."

"You ever been hog hunting?"

"No. My dad was a white tail deer man. Heard people talk but I don't really know much about the details."

"Okay, I'll back up here a bit."

Bill wondered why Wink's eyes kept darting to the tree line.

"A sounder's a small group of hogs, maybe one or two sows and their offspring. Wild hogs are social animals to a point. Most the adult boars go off on their own and I suppose that's nature's way because some boars will fight to the death with those tusks.

"They're intelligent animals, a little shy, secretive. They'll go nocturnal if they're under pressure from hunters. Better sense of smell than Hector's bloodhounds but don't go saying I said that. You know how sensitive Hector is about his dogs."

Bill chuckled. "I won't tell Hector."

"Okay, I'll take your word." Wink didn't smile.

"Wild hogs'll pick up scent from miles away and twenty five feet deep under the ground. I don't have any science on it so don't go telling Dr. Glassman I said that, but it's true. And they can hear about as good as they can smell. That's what makes them hard to hunt. So, where was I..."

"You were telling me about sounders up at Crow Foot Fork."

"Yeah, I was." Wink tapped the back of his hand against his mouth.

"There's a sounder and a big boar in that area I heard of so I parked the truck. I go around to help them get their gear out and they only got two bags. Most customers got their heated vests, heated boots, and battery operated gloves. It can get chilly that early."

Bill nodded. "All that high tech stuff and they still get lost in the woods. The low tech nose of a bloodhound rescued more than one."

"Well, these two fellas got none of that. They had knives, which struck me as strange. Knives are for f-ighting up close and personal. That's about the last thing you want is to get personal with wild hogs. I guessed knives are for probably taking meat.

"I noticed they had leggings they velcro around their calves, p-pulled them up, then hooked over their belts. Sorta like cowboy chaps but not leather. Don't know the material but you couldn't get a blackberry thorn or cockel burr to stick to it.

"So, you know me, I'm trying to make s-small talk but keeping quiet in the woods. The h-hogs are way down between the three forks and we're just waiting on Garl to come with his dogs. I poured a little coffee from my thermos and offered them some but they just kind of grunted so I supped it up and didn't offer anymore. I got the guns ready, laying on the tailgate, but these two don't ask me questions so's I guess they know'd about guns."

"Did they ask you anything at all? About the dogs, or what the plan was?"

"Nope, Bill. Not one word, but I'm getting to that."

Bill felt his stomach growl; Wink took his time telling the story.

The outfitter scratched his ear and continued. "Before too long, I see Garl's truck coming up the road. Garl runs Redbones and Catahoula cross curs he got in Louisiana, and he's got a little Pitbull catch dog. She's got the fire in her belly to do the job. My buddy down south calls that 'grit with no give.' Her name's Lights Out because when that Pittie catches the hog by its nose, Garl goes in with a gun and it's lights out for the hog.

"Garl gets five dogs out and is telling the customers how the hunt works. First, the dogs'll go down in the hollar and scatter the herd. They'll go after one hog and worry it. When they got the hog held, then Garl'll send in the c-catch dog. He said to let the c-catch dog do her job, then they come in with the .44 magnum pistols or whatever. Garl told them where to place a round to drop the hog. He says whatever you do, don't miss and go hitting the c-catch dog with the bullet. It can take a long time to train another. A good catch dog is worth a lot of money.

"Just before daylight, Garl and me begin walking the dogs into the fork. It's about a f-orty-five degree slant, maybe fifty in some spots and less in others, but we're being quiet and the dogs haven't hit on the hogs yet. Well, it didn't take long because Garl's got the best dogs in West Virginia."

Wink looked up at the light over their booth. "Well, there might be a pack comes close to him in Alabama, but maybe not. Anyway, the hogs smell the dogs and they start moving around, scattering."

He used both hands to wipe down his face and deflect the stutter. The outfitter tensed the muscles on his forehead a couple of times before he relaxed his face to continue.

"The d-dogs focus on the boar after the herd runs. He was rousted up but he ain't scattering. This boar is looking for a fight. I think he'd been hunted before and knew some tricks because he set himself up a defensive fighting perimeter. D-og would come in one side to nip at him and draw his attention, then a different dog w-would come in from a different side. See, the dogs worry a hog like that and wear him down.

"This boar was calculating. Like I said, he'd been hunted before and know'd with his size he c-ouldn't out run the dogs. I think he decided to stand his g-ground.

"He caught one of Garl's dogs with a tusk and tossed it. Dog shook it off and went back in. Didn't seem to be hurt, but you know when dogs get into hunting mode, there's a whole lot of s-tuff they don't notice and you don't notice til everything's over.

Wink used both hands to drink his coffee. The cup clattered as he tried to return it to the saucer. He got the cup on the saucer but managed to flip the spoon.

****

"Usually the dogs are holding it and Garl sends his c-catch dog in. S-she charges right up there and takes a hold of the hog by its nose. Usually the hog is in so much pain, it can't move. You walk up and give the hog the kill shot. Hunt's over. You know'd it, dogs know'd it, and the hog most certainly know'd it.

"But, it wasn't like that. Garl and I were so busy watching the d-dogs work we weren't looking for those two. Garl let Lights Out off the leash and she went running to snag that boar. She did her job and hung on good and tight to the nose.

"The boar shook her off and d-dang if she didn't take part of the hog's nose with her; she was hanging on that tight. There she s-stood, quivering with a chunk of hog nose in her mouth, totally surprised. She's never, and I mean *never*, had a hog shake her off. But, like I said, this was not your run of the mill boar."

Bill had to fight the urge to turn around when Wink looked at the woods.

"That said, this was not a normal hunt, not with Lights Out getting s-shook off a hog."

Wink was scared. Bill stopped rolling the stem of his coffee spoon and laid it down beside his cup.

"None of Garl's dogs are quitters." Wink continued. "Four dogs moved back in to get the b-boar held tight. It's time to drop the hog and end the hunt.

"But the boar w-ent down with a thud, almost crushed the one dog, and its howl set the other dog to letting loose. Brave little Lights Out went in on her own to grab the boar by its nose again. Like an issue of professional pride, but this time she didn't get ahold of the nose. Her timing was off. The boar hooked her by the shoulder and tossed her like a rag doll. He tossed all the dogs out of the kill zone.

"This was all gettin' out of hand so we slung our rifles over our s-s-shoulders and h-hurried down the hill. The Pittie was laying in the brush with b-blood coming from her side. We were gonna get Lights Out before the boar could crush her. The pack dogs were s-standing back, their sides heaving, looking at each other trying to figure out what's next because they never met a hog they couldn't worry, wear out, and hold.

"I'll say some of what happened was my f-ault. We just couldn't figure out that b-boar and the dogs. It didn't make sense what was going on.

"Those guys come up out of the bushes with tactical knives in each hand and started hacking and stabbing that boar. Blood was flying and they were screaming as they were hacking. They scared the dogs so bad that two Redbones slunk away peeing as they went.

"Garl's dog's are seasoned hunters. But they know'd in their dog brains that it wasn't supposed to happen like this. Those dogs know'd from experience there'll be a big bang and the hog is dead and the hunt is over. They know'd that, but what they didn't know was those two men, I mean they're big men, comin' out of the woods like savages from prehistoric times. The dogs never saw a human act like an animal.

"The one guy jumped on like a cowboy roping a steer. He sunk his knife in the boar's throat and twisted it to the ground. What kind of man straddles the back of a hog and stabs it?

"Stuck the knife right up to the hilt in that hog's throat, cutting its windpipe so poor pig couldn't give a death cry. The other guy was stabbing and hacking along the boar's back. Sliced the spinal column so the rear quarters didn't work. Was almost like a wrestling match with them tag teaming the boar.

"I noticed the dogs were backing away. Never saw that before, Bill. But I never saw a hog like that either. Must have been 550 pounds."
****

Amy quietly placed two glasses of water on the table when she made her round. Wink took his and drank it down. Bill moved his glass over to Wink, who was sweating through his shirt.

After a few deep breaths, Wink studied his hands, forcing them to stop trembling.

"Bill, a herd can charge. A sounder can take a notion and come to a group decision just like people can. A shoat startled up from the brush and got sliced with one of those tactical knives. It started screaming and squealing and dang if the sow didn't backtrack to the sound of her baby in pain. Well, the sow came charging right into the fricas and she was calling the other hogs to her. She was calling them to their death.

"The boar was done for and dead, but those two turned on the charging sow. They tag teamed her just like they did the boar. One of them jumps on the sow's back and hangs on to her tusks while he's stabbing her in the neck. The other guy rolled on the ground and cut the sow's hamstrings. Now momma hog is realizing she's no use of her hind legs. It's gone from being on the offense to realizing it's fighting for its own life.

"Hogs have tusks growing from their jaws; cutters on the top usually sharpened by the whetters on the bottom. They can slice your femoral artery and you bleed out in the woods. But those leggings I told you about couldn't be punctured by the tusks. When the boar tried to slash, the tusks just slipped off. When the sow tried to bite, her tusk wouldn't take hold. The hogs couldn't use their natural weapons."

Bill asked, "Do you think they were military people? Like Special Operations?"

"I don't know. You're the sheriff and I'll go with what you think. I got to finish this and get it off my chest."

"Sure, Wink. I'm sorry I interrupted you."

"Garl started to call the dogs but once they got to the outskirts of the killing madness, they snuck up the hill as best they could, their tails between their legs. The dogs know'd they'd been beat and got out of there to save their own lives."

Wink stared at his cup. He took a ragged breath and shook his head.

"It was pitiful to see those dogs defeated. Awful to see the look in their eyes." Wink briefly glanced around the diner to distract himself from the memory.

"But those two, Bill, those two were still flashin' knives and roaring. There was so much blood and screaming, that I couldn't tell the difference between the hogs screaming in death or those two men screaming because *they were Death*.

"We were just thunderstruck. This was an insult to nature. Put everything out of balance. It damaged the sanctity of the forest in the worst possible way.

"It was savagery. There was maybe eight additional hogs dead or dying when it all settled down. What hogs wasn't dead, they went around and stick 'em until they were. Then they stood in the middle of all the carnage, put their heads back and roared at the sky."

He didn't hold back the tears rolling down his cheeks as his mind replayed the scene.

"Just a second, Bill." Wink pulled a blue bandana out of his back pocket. He wiped his face and eyes, and blew his nose. "Excuse me, please. I'm okay."

****

"Garl got his dogs gathered in their travel crates and tucked away. Never seen d-dogs so depressed and shocked after a hunt. They just s-shook in their crates. Garl held Lights Out in his arms like he w-would a baby, she was still b-bleeding bad from the gash but her insides warn't coming out. Boar caught her just behind her vest. Could have tore her chest out but didn't."

Wink's eyes started to fill again, but he wiped them dry with the paper napkin from under the edge of the saucer.

"I spread plastic on the back seats. They got in the truck and didn't say a word. I kept my eyes on the road and dropped them off at the cabin. When I heard the cabin screen door slam shut, I drove straight down the road.

"I met Garl at Dr. Glassman's and helped with the dogs. Out of the total of six dogs, Garl had one with a broken leg, one with a cracked pelvis, and all them five got stitches someplace or another. The Pit got blood transfusion, stitches, and had to have her front leg taken off."

Bill asked, "Did you tell him how the dogs got hurt?"

"No. Just said it was a hunt that went bad." Wink cleared his throat.

"Then I helped Garl get three stitched dogs home, settled, cleaned up. Told him I would take care of Dr. Glassman's invoices. Last thing Garl said to me was he was done. Not going to hunt hogs anymore. His dogs are retired and so is he. He went in the house and shut the door."

"What'd you say to your wife?"

"When Hazel asked me how it went, I just said it was good. Took everything I had to keep my voice steady. I got a thousand dollar tip and I hid it in the truck. I couldn't tell her how I got the money so I didn't tell her at all. I didn't want to touch the bills with my bare hands.

"Hazel said they skedaddled out, took what belongings they brought, even cleaned up the bathroom and folded the sheets on the foot of the beds. Bathroom smelled like bleach. She found a hundred dollar bill under each of the pillows. They put extra cash on the hunting invoice, too.

"I could not look that woman in the face and tell what happened. The coward in me came out and *I lied*.

"I said it was a big tip for a good hunt and maybe we should put half of it in the church collection for the new handicapped steps or something. Well, it was two hundred dollars and you know Hazel's big heart, so she put it all in.

"It's the only way to sanitize money from people like that. And the thousand dollars they left me? Buried out in Dolly Sods bog. The earth will know what to do with it. Garl and me though you should know."

"I'm glad you did." Bill sat back in the booth, his mind working about what his next step would be.

"Garl said he'd verify what I say if you wanted, but he ain't getting out of the truck. He's still shocked. Maybe more than me. You know how he is about his dogs and I don't know how long it'll take him to get over it.

"When I was a kid I sometimes had nightmares about monsters. Always wondered if I dream about monsters, what do monsters dream about? Well, now I know. When monsters have nightmares it's about those two guys. That kind of savagery is found in the nightmares of monsters."

"Do you have any idea where they went when they left?"

"No. I can get you the address they registered with."

Bill drummed the table with his fingers once. "You call me if anything comes up. You rest and take care of those dogs."

"Thanks, Sheriff. I'll tell Garl." Wink wiped his face and eyes one more time before he left.

****

Mike slid into the seat vacated by Wink. Sheriff Harris looked up. "You heard?"

"All of it," Mike replied. "More than I wanted. I'd like to offer my services if you need them."

"I'm stretched pretty thin with two staff members to Waybird City for training. Hodding blew his knee falling out of a boat. Can you handle a gun? Any good in a fight?"

Mike Green's brain lit up with the images of shooting his way out of a cold recess of at the headwaters of *Ozero Bol'shoye Shcuch'uye* in Siberia "Yes, I can and yes, I am."

"Are you sure?" Bill smiled.

"Pretty sure."

Gracie sashayed her way to the booth. "Are you boys ready for breakfast? Dodger's chompin' at the bit to get cookin."

Mike grinned broadly. "Sure. Gracie, put this on my tab. I may need the good sheriff here to fix a speeding ticket some time."

"Fat chance of that, Mike. I've watched you drive." Bill thought he caught movement in the woods when he watched Wink's truck pull out.

"Gracie, tell Dodger I'm ready for breakfast and cook the eggs over hard or he's under arrest."

PENNI

THE BELL ABOVE THE grocery store door tinkled when Hector Cobb made a morning visit to the grocery store.

"Morning, Ambrie,"

"Morning, Hector. What can I do for you?" Ambrie adjusted her glasses. The heaviness of the lens made them ride down on her nose.

"Nothing much, Ambrie. Say, doll, you got any fresh coffee and a donut?"

"Hector, you know I do. You're such a scoundrel."

Ambrie chuckled as she took a napkin from the stack. "You smelled the coffee when you pulled up in the drive. You've got the same nose your bloodhounds do and before you ask, Bill's already been here and got his share of donuts. You know he just loves the ones I make on the weekends. Crunchy outside like his grandma made."

"I'll take a coffee and a donut then. Ambrie, you know if I was thirty years older I'd give you a whirl around the valley for those donuts."

"Hector, if I was thirty years younger, I just might take you up on it. Still want four sugars in the coffee?"

"Yes, please. Maybe five. Alice made me clean the house yesterday and I'm still feelin' a little weak from the exertion."

"You are a *liar!*"

Laughing, Ambrie came around the counter and filled a cup for Hector. She added five teaspoons of sugar, no cream, and put the last donut, plus the remaining half of a broken one, on a napkin. "When Dr. Glassman says you've got diabetes, don't come crying to me."

"Ambrie, I'm training dogs and I need all the sugar I can get to keep up with them."

"Who's in training now?"

"Well, I'm fine tuning Rip as a replacement for Dotty. She's past ten almost. A new pup is coming from a guy in Tennessee next week. There's Hank for conditioning, but he's a cadaver dog so I don't want to put him on anything alive. Alice thinks I should go find a dog from Mom's original lines."

"You better think long and hard about what Alice says. That girl's got enough brains to dish out a second helping to everyone in the Hollar."

"That she does, Miss Ambrie. That she does.'

"How's the donut?"

"Excellent, as always, doll."

"Whatcha got in the bag?"

"Just some more stuff for your lost and found board. One of my dogs brings home more than you can shake a stick at."

"What'd you mean?"

Hector pulled a stool out from under the counter, and seated, stirred his coffee. "I've got this girl who started digging under the fence. Never had a dog dig out like this one and I'm worried she'll get the other ones started."

"Oh, dear, no. Could get hit by a car or shot. Maybe even coyotes would get her in the wild."

"Yeah, I thought that, but she always comes back and brings me things."

"You don't mind if I do this while we talk, do you?" Ambrie held up a carton of shorts. "I gotta get the cigarette rack filled."

"No, go ahead. But, like I was saying, that dog digs out under the fence, then she's gone for hours. Always comes back but she, well, like here–I got a paper bag full." Hector took out items, laying them on the counter.

"Here's one shoe, a little girl shoe. Now, who lets their kid walk around in one shoe? And here–here's a gold hoop earring. And here's a hankie all embroidered with little designs all around the edges. And, hum...here's a kid's sock, and here's a piece of elastic with a hook on it–and here's a little silver bracelet."

"Lots of kids will lose one shoe. Sometimes they throw them out the car window and the parents don't know it. Same with the socks. That elastic looks like the strap off a woman's bra, the shoulder strap. Suppose she found some old campsite in the woods and all this stuff is left over from tourists?"

"Could be. But the stuff doesn't look like it's been out in the weather all year. No wear on the baby shoe. Mind if I put it up on the lost and found? That earring looks expensive."

"Go ahead. Give me the hankie. I'll wash it then put it up. Tourist might come around and want it back. The embroidery is beautiful."

"Thanks, Ambrie."

"I just thought of something, Hector. Why don't you follow her once? Besides, she might be trying to tell you something in her dog way."

"I just might do that."

"Which dog?"

"Penni. Her name is Penni."

****

"Alright, honey, Daddy's gonna be right behind you so I want you to take your little walk and show me where you been and what you're up to in the woods."

Hector kissed the bloodhound on the point of her head, adjusted her reflective collar, and patted her neck. Penni sat for a few moments, digging at the loose hair on her side. She shook her head, lacing Hector's pant leg with a string of drool, then ambled off into the woods with Hector close behind.

"K9 to Base. K9 to Base." Hector let go of the call button and waited for a response.

"Base to K9. This is Bill. What's up, K9?"

"Yeah, hey, Bill. I'm going on a little walk with Penni, so maybe just keep your ears open. If it's nothing, I'll let you know. Over.

"Copy K9. I'll be available. Over."

"Copy Base. K9 Out."

"Base Out."

****

Cleveland Coop sat across from Bill in the communications room.

"Sorry we didn't get the interviews from Aunt Gem. Cliffer warned you she probably wouldn't say anything."

"Some folk are like that, Sheriff. My mother was pretty closed-mouthed about everything even though dad said she talked him to death when they were alone." Coop took a sip from the soda can. "Hector out working his dog?"

"No, not in the traditional sense. He's got one that takes off now and again and brings crap back the tourists leave at the camp sites. His little dog is filling up Ambrie's board over at the store." Bill flipped through a couple of flyers from the Feds. "I see your associate arrived."

"What? He made the FBI Most Wanted?" Coop joked.

"Ha! I didn't mean he was in my pile, but, hey, I'll keep an eye out for him."

"Ubell Gant. Very astute in the lab handling unique evidence. He's been with the Bureau for a number of years. I would like to see if I could get him to work for the state, but I don't know how the benefits compare. With some experience in the field, I think he could be my replacement."

"Sounds like a good guy. Are you hungry? I think Gracie's got pulled pork, chips, and asparagus on special today."

"Pork sounds good to me." Coop gathered his briefcase and coat.

****

Hector checked his watch and GPS on his phone, matching everything with the compass his mom gave him when he made his first find with a bloodhound–"Just in case you need a compass, son, now you got one."

Penni was plodding along a trail only she could find. She stopped periodically, cast on the wind, and then carried on sorting through the moisture, moss, and debris. The webbing between her toes gave her sure footing in the muck. She trotted along in her own special way, not hurried, not pressured, just a dog out on a walk.

Hector whispered to himself, "I should have let Alice show you in the ring. That would put all of them scallywags in their place. You're dang near perfect conformation, classic head, and a smart nose to boot. Maybe a pup out of you."

Hector saved his route on his phone app. They covered several miles in the time they were moving.

Penni started circling a small area.

"Well, it's about time you showed Daddy what you've been up to. Here, let me see."

He picked up a stick and pushed back the edges of the plastic bag. The smell of an aged diaper hit his nose. "How'd you stand that, girl? Whew. What we got here?"

Using the stick to prod the bag, he found bloody clothes, socks, pairs of girl's panties, broken combs, cups, empty jars of baby food, and a store receipt from Syke's Grocery. A little deeper in the bag Hector used the stick to flip open a pink jewelry box.

"What in good hell?" He fished out a gold hoop earring. Looking at Penni, he watched her sit and cast on the currents coming off the cliff edge above them.

"Want to go up there, girl?" He snapped the lead onto her collar and gave the command seek.

Penni charged up the steep cliff with her handler keeping pace. Hector wasn't but six feet behind her. He leapt over a boulder and scanned the area as he brought his body up to the high ground. He pulled his Glock 19 out of the holster and was at the ready.

Penni walked slowly to a white bundle on the ground. She dropped to the down position and placed her head between her paws, signaling the search was over.

Hector could see what was beneath the thin veil. "Oh, my Lord."

PULLED PORK AND CHIPS

LUKE PULLED OUT THE chair and secured the bumper seat to the rails. Assured it was secure, he lifted his sister into the seat and pushed her up to the table. He sat Bentley in her lap.

Maggie pulled on Luke's shirt sleeve. "Luke, see it goes like this. The color goes right next to the line. But you don't put it outside over here because it always goes this side of the line. Not over here. Right here by the line and the other color goes by this line here, but not out of there over here."

"I see, Maggs. That's very good. Who showed you how to color?"

"Tater. And Mom. And Dad. But not you."

"Now that you've chastised your brother," Elsie smiled, "please color in your book while we order. Remember to tell Gracie thank you."

"Okay." She tapped Luke on the arm. "Here's the red color goes here on this part inside the line."

"Got it, Maggs."

"You said you had some friends meeting us here?" Howard added cream to his coffee.

"Yes, I think so. They called early this morning."

Elsie smiled at her son. "We don't have to order right now. We can wait awhile."

"Mom, Dad, I need to tell you something about them."

Elsie and Howard looked at each other then back to Luke, waiting for some bomb shell to hit.

"Son," Howard said, "if this is about S-E-X, maybe we should meet without someone..."

"Dad, no. Not at all."

"Okay, then what? Remember I don't want your sister exposed to..."

"Dad, don't jump to conclusions."

"What then?"

"They're in the Army. They're Rangers."

Howard opened a pack of crackers for Maggie. "Your mother and I don't live in the bottom half of a clamshell. We know about special forces. How'd you meet them?"

"Through work. I was asked to provide information about the geography of a place they were going to. We kind of hit it off and when they're in D.C., we all get together."

"I'm glad you made friends, Luke. I was concerned about you moving there. That "inside the beltway" I hear on the news, well, those folks don't share the same values we do." Elsie reached across the table and adjusted the bow on Maggie's hair. "I don't want you to lose your upbringing."

"Mom, they're a little rough around the edges, but highly intelligent and skilled in what they do."

Howard fed a teaspoon of his sugary coffee to Maggie. "And what do they do?"

"They each have specialties. Zero works in combat engineering, Scout in telecommunications, Cobalt is a linguist, and Diego is a medic."

"Honey, do you know their real names?" Elsie watched Maggie pick a new color from the box.

"No, but their code name is what they're always called."

"They all gots a cold, Luke?"

"No, Maggs. It's called 'code' names. Like special names."

"Do you like this one, Luke?" Maggie held up a purple and red dog.

"Yes, it's very good. Here, let me hold Bentley for you so you have more room to color."

Magdelyn handed the stuffed dog to her brother. "He got hurt but Dr. Andy fixed him."

Luke looked at his mother while he kept the toy under the table, feeling for the microchips inserted in Moscow.

"The twins can tell you better as it's their story to tell, but suffice to say Bentley was pretty torn up after a young coyote came into the yard. Your sister, the courageous soul that she is, wouldn't let go. After Nathan shot it, Magdelyn insisted we go to Dr. Glassman's for repairs. You can see one eye is a button. He did an amazing job taking care of all three of us."

"Nathan shot a coyote? With Maggs playing tug-o-war on the other end?"

Barbara came to the table with water glasses, and topped off the coffee. "Want another juice, Maggie?"

"No, thank you but you can come see how I color inside the lines."

"That's great, honey. Yes, we have purple and red critters in the Hollar just like that." She smiled at Elsie. "You folks ready?"

As Howard placed the order for the pulled pork sandwich specials and a grilled cheese for his daughter, Luke saw the black truck with darkened windows pull in the parking lot. Whoever was driving went to the far end making sure there was enough room for the trailer. Luke swallowed hard—*Lord knows what they brought with them.*

He watched his friends from the Afghanistan mission exit the truck. "Mom, Dad, they're here. Be right back."

Howard pushed an empty table to join theirs and placed four more chairs, as Barbara set extra place settings.

"Guys, this is my Mom and Dad, Elsie and Howard Perkins. And this is my sister, Maggie. Mom, Dad, Maggie, this is Zero, Cobalt, Scout, and Diego. These are the guys I did research for."

All four shook Howard's hand.

"Glad to meet you, Mrs. Perkins and Miss Perkins," Zero said.

"Gee, you guys take up the whole table," Maggie noticed.

"Magdelyn, don't be rude," Howard said.

"We are kind of big, Miss Perkins, but gentle as puppies. Do you mind if I sit next to you?" Cobalt smiled, immediately smitten by the little girl. Maybe some day he would father one just like her.

"Do you know how to color?"

"A little bit."

"I see someone colored on your arm." Maggie examined Cobalt's sleeve of tattoos.

"Yes, they did. Do you like them?" He felt the softness of her breath on his skin.

"Yep. They did a good job and stayed in the lines."

"Magdelyn, that's enough of staring at Mr. Cobalt's arm. Pay attention." Elsie handed her daughter a yellow crayon.

****

After Barbara took the extra orders, Howard asked Zero, "My son says he has done some research for you. Do you four always work together?"

Zero responded, "Not always, Mr. Perkins..."

"Please call me Howard."

"Okay, Howard, not always, but we've been together on several missions recently. The commander let us have some time off, so we decided to come here. Luke spoke highly of the area."

"We've got some of the best brook trout fishing in the state. And, if you're interested in exploring new places, my twins are pretty experienced cavers. They've got a lot of them mapped out."

Diego nodded. "Interesting. We've got several weeks, so that sounds like a good option for exercise."

"I'm hungry, Mom. When do they bring food?"

"Magdelyn, we don't interrupt when adults are talking. Here's a cracker." Elsie saw the police cruiser pull beside the black truck driven by Luke's friends. "Magdelyn, there's your favorite sheriff."

"Where?"

"Coming in the front door."

Luke saw his sister wiggle off her chair, assisted by Cobalt, then run across the dining room to jump into Sheriff Harris's arms. Mike Green and Special Agent Coop followed him in.

"How's my girl?"

"I'm good. Luke brought his friends home and guess what?"

"What?"

"That big one knows how to color!" Maggie pointed to Cobalt.

Elsie rolled her eyes and covered her face. "I'm sorry. She hasn't learned how to think before she speaks."

"Mrs. Perkins, I actually like her honesty. None of these guys ever tell me how well I stay within the lines." The Rangers smiled.

The sheriff put Maggie back in her bumper seat. Luke stood to make the introductions.

Mike gave no indication he knew the Rangers. "Nice to meet you, gentlemen."

"Feeling is mutual, I'm sure," Zero responded.

"I hope you boys enjoy your vacation here in the Hollar. Fishing is good. Do you boys hunt?" Bill asked.

"Well, yes, actually we do," Cobalt nodded.

****

Barbara seated Sheriff Bill, Coop, and Mike in the fourth booth by the window and took their orders. Bill made the formal introduction between Mike and Cleveland.

"Coop, I don't know if you've run into Mike since you've been here, but he was a deputy sheriff in Michigan. Mike, Cleveland here works with the state forensic lab in Charleston. He's here looking over our evidence protocols."

"Can't say that I've had the pleasure of meeting you, Mike. I'm sure the sheriff has a good eye for competent help. Will you be joining the department full time?"

"No, sir. I'm just filling in while Bill has deputies in training and on sick leave. I'll be happy to go back to my retirement activities of landscape painting and gardening."

"A painter?"

"Yes, I was in the business of evaluating art, coordinating exhibits, and connecting artists with agents."

"Sounds interesting. Did you travel a lot? I thought I detected a slight accent."

"You probably did, Cleveland. I lived in Europe for a number of years. I had to go where the museums are to make my living. Barcelona, London, Paris, and I was in Cairo for several years."

Coop nodded. "I had thought about traveling after retirement, but I'm more inclined to settle around this area. Amazingly calm and peaceful for an old man like myself."

"Is retirement close on the horizon?"

"Yes, Mike, I'm counting the weeks."

Barbara brought a cell phone over to Sheriff Harris. "Hector Cobb's trying to get you, Sheriff."

"Thanks, Barbara. Hector, what's up?"

"I need you up here."

"Where?"

"About 300 yards off the turn of Green Snake Falls."

"Penni took you that far?"

"Yeah. I think I found the owner of the baby shoe, maybe the earrings, too."

"We don't have tourists up there, Hector."

Bill looked across the table at his lunch guests. Mike and Coop watched the blood drain from his face. Bill stopped talking for a few seconds as he heard Hector break into sobs.

"Okay, we'll be there. Yes, I'll tell him." Bill laid the phone on the table and took a long drink of the ice water before he spoke.

"Gentlemen, duty calls. Coop, can you swing around and pick up Ubell and his equipment?"

"Yes, I can."

"Meet me and Mike at the office and you can follow us."

"Sounds serious."

"It is." He looked at Maggie Perkins happily selecting colors for Cobalt to use on the page she told him to color. "The worst kind of serious."

****

"Must be in a rush. They didn't get their order," Zero commented.

Barbara brought four extra pulled pork specials. "This is on Sheriff Bill. He said you big guys would need more to fill you up."

Howard gave his potato chips to Maggie. "What's going on, Barbara?"

"I don't know," she replied. "Hector and one of his dogs are up the other side of the mountain. We'll know soon enough the way talk flies down the hillside. Enjoy your meals."

<h1 style="text-align:center">ROLLED INTO THE
DEEP</h1>

"CLARENCE, YOU DON'T LOOK so good."

"I ain't, Jose. You gotta take me to the doctor. I got this coldness in my feet and legs...my chest hurts."

"How am I going to do that? Jiggy took the car and ain't come back. I told you not to give him money."

"I know, I know. But he'll be back any day. The truck here?"

"Yeah."

"Then get the keys and help me up. I can't lay in this bed anymore. I need some medicine...maybe a mustard plaster...I just ain't well, Jose."

"Okay, I got it. Hold on, Clarence. I'll be right back to get you."

Jose's eye began twitching as he fumbled putting the key into the ignition. Tears from the irritation fell down his cheek–"Come on, you *puta,* start!"

The motor turned over and Jose gunned the engine to keep it running. He backed up over a couple of garbage bags, then found first gear. He stomped on the accelerator, throwing sand from under the rear wheels as he drove toward the cabin. Jose took the front steps two at a time.

"Okay, partner, let me help you. I got the truck by the front door."

"Wait...wait." Clarence struggled to get his breath. "First...first...you gotta move the product...get them up to the cave. Gotta hide them. Not...here."

"But you said to get you to the doctors."

"Move them up to the cave, stupid. If Boss and his crew find their way here, they'll take the girls and all the plans are ruined." Clarence rolled to the side of the bed and coughed blood, brown phlegm, and mucus on the floor.

Jose hurried to the kitchen, gagging and throwing up in the sink. "Okay, okay. Just stay there."

He grabbed the keys to the shed and fumbled with them before he could get the key inserted. It was impossible to focus on the keyhole with one eye tearing and draining. Jose popped the padlock open and put his shoulder to the door.

The girls shuddered against the wall, shielding their eyes from the sudden light.

"Come on, come on," Jose growled. "Get moving." He herded them out of the shack and up the trail to the opening of the cave several yards behind the cabin. The youngest ones started to cry but were shushed by the older girls who held them tightly against their shoulders.

Jose unlocked the barred gate and slammed it shut behind the last one. There was already a group of four young girls in the cave, emaciated and filthy from neglect.

"And shut up. I'll be back." He raised his hand as if to back hand the one closest. They cowered, having felt his wrath before. Jose slammed the iron gate closed. He growled at the captives then pivoted to return to the cabin.

****

"Get me in the truck."

Jose put Clarence's arm over his shoulder and put his arm around Clarence's waist half carrying the gray skeletonized stick of a man down the steps. At the truck, Jose opened the passenger door and lifted Clarence into the seat.

"Fasten the seatbelt, Clarence."

"What do you think I'm a baby? It cuts off my air. Just...just get going...Oh, God, I can har..dly breathe."

"Okay, okay. Just hold on. I'll get you there, but Deacon's Hollar is closer."

"God, how I wish Franklin was here. He...he should have made contact by now. No, don't go to the Hollar. Ca..can't show my face there. But here." Clarence handed Jose a piece of paper as Jose drove the truck down the drive and turned onto the dirt road.

"What?"

"Here, a contact. Wal–Walter Venter. He's there. Get to him. Tell. Tell him I'm in Waybird. Walter knows...how...the plan."

"How come I never heard of him?"

"I just...for..got."

Jose stomped the accelerator in anger at the idea of a new name and face in the operation. Clarence was pinned back against the seat as the rear wheels dug into the gravel.

As Jose drove, his anger increased. He visualized Clarence and Venter dividing up Jose's share, piles of money Jose would never have, naked women he would never touch, or expensive tequila never tickling the back of his throat; all of it gone because Clarence took on another partner.

At the bottom of the S-turn, Jose handled the silver truck well but he came out of the curve and into the next turn too fast. He was close to the edge of the cliff. The passenger door popped open, and Clarence disappeared from the seat.

Jose slammed on the brakes. He jumped out of the truck and ran back to the curve. Looking down the cliff face, he watched Clarence make the last of his fall, caught by the thick branch of a dead tree projecting over the stones.

"Hey, Clarence. I told you to fasten your seatbelt."

Jose watched Clarence flail his arm, pointing to his legs.

"What's that? Your legs? They look broke. Tell you what," Jose shouted, "I'll go get help. You just stay there, you old cheating bastard. I'll be right back. Maybe with your friend Walter. Suck on that idea, *puta.*"

Jose looked across the valley at the village below. There was no evidence of a vehicle coming toward him, and no dust from the road behind him. He bit his lip and looked back down at Clarence waving at him.

"Yeah, I'll be right back." Jose walked to the truck and decided to go to Waybird City for a hamburger and a beer. He had to think about this Walter Venter guy.

****

"Oh, God," Clarence called. "I'm in so much pain."

He saw Jose peak over the edge and stare at him. His voice was cut short by the liquid pooling in his lungs. He moaned and drew irregular breaths. Rolling his head side to side, Clarence thought he saw a white dog staring at him.

"Come here, boy. Come. Keep old Clarence warm, just until Jose comes back with help."

The dog sat, gazing along Clarence's face, chest, legs. It heard him cry out when he moved his feet or a muscle spasm jerked his quad. The animal was joined by two others, all white as light with dazzling blue eyes. The threesome sat quietly while Clarence begged them to go for help; he pleaded with the dogs to go get their master.

"Then go to hell, you worthless curs. Go to hell."

They rose in unison and walked to Clarence as a gentle mist encompassed him, dampening his feverish forehead, sapping what air he had in his lungs.

"Worthless curs," were the last words he said as the strong jaws and sharp teeth clamped around his throat.

Angels

HECTOR VOMITED ONE MORE time, thinking that would be the last of it. He was wrong.

Sheriff Harris and Mike Green each got out of their marked cars, while Cleveland Coop and Ubell Gant parked just behind. The forensic men unloaded equipment to evaluate a crime scene.

Hector sat with his hand on Penni's head and kept his eyes averted from Bill's face.

"You okay, Hector?"

"Yeah, Bill." Hector stood and spun, emptying the bile from his stomach in the weeds.

"Just point what you want me to see."

After a few more dry heaves, the bloodhound handler picked up Penni's lead and clipped it to his belt.

"Back this way, Bill."

"Just a second, Hector," Coop said. "Let Ubell and me go first. Might be evidence along the way we need to collect."

"Sorry. I know better. You can see the broken brush where Penni and I came out. I carried Penni so there's just my trail."

"Hector, stay here with Mike." Bill nodded to Mike. "I've got some antacids in the first aid kit. If you feel like it, there's water and electrolytes. Might settle your guts."

"Thanks, Bill."

****

Mike shook water and powder in the bottle.

"If you think you can handle it, take just a sip, Hector. You're looking a little rough."

"Thanks. I normally have a pretty strong stomach, but this scene got to me."

"Sometimes that happens." Mike squeezed Hector's shoulder. "We all have our soft spots."

He reached down and patted the dog on the head. "Nice looking hound, Hector. She's sleek, shiny, not too big. Did you train her yourself?"

"Yeah, I train all my own. Have done some outside training for law enforcement, but that's tapered off."

"I should've had you train my pup. It kept running to the Crawford boy but the woman's boyfriend didn't like it so it was given to the little Perkins boy."

"Tater? Better off with Tater than that Venter guy Miss Crawford took up with."

"Yeah, that's what I thought."

"Those are good boys."

"They come up the mountain and spy on me."

"Elsie would tan their hides for bothering you."

"Nah. It's gotten to be a game. They think they're spies, international men of danger. It's something I look forward to."

"Well, if they get to be too much, send them home."

"Okay. Feeling better, Hector?"

"Yeah. Thanks. My stomach's settled."

****

The men were stony faced as they surveyed the area; scattered trash, torn garbage bags, and the form of a small child, then another, then another.

Coop took charge of the evidence collection. "We cordon off this area. We need to get Hector's input with his dogs and find out how many more bodies and then we'll try to piece together how they got here. Ubell and I can set up a field lab over there once Hector clears it."

"Good. Sounds like a plan." Sheriff Bill added, "I've got an undertaker in Waybird City can keep the bodies for examination by a coroner. He'll keep his mouth shut until we're ready to make an announcement. No sense getting people riled up before we know what we got."

"Bill," Coop said, "don't get your heart set on any definitive reports. These kids have been out here for a while. Ubell can take samples and send them into the state lab, but answers will probably be speculative."

"Doesn't Ubell work for the feds?" Bill asked.

"He's working under me for the time being."

Bill made his way back to the roadside. Hector looked better after getting fluids in him.

"Hector, we need a cadaver dog in the area. Coop wants to map just what we've got here."

"Sure, Bill. I'll radio Alice. She can drop off Cricket or Hank and pick up Penni."

"Mike, I'm making you full time immediately. There's extra uniforms at my office, badges in my center drawer, and I can get you a weapon."

"No need. I've guns at home. I can use those and save the county ammo."

"Good. Stop by Ambrie Sykes to let her know you'll be picking up her cash at closing. When we're done here, you and me can make some trips around the county and see what we can flush out of the brush."

****

Ubell plugged the battery charger into the car's outlet. He organized the batteries so two would always be full and ready. He checked the camera and video and inserted a clean recording stick, then checked the software with his computer. In the truck, he found plastic bags sorted by size. Ubell made sure he had six new marking pens, tape, a box of nitrile gloves, alcohol, forceps and tweezers. Specimen boxes were stacked according to size and the correct lids were contained with each. The rolls of labels were color coded. He wondered if eight flashlights were too many.

Mumbling to himself, "I'm sure I'm not missing anything." But he checked it again.

A whiff of decomposition made him stand up with a start.

"What the hell?" Ubell sniffed the area not unlike one of Hector's bloodhounds. He judged the air currents to be rising from the valley floor. Ubell saw the chrome bumper of a red car glint in the sunlight. Oozing down the side of the car was bloody material, some gelatinous, some liquid, some dried, but all of it goo.

"Coop! Coop!"

****

Jose parked the truck just off the main highway going through Waybird City. He needed time to think and he was hungry. The fat hamburger and a thick chocolate shake from the drive-in would energize him. "The bitch left the cheese off it," he said aloud.

He grabbed a pickle falling from the back of the sandwich before it dropped on the seat between his legs. Looking up he saw the two black Humvees stopped at the traffic light.

"Screw that all to hell. Boss is here. He'll call Clarence–where's the phone–I bet that bastard took it with him down the cliff." Feeling panicked, he searched the passenger side of the truck.

"Wait–it's on the floor–how do I cover Clarence being gone?" Jose watched the vehicles as they went through the intersection. "Yeah, Clarence stole the product and left me holding the bag. I can give Boss the ones I got, get paid, and Venter and me can take the next load."

Boss was followed by a large green truck with two men in it. He'd never seen them before: pale white skin, bald, and looking at people walking along the street like they were two tigers in a cage selecting a tourist for lunch. He couldn't help but shiver.

****

Mike went back to the sheriff's office. The pants on the shelf were too big but he did get a khaki shirt, badge, and equipment belt. He snagged a belt holster for the gun he would bring from home.

He saw a box of new uniforms still in their plastic. Interested to see if any were his size, he took the entire inventory out of the box, sorting them on the desk. Each stack reached its limit and slid to the floor.

"Blin."

He restacked the poly clear shirt bags and the whole pile slipped to the floor again.

"Blyat." Mike cursed in Russian. He put the box on the desk, picked up the wrapped pants from the floor. He sorted them one by one. He noticed the last pair of pants were his size. *"Suka sin,* for me."

His joy turned to grief as he turned and knocked the box over on the floor with his elbow.

"Dyavol! chert poberi. govno!"

Frustrated, he up righted the box and threw everything back in. Putting the container on the shelf, he glared at it. *"Davai suka, padai."* The box stayed put.

"I need coffee."

Mike filled the aluminum pot with cold water. He added what he thought would be enough grounds. He turned the heat on high.

He found a pair of handcuffs and a key; in the back closet, a hat.

In the interim, the coffee pot, missing its lid, began to boil. Not just boil, but boil with the fury of a volcano. Water and coffee grounds erupted over the desk, paperwork, and Bill's chair. Mike grabbed the handle of the coffee pot barehanded.

"Yob tvoyu mat!" Mike shook his burning fingers. With the pot holder, he moved the percolator to the unused heating coil. His palm started to redden. Mike's elbow hit the roll of paper towels which landed in a puddle of coffee water on the floor.

"Eto pizdets!"

"Where's Bill?" Ambrie's voice startled Mike and he slopped hot coffee on his hand.

"You scared the daylights out of me, Miss Sykes," he said. He smiled through the pain of his blistering skin.

"I guess I did. You look like a deer caught in the headlights. What was that you said? Eat pretzels?"

"Yeah, my dad taught me that so I wouldn't swear in front of my mom. Eat pretzels!"

"That's strange. Polite, but strange. Where's Bill? I got my deposit. What are you doing in one of his shirts?"

"He deputized me, Miss Sykes. I volunteered to help out."

"That's real nice of you. Here's my deposit. Bill runs it over to Waybird City between patrols. Sure will be easier when we get a branch office here."

"Yes, it will, Miss Sykes."

"How's your dog doing? I heard it kept running away to the Crawford place. Then Tater got it."

"He's fine, Miss Sykes. I guess I'm just not a dog person."

"I guess not. When you see Sheriff Bill, tell him that a red car was at the store the other day. I didn't like the guy when he came in. Something about him made my skin crawl. He bought a bunch of snacks. Like he needed it."

"Okay, Miss Sykes. Red car."

"I already wrote down the plate and description." She paused to take a deeper breath. "Oh, and by the way, Mike, you've been here long enough, I guess you can call me Ambrie."

"Thank you, Ambrie." Mike grinned through gritted teeth. His hand was on fire.

"And don't forget to tell Bill about that car. There's something funny going on around here."

"Yes, ma'am. I certainly will. The red car. Have a nice evening, Ambrie."

"You, too, Mike."

****

"Bill, Cricket found six bodies in this grid. I think that's a total of eleven."

"Yes, unfortunately," Sheriff Harris replied. "Penni's one, Cricket for four, and then six more."

"I marked my way and the finds. I'll go let Coop know."

"Good. I think we need to keep this under wraps."

"Yeah. At least I know what Penni was doing on her forays into the woods. Smart dog. She was bringing me to find those kids."

"If she takes off again, let me know."

"I will. Here comes Coop." Hector wiped his forehead with a red bandana, then wiped the drool from the cadaver dog's mouth.

Coop and Ubell rejoined the other men.

"Pretty obvious we have a dumping ground for children. Hector and his first dog found one, then the next dog found four in grid A1, then six in grid A2. The six have been here for a while. There doesn't seem to be any more, but I'd like Hector and his dog to check here, A3, B1 and B2."

"Got it. I'll get on that." Hector squatted and gave the dog a hug.

"Traffickers have specified routes they take to keep out of sight and off the radar. They can't move groups of women and children all at once, so they have layovers. I guess West Virginia is along a route coming out of Florida and headed to Canada, probably Montreal. It's a long distance so they move, layover, then move to the next spot. These kids didn't make the trip." Coop shook his head.

"Right under our noses." Bill looked up at the wind moving the leaves of the trees.

"That's why they're so successful," Coop said. "There's an immense amount of money involved and they have an endless supply of humans to move. They sell women and children over and over so they have a continual money stream. And most of it's in plain sight."

"Any way we can find out who these kids are?" Bill asked.

"I'll take DNA, finger prints, photos, and anything I can," Ubell offered, "but don't count on any identification any time soon. We might get lucky and find a hit using the law enforcement databases, but understand these are lost kids and we may never find out anything about them."

"Ubell," Hector asked, "What happens then? What happens to these kids if they are never claimed?"

"Well, we have to make the effort to identify them and try to find a next of kin. If we come up with nothing, then the state has jurisdiction. I'm sure there're laws in West Virginia covering that situation."

"Gentlemen," Coop said, "we've got two crime scenes. I'd bet even money they're related. Ubell, you start here. I'll start across the road. Bill, the funeral director in Waybird, can he be trusted to keep this confidential?"

"I'll make that clear, Coop."
****

It was almost dawn by the time the last task at the crime scene was completed. The mortician from Waybird City left with eleven small bodies sleeping side by side in the black hearse. The tail lights of Bowtie Crawford's tow truck disappeared in the shadows of the mountain, the flashers getting dimmer with each mile toward the village.

Bill let Hector and his dog sleep as he drove them to the valley floor. Coop and Ubell discussed Ubell's future with the FBI crime lab and a possible transfer to state service on their way to the bed and breakfast.

Three white dogs watched the caravan of vehicles leave the area then trotted up a mountain path into the twilight.

GETTING TO KNOW YOU

"Hello?" Jose's hand shook as he answered Clarence's phone. The icy pause scared him.

"Let me speak to Clarence."

"He...h...he and Jiggy took off. I don't know where they went."

"Who's this?"

"Jose. Garza. Jose Garza."

"Jose, I work for Boss."

If Jose was going to survive, he needed to be convincing.

"They took the red car and most of the product and left. I think they was meaning to cut you out, but I...I was looking out for Boss and I still got ten of them stashed. I was looking out for Boss and his investment."

"Just a minute."

Jose couldn't make out the muffled words. A cold chill ran down his back.

"Why didn't Clarence take his phone? Where's Frank Wells?"

"He...h...he musta forgot it. I mean, looks like they was in a rush to get out of here and get north. We never made contact with Frank. Clarence thinks he went to Georgia."

"Why didn't you go with them?"

"To Georgia? Frank was gone before we got here. Clarence said to wait and Frank would show up."

"No, why didn't you go with Clarence and Jiggy?"

"I didn't know nothing. I was in Waybird getting supplies just like Clarence told me and when I got back they were gone."

"They took product and just left?"

"Yeah, yeah, that's right. I'm here by myself."

"Where are you, Jose? What's the address?"

"I don't know. There's just a bunch of winding dirt roads and two tracks into the mountains. I can't tell you, but I can…" The line went dead. "Hello? Hello? Are you there?"

Jose knew phones could be traced with satellites and cell towers; The caller didn't ask for directions so they must have known their way to him or at least the area. With Boss and his crew in Waybird City, it would take at least forty-five minutes to an hour to the village. It was possible Jose could get to the gas station first, fill up the truck, and head for Miami. To hell with Montreal.

****

At the cabin, Jose tore Clarence's room apart and found a duffle bag of cash in the closet. He grabbed a few plastic bags of food and supplies, then jogged up the hill to the iron gate.

"Oh, shut up, *putas*." He growled at the whimpering girls and wide eyed children as he unlocked the gate.

"Here, eat this. It'll tide you over until I get back. You got food and blankets. Just shut up." He slammed the gate hearing it latch as he ran, but not hearing the keys fall through his pocket to the soft ground.

He threw the bag of cash in the truck ignoring several fifties picked up by the wind.

****

Cobalt grabbed Luke by his shirt collar and pulled him back into the shadows of the alley along Sykes' grocery. Across the street, the ghosts from Afghanistan exited Gracie's Place.

"Whoa, there. Look what I see."

"Smith and Jones. What the hell?"

"Did you send them an invite to the barbeque? Be honest."

"No."

"And what's behind curtain number three? What would they be doing in a remote town in the middle of nowhere Appalachian mountains? You're from around here, so what's the connection?"

"I don't know but it can't be anything good. Where's Zero and Diego?"

"Over at the hunting store. Diego's going to teach Zero how to fish without explosives. Let's hope they don't come out anytime soon."

They watched Smith and Jones get into a green truck and drive west along the valley road toward the freeway.

In a few minutes, Diego and Zero walked out of the hardware shop and crossed the street. They placed most of the bags in the back of the pickup truck.

"What the hell? Trying to give me a heart attack?" Scout sat up right, rubbing his eyes and moved the bags of ammunition Zero dumped on his chest.

"Dude, I need you to fire up your satellite and do some recon. We have un-friendlies in the area," Cobalt said.

"Got it." Scout turned on his laptop. "What's the deal?"

Cobalt leaned against the vehicle. "Remember those tracking sensors on the big bad black trucks I had you follow on the way down?"

"Yeah."

"Well, a couple of our desert buddies have suddenly shown up in the Hollar."

"What? Here? Just a second and I'll be up and running."

"I have no idea why they'd be here," Luke said. "There's nothing about the Hollar that would be on CIA or government radar. No mining here anymore, no industry, just tourists and hunting. There's campgrounds around the trailheads for hikers and spelunkers."

"Well, Scout had better spelunk some information and quick." Zero adjusted his ball cap. "We need to know why they're here and what they're up to."

"Here are your sensors, bro. Waybird City at a motel by the freeway. Just like when I checked this morning. They haven't moved." Scout pointed to the indicators on the GPS map.

"Check out the plate number of this truck. They headed west. You should be able to see them." Cobalt held out his arm where he had written down the plate number.

"Okay, give me a minute. You should have written *between* the tats, bro."

"There's no between the tats, bro. Not on this arm."

"Is that a seven? Okay, okay, got them. They're under the speed limit and projected to the highway. What's up?"

"Ranger rule number one: Don't forget nothing. Remember our spooky com-rades when we set the sensors in the 'Stan?"

"You mean Zik and Zak?"

"Yes. The boys are here in Luke's picturesque village."

"That can't be good," Scout said as he viewed the screen.

Cobalt slid into the seat next to Scout. "Keep an eye on my sensors. I want to know everything you can get about them."

Luke didn't like what he saw in Cobalt's eyes or the hard set of his jaw. "Is there anything I can do?"

"Yeah, maybe," Scout replied. "Looks like the bed and breakfast just beyond the center of town is the highest point besides climbing up the mountain. Is there any way I could get to the roof and set up an antenna?"

"There is. My mom used to clean rooms there and she took me along when I was a kid. The bedroom at the back, the one with the slanted wall behind the armoire, there's a door leading to stairs. Go up, get to the roof. Go down, come through a tunnel, and out a hidden entrance in the back garden."

"So mischievous. I bet you were a difficult child to raise." Diego pinched Luke's cheek.

"How's the Russian making out living in the US?" Zero picked at the plastic cover of rubber worms, not finding the opening.

Luke took the package from him and ripped off the cover, handing the worms back. "You don't need explosives to open that."

"How'd you know I was considering it?"

"You have a special look when you're thinking about blowing something up."

"Humm, I'll have to work on my poker face."

"Getting back to our Russian, he's fine. Almost no accent, seems to fit into the community. My little brother and his friend go up to his cabin and spy on him."

Cobalt laughed. "So suddenly he's *our* Russian? Interesting turn of events for an FSB agent."

"Retired KGB, Cobalt."

"What if," Zero proposed, "our mission in the 'Stan was somehow related to those two thugs being here? I mean, do we know why we had to set those sensors along the road? Why we had to take babysitters? There's too many questions about that mission in the first place and suddenly they show up in Luke's back yard? Somethin' ain't right."

"And while we're at it," Scout interjected, "does the CIA know who facilitated the relocation of a Russian into the comfort and beauty of the Blue Ridge Mountains?"

Luke grinned. "I'm not at liberty to say."

"Alex, I'll take 'Good Hell, No They Don't' for five hundred," Diego said, watching a spool of fishing line drop out of Zero's hands and roll across the parking lot.

"Hey, Zero, are you okay? If that was a grenade, we'd all be dead."

"Yeah, of course I'm okay. You got nothing to worry about. If it had been a grenade, I would've thrown Scout on it and he would've saved us."

"Oh, contraire my friend. I've got my Purple Heart."

Zero shook his head. "Dude, a pretty nurse pulling a roofing nail out of your butt cheek because you didn't watch where you were sitting really doesn't qualify."

"Bro, it was in a combat zone and she put me in for it. Besides, the nail was deep into my meat."

"Because you sat on the thing like a ton of bricks."

Laughing, Luke said, "Okay, guys, guys. I gotta get my Mom's grocery list filled at Sykes. You all just be up at my place for a cook out. We'll have a campfire and sort things out. The big truck is at the back. I'll take the pickup home."

"Yeah," Scout said. "Get extra hotdogs. This clean mountain air gives me an appetite."

"Zero, roll up that fishing line. I could use it in a pinch for suture material."

"Always a doctor, Diego."

****

After Luke was in the store, his friends gathered in a tight circle.

Cobalt explained his theory: "Those weren't military sensors. It was a ghost operation."

"Do you think Luke was in on it?" Zero rolled the fishing line on the spool as he spoke.

"No," Cobalt said. "Not at all. Scout, see what you can dig up with your satellite on the dark web."

"Who was in the trucks you had me put trackers on at the rest stop, Cobalt?" Diego searched his friend's deep violet eyes, not wanting to hear what came next, but the medic had an idea what was going to be said. They all did.

"Someone maybe involved in trafficking. Someone I used to know."

"Human trafficking? You're kidding? Right?" Zero stopped rolling the line.

"Wish I was."

Diego scratched his head and put his ball cap on backwards before he said, "Well, if you're sure about this, let's go get some beer and make a plan."

"I don't have all the facts yet, but if I'm correct we'll be taking care of two birds with one stone."

"And what's that, Cobalt?"

"The man in the light blue suit who went into the restaurant."

"You hid behind the *dieffenbachia* because of a chump in diamond shoes?"

"It wasn't *dieffenbachia*, it was *rhododendron*. I wasn't hiding. He was my old company commander. The one who set up my unit."

"Dead man walking," commented Scout.

****

Luke came out of the store with two bags of groceries.

"You guys are still hanging out in the parking lot? Get moving before you scare off the wildlife. Just be cleaned up and at the farm before 1130 hours. We'll eat about 1300. My Dad doesn't like cookouts held up."

"Got it," Scout said. "Zero is going to spring for the beers and I'll bring soda for the kiddies."

"See you later." Luke loaded the groceries and drove off.

****

"Cobalt, if you're right, and Luke's boss is part of this, we've got to keep Luke out of it."

"Agreed, Diego. We keep him clean."

"Tell me, Cobalt, why you are so sure there's trafficking going on?"

Cobalt pulled a small cloth from his pocket. "This is from the grocery store lost and found. Ambrie Sykes said one of Hector Cobb's dogs found it in the woods."

"And?" Zero asked.

"And the threads are not decoration. Those are Farci letters. This is a message. It says all along the edges *nejatam bedin*-rescue me. There's a girl up in the mountains who needs our assistance."

The men were silent.

Scout spoke first. "To tell you the truth, I don't think we can keep this to ourselves. We need to present our suspicions to Sheriff Harris. We're not in a battle zone and it's his jurisdiction. If we're going up in the mountains for a rescue, he should know."

"Scout's right" Diego added. "Sheriff Bill knows who in this community can be trusted. I really don't want Luke involved. There could be some serious blowback if there is CIA involvement. And, blowback for us with the regiment."

"Yeah, but this is Luke's home where his people are," Cobalt said. "You won't keep it from him and you won't keep him out of it."

They saw a red car being towed by Crawford's Garage with what looked like old blood on the side. Sheriff Harris pulled into his space in front of the jail. Hector Cobb got out of the passenger's side then opened the back door, a bloodhound following him to the sheriff's office.

Cobalt tapped Scout on the arm. "Gentlemen, I think the pieces of the puzzle are coming together. Mike Oscar."

****

Sheriff Harris looked up as Luke's friends entered. He had just filled the percolator and turned on the hot plate.

"Come in, guys. I don't have anyone locked up so I know you're not here to facilitate a breakout. Say, Hector," he called toward the back, "bring up four more chairs, will you? We've got company."

Zero and Diego walked to the rear office door and helped Hector with the chairs. Cricket, snuggled against Cobalt's leg.

"Come in, have a seat."

"We wanted to thank you for the extra pulled pork lunches. It was much appreciated," Diego said.

"You're quite welcome. One of those days where I had to cut and run. Skipping lunch helps to balance out the donuts Gracie tells me I shouldn't have. What can I do for you? Hector and I had a rough night. We just got back from a big breakfast with Cricket and we're ready for a nap."

The Ranger's looked at each other first, then at the sheriff—*did he really go to breakfast with a dog?* They smiled in unison.

"But let me not forget my manners. Hector, they are friends of Luke's. Introduce yourselves to Hector while I check the coffee pot."

"I'm Scout, this is Diego, Zero, and that scary man petting the dog, is Cobalt. I don't know what Luke told you about us, but we are...ah...in the same Army unit. My specialty is in the cyber electromagnetics activities. Cobalt is in counterintelligence. Diego is the medical professional attached, and Zero's area of expertise is general demolitions. That's about all I can tell you, Sheriff."

Hector and Bill exchanged glances.

"Nice to meet you," Hector said.

"I presume you gentlemen are not making this a social call?"

"It's not, Sheriff," Diego said.

"Okay, you'll have to bear with us while Hector and I play hostess. Sugars? Creams?"

After the mugs were passed around, a silence descended on the room until Hector called Cricket to his side. "I think she's gotten enough spittle on your pant leg there, Cobalt."

"That's fine, Mr. Cobb," the tattooed Ranger replied. "These pants have seen worse."

"You can call me Hector. Don't need to be so formal."

Bill's curiosity was getting the better of him. "Okay, boys, what's on your mind?"

****

Jose started shaking as he felt around in his backpack searching for his wallet and coming up empty handed. He had to go back to retrieve it and the maps. Jose turned the truck around and hit the accelerator.

He took the curves at speed. His life depended on getting his wallet. He absentmindedly reached into his shirt pocket for a stick of gum and instead pulled out the slip of paper with Walter Venter's name and phone number on it.

Jose spun into the drive of the cabin. He slammed the transmission into park and then ran up the stairs into the living room where he grabbed the maps but couldn't find his wallet. He jumped down the steps, right into the smiling face of his worst nightmare. Skull handed Jose his wallet.

"This must be yours. I found it on the ground. Left in a hurry?"

"Hey, thanks, I was looking for it."

"Where you going, little fella?" Skull flicked Jose across the face with the back of his hand as a distraction, then picked him up with one arm and took him back into the cabin. "We need to have a talk about product retention and loss."

Skull slammed Jose into a chair. "Now you stay right there while I look around and see what Clarence and Jiggy left behind."

Staying with Skull was a death sentence. Jose saw a dirty steak knife that had dropped to the floor and under a chair. It was his only chance.

With the artistry of a generational circus performer, he threw it, penetrating Skull's neck about an inch below his right earring. The knife sliced neatly through the carotid artery.

Skull pulled the knife out of his neck. Dropping to the floor, he saw Jose disappear out the door. Skull watched as the blood pumped from his neck, down his shirt and pool between his legs. He bled out on the dirty black and white linoleum.

****

Jose gunned the truck as the image of the cabin faded in the rear view mirror. Along Highway 219, Jose stopped at a gas station to refuel and buy a burner phone. In the parking lot he made the call.

"Is this Walter Venter?"

"Who's asking?"

"A friend of Clarence...Clarence Wells. He...he was a business associate of yours."

"What do you mean was?

"He's taken off for Kansas. He left. He said you were part of the plan."

"Who's this?"

"Jose. Jose Garza."

"Jose Garza? Yeah, I know about you. So what's up?"

"Walter, I need a place to hide out...rest up...Boss and his gang are in the area."

"Do they know where you are? Where's the product?"

"No, they don't know where I am and I've got product stashed in a cave. It's all good for at least a few days anyway. I just need a place where I can breathe. I got money to pay you."

Walter wasn't sure what to do but he knew with Clarence out of the way he'd have a two way split of the profits. It would be worth checking out. "Write down how to get here."

"Okay, I got a pen. I won't be there until tomorrow. I want to stay away from Deacon's Hollar tonight, just in case. Anyone there with you? I'm just a little nervous about how Clarence ditched the whole operation."

"Ain't no thing, Jose."

"Who's at your place?"

"Just a woman and a boy. They ain't gonna say anything. I'm the man around here. Come tomorrow. The mailbox down at the road says "Crawford" on it. That's the place to come into."

"Got it. I'll call you."

"Just be here. New plans need to be made."

Jose hung up the call, but not before he heard Venter yell at someone to shut up or he would beat the shut up out of them. "Humm...nice guy" Jose said to the phone.

****

Howard's truck kicked up a little dry summer dust from the driveway as he parked in front of the house.

"Honey, ring the bell, please," Elsie called from the screen door. "The twins have Maggie with them."

"Got it, my love." Before the last sound disappeared between the big pines, his daughter and sons came out of the woods. Maggie wore the two hind legs off a rabbit at her waist; feathers and debris caught among her golden red curls. Tobias had the rest of the legless rabbit plus another dead one. Nathan carried his rifle in the manner Howard taught him for safety.

"Daddy, daddy, we got rabbits." Maggie squealed as she ran up the drive to her father. She had blood on her hands and dirt across her face.

"I guess you do. Will we make bunny pie this weekend?" Turning to his sons, he said, "You boys teaching her how to behave in the woods?"

"Yes, sir," Nathan replied. "She follows the safety rules we give her and she isn't squeamish about dressing out the rabbits. She wants to know all the inside parts."

"That's my girl. I think she needs a bath and her hair combed before company comes."

"Who's coming, Dad?"

"Luke's friends from Washington will be joining us for a cookout. I want you boys to bring wood for the fire pit."

"Great. Can we get something to eat first? Kinda hungry," Tobias asked.

"Put your equipment away. One of you can finish dressing the rabbits while the other gets wood. You can eat when the guests arrive. It won't kill you to wait."

"Is this another lesson, Dad?"

"Yes. In sacrifice. Now get your chores done."

Elsie stood on the porch staring at her daughter. "What have you boys done to your sister?"

"She went hunting, Mom."

"Really. And what are the feathers and branches in her hair?"

"I a Viking Princess, Mom."

"I am a Viking Princess," Elsie corrected.

Howard scooped his daughter up in his arms. "Let's get you upstairs for a bath, young lady."

"I am a Viking Princess, Dad."

"Okay. What does a Viking Princess do, Magdelyn?"

Making a fist of her chubby hand and holding it high above her head, she shouted, "I drinks from the skulls of mine enemies."

Howard looked with raised eyebrows at his sons.

Elsie said, "You wanted a daddy's girl. She's yours, I promise."

Howard laughed and kissed his wife on the nose. "I wouldn't have her any other way."

Addressing his twins, he said, "Boys, remember to clean your rifles."

"Yes, Dad," Nathan said. "We know."

****

"I told you not to listen on my phone calls. I told you not to put this garbage on the table and try to call it food. How many times do I have to beat it into you? Huh? How many times?" Walter Venter swept his hand across the table throwing the food, plates, dishes, and cups onto the floor with a crash.

"I'm s..sorry, Walter. I thought you liked the way...but I forget..."

"Shut up, bitch, just shut up." He backhanded Agnes Crawford across the mouth, sending her against the open kitchen drawer. The force broke the facing, scattering kitchen utensils across the floor.

He grabbed her by the hair and dragged her back to the stove. "Get it right, get it right," he screamed as Agnes huddled against the oven door. "How many times do I have to tell you?" He punched her in the head three times, the blood pouring from her nose.

"Leave her alone." Fishbone's voice was even, steady, and loud. It had an unusual maturity to it. There was no response from Walter as he stood over Agnes.

"I said leave her alone."

"And just what do you think you're gonna do about it, brat?" He turned to face the seven year old. "I'm the man in this house."

"No. Today, I am." Fishbone pulled the trigger, putting all but one of five rounds into Walter's broad chest.

Walter collapsed in a heap, a pool of blood poured from his wounds, making the floor a sticky mess.

"Oh, my God. What have you done?" Agnes was hysterical. "Oh, my God you'll go to prison." She gasped for air as she clutched the front of her blouse, blood dripping from her nose.

"Come on, Mom. Come outside. Let's sit on the porch." He placed the revolver on the table.

The boy helped Agnes step over the body of her abuser and when his mother was in her chair, he returned to the kitchen. He put ice in a towel for her face. He kicked Walter's head.

"That's for hurting my mom. And that's for saying you'd make me disappear. Who's disappeared now?"

Fishbone blotted the tears from his mother's swollen cheek, and kissed her bruised forehead. He didn't cry until he heard his uncle's voice on the phone.

"Uncle Bowtie?"

"Hey, Fishbone. What's up?"

"I...I..."

"Boy, it's alright. Stop. Tell me what happened."

"I did what you said. I protected my mom. That's my job, isn't it?"

"Yes, that's right. What happened?"

"I shot Walter. He's dead on the kitchen floor, he was beating my mom, she's bloody again. I made him stop."

"Just stay with your mom. I'm coming right now. Where's the gun?"

"In the house."

"Leave it there. Don't touch it. I'm on my way."

"Okay, Uncle Bowtie."

"I love you, boy."

****

When Sheriff Bill and Deputy Johnson arrived, Bowtie, Agnes, and Fishbone were sitting quietly on the porch. The scene was certainly deceiving compared to the call:

"Bill, Bowtie here. You better get to Agnes' place. I just shot and killed Walter Venter. He was beating on her when I walked in so I shot him. That's it."

"What?"

"That's my confession. No need for a trial. Judge Dietz can sentence me. It's done."

"I'm on my way, Bowtie."

"Don't worry. I ain't going anywhere."

****

Bill and Deputy Johnson entered the house. They found evidence of a struggle in the kitchen, the gun on the table, and Venter dead. Johnson bagged the weapon.

Bill sat on the steps and adjusted his headgear. "Okay, what happened?"

"I told you what happened. That's it. Arrest me."

The boy left his mother to go back into the house but Deputy Johnson stopped him. "Crime scene, Fishbone. You can't go in there."

"I'll be getting my mom some more ice for her face," he said as he skirted around the officer and went into the cool darkness of the house.

Johnson turned to follow him but Bill said, "Let him go. It's okay. I'm going to make a call."

Bill went to the patrol car. His voice crackled over the radio to the base station in his office. Mike Green picked up the mic.

"Deputy Green. Over."

"Yeah, Mike. Call Cleveland Coop and get him and Ubell Gant up to the Crawford's place with all their equipment."

"Got it. Out."

"Copy. Out." Bill studied the small mountain home. Bowtie didn't kill Walter Venter, but Agnes did. There was no way Judge Dietz was going to punish a woman with a cauliflower ear.

"Are you going to arrest me, Sheriff?"

"Yeah, I guess so. Agnes and Fishbone, you'll need to go into town. I don't want you here for a while."

"I don't have money for that, Bill," Agnes mumbled from her swollen and painful mouth.

"I'll take care of it."

****

Mike handed Bill a cold soda from the cooler in the squad car.

"Is there anything else I can do, Bill?"

"No, not now, Mike. Johnson will drop Agnes and Fishbone off at the B&B, then he'll lock up Bowtie."

"Want me to put up crime scene tape?"

"Yeah, go ahead."

"Undertaker will be here. I told him not to rush because the scene needs to be cleared by Coop."

"While we're waiting, Mike, have you seen anything of those guys Wink Decker was all shaken up about?"

Now was not the time to tell Sheriff Harris the truth, and the truth was Mike had been stalking them via the special equipment secured in his western bedroom.

"Nah, haven't been into town too often, Bill. But I'll keep my eyes out."

"Open, Mike. Keep your eyes open." Bill started to laugh. "It's been a long day."

Mike laughed too but reminded himself to be more careful. "Did you call Dr. Glassman?"

"Yes. He's going to check Agnes and the boy. No sense dragging them through the village. Word will get out soon enough."

When Coop arrived, Mike helped Ubell bring the equipment up to the house then returned to the steps, waiting with Bill.

"What do you think, Bill?"

"About this? There's no way Bowtie did this. He's protecting his sister-in-law."

After about an hour, they both stood when Coop walked on a squeaky porch board as he exited the house.

"Preliminary, Coop?" Bill turned to face the forensic officer.

"I've got one, but what's yours?"

"Agnes had enough and blasted Walter when he was attacking her."

"Reasonable, but I think the evidence says you're wrong."

"How's that?"

"From the trajectory of a bullet I found in the dish cabinet, we have to rule out Agnes as a suspect."

"Okay. Then it's Bowtie."

"No, Bill,"

"Why?"

"Our shooter is about four feet tall."

"Oh, my God." Bill grabbed the railing and sank back to the steps.

THE COOKOUT

Maggie Perkins balanced herself on the porch railing waiting for a bird to come and take a cracker from her fingers. A black Excursion pulled into the drive and parked behind her father's truck.

"Who be them, Tater?" Her brother sat in a rocking chair picking his nose.

"Luke's friends."

"Momma," she shouted, "they here!"

Cobalt, Diego, Zero, and Scout piled out of the vehicle.

"Coblew, Coblew, catch me!" Maggie jumped up and down on the railing with excitement. Cobalt ran to the porch, catching the little girl as she jumped into his arms.

"I guess Cobalt's got a special friend," joked Diego.

Scout nodded. "He sure does. She opened him up."

Zero and Scout unloaded the coolers of beer and soda, while Diego brought bundles of badminton, croquet, and ring toss.

"You guys went shopping?" Luke said.

"Yeah. Zero said his folks have this at family cookouts. Where do you want it set up?"

"Over in the side and backyard. Plenty of room. By the time we play a couple games, it'll be time to eat."

Luke made the introductions as Elsie and the twins set the picnic tables with silverware and plates.

"Guys, you know my parents and Maggs, but this is my little brother Tater, and the twins, Tobias and Nathan. Everyone, this is Zero, Diego, Scout, and Cobalt.

"Manning the grill is John Seven Star, and setting out the salads is his wife, Running Deer. The two men over there by the fire pit are their sons, Sam White Owl and Spencer Tuttle.

"Feel free to walk around. Maggs will show you her swing set, I'm sure. However, when Mom rings the dinner bell, you had better be ready. This crowd waits for you like one hog waits for another at feeding time."

Zero and Sam assembled the badminton set while Spencer and Diego laid out the croquet course. Scout and Cobalt were given a tour by Tater and Maggie.

"What are you building here, Tater?" Scout surveyed the two by fours, roofing, and bags of cement.

"Dad's getting Maggie a pony and here's where it lives. Can't come in the house like my dog."

"What kind of dog do you have?"

"It was gaven to me from Mr. Green. Wouldn't stay up with him so he said he could stay here with me. Won't hunt. Just a pet. Here, I'll call him for you." Tater took a deep breath and shouted through cupped hands, "Mr. Green's Dog. Come'ere boy."

Cobalt, with Maggie still on his arm, asked, "The dog's name is Mr. Green's Dog?"

"Yeah. That way the dog knows where he come from if he wants to go back."

"Solid thinking, Tater." Scout winked at Cobalt.

Out from under the coolness of a shed came Mr. Green's Dog. Short and stocky, looking like a Beagle of sorts, in basic white hair coat with splotches of brown, black, and a scattered ticking of tan among the white. Not in any hurry, the dog ambled to Tater and fell on its side, exposing its belly.

"Nice dog, Tater." Cobalt went down on one knee, careful not to jostle Maggie, and obliged the dog for a tummy scratch.

"Yeah, he sleeps on my bed. Keeps booger men away at night."

"Tater," Maggie corrected, "it ain't booger men. That's what comes out you nose. It's boogie men. *Boo-gee.*"

The boy rolled his eyes. "Okay, Maggs."

The clang of the dinner bell interrupted the tour.

"You better hurry up and wash your hands before Dad says grace. I'll beat you, Maggs."

****

Once everyone was seated at the long table, Howard said the blessing.

"Lord, thank you for the beautiful day.

"Lord, thank you for the beautiful people who are gathered here in friendship and love.

"Lord, thank you for the food we are about to eat and for all the land and people who produced it.

"Lord, help us to serve others before we serve ourselves. In the name of your Son, we ask. Amen."

The 'amen' was echoed around the table.

"Dad, it's time I was served." Tater held his plate up.

"Thank you for waiting through the exceptionally long prayer, Elias."

"You're welcome, Dad. Now, someone pass me them potatoes."

"Sorry, gentlemen, sometimes my son forgets we serve guests first, don't we, Tater?" Elsie patted the top of his head.

"Yeah, they get first spoons cuz if they get sick we know'd not to eat it."

"Who told you that, Tater?" Howard asked.

"Tobias said it."

Nodding at his twins, Howard said, "Thank you for helping me raise your little brother."

Tobias grinned, "You're welcome, Dad."

Elsie looked over the table of food. "Everyone eat up and don't be shy. There's more in the house for seconds and thirds. John has plenty of dogs, burgers, and brats on the grill."

Running Deer brought a platter of roasted ears to the table. "For you newcomers, peel back the husk and roll the corn in the melted butter. Add salt to taste. Be careful, it's very very hot."

"Helps me with mine?" Maggie looked into Cobalt's dark eyes.

"Sure, Miss Perkins. Careful."

John Seven Star called out, "Coming through," as he brought a steaming platter of meat to the table. Running Deer divided the meat onto three smaller platters and placed them at intervals along the center of the table.

"This is family style," Luke reminded everyone. "Ask and you shall receive."

For a few moments the conversation was hushed as men, women, and children ate hamburgers, corn on the cob, and potato salad. Short threads of conversation floated on the warm breeze like the aroma of steaming breads and beans.

"Maggie, Tater, chew slowly."

"Yes, Mom."

"I see your tat. How long in the Corps?"

"Me and Sam were active for three years."

"Honey, we need more butter for the corn."

"Spencer, pass the beans, please."

"Tater, are you feeding the dog under the table?"

"No, Dad. I just accidentally dropped some."

"Beautiful day for a cookout. Anyone want another beer?"

"Nathan, go in the cooler and get that other dish of potato salad, please."

"Who needs what? John? Running Deer? Howard, pass the green beans down Spencer's way. Thanks."

"So you guys know Luke from D.C.?"

"My family was in the fireworks display business. Been around it all my life."

"Zero, will you crocket with me?"

"Maggs, it's *crow-kay*."

"I didn't ask you, Tater."

"My mom and my sister are back home. Sis is in junior college and my mom works part time as a customer service rep online."

"Yes, I've always been interested in medicine which is why I took the schooling in the Army. I come from a medical family in Boston."

"Were you at Walter Reed for very long?"

"Pass the chips and ketchup, please."

"Both me and Sam were there until Mom and Dad came and busted us out, just like a raiding party. Glad to get home."

"Tater, are you still feeding the dog under the table?"

"No, ma'am but maybe a little bit dropped on the grass."

"According to the research, I'm descended from the Conoy tribes and Shawnee, but historians and archaeologists have gaps in the history of West Virginia. My wife's Cherokee. She's got a way with plants and animals."

"Last I heard, Birdie is doing good. You know these old gals are a part of the mountains just like the trees and grasses."

"My boys are going to get her set with wood for the winter."

"I haven't eaten this good for ages. Thank you, Mrs. Perkins, John, Running Deer."

"Thank you, gentlemen. You're all welcome to come back."

"Cherry pie cuts first," shouted the little girl with red hair and baked bean sauce around her mouth.

"Lemon is next."

"Tobias, get the ice cream and dipper out of the house. Thanks, honey."

"Sam, Spencer, collect the plates for Elsie and take them into the house, please."

"Yes, ma'am."

"Here, Coblew. You can share my pie."

"Thank you, Miss Perkins."

"Did Running Deer make blueberry? I'd like some of that."

"Seconds on anything? Salads? Brats? Desserts?"

The dinner was done. Adults sat back in lawn chairs waiting for the meal to settle while Nathan and Tobias read to Maggie and Tater under the shade of a white oak tree.

Zero leaned over and spoke, "Luke, is your Mom and Running Deer going to do all these dishes?"

"The twins will help."

"Nah. We'll do them."

"Mrs. Perkins, we'd like to help with the clean up if you don't mind."

"Zero, that is very kind. Luke, you know the way around my kitchen. There's plenty of containers for leftovers in the pantry. I think Running Deer and I would like to just sit and rest. Thank you."

"John," Howard said, "I've got some venison summer sausage for you. Had it mixed with Holstein beef. A little dry, but not greasy like with pork." John patted Howard on the back; they had escaped the cleanup.

****

In the kitchen, Diego approached Luke. "Dude, we want to run something by you." He and Luke were drying the dishes Cobalt washed and put through the rinse water.

"What?"

The room was suddenly quiet as Luke looked from face to face.

"We think, and we talked to Sheriff Harris and Hector Cobb about it, we think you've got traffickers in the area."

"How?"

Scout picked up the conversation. "I've used some satellite data to track Cobalt's old company commander. He's in Waybird City, along with Jones and Smith. We concur that Afghanistan wasn't a CIA sanctioned mission. We also concur that your boss and Cobalt's CO set us up to help track shipments of women and children across the 'Stan. That particular area is one of the major trafficking routes out of Central Asia. They used us to ensure they knew when their product was coming through so they couldn't be traced."

"One of Hector's dogs kept bringing him items from the woods. She finally brought him a white rag with embroidery on the edges," Diego added. "It was Cobalt who found the cloth in the grocery lost and found. You want to take it from there?"

Cobalt placed a stack of dishes in the cupboard Luke indicated. "It's Farsi. The letters are a repetition of the phrase 'rescue me' all around the edges. Have any Farsi speakers in the Hollar, Luke? I thought not. You've got a problem, bro."

Zero added, "Cobb and his dog found bodies of the kids."

Luke wiped his face. "So you think we were in Afghanistan to set up landing lights for a smuggling operation run by a prior service Ranger and a deputy director of the CIA?"

The Rangers nodded.

"This is dangerous information."

The Rangers nodded.

"Did you come up with a plan? You guys and Sheriff Harris?"

The Rangers nodded.

"And that is?"

The violet blue eyes of the deadliest Ranger of them all, narrowed to slits, as Cobalt replied, "We will do what we do best."
****

Elsie Perkins brought a slice of cherry pie into the kitchen. "I couldn't give this away, everyone's so full." She stopped short. "Why so serious, gentlemen? I hope you didn't have second thoughts about doing the dishes?"

"Mom, not at all. These guys have been talking so much, I think they are getting hungry again. Dishes are all done, and put away."

"If you want any more to eat, there's paper plates in the pantry. It looks spotless here. Thank you."

"I'll bring the tray out if you find out who wants coffee, Mom."

"Okay, honey, I'll take a head count and be right back."

After Luke was sure his mother was out of earshot he said, "We'll talk later."
****

Sam White Owl started the fire in the pit while Spencer helped Maggie and Tater poke a stick through their marshmallows.

"Not too big fire, Sam," Maggie warned. "My dad said so."

"Magdelyn, we don't order Sam around," Elsie reminded her.

"Mrs. Perkins, I don't mind. She's a lot cuter than my drill instructors." Stretching out his sore leg, he motioned the little girl, "Come here, Maggie. I'll help you roast your marshmallow."

Freshly bathed and in her slippers and robe, she laid her arm on the back of Sam's neck and leaned against his shoulder as he cooked the sugary treat.

"Is that okay, Maggs?"

"Yep."

"It's hot so blow on it first." Sam repositioned himself as he gave her the stick. "I'll make you another one if you want."

Howard and John offered beer to the adults around the fire. A peaceful quiet descended on the group as the sun was setting behind the tree line of the mountain. The crickets and night insects began to sing. When the temperature started to drop off, Maggie wormed her way onto Cobalt's lap. She yawned.

"That was a big yawn for a little girl. What did you do today that made you tired?" He fluffed her curls and watched the gold highlights dance from the light of the fire.

"Killed rabbits for Dad's bunny pie."

"Really?"

"Yeah, and played Vikings. I'm a Viking Princess."

"Oh, that's great. What does a Viking Princess do?"

Maggie jumped up on Cobalt's leg, thrusting her fist skyward. "I drinks from the skulls of mine enemies."

Cobalt hugged the child and put a kiss on her cheek as he laughed. "Diego, I think we can make a Ranger out of her."

"Can? She is already. Get her a regimental tab for her jammies."

"TATER, YOU AND MAGGIE stay here. I'll be in the other room over there and I'll leave the door cracked so you can see me."

"Is Cloblew there?" Maggie looked under the table toward the private room at the diner.

"Not yet. When I'm done with my work, we'll all have some ice cream. Would you like that?"

"When's Mom and Dad coming back?" Tater played with a spoon.

"Tomorrow. They went to Waybird City for a movie and shopping. I'm your babysitter."

"You ain't so good as a babysitter, Luke."

"Then you can tell Mom when she gets back."

Tater had been grouchy all morning. Luke tried to distract and redirect, but nothing worked.

"Barbara and Gracie will get you anything you want. If you're hungry, just tell them."

"But we stay right here." Maggie placed Bentley on the table beside her plate. "Bentley wants a hamburger, Luke."

"Just tell Gracie. The two of you stay here. If you need anything, I'll be right in this room. See? There's a table and I'll be there."

"We ain't stupid, Luke."

"Tater, just do what you're told."

****

Luke heard Barbara say six steaks would be too much at one time when Tater placed his order.

"They okay out there?" Scout asked.

"Yeah, they're good kids," Luke responded.

"The joy of children." Diego unrolled a map of the area and spread it across the table.

"Cobalt coming?"

"Not yet. He stopped at the grocery store to get a few things. Should be here shortly."

Luke, Zero, Diego, and Scout studied the map.

"According to Hector, his bloodhound found the bodies about here," Scout indicated to a small flat area.

"You got aerial photos of this, Scout?"

"Yep. Here. The bloodhound took Hector the hard way, up the escarpment, but you can see there is a road or two track a sixty meters on the other side."

Luke circled a point on the photograph, coordinating it with the map. "Here's where Sheriff Harris found the red car. Coop and Gant have gone over it but I don't know any results. Some kind of goo."

Zero pursed his lips. "Goo, you say? Like the doughy stuff kids play with?"

"Idk. He just said goo. More like what's left over after an airstrike or Howitzer, I guess," Luke replied.

"As the combat engineer and explosives expert, goo isn't left by a Howitzer. That would be more like pink mist." Zero checked his watch. "Blue eyes should be here."

Diego returned to study the map and photographs. "The route in red is where the dog takes Hector from his farm to the trash, and then to the bodies the back way as Scout indicated.

"They had to have driven the car from someplace in the area to the dumping ground. They wouldn't want the disposal to be too close to where they were hiding. Let's make concentric circles from the dumping ground then matrix it with a grid pattern."

"On it, Diego." Scout was busy commanding his computer and satellite to make the required patterns over the photos of the vegetation.

Luke looked into the dining room. The kids were eating French fries. He couldn't see Gracie but Barbara was filling salt and pepper shakers at the far end of the counter.

Zero looked at his watch again. "I thought Cobalt would be here before now. We really can't go any further with operations with one missing."

Diego put his feet up on an adjacent chair and positioned his visor over his eyes for a snooze. "Let's give him five more minutes before we call in the National Guard to go looking for a Ranger lost in the woods."

The quiet of the room was shattered when Tater burst through the door screaming, "Luke, that man gots Maggie!"

****

Jose didn't want to go into Deacon's Hollar but he was almost out of gas. It was a chance he would have to take hoping he wouldn't run into Boss. He needed a bargaining chip if he did.

There she was, the answer to all his problems, walking down the sidewalk. Jose could return all the product to Boss plus this red headed dream that just dropped into his hands. Jose's luck would finally change.

He parked the truck along the curb. He crossed the street and walked quickly but quietly. With the coast clear, he grabbed her from behind, putting his hand over her mouth, then doubled timed it across the street to his vehicle. He heard a scream, but he ignored it and pushed the little girl into the truck.

Luke shouted from the restaurant as he ran onto the street, "Stop that truck. He's got Maggie!"

A short distance away from each other, Cobalt and John Seven Star saw a strange man grab Maggie, and toss her into his vehicle.

Cobalt dropped his bags. He jumped into the pickup bed, then catapulted himself from the bed, landing on the ground by the driver's door. Cobalt reached in and grabbed Jose by the throat. On the other side of the truck, John pulled open the door and lifted the wide eyed little girl from the passenger footwell.

"Going somewhere, friend?" Cobalt loosened his hold when Jose's eyes bugged out of his face.

"Come here, Maggie. Uncle John's got you. You're okay, sweetie." John walked away from the truck with Maggie sobbing in his neck.

Luke rushed up to John, taking Maggie from his arms.

He nodded thanks to John.

"Let's go back and see Gracie, okay, Maggie?" Luke took his sister to the diner while Cobalt pulled Jose Garza out through the driver's side window.

"What you got here, Cobalt?" John asked.

"Just the fish I've been looking for. This one will do nicely over my mantle."

"Here, let me help you with him. Looks like he might start flopping now he's out of the water."

John looked in the bed of Jose's truck. "Just what we need so he doesn't head for the creek." John ran the cable ties around Jose's wrists.

"You *bastardos* can't do this. I was gonna help the little girl find her mother. I want a lawyer."

"John, this town have a lawyer?" Cobalt asked.

"There's Judge Dietz. He might be in Waybird so it could be a while," John replied with a grin.

"Need any help?" Zero and Scout came to the truck.

"Nah. John and I can get him to the sheriff's office for an interview. Diego, take a look at the little one. Make sure this scum didn't hurt her."

****

"Why'd you let her go, Tater? I told you to stay here." Luke was on his knees talking to his brother.

"She just took off, Luke."

"That man grabbed her and could have hurt her."

"It ain't my fault! I'm just a kid. She got mad and left. You supposed to keep us safe. That's what Dad says. Nathan and Tobias never leave us." Tater burst into tears.

Luke gathered Tater into his arms and held him tight. "You're right. It isn't your fault, it's mine. And I'm sorry. I'm so sorry." He rocked his brother back and forth shouldering the boy's fear and rage.

"Tater, you did the right thing. You came and got me right away. You saw what happened and you did what was right. It was very brave. Dad will be proud of you."

****

Scout came into the dining room holding Bentley. "See who was looking for you outside?"

"Thank you." Maggie cuddled her toy.

In the diner, Barbara motioned to Luke. "Bring them into to Gracie's office. Next shift will be here in five minutes and I'll read to them or color in the kid's books."

"Thanks, Barbara," Luke said. "I really messed this day up for them."

"It's alright. When Tater started shouting and I realized she left, you were already on it. It's over. It'll be okay."

****

The short walk to the sheriff's office wasn't pleasant for Jose. Cobalt applied a choke hold every time Jose screamed for a lawyer.

"Cobalt, get a grip," John grinned. "That's the second time you dropped him when I went to scratch my nose."

Cobalt smiled. "I need to work out more."

Sheriff Bill opened the door. "What do we have here, gentlemen?"

"Confidential informant," Cobalt said.

"Is he alive?"

John checks for a pulse. "He's good."

"Okay, put him in my interrogation room. I'll need a statement, John." The sheriff knew Cobalt wouldn't sign anything.

"I'd like to be with him when he wakes up, Sheriff."

"I can arrange that, Cobalt. Ambrie Sykes already called me. She said you boys had everything in hand and were on the way to my end of town."

John found a rubber band on the desk. He pulled his long black hair back away from his face and secured it as he read the witness form.

****

Jose woke to the stare of a monster with violet eyes.

Cobalt had reversed his chair, his chin resting on his folded arms. The deep black of his unshaven beard and uncut hair framed his face, making the blue violet of his eyes more piercing.

"I want a lawyer."

"Wrong answer."

"You can't grab innocent people off the street."

"That's ironic, *and* the wrong answer."

"Honestly, I thought she was just a lost little girl and was…"

"Wrong answer."

"You can't keep me here."

"Wrong answer."

Jose lunged forward.

Cobalt straightened his arm. Jose fell to the floor, knocked out cold.

"Again, wrong answer."

Diego opened the door. "He say anything?"

"No, but I haven't added the habaneros to the sauce yet. Watch him for a minute. I want to take a leak and get a cup of coffee."

"Sure. Take your time. Sleeping Beauty will be out for a minute or two."

Pausing at the door, Cobalt asked, "Are the kids alright?"

"Yeah. Everything's good. Tater forgave Luke and Maggie is feeding ice cream to Bentley. Bring me a coffee when you come back. The sheriff's homebrew kind of grows on me."

As soon as Jose started to moan, Diego grabbed him by his collar and belt, then slammed him back in the chair.

"Time to wake up, dude."

"What? What happened."

"Your glass jaw caused a drop in your blood pressure."

"That guy scares me." Jose shook his head.

"He scares me, too, dude, but in your position, I can think of only one way to relieve your anxiety."

"Huh?"

"You need to talk to him or he'll slice the truth out of you."

"He'd cut me?"

"In a heartbeat, bro."

"You're kidding me?"

"Nope. Serious as a novice taking her vows."

"He's dangerous."

"That he is, bro, but more than that."

"What?" Jose sat back as Diego leaned in to speak in a whisper.

"When he cuts you, well, he's so fast, I saw him slice the face off a Taliban leader who didn't know his face was gone until my buddy held up a mirror."

"I don't believe that."

"Yeah? You're from Mexico, aren't you?"

"Yeah."

"So's my family. Came to the US for a better life two generations ago. We could be related, *bato*."

"Yeah, I guess." Jose started to relax.

"Familiar with the cartels down that way, *amigo*?"

"Yea...yeah." Jose swallowed hard.

"They taught my friend everything he knows. He did time in prison down in South Texas. They had a special cemetery for the dudes he killed. He would have stayed there but the government needed his skills overseas. Critical assignments."

Diego leaned back in his chair and took out a pocket knife, cleaning under his nails. "He takes pleasure in his work if you know what I mean, bro."

Jose flashed on the bloody cartel wars. He began to shake and sweat as the bile rose in this throat.

"Hey, *primo*, I didn't mean to scare you. But maybe there's a way I can help you out of this *torpeza*. See, I convince my buddy you'll leave this hillbilly town never to return, you know, bro? Maybe help you get to Miami or someplace safe, you know, bro?"

"You'd do that? For me? Save me from that purple eyed *brujo*?"

"Sure, *perro*. Us Latinos gotta stick together, bro."

"I can trust you?"

"Here, I'll cut those zip ties off your wrists to show you."

Diego stepped behind the chair and sliced the ties. Suddenly freed, Jose rubbed his hands to restore the circulation.

"Thanks, man. I thought I was going to lose my hands."

"Dude, fill me in on how you got to this backwater hole." Diego smiled as he put his pocket knife away.

The friendly voice relaxed Jose and he vomited his story to Diego about Boss, Skull, Jiggy, Racy, and Allen. He told about watching Clarence get sicker and sicker and how he lost Clarence out of the vehicle and down the gully. He told how he threw the knife, stabbing Skull in the throat.

"If I can get to this Walter Venter guy, we can split the money three ways."

"Three way split? With me?" Diego asked.

"Yeah. We're *compadres*. I called Walter once but couldn't meet."

"What were you going to do with the little girl they caught you with?"

"Promise you don't snitch me out?"

"What? You think I look like a snitch?" Diego said with a smile, "We are *compadres, si*?

Garza lowered his voice, "Sorry, sorry. I was going to give her to Boss. He likes them that young and he gets more money for the ones that are different. You know, like the white blondes, real dark ones with long hair, and redheads."

"What about the ones you have now?" Diego enquired while he stretched his arms up toward the ceiling and then down and out toward the walls, crossing his arms over his chest to keep himself from beating Jose to death.

Jose took the bait. "Up in a cave behind the cabin. I threw food in there a few days ago."

"How many you got?"

"Five or six, maybe ten I think unless another one died on us. They was going to Canada."

"So how'd you get them into Canada?"

"There's a lot of roads that are unmanned and unprotected. Just gotta know where they are, what time to cross, who to pay off, and suddenly you're in Canada and hooked up with another part of the network. One's in Maine. We use that to funnel product into Quebec."

"So where's the product now?"

"In a cave up in the mountain, I said. Behind the cabin."

"A cave behind the cabin? Boss is from around here?"

"He's not but he knows Clarence and Franklin Wells somehow. I don't know how they met cuz I was brought on later. Maybe in the Army. I was told Boss was in the Army once."

"Think you could find that cabin?"

"Oh, yeah. It's well hidden because it's off the road and down a two track."

"Really?"

"You head north out of here, go about three miles on the 219. There's a big old boulder by the side of the road and the cut off is just beyond that."

"And the cabin is up there somewhere and the cave behind that?"

"Yeah."

"Jose, bro, do you think you could give those instructions to Boss and they could find the place?"

"Oh, yeah. I'm sure of it. But why? I want to get away from him."

"Well, bro, I think my buddy and me can get Boss and his friends off your back for good but in order to spring the trap, you need to bring them into the area. *Si?*" Diego smiled. "Here's your phone, bro. I found it on the ground by your truck."

Jose stuttered through the instructions to the man who answered. He hoped he sounded genuine. Garza smiled as he handed the phone back.

"Done."

"Bro, I'm proud of you."

Diego got up and walked around behind Jose. Before he could react, Jose found himself secured with handcuffs.

"What's this, *bato?*"

"I ain't your bro. I ain't nothing like you...*bro.*"

Jose started to cry when Cobalt stepped back into the room.

****

Sheriff Bill turned off the monitor. "Will Cobalt skin him?"

Diego wrinkled his brow and shook his head. "Not now, anyway. Maybe later...or not." Diego paused. "So serious, Sheriff Bill. I'm just kidding. He'll sit across from him, drinking coffee and staring, until Jose pisses his pants. No worry."

"Did he serve time in South Texas?"

"Negative, Sheriff. I just made that up. Pretty creative, eh?"

John Seven Star finished his statement. "Did you get the information you wanted?" he asked Bill.

"Yes, sir. I've got a general idea but will need your help locating this cabin once we get there."

"If you think you have traffickers in the area looking for their source of income, you'll need to go in with plenty of firepower. They'll have back up of their own," John paused. "Come to think of it, isn't that the homestead of Tony and Arvilla Wells? That's on Green Snake Falls Road. Clarence and Frank were raised around there. Devil's Rooms isn't too far."

"John, that's the connection. We need to find those children before Boss and his gang." Bill took his hat off the hook by the door.

"Maybe contact Walter Venter up at Crawford's place?" John asked.

Sheriff Bill blanched. "Not an option." He tried to relax the tightness in his chest.

Bill grabbed a set of keys from the key safe and opened the door to the interrogation room. He saw Jose sitting in a pool of his own urine; Cobalt was still staring.

"Excuse me, but I think I need to secure our visitor before I leave. You've made a mess of yourself, young man."

Jose was relieved to get away from Cobalt.

He was placed next to Bowtie Crawford.

****

"Do you know the area, John?" Sheriff Bill studied the map and the photographs back at Gracie's diner.

"If I understand, this is the back way Hector's dog took, along the north-south valley line. Probably scent came from higher and settled along the creek here. Here is the burial, and this road here will take you around Green Snake Falls. Not too far from the Wells homestead. And down along here," John ran his finger along a tree line, "is the old railroad line. Probably pretty over grown but I think you could get a truck down there in most places."

Gracie held the door for Dodger who pushed in a cart filled with cookies, small sandwiches, and a coffee urn. "Thanks, Dodger. Appreciate your help, honey."

"I see all'ya'll have turned my dining room into a command center. Mind tellin' me what's going on? I got two scared kids in my office and Tater's tellin' me some guy tried to kidnap Maggie. He might have gotten away with it if it hadn't been for Mr. Cobalt and John."

"Gracie," Bill started, "we think the Hollar is a stopping point for a group of human traffickers."

"Are you serious? In the Hollar?"

"It's my best guess the one locked in the jail made the attempt to take Maggie for..."

"Oh, my God, Bill. I need to sit down."

Zero, Luke, Scout, and John Seven Star gathered around the cart and helped themselves.

"What are you goin' to do, Bill?"

"We're going to stop it, Grace."

Luke sat beside her. "Miss Gracie, you need to keep this confidential."

"Well, yes, but it's up and down the street that some guy tried to snatch Maggie."

"What I don't want anyone to know is there might be more. Everyone in this room except for you, is going to conduct a search. We can't have the whole community traipsing through the woods trying to be heroes. These gangs of traffickers are armed and dangerous."

"I know that, Luke, but what are you doin' out there? You're a librarian for Pete's sake."

Cobalt gagged on his coffee but covered his mouth with a napkin, not daring to look at Luke. Zero pressed his forehead against the back window, biting his tongue.

"Gracie, I can handle myself. Besides, I took some self defense classes in D.C."

"Don't worry, Miss Gracie," Diego said. "I know he looks like the scrawny type, but I think he can handle himself. We'll look after him, keep him at the back so he's safe."

Ignoring the comment, Luke continued. "It's important that the rest of the village thinks it's a one time thing and it's over. The guy is caught, Maggie is unharmed, and things can go back to normal."

Gracie nodded in agreement.

Bill started to take a sugar cookie, but after looking at Gracie, he chose the tuna salad sandwich.

"Okay, Luke, I got it and I'll make sure we stick to the same story. If ya'll need anything that I can help with, just let me know." She gave Bill a kiss on the cheek and went back to managing the kitchen.

Zero raised his eyebrows. "Oh, someone's sweet on the Sheriff."

"You should be so lucky to find a woman like her, Zero." Bill blushed slightly. "Ever since high school. Now gentleman, let's make a plan."

"Just a minute," Luke said. "I've got to make a call. I know two men who know that area."

****

Scout's computer began to beep. "Cobalt, they've left Waybird. Projected route brings them here in maybe forty minutes without any stops. I might be able to hack into the engine if you need more time."

"Good."

"That's not illegal in West Virginia, is it sheriff?" Scout asked innocently

"Hacking into someone's car? Not in my county it isn't. Go ahead. We'll need a few hours." Bill smoothed his hair back from his forehead.

"Let's go over the terrain, again," Luke said. "The ridge runs north/south pretty much. This road is east/west for the most part and is south of the caves which dot the ridge here. Right so far, John?"

Seven Star nodded. "A little west is an old logging trail I used to patrol on horseback. The last it was cleared for hikers was maybe two to three years ago. I would think it's still passable."

"Good. Cobalt, Diego, and I will start here at the Stone Path trailhead. Zero, just off the east/west road here and let us know when they arrive. And permission granted for you to do your thing."

"Got it."

"Scout, you take the high ground for reception and overview."

"Maybe here?" Scout pointed.

"Wherever you can get the best signal and direct the action. There's a lot of thick vegetation, trees, and brush. We'll need eagle eyes."

"Affirmative."

"The Stone Path serpentines along the hillside. You'll have some hairpin turns due to the sharp increase in elevation in places. Mostly from the trailhead it goes west, upward, then makes a sharp left to the south. Continues south when it makes a hairpin turn and goes back north for maybe half a mile. The next turn, which takes you up to the caves, is more gradual, but you'll be out in the open for fifty meters until you have tree cover again." Luke looked around the room at the concerned faces.

"This will be a grab and go. We locate the kids, get out. Get back to the rendezvous."

"When we go back to get the scum, take no prisoners?" Cobalt asked.

Everyone looked at the sheriff.

"Gentlemen, the only thing that stopped Maggie from disappearing into the nightmare was Mr. Cobalt and John Seven Star. Your call."

TWINNING IT

"WHAT WAS THAT ABOUT?" Tobias turned the page in his science book.

"Luke wanted to know about the caves where Dad took us a couple years ago."

"Devil's Rooms?"

"Yeah."

"Why does he want to know about that?"

"I don't know. He's got Tater and Maggs with him so why would he want to go caving? And without us?"

Nathan made a sandwich at the counter.

"Luke never liked caves." After two bites he suggested, "Wanna go up there and look around?"

Tobias grinned. "Sure. I'll get the rifles and you get the ammunition. Our gear is in the utility room."

"Got the keys to the truck?"

"Yeah, but you know we aren't supposed to drive unless it's an emergency."

"Well, if Luke gets lost looking in those caves, I guess we got ourselves an emergency."

"You are so smart, Nate."

"You, too, Tobes."
****

Nathan parked in a grove of pines. They camouflaged the truck by breaking fallen boughs, tucking them around the vehicle's bumpers, and door handles. They used bushy plants and branches across the hood and cab roof.

"You know, Tobes, we've got the truck pretty well hidden, but who's going to come up here anyway?"

"Probably no one, but it's good practice."

Nathan asked, "If Luke is so interested in Devil's Rooms and coming up here, I wonder what he did with the little ones? He was supposed to babysit."

"I bet he doesn't have them with him now. Probably stashed them with Miss Amelia. I also bet he's going to bring his Army buddies up here and show off. He'll be surprised to see us when we jump out at him."

"You got that right. We got everything? Ropes? Ammo? Knives? First aid kit?"

"I think we got it all, Tobes.

"Let's hit it."

****

The Stone Path was a trail laid in the mountain predating the Civil War. At first, Howard told his sons it was used to hide pirate treasure but stopped when they questioned how pirates hauled treasure over the mountains to landlocked West Virginia.

"Actually, and this is the truth, the caves were used to hide whiskey from being taxed by the government. Thomas Jefferson wanted to pay war loans, but the farmers and distillers wanted profits rather than pay taxes. It was cause of the Whiskey Rebellion in July1791."

"Dad, let's just stick to the facts. We never believed the pirate thing."

"Okay, men, you got me there. I just wanted to make it exciting for you."

"Dad, we're exploring with you. Pirates or not." It remained one of his special "dad moments" for the rest of his life.

Now, they were on their own. The moment they headed out on the trail, they found their way along the Stone Path and up the mountain.

Reaching the first of the caves, Nathan approached with his weapon at the ready. Tobias threw a decent sized stone into the darkened cave. A bird flew out. He got closer and threw another, hearing it bounce off one of the walls. With Nathan covering him, Tobias turned his high beam flashlight around the inside of the shallow cave.

"Nothing here, Nate. Let's go to the next one. Should be about fifty feet up of this one."

"Yeah. I remember there were four. When was we here last, Tobes?"

"It's 'were' and I think it was with Dad two years ago. Something like that. They're spaced out about the same distance from each other. There's one at the top I think. Should have brought my journal."

"Don't worry. It'll come back as we search."

At each cave, Tobias examined the area leading to the cave entrance, then the cave itself.

"Nate, why was Luke so curious about these caves? There's nothing in them."

"I don't know. He never asks about stuff and all of a sudden he wants to know how many caves, exactly where they are, and feet between them."

"Maybe he's gone all stupid living in D.C."

"I'll tell you, when he comes home tonight, I'm going to question his butt about why he was questioning my butt."

"I want to hear how he answers you."

"Yeah. We've got one more up around those rocks. That's the one with the door."

"Go about 125 feet and we should be close."

Nathan and Tobias continued up to the last cave. They heard voices coming from the darkness.

"Ain't nobody should be around here, Tobes."

"See? The grating is locked with a new padlock. There's people in there, I swear it."

"What're we going to do?"

"Probably let them out. Toss a stone in there and let's see what happens first."

Tobias threw a stone. In seconds it was thrown back out. A small child, underweight with matted hair, appeared at the gate waving a skinny arm.

"Dang it, Nate. There's a kid in there. Looks like a little girl. How'd she get there?"

"I don't know but we'd better do something about getting her out."

The boys approached the cave so they could be seen.

"Hello. We come to get you out. I'm Nathan and this is Tobias."

"*Mira, mira...la clave...aqui, aqui.*"

"That's Spanish," Tobias said.

"What's she say?"

"I don't know what *la clave* is but let's look around and maybe we'll see what she's talking about."

The boys fanned out while the child kept repeating *"la clave, la clave."*

"Here, I got it. It's a set of keys."

Three more young girls crowded around the gate when they saw the twins.

As Tobias fumbled with the keys trying each one in the lock, Nathan looked at the faces of the children, gaunt, dirty, with eyes that had lost their sparkle and luster.

"Tobes, we gotta get them out of here. Get the dang door open before someone comes."

"I got it, I got it." Tobias swung the door open and was swarmed by several children. "Hey, hey, it's okay." He didn't understand what they were trying to tell him but they pointed to the path.

"Tobias, we need to get them to the truck and to Sheriff Bill."

"They don't need to be arrested, Nate."

"I'm not saying that but he'll know what to do, where to look for missing children reports nationwide."

"I think we get them to Aunt Gem's. Look, that one's got an infected hand, and that girl is limping. They need food first and medical treatment, Nate."

"They seem awful scared about that trail over there. But you're right, Tobes. You piggyback the limping one and go first. How many we got? Seven? Crap, Tobes, here comes two holding babies."

"Shit dang it to hell. Nathan, get the rope and tie the ones who can walk around the waist to each other. They won't get lost that way and we can get them down the hill with me at the front and you'll bring up the rear." Tobias took a section of rope from his pack.

Nate placed the little girl on Tobias' back. With the children in line following each other, Nathan mimed how they were all to hold on to the rope. "Don't let go...hold on, like this. See? Put your hand around it and hold on. Like this, see?"

Everyone complied except the last girl who kept pointing to the cave.

"Tobias, I think there's someone back in there. Wait a second."

Nathan paused at the opening. The tactical beam illuminated the cave. At first all he saw was a bundle of rags in the corner. Then it moved.

He knelt down. "Are you okay?"

The dirty face with dark brown eyes turned at the sound of his voice.

"*Nejatam bedin.*"

"I don't know what that means but me and my brother are going to get you out of here. Can you walk?" Nathan mimed walking out of the cave, signaling for her to follow.

In broken English she replied, "No, no. No walk."

Nathan returned to the mouth of the cave. "There's a lady in here. She can't walk, Tobes." He adjusted his rifle slung over his back.

"What should we do?"

Nathan paused. He looked at the ragged children hanging on to the rope behind his brother.

"Got no other choice, Tobes. You get them down to the truck and over to Aunt Gem's. I'll stay here with this one until you get back and the two of us can get her down the mountain."

"What if whoever locked them in the cave comes back?"

"Give me the extra box of ammo you got in your backpack."

"Seriously, Nate?"

"Whoever done what they did to little girls by starving them and keeping them locked up in an old dark cave won't deserve a friendly welcome."

Tobias tossed his twin the ammo. "I'll be back as soon as I can."

"Get to Aunt Gem's. I'll be okay here." Nathan propped the gate back so it would appear that it was still shut. He watched his brother lead the children down the path.

"You got her, Tobes?"

"Yeah. She doesn't weigh nothing. Light as a bird."

****

"Here," Nathan said as he helped the girl sit up, "just take sips of water. You'll throw up if you take too much."

She seemed to understand. Pointing to herself, she said, "Esin."

"Esin. That's a pretty name. I'm Nathan." He repeated the gesture.

"Nathan," She said, forcing a smile.

From his backpack, he retrieved an energy bar.

She nibbled at the food between drinks of water. While she ate, Nathan cleaned the cuts and sores on her feet. He applied clean 4x4 pads and wound rolled gauze around them. He finished with an Ace wrap.

"We need to get you out of here. This cave smells and is dirty. If you can get on my back, I can get you outside in the air."

Nathan pantomimed walking outside, then filling his lungs with air.

Esin nodded her head.

Nathan piggybacked her out. She squinted when the light hit her eyes. Nathan indicated a stop; she slumped off his back in a pile, exhausted. He cut several boughs from nearby pine trees and made a bed for her. He covered her with the survival blanket and his backpack served as a pillow.

Nathan took her pulse, made sure she was tucked in all around by the blanket. He loaded his rifle with eleven .17 HMR rounds, and placed one row of eleven rounds on standby for reloading quickly. There was another spot approximately fifteen feet from his first post. He lined up more rounds on a small stone behind cover. At a third place, he repeated the layout of bullets. If he had to move, he had ammo ready plus more in his pouch.

Once everything was set, he checked his watch against what he saw of the sun. He could see the mouth of the cave and the path leading up to it. If he had to fire, he had the element of surprise on his side. He began his wait.

Of Our Own Accord

Luke spread the map of the area across the hood of the truck.

"Pre-mission review." He passed copies to Zero, Cobalt, Scout, and Diego.

"We are here, and the turnoff from Highway 219 is south. This is the two track Diego and Cobalt will come in on from the north. The trailhead is here where I'll be. Vehicles secured here.

"Scout, you can take the high ground here. Zero, watch the road here." The men nodded as Luke pointed locations on the map.

"We will come in from the south and the north and meet at the last cave. Grab the kids and go. I'll come up on the Stone Path from this point. I'll cover your six."

Luke paused to look at the darkening rain filled clouds. They had to get the kids out of the mountains before it broke. "Update on their movement?"

Scout checked his computer. "There are two Humvee's coming our way. I've checked back to Waybird City. There were three of them yesterday at the motel, but I have trackers on only two. Can't find the third truck."

"If we have two coming, that drops the count down to maybe sixteen or so." Zero adjusted his equipment belt as he tried to count. "Driver and shotgun, three in the middle seat, and three in the back."

"Wrong answer," Cobalt corrected. "They need room for weapons, so take out three from each vehicle. Guys like that don't travel light and if they're going to take the kids, they'll need room."

"So, that's twelve."

"No wonder you blow everything up. You don't do the correct math."

"Hey, I got a computer that figures that out for me."

"Yeah, but you won't use it." Scout ratted on him.

"Don't argue with success. My estimates are better than most guys' calculations."

"Weather for tonight is rain. There's a front coming in from the southwest. Lightening, some wind, thunder." Luke put his phone back in his chest pocket.

"Ah," Diego said. "Ranger weather."

"Once everything is secure, we put an end to this."

"Roger that." Scout rechecked his satellite.

The others watched Cobalt staring into the woods, waiting for the inner storm to be unleashed.

****

Luke made his way along the worn trail until he came to the Stone Path trailhead. He found plenty of brush to hide his equipment. While he waited for the first radio check, Luke examined his side arm, magazines for his Glock 19, and familiarized himself with the M16 SCAR-L Zero issued.

"I wonder how much this set the taxpayer back?" he said softly to himself. He had three thirty round magazines, three grenades in his pack, two smoke canisters, and several flash bangs. The walkie talkie was tossed into his pack by Diego. "Just in case Scout's satellite drops from the sky."

The team would come in hard to destroy the snake nest in the mountains surrounding his home. Luke was sure his barbarians would descend on the traffickers with violence in action so swift they wouldn't know what hit them.

"In position, radio check all units. Scout, radio check with Sheriff Harris. Copy."

Luke froze at the sound of a branch breaking close by and a moan of pain.

****

Nathan gave Esin more to drink and offered her a chocolate bar, which she nibbled before falling asleep again. He left her to search the immediate area looking for more camouflage.

The branch snapping under his weight alerted squirrel chatter. Nathan ducked behind the thickness of the minni bush at the base of an old growth chestnut tree. He breathed through his mouth, feeling his heartbeat slow. Nathan heard a familiar voice.

"Luke?" His voice was hoarse as he whispered. Nathan saw his brother through the leaves.

"Nathan? Tobes?"

The boy stood. "Nathan. I could use your help."

"Stand down, all units, stand down," Luke called into his com.

"Copy." came from all four men at once.

Scout's voice came over the earpiece. "What's up, CB?"

"My brother's here. Standby."

****

"What in good hell are you doing here, Nathan?"

"I can ask you the same thing, Luke."

"I asked first."

"You're the one who called all hot and bothered about the trails and caves up here. You never went caving with Dad and us. Not once. All of a sudden you want to know everything about this place. Tobias and I..."

"You got Tobias here? Where?"

"He drove all the kids that could go to Aunt Gem's to get taken care of."

"Drove? You took Dad's truck?"

"Yeah, and it's a good thing we did so we could rescue those kids."

"I don't believe this." Luke sat down hard on the ground and wiped his hands over his face.

"So, what are you doing here?"

"Well, my team was going to save those kids, but I guess you and Tobes did already."

"There's one more over here, Luke. She needs help. You can chew Tobes and me out later."

Luke touched his earpiece. "Diego and Cobalt, come to my position. We have a female for transport. Over."

"Copy, CB. Out."

"Scout. I need some time. Can you delay the guests? Over."

"Affirmative. Looks like their engine light is on and a flat tire in 3,2,1. Out."

****

"Luke, what are they doing here? How come they call you CB?"

"It's a long story. How long since Tobias left?"

"I don't remember. But come here and see Esin."

"You've got her name?"

"Yeah. She's not afraid of me."

Nathan touched Esin on her shoulder. She opened her eyes to see a man talking to her. He put his arm around her shoulders and raised her into a sitting position, her back resting against his chest, cradled in his arm.

"Nate, go get a bottle of water and one of the energy pouches in my ruck."

What little water that was left in Nate's bottle, Luke used to dampen a cloth from his shirt pocket. He patted her forehead, her cheeks, and around her neck. She smiled at him.

"Mix the powder with the water and let's try to get some of that into her. What you did was very brave."

"You going to tell Dad that after you tell him we took the truck?"

"The truck is immaterial. You could've come up here, looked around and went home with no one none the wiser. You could've left those kids in the cave and kept your mouth shut."

"We weren't raised like that."

"No, you weren't. Dad will be pleased."

"Luke, someone's coming."

"That'll be Diego and Cobalt. Go show them the way up."

In a few moments, Diego unpacked his medical kit. He took Esin's blood pressure, checked her heart, oxygen levels, and pupils.

"Cobalt, she looks Afghan. Tell her we'll get her out of here."

In Farci, Cobalt explained that they would help her. Diego is a doctor. Esin nodded.

"She's in the Baha'i community. She's Christian. That's probably why she was caught and sold."

"Scout. We're transporting now. Over."

"Copy. Sheriff Harris can meet you halfway to the highway. Out."

Cobalt gingerly picked up Esin in his arms. He and Diego disappeared into the moist vegetation.

****

"When Tobias gets here, you and him go."

"What about Tater and Maggs?"

"I've got them taken care of until Mom and Dad get home."

"You ain't no librarian are you, Luke." Nathan spoke not a question but a fact and Luke knew Nate wasn't going to quit until he had the truth.

"No, I'm not."

"And your friends, are they really Rangers?"

"Yes, they are.

"So all the postcards you send from overseas, were you really there when you sent them?"

"Yes."

"The government sends you to all those places for your work and not vacations like you wrote to Mom?"

"Yes."

"Why did you tell Mom and Dad those were vacations?"

"I'm not going to tell you all I do, Nate. And I want your word, man to man, that you don't betray my confidence to the folks, or even to Tobias. I need you to promise me that."

"Not tell my twin?"

"No."

It was Nathan's turn to be hesitant. He knew he had crossed the threshold from child to man.

"Okay, I promise."

"Sometimes we have to tell good lies so that the truth doesn't hurt the ones we love. Mom thinks I work for the Library of Congress. Sometimes I do, but it isn't to help people write books. It's because I want information. I work across Agency lines..."

"Agency? That's another word for the CIA? Where they train spies?"

"Yes. I'm not a spy like in the movies. I can't tell you what I do. I'm benefiting the country, and I'm surrounded by good people who assist me."

"The Rangers? Zero, Diego..."

"They are brothers to me. Anyone of them would die protecting our family."

"Well, Maggs sure has taken to Cobalt."

"She likes him because she thinks he 'colors inside the lines verwy, verwy well.'"

Nathan smiled at the imitation of his sister. "What happens next?"

"We'll wait for Tobias, then you leave. When the bad guys arrive, it could get nasty around here. I don't want the team to have to worry about where you are."

"What if you need back up? You remember Tobes and me won these rifles in a shooting competition."

"Yes, Dad called me when he found out."

"Where were you?"

"On a mountain outside Lhasa, Tibet."

"I made you a promise, now you make me one."

"If I can."

"Someday you'll tell me everything. All of it. I want to know where you went and what you did. I want every detail."

"Nate, someday I will. I promise."

The sound of the pickup truck echoed up the hill. Shortly, Tobias came through the brush and stopped when he saw Luke and Nate sitting on a log.

"You waiting for me?"

"What did Aunt Gem say about the kids?" Luke wanted to steer the discussion in another direction.

"I told Aunt Gem what happened and what we did and where we got the kids. Gem wanted me to stay but I told her I had to get back. I left when Running Deer and Birdie were pulling in the yard. That's all I know so far."

"You guys did really well, but now you need to go home. I don't know how much time we have..."

Scout's voice cut in "CB. They're on the move. I repeat, they're on the move. Copy."

"Copy. ETA? Over." Luke responded.

"They've put the juice to it, ignoring the check engine light. Over."

"Scout. We've got a wrinkle. My two brothers are here. The kids are gone and are safe. This is a cleanup operation. Over."

"What are the orders? Over."

"Standby."

"No can do. From what I see on Mount Olympus, the lost third vehicle will be parking just below you in thirty-three minutes. Other two vehicles arriving in Zero's location in twenty-eight. Standby. Over."

"Suggestions? Over."

Zero's voice came over the com. "CB, send the boys up to Scout on the high ground. They can help monitor below. Over."

"Copy. Everyone standby until Diego and Cobalt return. Out."

The team maintained radio silence until the voice they all wanted to hear came over the channel: "On your six. Copy."

"Copy, Cobalt. Out." Luke turned to his brothers. "You get up to the ridge." He used his map to show them how to get to Scout.

"No, Luke," Tobias said. "There's the deer path just inside the tree line. The only open ground we have to worry about is here, and we can cross that before the bad guys get here. Nate said that when you called."

"Correct. Good looking out."

Luke stood and brought the twins in to hug them. He kissed them on the head and ruffled their hair.

"You know I hate when you do that, Luke," Tobias said.

"Dad does it all the time."

"Yeah, but he's Dad. You're just a brother."

Luke did it again because he was older and he could.

"You gather your stuff and get going. Scout will be looking for you, but keep quiet and move quickly."

"Luke, we ain't stupid."

"I've been hearing that a lot lately."

The young CIA agent watched the twins, their backpacks and prized Golden Boys, disappear up the Stone Path to the ridge. He said a silent prayer that everything would turn out alright. God help him if it didn't.

Warrior

He carries her, carefully, tenderly. He speaks in her language.

She is confused. Angels from God do not have beards. Is this a dream? Is she dead? Where does he take her? To Heaven? To Hell? Surely she goes to Hell for what she has done, for what has become of her. She is innocent but it is too late.

She keeps her eyelids firmly closed. She does not want to see the gates of fire open for her.

****

"Diego, she keeps going in and out."

Gentle hands touch her arms, ribs, and softly prod her abdomen, her back.

"I don't see any signs of internal bleeding."

"Cobalt. Over."

"Cobalt. Go."

"Harris is at rendezvous coordinates. Over."

"Copy. Almost there. Over."

"Eye in the sky says the visitors are in route to our location. ETA thirty minutes. Over."

"Copy. Out."

"Diego, can we get back in that time frame?"

"Sure. Let's make it happen, cap'n."

****

Floating in the arms of the dark angel, she willingly accepts the pain of the damned because it is less than the pain of the living.

He puts something in her hand. She knows the white cloth with its black embroidery around the edges. Her fingertips know each letter, each knot, each thread: *nejatam bedin.* It is the sign she waited for.

God collected her tears.

He recorded them in His book.

She was not forgotten.

He unleashed His warrior to save her.

****

The western sky darkens with the oncoming storm. Mrs. Cunningham shutters her downstairs windows preventing yard debris breaking the glass. Mr. and Mrs. Brubaker unplug their computer and TV; they'd been hit by lightning before. Ambrie Sykes checks the portable generator and gas cans satisfied she can keep the freezers running. Elsie and Howard Perkins complete their shopping. Confident everything is well at home, they decide to go back to the hotel for dinner and stay another night. Hector and Alice Cobb finish feeding the dogs. The kennel is secure against the coming high winds. Special Agent Cleveland Coop and FBI Forensic Specialist GS-9 Ubell Gant sort through evidence bags for their report. Agnes and Fishbone Crawford share a room down the hall. Mike Green makes an emergency trip with Sheriff Harris and they transport a young woman to Glassman's clinic. Running Deer and Aunt Gem each sit in a rocking chair, cuddling children who don't understand the lullabies but who are comforted by their compassion. The other ladies give baths, tend to wounds, and dress the children in clean clothes. Birdie Spry cuddles a little boy, patting his back as if he was her own. While she rocks, she plots.

On the unnamed sandy two track, three men in black stand at the side urinating. They act like little boys shooting their streams in the weeds. Another man waits at the front of the vehicle smoking a cigarette. The fifth man sorts through weapons at the back of the Humvee.

The sound of thunder gives him cover. Cobalt takes three strides and places his left arm around the throat of the man at the rear of the truck. He plunges his Tanto knife into the man's *medulla oblongata* for the silent kill. Cobalt lowers him to the ground with the first drops of rain.

"Ain't you guys done taking a leak?"

Diego gives no warning from behind. In one fluid movement, he breaks the smoker's neck.

CB hears six shots ring out in rapid succession. "And so it begins."

THE PARTY'S OVER

CB WAS RELEAVED TO see the two Rangers come up the hill. "Everything okay?"

Diego replied, "Yes. She's stable and we handed her over to Harris and Mike, who, I must say, looks very dapper in his new uniform as a deputy."

"Good. Brief me on the Hummer on the north end of the trail."

"Cobalt neutralized them when they stopped for a smoke and a leak."

"Who pissed the furthest?"

"Cobalt shot them before I could ask."

"And the one smoking?"

Diego grinned. "Let's say he won't have to worry about lung cancer."

"CB. Over." Scout called from the ridge.

"CB. Go."

"I've got the junior Rangers with me tracking your movements. Over."

"Copy."

Diego was surprised. "How'd your brothers get here?"

"They laid out the whole area for me when I called from Gracie's. Because they're smart, they were curious why I was interested in the caves. They packed up, found the kids in the cave, and took it from there."

"Ten years in the Rangers and I get out maneuvered by twelve year old's. I'm heading over to give Zero cover." Cobalt tapped his earpiece. "Zero. In route. Copy."

"Hey, big guy, slow down. Guests headed up the trail to the cabin. Over."

"Copy. Will cover your six. Over."

"Make it my three. Out."

Cobalt nodded to Luke and Diego, then walked into the misty rain and out of sight.

****

"Tobias, use this tablet to track our men. There's a special sensor on each of them. The letter you see below the dot tells you which soldier belongs to that dot. The C-1 is for Cobalt. There he is. He's moving toward Zero. Look at the map, then out over the valley. Keep watching as he moves closer to the Z."

"Nathan, this is an ENVG-B or Enhanced Night Vision Goggle-Binocular."

"Like the ones that when you look through them it's all green?"

"That's right."

"My Dad has those for watching deer in the woods."

"Look, these are better. You can outline human sized targets. Check this out." Scout adjusted the high tech binoculars. "Now look through them."

"Looks like a video game."

"A lot of recruits were raised on video games and they really bust out on these."

Scout handed a thermal imaging camera to Tobias.

"Now this beauty uses thermal infrared. You're seeing heat instead of light. It works by detecting heat and then translates the heat into temperature variations. This is in a grayscale. The brighter shades are hot and the darker ones are cold or cooler."

"Wow. I can see Zero, Cobalt. There's Luke...er, CB."

"Guys, here's the important part: you keep watching our men. This is our zone of action."

"What's that?"

"This is where we do all our work. Our team depends on us to have oversight and help direct them to, umm, take care of the enemy. We can see what they can't."

They nodded.

Tobias asked, "Scout, are you guys gonna get in trouble for all this?"

"You mean taking military equipment and having a firefight in the mountains with civilians?" He paused, then added, "Nah."

Scout scanned the area and checked his calculations of the terrain.

"From here on in, we practice sound discipline. We don't want our voices to echo and let the enemy know where we are. Only talk when we have to. Got it?"

"Yes, sir."

"Yes, sir."

"And also, you stay behind me when you hear gunfire. Just put the equipment down and get behind me on the ground. That's an order."

"Yes, Scout."

"Yeah, Scout."

"Zero. Over." Scout detected movement.

"Zero. Go."

"You've got six from the south. Over."

"Copy."

"Zero. Over."

"Zero. Go CB."

"Let them get in the cabin. They'll be off guard when they find the body. Copy."

CB and Diego started on the Stone Path.

"Copy. Visual confirmed. Zero Out."

****

Allen, Racy, and four hand picked guards walked single file along the path to the cabin.

"How far?" one of them asked Allen.

"When we get there is how far. You sound like a kid in the back seat."

In his thick Bronx accent, Racy said, "Not far. Clarence said he picked this place cuz it's outta the way. No cops out herah. Keeps the food chain rollin', ya know whad I mean?"

They walked past the camouflaged Ranger. Zero kept them in the cross hairs, his trigger finger ready.

Allen pulled out his weapon when he saw the cabin door wide open. "Something ain't right, something ain't right."

One of the guards phoned back to the lead vehicle. "Boss, looks like we got trouble."

The passenger door of the Humvee opened. The man in the tailored suit stepped out onto the road, avoiding the mud puddle forming from the rain. He shouted into his phone.

"What's wrong? Skull should be there by now. Where's Garza?"

"Boss, the front door's wide open," Allen said. "There ain't nobody here."

"Get my raincoat from the back," he growled at his assistant. "Damnit, I have to do everything myself." By the time he got across the sandy road, he was fuming. He turned back to shout at his driver.

"Derrick, call the other vehicle. Find out what the hell they are doing and where they are."

"They don't respond, Boss."

"Then keep calling until they do. One of you stays with Derrick and watch the trucks, while the rest come with me." Several armed men followed Boss up the path.

****

Zero whispered, "Six up and on on the way. Copy."

"Copy," Cobalt whispered. "Scout, get eyes on them. Over."

"Copy." Scout searched over the area.

"Play out. Over." CB called.

"Copy. All units standby. Out." Scout took the tablet, showing Nathan and Tobias where the team was located.

Nathan kept his voice just above a whisper. "I can see CB over there."

"Stay frosty, gentlemen." Scout winked at the boys.

****

"Good Jezz." Allen ran out the door after seeing the dead man slumped on the floor. Racy heard him vomit in the grass.

"What in hell? Did he kill hisself? Look, dude," Racy said to the bodyguard. "He's holding the knife in his hand. That don't make sense."

The other guards entered, one already on the phone. "Boss, Skull's dead."

"Where's the product?"

"I don't know but there's no one here. I see one bedroom all tore up, looks like someone was there, but it's empty."

"Check the other rooms." Boss found a fifty dollar bill on the ground. "Look for the money."

Boss was furious. With Clarence gone, Garza not answering the phone, Skull dead, it could only mean one of two things: a competitor tried to take over or Clarence and Jiggy actually stole the money and the product.

"Nothing here except boxes of diapers, clothes, and food wrappers. They're gone."

"I know they're gone. But where'd they go?"

Boss was at the cabin and up the steps, his designer raincoat flaring out as he tossed the phone to the man behind him.

In the tree, Cobalt relaxed his trigger finger. Zero signaled he was going south to the road.

Like a shadow in the night, the demolition expert left his position and blended with the foliage, never disturbing even a mosquito on his way to the road.

Derrick, his back to the vehicles, raised his phone trying to get a signal. The other man was down the edge of the shoulder, smoking. Diego attached a small amount of C4 to the front wheel well of the first Humvee, then stepped silently to the second. He placed a cigarette pack sized amount to the frame just behind the grill and bumper. After he re-crossed the road, he popped a smoke grenade under the first vehicle and a frag grenade under the second.

From behind a shelf of rock, Zero counted, "Four, three, two..." The explosion blew the first Humvee into the culvert, killing the smoker. The grenade/C4 combo flipped the second up and over, killing Derrick.

"I bet you guys never saw that coming." Zero disappeared the way he came. About sixty meters in, he turned to examine his handiwork. "Probably should have used more C4."

"You got it, Zero. Don't worry about it, I can see it from here," Scout said.

****

The shock wave blew the front windows into the cabin. Boss dove to the ground. Two body guards fell over him. Roof shingles and eavestroughs were scattered among the trees and yard.

"Get off me you idiots. We're under attack. Gun, give me a gun." One of them put a Glock in his hand. Using the doorframe for cover, Boss looked down the trail, then left, then right.

"How do we get out of here?"

"Boss, there's a back way up by the caves," Allen said. "It's how we got product to a back road."

"Okay, move, move," Boss ordered. If the explosion came from a competitor, they were special forces trained. He knew how they worked.

"Get out the back and split up," Boss said. He ducked behind one of his bodyguards, pushing the man until Boss found a tree stump for cover. Just as Boss dove behind the rotted stump, the two men behind him were eliminated by Cobalt, hidden in a Pitch Pine tree.

Scout looked at the twins behind him, flat to the ground as instructed. "Just a few more minutes, guys, then we'll go for ice cream."

The boys were wide eyed gripping their rifles.

"This ain't nothing like deer hunting with Dad," Tobias said.

"Three on the north side of the trail. Fifteen meters from Cobalt. Over." Scout scanned the area.

"Cobalt, you're slipping," Diego admonished. "You need to up your game. Over."

Three shots rang out.

"My apologies, my man. I'm humbled. Out."

"Scout, where's the rain coat guy?" Cobalt radioed.

"Still hunkered down behind the big stump to your left. He's got two, maybe three men with him. Two more are still on the back porch. One is running up the hill, just past the first cave, and two running to Diego. Copy."

"*Dos coyotes.* Copy." Diego wiped the rain from his face as he shouldered his MK16. The first man slipped on the wet ground and tumbled to the side. The Ranger fired, catching the second one center mass.

"You missed one," Cobalt chided.

"He's yours. I didn't want to hurt your feelings."

From inside the cabin, Allen and Racy fire pistols frantically into the under-brush. They emptied their weapons and ran through the front door and down the path. The sight of the two vehicles blazing made them pivot, and run back to the cabin.

****

"How're we going to get out of here, Allen? We ain't got nothing to do with this, we didn't start this...it's all Boss's operation."

"Now's not the time to be a coward, Racy."

"I ain't a coward. Maybe if we go out the back with our hands up, we can surrender?"

"There's bullets whizzing around. Besides, who do we surrender to?"

The door frame exploded from a round, spewing slivers of wood above their heads.

"Hello, gentleman." A man's silhouette appeared several yards down the path.

"We surrender." Racy stood with his hands up walking slowly across the living room.

Zero smiled under his camo painted face. "Too late, man. Fire in the hole."

The Ranger rolled over the ground and behind a buttress of limestone rock. He pressed a button as he took cover. The first charge crumbled the carrier beams under the floor. Racy and Allen fell screaming into the basement as the secondary charge collapsed the roof and walls, burying them under tons of debris. The third charge started the fire which consumed the structure.

"Perfectamundo. I call that a ten." Scout looked at the twins. "You guys still okay?"

"Yeah. It's pretty amazing. I mean...Shit, I don't know what I mean." Nathan was shaking.

"Language," reminded Tobias.

"It's normal. We'll talk about it later with CB. You're good soldiers."

Scout scanned the area with his thermal camera.

"CB. Diego. Green truck parked on the road. I don't think they stopped for weenies and marshmallows. Two males. Well, I'll be. It's our babysitters from the 'Stan. Over."

"Are they getting out? Over."

"Not yet. Just watching the burn pile. Over."

"Copy. Out." CB signaled Diego to go high while CB would go low on the slant of the trail. A bullet flew past CB's head and through the rim of Diego's hat, knocking it off his head. CB spun, firing a round from his Glock 19 into the man's chest.

"Nice dance move. Thanks."

"How many of these guys are there? They pop up like poison ivy after a rain."

"Who knows for sure. Zero counted them. Where's my boonie?"

***

Boss was pinned down behind the tree trunk.

"Listen," he shouted, "we can make a deal where everyone comes out on top. There's plenty of money to go around."

Boss whispered to a bodyguard behind a boulder, "Get up to that ridge. There's a spotter up there and take him out. I'll cover you."

He fired a barrage of bullets, aiming at where he thought the lookout would be. The guard took a round to the head from Cobalt's first shot; the stump took the second, scattering bark over Boss's head.

"That'll teach him to shoot at me," Scout spoke into his mic.

Boss ordered the second guard up toward the caves.

"I'll give you a hundred thousand to take out the spotter."

"Done deal, Boss." The thug in black stayed low and behind available cover as he started the climb.

Boss tried to open up a dialogue. He shouted, "Guys, I mean there's a lot of money. I can cut you in for a third and you'll get 200k to begin with. Now, how many ways do we make it?"

Zero tossed a grenade toward the sound of his voice.

After the smoke cleared, Boss shouted again "I take it that's a no. Listen, we can keep this up all day."

Diego whispered over his com, "I doubt that. Not with Zero's inventory."

"Fellas, let's just take five minutes to think about my offer. More money than you've ever made or ever will make. Women, booze, travel. Whatever you want. Even the kinky stuff. I can make it happen." He tried to see how far up his man was, but the foliage impeded his view.

****

Tobias followed the heat signals on the tablet. All CB's men were accounted for but there was an extra figure coming up the ridge.

"Nate, look. I think this one is headed toward us."

The gunfire started again.

"What do we do?"

"Grab your rifle and keep low."

The two boys crawled on their bellies, then stayed in the underbrush.

The man was big, dressed in black, blending with the darkness of the fading light and the rain. He anticipated traveling up the ridge, quietly coming behind the spotter and taking the high ground after killing whoever was there directing fire.

Nathan nodded to Tobias and Tobias nodded back. With one mind, they opened fire. The figure screamed, grabbing his legs, as the rounds entered and then went through his calf and thigh, shattering bone. He stumbled, fell, and rolled over a cliff into a ravine.

Tobias picked up the handgun as he looked over the edge. There was no movement below.

Over his shoulder Scout said, "I thought I told you to stay here and stay low. Is it good?"

"Yes, sir. All good," Nathan promised.

"CB. One six meters south of your position. He's standing next to the tree reloading his magazine. Over."

CB fired. The man dropped and did not move.

"That's a hit. Over."

"What's the count? Over."

"The one who won't shut up is still behind the log. I think your brothers took out the one that was going to overrun our position. Over."

"They killed him? Over."

"No, I don't think so, but the sudden stop in the ravine did. They have his weapon. Over."

"Are they okay? Over."

"Yeah, shaking, but they're tough little Perkins. Over."

"Location of Smith and Jones. Over."

"On the road by the Humvee barbeque. No movement. Over."

Still in the pine, Cobalt adjusted his boonie hat. "I knew they were cowards."

"Awaiting orders, CB. Over."

"I've got to get my brothers off the mountain. Over."

"They're good where they are. Over."

With a massive bolt of lightening and an earth shaking roll of thunder, the heavens poured a continuous gray curtain of water.

"CB. Over."

"CB. Go."

"I'm blind. Nothing works in rain like this. The zombie dudes got back in their truck and are heading east. But I lost one, maybe two of the others. Over."

"I'm on the way up but not blind. Over."

Tobias tapped Scout's shoulder. "What's that mean?"

"They want to get up here with us but not without knowing where the rest of the bad guys are."

"Tell CB to go a couple yards north of the Stone Path. There's a deer trail that'll take him up here. Sheesh, I told him that once already."

Nathan wiped the rain off his rifle, then tucked it under his raincoat. "He's like Maggie. She don't listen either."

****

CB and Diego made their way along the hillside using the rain and the foliage to hide themselves along the deer trail.

"Cobalt. Over."

"Cobalt. Go."

"You can come out of the trees, monkey. And bring your little buddy with you. Over."

"Turn around." Cobalt stood behind CB, dressed in a ghillie suit of pine boughs. "Zero is admiring his handiwork at the road."

A break in the downpour brought Scout's equipment back on line.

"Zero. Two south of you. Over."

"Copy."

Cobalt's deep voice came over the com. "And where are we on let's make a deal? The car or what's behind curtain number two?"

"You've got your game shows mixed up, bro. But, he's leaving, too. Cancel the table reservation for three by the fireplace. Over." Scout waited for a reply.

"Scout. Over." CB holstered his Glock.

"Scout. Go."

"Make a diversion until we rendezvous at your location. Over."

"Copy. Out."

Scout looked at the twins, rain dripping off their hats, eyes wide, and shaking. The Ranger didn't know if it was with excitement or cold, but he knew they were game for what came next.

"Do you boys think you can stir up enough firepower with those rifles and buy our soldiers time to get here?"

They nodded in unison. "Sure."

"I've got two West Virginia Rangers laying down suppressing fire. Be ready to move." To the twins he said, "Aim high. We just want to make noise and cover our guys."

Scout gave the order. "Fire when ready. Light 'em up."

The first sounds of the rifles reverberated off the hillside. The twins kept firing while CB, Cobalt and Diego ran up the trail. Zero moved his position from the south of the first hairpin turn of the Stone Path and dove into the underbrush at the base of the lime rock walls supporting the path and the caves. The twins kept firing into the trees until Scout waved them to stop.

CB understood his barbarians were not going to let anyone get away. He figured Zero and Diego would follow the two men, while Scout directed the movement. Cobalt would go on his own.

"Dude," CB started to say but was stopped by the look of determination on Cobalt's face.

"'There is no hunting like the hunting of men, and those who have hunted armed men long enough and like it, never care for anything else thereafter.'" Cobalt looked into the rising fog.

"I know," CB said so only Cobalt could hear him.

"I am what I am, CB."

"Then, happy hunting." They shook hands and hugged.

The three Rangers began their track. CB heard Zero ask, "Who were you quoting, Cobalt?"

"Hemingway."

"I thought it was Bart Simpson. Hemingway? Are you sure?"

Cobalt put his arm around Zero. "Pretty sure."

****

The clouds parted, giving way to a blue sky. Scout handed CB a phone.

"It's for you. Director of Homeland Security."

CB took the phone, a puzzled look on his face, but he broke into a smile when he heard the voice on the other end.

"Hey, Mom. Yep, everything's fine."

****

"Guys, you stay here with Scout and pack up equipment. I'm going to check for evidence. I'll be right back."

Tobias was interested in every aspect of Scout's equipment and began asking rapid fire questions about his education, time in the military and training. Nathan was more interested in watching CB leave the high ground. He waited a few minutes before following his brother.

CB was careful as he picked his way along the path. Some stones were slippery while the muddy water hid the spaces between others; easy ankle breakers if he wasn't cautious.

The first three caves were empty. The fourth one was different. He pushed the grated door the rest of the way open. The light from his tactical flashlight illuminated the walls and ceiling.

CB kicked a couple of paper bags and flashed his light on a pile of rugs in the corner. It was only when he turned to go he realized his mistake; the pile of rags hid the man who suddenly tightened his arm around CB's throat.

He tucked his chin in the bend of the attacker's elbow, then rolled his right shoulder over to his left knee as he jutted his buttocks back into the man's groin. The man was thrown over CB's back and on the ground. The flashlight rolled across the floor plunging the cave into darkness except for illumination against the back wall.

Whoosh. The punch was coming but CB couldn't avoid it. The attacker caught CB on the right side just behind his ear. It stunned him but didn't disable him. As his eyes adjusted to the dim light, CB threw a left uppercut; he followed through with a right close jab, connecting with the man's face.

The young CIA officer grabbed the flashlight and stuck the end into the soft ground.

"The better to see you with, my dear. Wanna fight? Come on, then. You hit like a girl." CB felt the weight of his Glock gone from his hip, scattered in the cavern someplace.

The man roared something in a Slavic tongue. CB knew it wasn't Russian but by the looks of him, the man was from someplace in Central Asia. He wasn't so tall, but thick, stocky.

"Okay, dude, let's see what all those hours in the gym did for you."

The man put his hands up in front of his face, trying to look menacing over his fists.

"Right. Boxing it is," CB said as he came in for a roundhouse kick. to the man's head. The Slav ducked but grabbed CB's ankle and twisted. They both fell to the gravel floor.

CB was up first but a quick roll by the attacker in the tight space caught him by surprise. He tripped backward against the wall. The Slav rose to his feet immediately, and grabbing CB by the front of his jacket, landed jab after jab to CB's face.

CB feigned sliding down the wall as if passed out, but slammed a fist into the man's groin. It didn't phase him.

The attacker took long enough to laugh at CB's wasted effort, but that was all the time CB needed. Using his right fist, he slammed everything he had into the man's solar plexus, bowling him over and against the far wall.

"Don't run away. I'm not done with you." CB took in deep gulps of air, balanced his stance, and waited to see what the attacker would do next.

"Run out of tricks?" CB asked.

"Not yet, little man," came the reply.

"So you do speak English."

In a thick accent he said, "Is not important for you. You not hear because you dead."

He rushed across the cave like a charging bull elk, waving arms in place of antlers. CB pushed off the wall and aimed a two heel drop kick to the man's chest. At the last possible second the man veered, avoiding the full force of the kick. CB dropped to the floor and the man dove on top, the flash of a knife blade in his hand.

The two of them rolled side to side, each trying to find a weakness in the other. The attacker held his forearm across CB's throat. His free hand holding the blade, closer and closer to CB's eye.

Boom! The sound of the exploding round filled the cave, reverberating wall to wall, ceiling to floor, echoing like a caged lion pacing against the bars. The man's hand, still holding the knife, fell on CB's chest as the attacker screamed. CB grabbed the handle, and deftly inserted the blade at a forty five degree angle midway between the jaws. He shoved it all the way to the hilt, bisecting his attacker's tongue at its base, through the epiglottis, dragging on bone between C1 and C2 vertebrae, but finally exiting at the cerebellum. With disgust, he pushed the man off.

The slight figure stood silhouetted at the mouth of the cave, smoke coming from the barrel of the rifle.

"How long have you been standing there?"

"Long enough to see you were getting your ass kicked."

"Thanks. A little slow on the draw, but thanks."

"I wanted to make sure I had a clean shot. Did I kill him?"

"No, I did. You just shot his hand off."

"It looked like you were getting the raw end of it. Lot of blows to the face..."

"I get it, Nathan."

"Yeah, he was really hammering you. A left, then a right, then..."

"Nathan, okay."

"First time I've ever seen a Perkins get a ass whippin' like that."

"It will be the second time you see a Perkins get an ass whippin' if you don't..." He saw his brother smiling.

"I appreciate your skill, Nathan." CB painfully got up from the stony floor of the cave.

Nathan flashed the light across CB's face. "Whew. Look at that."

"Is it bad?"

"What are you going to tell Mom?"

"That I fell?"

"She ain't gonna believe that. Tobias used it the last time he got in a fight on the school yard. Better find another excuse."

BREAKFAST AT BIRDIE'S

THE RANGERS PARTED WAYS at the road. The acrid smell of burning tires permeated the air.

"I guess this is it," Diego said. "Another enjoyable retreat at the OK Corral."

"Happy hunting, gentlemen," Cobalt replied. "I'll see you at Shorty's for Leadslingers and beer."

"Happy hunting, dude," Zero said. They shook hands and hugged.

Zero and Diego watched Cobalt adjust his cover as he disappeared into the wet brush and fog.

****

"Scout, you got any images for me? Over." Diego checked the monitor.

"Sending. Quality isn't good. Over."

Zero looked at the screen. "They're about one click to the southeast."

"Copy. Happy hunting. Out."

They checked their weapons, magazines, and adjusted their ruck.

"Touch up your face paint, bro. You won't make the cover of Vogue like that."

"You're still ugly as ever, Zero."

"Said the man to the mirror."

"How much should we take?"

"We don't need all of it. Poncho, ammo, boonie hat, ammo, energy bars, ammo..."

"Zero, I got it."

Satisfied everything was in order, they started down the embankment through the trees, silently, deadly, and determined.

****

The blond man was struggling to make it through the boggy muck as he tried to dodge branches slapping across his face from his partner ahead of him. "Do you think any of them will follow us?"

"What do you think? You've had military training. Do you think after all that firepower they'll just drop the whole thing and ignore that we got away?"

"I was in the Air Force."

"Oh. That sucks."

"Maybe they'll be too busy to notice we're missing. We must've gone a couple of miles. My feet are freezing."

"If they've come after us, cold feet will be the least of your worries. Keep your voice down."

****

Diego brought the ENVG-B binoculars up to his eyes and began scanning the area.

Zero was shocked. "You got Scout's new spy glasses? He'll be pissed. You know how he is about his equipment."

"Like you are about your grenades?"

"Well, yeah. What're you gonna tell him?"

"Nothing. I'll put them in the case when we're done and he'll never know."

Scout's voice came over their earpieces. "You both will be court martialed and confined to Leavenworth for the rest of your natural lives."

"Diego, he still loves us."

****

Wave after wave of rain pelted the mountain side. The two men found a thick pine tree to huddle under. Drops of rain collided, forming long drizzles of water from the branches, sometimes missing them and sometimes making a direct hit on their necks; the jackets were worthless as the chilling molecules penetrated the threads. Each time a thunderbolt hit the mountainside, they shuddered.

"They've got some hellish storms around here. We can't stay like this all night."

"You really are a coward. Where do you want to go? San Fran? Atlanta? We're stuck here until we can get off this mountain."

"Yeah, yeah, I get it. But how are we going to get paid?"

"There's only so many places that welcome a guy like Boss. We've been to most of them. Once we get out of here, we'll find him and collect. He knows he owes us." He took another drag from the cigarette just before a cord of raindrops hit it and put it out.

"Damn it. Just stay away from the low spots. A little stream around here will be a raging river with this rain."

"Got another dry smoke?"

"Yeah. Can't do anything else."

****

A break in the clouds gave Scout what he needed. "They're under a pine tree, maybe 500 meters south and east of you. You'll have to cross an open field. Over."

"Got it. I see them. Over."

"What's your plan? Over."

"Don't know. We might play with them a little first. Out."

"We're going to edge the field?"

"I think so, Zero. They're tired and miserable by now. We can cover ground they can't."

Zero sniffed the wind. "Wait. I smell cigarette smoke."

"Our lucky strike."

"Mike Oscar, bro."

****

"What was that? Someone coming?"

"No one's coming. They'd have caught us by now if they were."

"I told you, I heard something. There's something out there."

"Yes, you're right. There's raccoon, opossum, bats, and night birds. So, yes, probably some dumb deer stepping on twigs. That's your second cigarette. You done?"

"Yeah. Which way do we go? I don't know where the road is."

"I think we keep going up to the ridge. See? Just over there. You can barely see it."

"I'm tired. Can't we rest?"

"You've had your rest. You want to stay here and have bears eat you?"

"Damn it. There's something trying to get me. It just hit my head."

"We're under a pine tree. Probably a pine cone or bird crap. Let's go."

The clouds closed over the mountain releasing not a torrent but a soft misty rain. The terrain became more and more difficult to traverse. It seemed the branches and vines reached out, curling around their legs, dragging them into the boggy ground. Their chests strained inhaling air heavy laiden with moisture. Each step forward to the ridge was fraught with the danger of slipping and tumbling back down the mountain side.

"How many times have we fallen? I think I've blown my ACL on that last spill. God, I can hardly walk. How long have we been going? I'm ready for another cigarette."

"Shut up. Your voice carries all over the place."

"Well, if we're alone out here, I guess it doesn't matter. And stop telling me to shut up. You're in this just as deep as I am."

"It won't be long. The rain's let up. Here's a smoke."

"This route through West Virginia was supposed to be easy. Clarence and his dimwit brother sold Boss on this stop over. I still think we should have just gassed it all the way to Buffalo, stashed the product, then over to Toronto. We get paid, and they get their product to Montreal however the hell they want."

"So, let's have a do-over okay? We'll just go back in time. Are you crazy? Stop bellyaching about it. We need to get back to civilization and make contact."

"When we catch up with Clarence and Franklin Wells, I'd shoot them both in the head and never look back."

"Agreed. Them and that moron Garza cost us the whole operation. Both our vehicles are gone, Derrick, Jimmy, Allen…"

They smoked in silence until the tall man said, "You done? Once we get to the top, it's clear enough we should be able to see the road and get an idea of just where the hell we are."

"What's that sound?"

"Nothing."

"What about that one?"

"Again, nothing. Just smoke and shut up.

"Give me five minutes

"Okay. Just five."

They sat back against the trunk of a tree, softly snoring in two.
****

Zero and Diego hid along the edge of the trail.

"They've been sleeping long enough. Time to wake the boys up." Diego performed his impression of an owl. Then he cupped his hand over his mouth and made a half whistle half caw sound.

"What was that?" whispered Zero. "I know an owl when I hear it, but what was the second one?"

"I don't know. I just made it up."

Scout's voice came over the com line. "Status. Over."

"Stationary. They needed a night-night break. Over."

"I thought you'd be done by now. Over."

"Yeah. Diego wanted to play tag. Everything cleaned up? Over."

"Affirmative. There was one hiding in the last cave. CB took care of it but he got his ass beat. Over."

"He got his ass beat? Over."

"Yeah. Nathan said it was primo. All good. Over."

"Any word about the little chicks? Over."

"Baby chicks are with Mother Hen and doing fine. Standby."

While they were waiting, Zero and Diego munched on an energy bar and each downed a bottle of water.

"Scout. Over."

"Go."

"What's the terrain on the other side of this hill? Over."

"It will start going down. Over."

"Okay, wise ass. What do we got for buildings and roads? Over."

"CB indicated there was an old lady living in a cabin at the top. He said to tell you she is armed and possibly dangerous, but she's good people. Just doesn't like strangers. Out."

Zero and Diego looked at each other.

"Reminds me of Burma," Diego said.

"Reminds me of Bolivia. Madidi National Park."

"What were you doing there?"

"Chasing the head of a drug cartel. He dipped into the forest and I lost him."

"Too bad. Who'd you work with?"

"Cuerpo de Policía Nacional. My contact was a gal named Maria. For a girl, she was a pretty tough dude. She shot first, then forgot the questions."

"So they found him?"

"Well, not really. A couple days later a guide was taking a bunch of scientists through the jungle. One of them photographed a panther in a tree."

"So?"

"It was in a tree chomping on a leg with a Nike shoe on the foot. The guide said it looked fresh so Maria figured it was our guy."

"Interesting end to an foray in the tropics."

"For the panther, *si*. For the dealer, *no*. "

****

"Come on, wake up. It's almost sunrise."

"Yeah, yeah. Got a smoke?"

"Not until we get to the peak of the ridge."

At the top, they saw a mercury vapor light on a weathered barn.

"Hey, here's our ticket out of here. Some old farmer. He's got a truck."

"Wait, it's still early. Let's stay out of sight until we see how many are there. Got your gun?"

"Yeah. Of course I got my gun. Why'd you ask?"

"Because you said you were in the Air Force. I never knew a zoombag who could keep track of anything smaller than an F-15."

"Funny. I wasn't a pilot. I was in administration."

"Good God, that's even worse. The sun will be up in a few minutes. We can see anyone coming or going from here. Nice and easy and don't make any sound."

****

Birdie left her porch, walking to the bridge at the end of her drive. The water was up and frothy, but she saw the high mark and knew from experience it was receding. She noted that there didn't seem to be any washout from around the pylons but she would have the Morris brothers take a look at it just to be sure. Her days of inspecting the bridge were over. Time does that to a body. Sun was coming up and she was ready for breakfast.

****

She put water over for coffee when the phone rang.

"Birdie here," she said as she picked up the handset.

Birdie nodded her head. "Yes, I hear you. Did the children settle down after I left last night? Oh, good...hum...Now, Gem don't you go to crying or you'll get those little ones all upset like they ain't been upset enough...yeah, yeah.

"So John went to Waybird City for bandages? What about Dr. Glassman's place? That'd be closer.

"Yeah, yes. Glassman's getting a pediatrician he knows to come check the babies? That's nice. Good he did that."

When the water came to a boil, Birdie added a handful of fresh coffee grounds and an eggshell to the brew. After a few moments of listening to Gem, she turned the heat to medium. She saw the bushes at the edge of her driveway move in the first rays of sun on a windless morning.

As Gem talked, Birdie place a sugar and creamer dish on the kitchen table. She emptied the contents of a pint jar into a glass pitcher and sat that in the center, along with a one pound block of butter on an enameled blue and white saucer.

"So what started all this? Tried to kidnap Magdelyn Perkins? You don't say. Luke's friend and John Seven Star saved her?

"Now, Gem, don't cry. You know there'll be retribution. Your people have been in the Hollar as long as mine, and you know there'll be retribution as sure as we're talking on the phone right now. You always were too soft hearted. It'll turn out the way it is supposed to. Time to get around for breakfast. You've got hungry kids to feed.

"Say, Gem, did Luke say any of them got away? Not sure, eh? Well, I'll certainly look out for any strangers. Oh, and Gem, I'll bring some things down from my pantry, help calm the children. And something for you, too. Okay, Gem. Bye bye."

****

She saw the tall man step on her periwinkle at the edge of the drive. When two men staggered into her yard, she wasn't surprised.

She came out on the porch.

"My, my. You boys all wet."

"It's been tough ma'am. We were camping and got separated from our group. We've been out all night in the rain."

"Well, I say it looks like you have. We can't have you catch your death of cold here, can we. You come in and get dried off. I've a warm fire, coffee, and can rustle you up some pancakes. How's that sound?"

The men looked at each other and smiled. She would be easy to overcome.

Birdie took their jackets. "You boys just stand by the fire and dry out. Sorry ya'll got lost. It's not good to be strangers in these hills, no sir. Just stand next to the fire and get dried out. The coffee's just about ready and the griddle is hot. I hope you want to join me in pancakes and bacon breakfast."

"Thank you so much, ma'am. It was really tough trying to make it through the night," the tall one said.

"Well, it can get scary around here. Folks talk that the mountains are haunted and such nonsense. But I don't believe that, do you boys?"

"No, ma'am," said the blond one. "We don't."

"What do you boys take in your coffee?"

"Just black for mine"

"I'd like a little cream if you have it, ma'am."

Birdie brought the mugs of coffee to them at the fireplace. "There you go, boys."

The slices of bacon started to sputter and spit in the grill, filling the cabin with the unbearably beautiful, tantalizing aroma of corn fed meat.

"What did you say your name was?" asked the tall man.

"I didn't but my name is Birdie. Birdie Spry."

"That's an interesting name, Miss Spry."

They didn't see Birdie wince as she poured the batter on the griddle.

"Last night sure came down in buckets, don't you think? Thunder, lightning like I haven't seen since I was a child, ahuh, that's right." The circular flapjacks were golden brown on one side and as they bubbled, she babbled.

"It certainly takes experienced campers to get through bad weather, don't ya'll think?"

"Yes, Miss Spry. We were looking for firewood and got turned around. Then the rain came. We had to get through the night and then look for help. We're happy we found your place. Do you have a car? We'd appreciate a lift into town."

Birdie flipped the pancakes to cook through the other side. The bacon started to curl so she placed the flat iron on it, keeping it straight.

"Why, yes I do. I'd be happy to give you a lift into the Hollar. But let's have breakfast first, shall we?"

****

"What she doing, Zero?" The Rangers were hidden in the tree line.

"Looks like she's feeding them breakfast. We'll take them when they steal her truck."

"Copy that, bro."

****

"It smells great, Miss Spry."

"Oh, you don't have to call me Miss Spry. Birdie is good enough."

"Okay."

"Now here's your plate and here's yours. This is what we call a short stack. Here's the butter. I made this myself yesterday so ya'lls know it's fresh."

"Thank you. Thank you. This looks great. Is there any more coffee, Miss Spry?"

Birdie winced again but her back was to her guests.

"Yes, let me top off your cups. Sorry, I'm out of maple syrup, but here's some elderberry I made. It's awful good for the immune system. Tastes delightful. I add just a touch of honey, smooths out the berry. Hope you like it. Is there plenty of cream in the pitcher? Yes, well, I guess you're all set then." She stopped fussing and watched them eat.

The men smothered the steaming pancakes with butter, placing generous pats between each golden layer. They drizzled thick syrup over the cakes, even using their finger to swipe a droplet off the edge of the plate.

In five bites, they were done. Birdie served them seconds. The elderberry sweetness dripped from the sides and blended with the melted butter forming a purple and yellow pool on the china dishes.

Halfway into the second serving, the tall man said, "I don't feel so good."

"Oh, I'm sure you just ate too fast," Birdie said as she looked into his eyes.

"Me either," said the other. "My legs are trembling. My heart's pounding."

"Well, it's not polite for a guest to throw up a charitable meal, but you do look a little green. If you think you're going to upchuck, get outside, quick."

They rose, almost tipsy, as Birdie shoved them out the door. They fell down the steps and on the lawn. First one, and then the other, started to scream in agony, froth pouring from their mouths, gagging on pancake vomitus pouring into their lungs. In a few short moments they were dead.

****

"Dude, she took them out," Zero said, stunned at what he saw.

Diego nodded. "Old girl poisoned them. Damn, bro."

They receded into the woods. They were never there.

****

Birdie sipped her morning coffee as she surveyed the front yard. She took her journal from under her arm and settled into her rocking chair, fluffing up the pillow at her back. Examining the pages, she found the one she wanted and wrote:

"Swamp hemlock mixes well with elderberry syrup and remains highly effective."

RIGHTIOUS KILL

"What do you mean you can't get a fix? The GPS on my phone should lead you right to me."

"The GPS is jammed, sir."

"Jammed? Well unjam it."

"I don't know if it's possible, sir...I..."

"Then get someone who can. I'm not paying for idiots."

"Boss." A male voice, with just a touch of an East European accent, came over the phone. "He's not lying to you. He's trying his best to locate you."

"So, Anderson, you're the new peacekeeper?"

"You pay me to make things work and that's what I'm doing now. I'm isolating your location for the evac."

"Why you didn't you warn me about the ambush a few hours ago? Eh? Two, maybe three, vehicles disabled. Derrick is dead, along with seven men I know of, more than that missing and presumed dead. All of the product for this shipment is gone. What kind of security is this?"

"Sir, the mountains of West Virginia propose problems for any technology. We can talk about that later. My concern is your rescue. A very strong storm system is across the Appalachian Plateau and once it hits the mountains, I don't know when or how we can get to you. For now, find a high place and just sit tight."

"What the hell else do you think I can do? You had better fix this, Anderson, and do it now."

"Sir, you're breaking up. Sir? Sir?"

"Anderson? Damn it all to hell." Boss stuffed his phone in his chest pocket as the raindrops began to fall.

Three meters away, covered in grass, leaves, and the branches of black huckleberry, Cobalt lay in wait, breathing slowly, relaxed, and studying his prey.

****

In the computer center, Anderson patted his IT apprentice on the shoulder. "Don't worry about what he said. You work for me, simple as that."

"But..."

"No but's, no excuses. Why don't you and your associates take an early lunch?"

"Really?"

"Really. And here," Anderson reached in his pocket. He was careful to cover the insignia of St. Michael across the money clip.

"Yes. Lunch is on me." He pulled out three one hundred dollar bills. "Make it a long lunch. Better yet, take the afternoon off. All of you."

Stuttering his thanks, the associate signaled to the others in the office to follow him.

Sitting at the console, Anderson, whose passport was in the name Olesksandr Tymofiy Pavlenko, code name Alex, typed in a series of numbers relayed to several IP addresses on the dark web. His signal bounced between two satellites then traveled to the earpiece of Dayvd Vladimirovich Vovk. The message was simple, "*Hutsulshchyna.*"

"Going dark," was Cobalt's response.

The hunt was on.

****

Boss stumbled in the darkness. The rain stopped but not the thunder and lightning. Bright flashes illuminated his way up the hillside. His diamond studded shoes and Kennsington trench coat were no match for the thorns and brambles tearing at his ankles and legs as he scrambled among the rocks. He used the flashlight on his phone to search the underbrush.

Too many five star dinners at European hotels and too few hours in the gym taxed his heart and leg muscles as he fought the briars and branches slapping him across the face. The last vine hit him so hard it lacerated his forehead. He cursed the blood dripping into his eyes. Without moving a step, another vine slashed the side of his head, opening a second wound to his ear.

"Damn it. I'll burn this place down." He reached for the vine to tear it from its roots but couldn't find it in the dark. Another vine wrapped around his ankle and he fell back fifteen feet of precious ground gained. Pausing to catch his breath, he made another call.

"The rain is letting up. Can you hear me?"

"Yes, sir. I'm locating your position now."

"How long will it take? I'm freezing."

"We'll have to find a place for the chopper to land. The terrain is very rugged. This might take some time, sir."

"I don't know how long I can last out here. I haven't eaten, have no water, no way to build a fire."

"The extraction team is organizing now."

"Did you locate any of the men? Are there any vehicles available?"

"I have one parked on a sand track. There are five bodies around it. No one is moving."

"Damn it. Damn it to hell. Keep looking. And get that chopper here. You've got my money. And remember, I've got friends in high places in Washington. I'm not in this alone and some of my friends are very dangerous."

"Yes, sir. Please save your battery. I'll call again." Anderson entered more code bringing up two heat signals. He smiled.

Boss continued crawling up the hillside. He felt the icy water trickle down the front of his silk shirt; it flooded his shoes and encircled his toes.

A limestone outcropping appeared in the flash of lightning. Another vine slashed across his face but before he finished crying out, he heard the crack of a breaking branch and everything went black.

****

The warmth of the fire woke him. He peeked through one swollen eye at the fire, and then around the cave. A camo pack leaned against the wall with a bottle of water next to it. Plastic ties restrained his wrists and ankles.

The image of a man at the opening was silhouetted by the next bolt of lightening

"Jesus, you scared me. Help me. Something hit me on the head."

"That was me."

Boss hesitated when he recognized the voice. "Vovk? Is that you? What the hell? Untie me."

"I don't take orders from you any more."

"And who do you take orders from?"

"Someone you wouldn't know."

"Cobalt, untie me. Come on, man. We're tight back in the day. There's a lot to tell you."

"I heard what you had to say."

"So it *was* you. Once I saw how things were going, I knew it wasn't a competitor. Got the whole gang with you?" Boss bit his tongue at a flash of memory.

"You had them killed in Afghanistan. If you had told me the truth, I would have killed you then."

Cobalt watched his former commander struggle against his bonds.

"It wasn't until I was assigned to provide cover for a CIA case officer, it occurred to me what was going on. Once we placed the sensors, I knew we were replacing the ones we lost on the first attempt. We were installing communications to facilitate your shipments of product. You used us to help you traffic kids out of

Eastern Europe, get them across the mountains to waiting vehicles for transport. It never was about enemy recon."

Cobalt used a stick to poke at the small fire. He tossed a few more branches in the center. The flame crackled with joy, sending up small sparks.

"Where'd you find the dry wood?"

"I'm a Ranger."

"Untie me and let's talk man-to-man."

"You're talking now. Untying you won't make any difference."

Boss smiled. "But it's a little uncomfortable."

"I hope so."

"Come on, man. There's no need for this. I can make you rich. You'll have more money than the Army could ever pay you. Going to retire on that pittance and go to the VA for your knee replacements? Eh? Got those aches and pains in your joints from climbing someone else's mountains? I know you carry horse liniment in your kit. There's no need for that. For you or your team. You had help back there, I know."

"What's your offer?" Cobalt asked.

Boss studied the flames of the small fire. He was getting warm, at least the chills had stopped. If he had any chance of being released, he had to figure out how to sway Cobalt to his side. If not released, then keep him talking until the extraction team arrived. He was sure Cobalt would be killed.

"For you? Thirty percent. Ten percent for each of your crew after delivery of the product."

"That sounds tight."

"And...and pick any of them, male or female. It doesn't matter. But you can't touch the special orders. They have to stay clean. Better price that way."

"And what about the children?"

Cobalt moved his neck in slow rotations to loosen his *levator scapulae*. He made a couple of circles relaxing his shoulder muscles. Boss was right about one thing, Cobalt could use some liniment at the moment.

"Depends. If they're Scandinavian, there's always a market for white hair among the Middle Eastern clients. Virgins of any skin color, well, there's a market for them, too. Good price. Then the ugly ones go for housekeeping and drudge work."

"Really? How much?" The Ranger continued his warmup by stretching with elbow pulls on each side.

Boss was calm as he continued his business proposition with the black haired warrior he previously commanded.

"Depends upon the market at the time and the customer. My top of the line products are Four Seasons for as long as they last. They're clean, healthy, and well dressed. Some of them even learn to tailor their attire to the client like, um, a maid, a nurse, you know, that kind of thing. With an international clientele, there are special requests, for a price of course." He paused.

"They all like what they do?"

"In a manner of speaking. They come around after getting some of the perks but if they don't, they get cycled out."

"How much does each one generate in profits?" Cobalt performed a couple of heel rises, stretching his calves; a few squats stretched his quads. He felt good, loose, ready.

"I average, that's on a yearly basis and only average, about $195,000 to $250,00 a year."

"Per item?"

"Per item. Then there's income from organ donations, but that's separate through China in Hong Kong and Mexico at the southern border. Add a few hundred thousand for that market."

"So how much for the ones you had stashed here?"

"Not that much because they were lower quality. More like spare change. But there are secret auctions, some online, some in the Middle East, Moscow, Budapest, Paris, where they start at a million. I'm in that market now and the sky's the limit."

Cobalt walked to the opening of the cave. He stretched his arms out wide, then brought them across his chest.

"Hey, wait a minute. You can't leave me like this."

"I'm not leaving you."

"There's an extraction coming, my man. You can join my team. I'll take you on in a heartbeat. I think we can patch things up. Like old times."

"No, I don't think so."

"What? You don't want to make money?"

"No, there isn't an extraction team coming."

"Yes, there is. They'll be here via chopper."

"No, they won't."

"And just how the hell do you think you know?"

"The man you call Anderson is a friend of mine. Actually a cousin. We grew up together in New York City in the section of 6th and 7th streets between 1st and 3rd Ave. They called it "Little Ukraine" back in the day. Maybe they still do. I haven't been there for a long time.

"Anyway, when Anderson and I, or Alex as I call him, were kids, we walked with our grandmother to St. George Ukrainian Catholic Church every day before school. The three of us would go into the church and my grandmother would buy a candle. Old girl must have spent ten grand on candles over the years."

"Please, Cobalt, you're breaking my heart. We've business to discuss."

"Every day she prayed for the return of her sister. She was taken on her way home from school."

"But..."

"She vanished into thin air."

"I didn't have anything to do with that."

"No, you didn't, but it doesn't matter. Alex and I made a promise to our grandmother and to each other we would do whatever it took to stop men like you. We're keeping our promise."

"There's no extraction team?"

"No."

Boss laughed. "And the cavalry isn't coming?"

"No."

Cobalt stared over the tips of the flames of the campfire. He recalled the faces of his brothers. He remembered digging through the stones and sand trying to find something, anything.

"They were vaporized in the bombing in an area they should never have been. Erased from the universe. I couldn't find enough to bring back to their wives to bury."

"You don't love life, do you Cobalt."

"I'm a Ranger. I can't afford it."

"Oh, yes, the heroic solitary warrior. You forget I've read your file. It's why I picked you for the operations no one else wanted or could do. You've got nothing to lose. There's no one gives a crap about you, your achy knees, your suicide missions overseas. Here's your chance to change all that."

The thought of Maggie Perkins in the hands of Boss flashed through Cobalt's mind. It steeled him for what was to come.

"How was I to know the Marines called in an airstrike? By the time I found out, it was too late. I tried."

"Lopez, Juan Louis, Staff Sergeant." Cobalt flicks an ember from the coals. It lands in Boss's eye. He screams.

"Collins, Ronald M., Sergeant." The next ember lands on Boss's chest and burns a hole through his silk shirt to his nipple. Again, he screams.

"Poole, Lashawn Lado. Sergeant. Poole's daughter was born two days after he was blown up. I attended her christening as her godfather." A larger coal lands on Boss's left testicle. He begins to sob.

Cobalt, never taking his eyes off Boss, removes his Tanto from its sheath.

****

The next front rolled in. Ribbons of lightening shattered tall pines, exploding the trunks into splinters; torrents of rain fell from the sky engorging the streams, and the thunder vibrated between the mountains and down into the valleys.

From the cave, Boss's screams fought their way skyward. His pleas for forgiveness were blocked by the cumulonimbus clouds, sealing off any response from the heavens.

MOUNTAIN MISTS

Cobalt rolled the cheroot between his thumb and index finger, gently pulling the smoke across his palette. It had been a while since he enjoyed hand rolled Cuban tobacco. To avoid the rush of nicotine, he nibbled on a piece of Puccini Bomboni chocolate. He carried a square of it whenever he carried a cigar. A woman in Amsterdam said it was the best. She was beautiful and he believed almost everything she said until the day she left.

He watched the eastern sky turn pink in contrast to the haze of the Appalachian Mountains. He was sure the furthest range, the one that touched the sky this morning, was the Blue Ridge. The colors in the early morning, the mist drifting down the valleys as the sun warmed the droplets, and the calls of the birds, gave him a peace he longed for. Maybe he could settle here.

He blew three small smoke rings and watched them drift skyward. Now what? His mission was complete, debt paid in full, there was no more that was due. What would it take to calm the savage within? Right now, the Montecristo Linea 1935 was doing the trick. He would save the cigar band for little Maggie Perkins. She would like that.

The charges were set. All he had to do was push the button. What stopped him? He rested and then put the finished cigar on the rock beside him. It would go out in time, as would his rage. At least he hoped so.

He shouldered his kit and started down the hill. Pausing, he turned to take one last look at the cave. A surprise bullet came from a single shot Walther hidden in a coat lining and held in a bloody broken hand. Cobalt felt the burning round enter his body just above his left belt line. Instinctively he pushed the button and the charges exploded, sealing the cave opening in a dusty curtain of limestone rock; its secrets buried forever.

The shock wave sent him tumbling down the path, rolling, crashing, twisting over stone, brush, and low branches. The momentum of his fall slowed only by his ruck sack snagging on a thick low hanging branch. Cobalt fell over a small abutment of limestone. He dropped six feet landing on a boulder, breaking three ribs; the air forced out of his lungs.

He rolled off the rock, his fingers feeling for an opening to grip as he slid down it's face. Reaching out, he grabbed a vine growing among the rocks. It pulled free from the saturated earth. Sliding down along a shallow gully, Cobalt started to roll again. He was jerked to a halt when his kit was wedged in the fork of a branch jammed between two boulders.

Unconscious and suspended above the ground by a few inches, Cobalt was deaf to the calls from his earpiece as the raindrops fell from the brim of his hat.

****

"How long do storms like this last?" Scout was entering, re-entering, and rebooting his laptop trying to get through the thunderheads and contact his appropriated satellite. In frustration he put the communication pad on the ground beside him.

CB repositioned the sleeping Tobias from his shoulder to the floor of the cave. Nathan was still awake.

"Storms come across the Great Plains then get stalled on the mountains. This one looks like it has several fronts to it. We've gone through two but there's a lot of thunder coming from the west. It could go on for a while. How's the connection?"

"Your lovely mountains are not making it easy for me. Still can't get a line on Cobalt."

"What about Zero and Diego?"

"As soon as I can get back up, I'll call them." He tapped the face of the pad. "We're a go. Back up and running. Here. Down by the back road. Look."

CB watched Smith and Jones examine the back road where Cobalt and Diego neutralized five men. They paused inspecting the Humvee without touching anything. They changed direction and went back to the road where their vehicle was parked.

"They missed a bullet this time. Took them long enough to find the back door. Must have gotten lost."

"It's easy to do in this wilderness. But they know the party's over. What now?"

Nathan spoke up. "You've got to kill them. There's no other choice."

Both CB and Scout looked at the boy who made a man's decision.

"If you don't, they'll come back, maybe try to kidnap more kids. The children Tobes took to Aunt Gem's...kids shouldn't be kept like that. As long as those men are alive, everyone in the Hollar is at risk."

CB and Scout let his words sink in.

"He's right, CB," Scout said. "It needs to be finished now. Everything erased. That's how to protect your family and the village."

"See if you can call Diego and Zero. Keep an eye on those other two. We'll need to make a plan."

****

Sheriff Harris paced back and forth in his office. John Seven Star poured two more coffees, adding sugar and cream to his own, leaving the Sheriff's black.

"I don't suppose I need anymore caffeine." Bill blew on his coffee.

"No, and neither do I. However, under the circumstances, it's easier dealing with caffeine. Our history with alcohol isn't something we want to repeat."

Bill smiled.

"It's nerve wracking not knowing how Luke and his friends are making out. Why are you so relaxed?"

John laughed. "My wife makes these little herb packs. Here, take one. Just put it between your cheek and gum. Juice it up a little, and chill."

Bill did as instructed. In a few moments he did feel a bit calmer. "I'll put in an order if she'll make more. I could use these around the tourist season."

They passed time looking at FBI Most Wanted posters on the wall.

"Looks like my brother-in-law, Bill. Is this guy still on the run?" John pointed to the third one from the front.

"Nope, that one was caught in Ohio. But this will send chills up your back. The next one...no, not the guy with fisheyes...the next one, yep. Looks like my dad, doesn't it? Looks like old Sheriff Bill Harris, Sr." He started to laugh.

"It sure does. That's why you keep it at the back?"

"Hum, yep."

The radio crackled, startling both men.

"Base. Over." They recognized Luke's voice.

"Base. Go."

"I want you to keep an eye out for two hefty men in a green truck. Over."

"Copy that. Part of the crew you boys were hunting? Over."

"Yes. They're armed and dangerous. Over."

"Copy that."

"I'll tell you about it later. Out."

"At least we know they're okay," John said. "More coffee, Bill?"

****

"Call Diego and Zero. We'll rendezvous at the vehicles."

"What about Dad's truck?" Tobias asked.

"How long have you been awake, little bro?"

"Ever since Nathan told you to kill the last two men."

"I won't tell Mom you were eavesdropping on my conversation."

"And I won't tell Mom you killed that guy."

"Checkmate."

Scout smiled.

CB paused, then added, "Here's the plan. Nathan and Tobias, get the truck and go home. Mom and Dad are staying an extra night so we don't have to worry about them for another day. I think the explaining is better left to me."

"CB, I'll pack up here. See you later." Scout paused at the entrance of the cave. "You boys are real operators."

"Thank you, Scout."

"Thanks, Scout."

"Let's get going." CB led his brothers out of the cave and down the trail.

****

"Diego. Zero. Over."

"Right behind you, Scout." Diego and Zero emerged from the culvert below the road.

Scout began packing his equipment in the Excursion. "You get what you were looking for?"

"Yeah, yeah, we did." Diego exchanged glances with Zero.

"Did you get rid of the bodies?"

"All taken care of, bro. We got this. Not our first time at the rodeo." Zero broke down his weapon for transportation. He removed his equipment belt, and used his boonie hat to wipe the sweat and rain from his face before putting it back on his head. "All taken care of," he said again as he winked at Diego.

"Have you heard from Cobalt?"

"No. I'm going to call again in a few. CB is escorting his brothers off the mountain then he'll meet us here. You ever seen kids like those?" Scout adjusted the suitcase containing his sensitive equipment, then turned and sat on the edge of the cargo hold. "I mean, they're mature, intelligent, and they can shoot. Must be some Daniel Boone blood in them."

Zero put three grenades back in the box. "We should've heard something from Cobalt. Looks like more rain will be coming from the west. I don't think we want to be caught in a flash flood."

Diego passed around small mugs of bitter coffee.

"Good hell!" Zero spit his out on the ground. "You tryin' to kill me? Please use a bullet."

"What are you whining about? That's the same brew Sheriff Billy has. You liked it when we sat in his office."

"Yeah, because he didn't have it fermenting in the butt of a bear for three days."

"Ladies," Scout said, "let's mind our manners. Here's sugar and cream, and a splash of Leadslingers."

"Whew, much better. You, sir, are a scholar and gentleman."

It was the echo of gun fire that made the Rangers drop their mugs and grab their gear. They ran toward the sound.

****

Tobias looked in the rearview mirror for a second time and saw CB wave at them. The third time he glanced, he slammed on the breaks.

"He's trying to kill Luke." The man-child jammed the transmission into park.

Tobias and Nathan were out of the truck and sighting in on the man who was in a life and death struggle with their brother.

The boys steadied their rifles on the edge of the rear panel, waiting for the shot. CB pivoted, exposing the back of the aggressor to the truck. The Golden Boys were fired at the same time. The man in black pitched backward as the .17 HMR rounds hit his buttocks. He screamed in agony as he turned to see who was shooting at him.

A millisecond was all CB needed. He slashed the attacker's throat with his K-Bar. Blood gushed into the air as large drops spattered CB in the face. The man dropped to his knees and then the ground.

CB ran to his brothers. "Come, take cover, we don't know how many more there are." They hid in the underbrush until Diego's voice came over the com.

"Area secured."

The three brothers exited from the brush. CB put his Glock back in his holster.

"Did we ki..ill him?" Tobias asked.

"No, I did. You boys saved my life a second time."

Nathan put his arm around his twin. "That's what Dad told us. Men protect their families. Besides, it looked like you were getting your ass beat again. That's twice in one day. Dad ain't gonna like that."

"When'd he get his ass beat before?" Tobias asked.

"A few hours ago up in the cave when you were looking at Scout's stuff. That's how his face got all messed up."

"So he didn't fall down the hill?"

"Okay, Nate..."

"No. He got whipped."

"How bad was he losing?"

"Bad. I mean really bad. He was getting hammered. I thought he was gonna take the count."

"Nate, okay, that..."

"We never got our ass beat on the school yard. Even by the big Monroe boys."

"I know, but he was taking a real whipping."

"Twice in one day? That's a Perkins family record. Mom needs to write that in her Bible."

"No one is telling Dad or Mom anything until I talk to them first."

"Yeah, but I got dibs on telling him how you got your ass beat."

"Yes, you can tell Dad." CB cleared his throat. "I'm sorry you got dragged into this." He put his arms around his brothers. "I am so sorry. For God's sake, you're only twelve years old."

"Nothing to be sorry about. Tobes and I made the decision to come. It worked out the way it worked out. We just have to deal with it."

CB hugged them to his chest and kissed each of them on the forehead.

"CB, we need to clean this up. Also, Cobalt hasn't checked in." Zero moved the situation along.

"Got it."

He walked his brothers to the truck while Diego and Zero dragged the body off of the road and into the ditch. They removed the other five bodies by the Humvee.

"We'll talk soon. Just the three of us." CB tousled their hair.

Tobias shook his head. "You didn't learn this at the library."

They watched the twins drive away.

"Those boys are something, CB."

"I've been away for a while and missed seeing them grow up, but my dad did a hell of a job turning them into men."

Diego put his hand on CB's shoulder. "Maybe extend your leave by a few weeks. This is a lot for kids to digest. They'll need you around to help them work out what they've been through."

****

Scout turned away from the conversation at the truck. His laptop was buzzing in a way he hadn't seen before. He turned up the volume as a slow deep voice came over the com.

"I'm sending you coordinates to find your friend. He has not moved in thirty minutes. The next weather front will reach his position in approximately two hours. I would advise the utmost speed. Out."

"What the hell was that? Somebody cut in on my satellite."

"Your satellite? You stole it from the government if I recall." Diego adjusted his pack.

Zero tossed a stone up and caught it. "Don't you mean *who* the hell was that?"

"Scout, is it real?"

"CB, that's the direction I last had him. I say we head for those coordinates before the next storm."

Taking Scout's tablet, CB said, "It looks like we can drive until here. Then we'll have to go the rest of the way on foot."

"Copy. Let's go, gentleman."

****

Smith turned on the headlights. "I hate these old trucks. Everything is low tech shit," he said.

"We blend in easier. How many new vehicles do you see around here?"

"Not many. What's next?"

Jones slumped in the seat. "I say we go to Waybird and back to the motel. Get something to eat. We'll have to figure out the loose ends and when it's all wrapped up, we get out. There are plenty of other crews to work with. Boss isn't the only one."

"But he's the only one who understands our quirks."

"I told you we shouldn't have dropped Pink Molly when we were here last. Things got out of control with the pig hunter."

"So what? He got paid more than he's gotten in his miserable life. Forget about it.

"Put the wipers on. It's getting hard to see in this fog. Fog or rain, it needs to make up its mind. I'll tell you the one loose end is Jose Garza. We ain't finished until he is."

"No one got out of that operation alive. Two vehicles blown to hell, the cabin on fire, and five dead at the rear. Somebody's trying to move in on this operation. Better we find out who it is and make a deal if we are going to salvage anything."

"Yeah. yeah."

Smith and Jones drove through the mountains. They picked up the bypass on route 219.

****

Cobalt moaned as he fought to remain conscious. The blood from his head wound seeped into his eyes. Every breath was a stabbing pain in his side. The leg was broken for sure.

Something was tugging on him, pulling him out of the rushing water. He felt the water at his knees, aware it was rising.

"Guys, let me help," he said. He raised his hand toward Diego, only grabbing at air.

The sound of his name by a familiar voice stimulated him to open his eyes but he was too weak from blood loss to respond. He knew he was hallucinating when he saw a white dog licking his face.

Judge Dietz

Thaddeous Copperfield Dietz parked in his reserved space in front of the jail. He stood on the sidewalk gazing at his 1970 Chevrolet Chevelle SS, with the look men have when they're in love with a car. Was he trying to relive his misspent youth? Maybe. However, the car was worth not answering the question.

"Sheriff Bill. Hello." He tipped his hat to Agnes Crawford and her son sitting on the lobby bench.

"Judge."

"Everyone here? Gladys ready to record the proceedings?" He hung up his coat and hat.

"Yes, sir."

"Thanks, Bill. Give me a few minutes to get ready and we can proceed."

"Coffee, Judge?"

"Did you make it or Gladys?"

"Gladys."

"Ok, I'll have some. Yours gives me heart palpitations."

"It will be on your desk when you're ready."

****

Judge Dietz adjusted the chair for Gladys to be seated at her recording equipment, then seated himself in a chair behind the desk. He sorted through papers, glancing at names, dates, and charges. There was a note on one file: "Please talk to Fishbone Crawford in my office–B."

"Gladys, all set?"

"Yes, Your honor."

"There's not much on the docket today so I'll dispense with all the blah blah blah stuff. You can just fill it in like you always do so we can forward copies to the state."

"Yes, Judge." Gladys smiled and adjusted her recording equipment. Her cameras were in focus and feeding into the computer.

"Okay, the first case. You've got the numbers and everything, Gladys?"

"Yes, Your Honor."

"The first case is that of Jose Garza. Bill, bring him in, please."

In a few moments Jose found himself in front of Judge Dietz.

"Hello, Mr. Garza."

"Hello, Your Honorship."

"Just 'Your honor' will do." He smiled at Jose. "I see you were arrested by Sheriff Harris and brought to the Deacon's Hollar Jail for temporary confinement. The charges are attempted kidnapping of a minor child under the age of thirteen. How do you plead?"

"Not guilty, Your Honor."

"So, Mr. Garza, you're telling me that you did not abduct a minor child under the age of thirteen years from in front of Gracie's Place diner and put said child in your vehicle with the intent of driving away with her?"

"Well...I...I thought she was lost and was going to take her back to her mother."

Sheriff Harris let fly from his rubber band slingshot a spitball which struck and then bounced off the tat on the prisoner's neck. Jose flinched.

"Well, what I mean to say is that..."

"Did you know the child's mother in order to return the child to the mother?"

"No."

"Do you deny the charges?"

"I want an attorney." Jose was getting nervous.

Judge Dietz removed his judicial nameplate from the front of his desk replacing it with one that read: T.C. Dietz, Esq. Attorney at Law.

"Wait a minute, you can't be the judge and my attorney at the same time."

"I'm not. Right now, I'm your attorney. You said you wanted an attorney. So, here I am. What would you like to say?"

"I...I...made a deal with the Sheriff. I get the benefits of the deal."

"That you do, but what was the deal you made with the sheriff?"

"Well, it wasn't actually the sheriff."

"So you didn't make a deal with the sheriff?"

Jose shifted his feet. Sheriff Bill was locked and loaded with another spitball.

"No, but I...I told all about Clarence Wells, Boss, and the crew about bringing product..."

Attorney Dietz cleared his throat. "Product? What was the product?"

"Ah, I didn't have anything to do with..."

Zing! Bill's second spitball hit Jose in the crease between his hairline and left ear.

"They was kids. We were moving girls and women from Miami to Montreal. Deacon's Hollar was a halfway point so we could rest up before getting to the border with Canada. I'm innocent."

Replacing the nameplate, Thaddeous became a judge once more. "On that, I'll enter a plea of not guilty."

The judge shuffled several papers, paused, then handed them to Gladys.

Jose started to turn, a warning Sheriff Harris to stop, when Bill's third spitball landed on Jose's left nostril, this time making him yelp.

"Mr. Garza, please show some decorum in the court. We may be small and informal at times, but this is still a courtroom."

"Yes, sir, but he keeps hitting me with projectiles."

"Bill?"

"Your Honor, I think what Mr. Garza is referring to is small pieces of ceiling plaster falling. I've been trying to convince the county to fix that."

Jose looked up. "I don't see any cracks in the ceiling."

Bill placed a fatherly hand high on Jose's shoulder. "You need to turn around and face the judge." He gave Jose's neck a rather unfatherly squeeze.

"Mr. Garza, I have before me a sworn witness statement from Mr. John Seven Star about the abduction of a minor child, a transcribed account of your confession, and all the information you provided to Sheriff Harris and his deputies."

"So you're not my attorney any more? About those deputies, Your Honor. I don't think they were really deputies at all. In fact..."

Zing! The tiny wet object hurtling through space landed on the lobe of Jose's right ear. "Ouch."

Judge Dietz looked up at the silent defendant. "Anything else you'd like to say?"

"Just that this is a kangaroo court, and I'm being subjected to cruel and unusual punishment in violation of the First Amendment."

"It's the Fourth Amendment and what's cruel and unusual about it, Mr. Garza?"

"The Sheriff keeps hitting me with stuff."

"Nothing cruel because you aren't bleeding and nothing unusual because he does that all the time. I'm going to remand you back to the custody of the Sheriff and you will remain there until trial on attempted kidnapping. Next case."

Jose was led back to his cell by Deputy Johnson. "Not a good day, eh, Mr. Garza?"

****

Bowtie stood before Judge Dietz.

"The next case is the State of West Virginia versus Bowtie Crawford. Gladys, make sure you use his birth certificate name before you send that in."

"Yes, Judge." The court recorder made a note on her steno pad.

"Bowtie, do you want a lawyer?"

"No, thank you. I waive all my rights."

"Do you want to tell me what happened?"

"I shot Walter Vender. He was beating up on my sister-in-law, and I took a gun and shot him. Simple as that, Thaddeous. I'm ready to pay for the crime."

"Any witnesses?"

"No. Agnes and Fishbone were outside when I shot Walter. They didn't see anything. That's it. You have my confession."

"Well, that's part of it, Bowtie, but I also have a forensic report from Special Agent Cleveland Coop which leads me to believe that there is more to the story than you're telling me. Stay here. We'll have a short recess." He struck the gavel. He winked at Gladys. "I really like doing that."

"But I..."

"Bowtie, let me do my job." He hit the plate again.

Judge Dietz excused himself from the courtroom. "Gladys, I'm going to be in the next room if you need me. Go ahead and do whatever it is you do to make the county look good. Be right back."

"What would you do without me, Judge?"

"I'd probably be in prison myself, dear."

****

Thaddeous was seated in Sheriff Bill's inner office when Fishbone entered, wide eyed and teary. The boy sat in the chair across from the judge.

"Do you know who I am, Fishbone, and why we're here?"

"Yes, sir. Uncle Bowtie works on your race car and says you're a judge."

"Yes, he does and I am. Let me ask you something, do you love your uncle?"

"Yes, sir."

"Would you do anything for him if it would help him?"

"Yes, sir. Sometimes he lets me help him at the garage."

Dietz smiled. "Let me ask you something else. Do you know the difference between the truth and a lie?"

"Yes, sir."

"And what is that?"

"The truth is what is, and a lie is what ain't in place of what is."

"That's good enough. Fishbone, why don't you bring that stool over here so I don't have to talk to you across this big desk. And, here, grab us both a soda out of the little refrigerator...yes, that one with books on the top. Let's just sit here and talk man to man. Are you comfortable with that?"

"Yes, sir."

"I have to ask you a couple of questions. It may be difficult for you to answer, but it is important that you tell me the honest to God's truth. Do you understand?"

The boy took another sip from the soda can. An unexpected burp put them both into giggles.

"Wow, Judge! That was a big one!"

"Yes, it was. Wait, let me do one." Dietz burped. "Not as big as yours, but a good one."

The judge paused, then looked at the boy, the humor gone from his face.

"I've got to change the subject, Fishbone. I want you to tell me what happened at your house when Walter Venter died."

Fishbone's giggle vanished.

"Walter was beating up on my mom...she was crying and screaming and her face was bleeding. He smashed her against the stove and then the sink. I-I went and got the gun from under the floorboard in Joseph's room."

"Joseph was your brother?"

"Yes, sir. He left a long time ago."

"Do you know where he is?"

"No, sir. My mom told me about the gun and not to touch it unless a wild animal came into the yard."

"So, what happened after you got the gun?"

"I went into the kitchen. Walter was slapping my mom in the face. I told him to s-stop. He turned around and I shot him and shot him and shot him and he fell down and my mom said I was going to jail."

Judge Dietz opened his arms. The boy crawled onto his lap and buried his head in the judicial robes, sobbing.

Thaddeous told himself after his wife and son died, he would never get close to another human being. Holding Fishbone to his chest, he broke that promise. He rocked back and forth until the boy stopped crying and slept.

****

"They've been in there a long time, Sheriff."

"Don't worry, Bowtie. Do you want a coffee or a soda?"

"Coffee would be good, Bill. Thanks."

When Bill returned, Bowtie asked if he knew anything about the state prison.

"Not really, at least anymore. I took a tour when I was taking classes to be a sheriff, but you know the state keeps coming out with updates as the law changes. I wish I could tell you something but I can't. Sorry."

"That's okay, Bill. I can make it on my own."

They sipped their coffee in silence until Judge Dietz entered the courtroom. A sleepy Fishbone went back into the lobby to his mother.

Bill called the courtroom back in session with his, "All Rise" monologue.

"I'm going to release you, Bowtie. There isn't any evidence to hold you."

"My prints were on the gun, Thaddeous."

"I'm calling this a suicide, Bowtie."

"What? A suicide? I told you I did it."

Judge Dietz replaced his name plate with one embossed in gold, "T. Copperfield Dietz, Coroner."

"Thaddeous, how can you call that a suicide?"

"Bowtie, any man who beats up a woman has planted the seeds for his own destruction, morally or physically, or both. So, by extension of logic, Walter Venter killed himself, responsible for creating the environment that lead to his demise. Furthermore, the evidence I have from Special Agent Coop eliminates you as a suspect. That's all I'm going to say about that."

He swapped out the name plate.

"Excuse me, but that's your attorney one," said Bill.

"Oops. Here...here's the correct one." Dietz was a judge again.

"I hereby order this case dismissed." He leaned over to Gladys. "Let me know when you have that ready for a signature. I'm going over to Gracie's for lunch."

"Yes, sir. In about an hour so."

"Good." He tossed his car keys at Bowtie who caught them in midair. "I need the oil changed and a tune up. Can you get that done for me by four?"

"Yes, Your Honor."

"Bill, let's go. That chair hurts my butt."

Vovky

"CB, there's a road along here. Do you know it?"

"Not really. I haven't run these hills in a while. Where's Cobalt according to the coordinates?"

"Here."

Diego checked his RATS pack. "I've got everything we'll need for the evac. I'm sure he's just taking a Ranger nap after a cigar and some Leadslingers. Bet he has a book with him."

"I wouldn't be surprised if that snake eater was ten feet away from us sacking out while we go humping around the mountain in a rainstorm looking for his sorry ass." Zero scanned the brush.

"It's getting dark. And by the next front, it'll be pitch black in the mountains." CB checked his watch.

"No matter," Scout said. "We've got what we need. Okay, punch it."

Zero drove while Scout watched the roads and cutoffs available on his GPS.

"Zero, here, turn in here."

Zero pulled the truck over to the side and started down a trail.

"Wait," CB said. "Let me walk it. The road may have washed out. I'll take Diego and will signal if it is safe to bring the truck in. Otherwise, just park it here."

****

Under the canopy of the trees, microns of mist coagulated into spray, then enlarged into droplets streaming from leaf to leaf and falling without grace on the boonie hats of the team as they made their way to the coordinates given by a stranger. From the west, the men heard the thunder and saw distant flashes of lightning between the tree trunks. The massive front was on its way.

"The terrain will rise sharply about ten meters this way," Scout pointed out. "If our friend gave us the right info, Cobalt should be about here." He pointed to the screen of his small computer.

"Will we need the ropes?" Zero adjusted the collapsible stretcher bag attached to his kit.

"I'm not sure. If we can't find a trail, we might have to lower him on the stretcher to where we are now. We'll just have to see." A clap of thunder broke over their heads, shaking the ground.

"Cobalt. Cobalt. Can you hear me? Make a sound, dude." Zero's voice was drowned out by the heavy rain.

Except for the thunder, there was no reply. They continued to search the area.

"We should be about on top of him."

"Here's part of his kit. Broke strap. Spread out."

It was CB who first noticed the bluish mist floating about five meters away from his position. In spite of the wind from the coming storm, the mist didn't move. He was afraid and grateful at the same time.

"I know where he is. Stay here, guys."

"CB, I'm picking up movement in the area. Maybe animals about where Cobalt should be." Scout watched the moving figures on his screen. "There, I got him. I got the heat signal. He's alive."

"Stay here. Don't move. Don't advance. Let me."

"Wolves?" Zero grabbed his sidearm.

"Zero, don't," CB commanded.

As CB moved forward, two of the low lying clouds dissipated.

The Rangers watched the CIA agent slowly approach the body of their brother. They heard him whisper over the com.

"It's okay...we're here to help...you remember me, don't you?"

The animal was on its belly, stretching its full length beside the unconscious Cobalt. CB removed his night vision scope, and turned on this flashlight, keeping the beam away from the animal's eyes.

Another step. "You remember me, boy, don't you. A long time ago you came to me..."

Another step.

"You kept me safe from the cougar..."

Another step.

"Ain't supposed to be cougar in these parts, but we saw one didn't we."

The animal moved. CB stopped and stayed crouched.

"I just want to check my friend."

Another step. CB could see the blue hues in the animal's eyes moving, being stirred by its emotions and instincts.

"I know he's hurt or you wouldn't be here keeping him safe. But it's okay now."

Another step.

"I can take over and you can go back to the woods, like you did when my Dad found me."

Another step.

"You went back into the woods with your brothers once you knew I was safe."

The wolf-dog stood, magnificent, dignified, majestic. It carefully backed away from CB and the now moaning Cobalt.

"It's okay. I'll take care of him."

He felt the bullet pass his head before he heard the retort from the barrel.

The animal yelped, screamed, and then ran off into the darkness.

"What the hell did you do?" CB said as he knelt over Cobalt. He was pissed, relieved, and amazed all at the same time.

"I didn't give it a chance to eat more off my bro."

Zero, Diego, and Scout rushed up to Cobalt. They unpacked their gear from their kits and hondo bags.

Zero opened Diego's RATS pack. From each side, Zero removed IV fluid bags while Diego began his evaluation. "I didn't want it to eat my bro," he mumbled.

"Heart rate's okay but not ideal, he's breathing on his own. He's broken rib numbers five, six, and seven on the right chest from the feel of them."

He moved the stethoscope over Cobalt's chest. "No indication of a punctured lung. That's good. Looks like a fracture of his right leg by the ankle but it isn't compound. Where's the bleeding coming from? CB, check out that spot on your side above his belt."

"Here. I see blood running out. Seems like there's a lot on the ground."

"Well, I can't put it back in. He's pale." Diego moved to CB's side and examined the wound.

"Scout," Diego said pointing, "give me the red one. Time to plug this soldier." Diego tore open the pouch and took out a long folded bandage. Inch by inch, he stuffed it into the hole of Cobalt's wound.

"CB, press on this for one minute." Diego then started two IV lines, and injected a clear liquid into Cobalt's vein. Tearing open the T3 pouch, Diego wrapped the military grade bandage around Cobalt's belly. "Got some love handles there, Cobalt. Better cut back on the carbs."

CB watched the medic deftly evaluate and bandage the wounded Ranger. Precise, confident, and almost artistic, Diego went about his business like the consummate professional he was.

Finishing the bandages, Diego asked, "Everyone been screened and cleaned?" They all nodded. "That's good. Who's got B Neg blood?"

"O Pos," said Zero.

"I'm O Neg," added Scout.

"I guess you got me." CB tucked the heat retaining emergency blanket around Cobalt. "We're about to become blood brothers, dude."

"Scout, find me a place where we can move him. I'd like a cave but I'll take rocks as long as there's an overhang."

"On it," Scout said and disappeared in the dark.

CB held the bag of fluids and focused the flashlight as Diego peeked at the dressing over the wound.

"How is it?"

"Celox stopped the bleeding. Eyes react the same to light but I don't like the cut on his forehead. Scout, hand me that bandage. I'm sure he's got an injury to his right elbow, but it doesn't seem broken. All that's secondary to the GSW. The bullet needs to come out of there soon because man does not live by lead alone."

"You got the stretcher ready?" CB asked.

"Yeah." Zero laid the stretcher by Cobalt's body.

"You got a place for us?" Diego shouted in the dark. "I need a private room with a view, Scout."

"Yeah, Doc. We just got to go up a bit and over. Got a cave that'll do."

Diego moved Cobalt's uninjured leg alongside the broken one. He secured the two legs together, using the good leg as a splint, then wrapped more gauze in a figure eight to secure Cobalt's lower body. He put pads between the calves and knees.

"Okay," Diego said, "let's roll him on his side. Get the stretcher under him...and now bring him back."

Diego used two straps to secure Cobalt to the stretcher. "We're ready to move him. CB, keep the IV up at least twenty-four inches. Damn, it's starting to rain again. Give me a poncho."

They were silent as they struggled through the brush, the leader using a flashlight and machete to cut undergrowth. The tactical flashlight exposed an outcropping of stone that hung over the opening to the cave. It was large enough to accommodate all five of them.

While Diego checked the IV fluids, Scout and CB searched the area for boughs that would support waterproof ponchos on the entrance. Zero returned with wood and started a small fire to remove the dampness and keep Cobalt warm.

"Where'd you find dry wood, bro?" Diego asked.

"I'm a Ranger. I can find anything."

"So am I but I'd be hard pressed to find burnable wood after these rains."

"Well, some of us can and some of us can't. Embrace your weaknesses and grow stronger, bro."

"You've been around Cobalt too long."

"How is he?"

Diego finished taking Cobalt's vitals. "The sooner I can get a pint into him, the better. So far, so good. CB, roll up your sleeve. Let me see those vessels said the vampire to the virgin."

Cobalt's stretcher was balanced on pieces of wood while CB stretched out on a narrow ledge three feet above. "This okay, Doc? "

"Yeah. When I tell you, you start pumping your fist. Quit when I tell you. Scout, come across with the energy powder and bars. CB, eat and drink, my son."

The warm blood filled the plastic tube. Diego attached it to the hub of the needle in Cobalt's arm. "Now we wait."

Zero passed protein bars then began making a meal out of a combination of MRE's and Spam. Something warm would do them all good.

"Zero, my man, this is five star all the way. I apologize for not bringing the wine." Scout sampled the concoction.

"CB, I'm sorry I shot your wolf. Once we get Cobalt taken care of, I'll come back out and finish it off so it won't suffer. Guess I was too much in the moment."

"You won't find it, I'm sure."

Cobalt moaned.

"How much pain is he in, Doc?"

"Some for sure, but I don't want him to have a lot of meds. I'm keeping him on the light side until I can get more help. You can stop pumping, CB. I'll unhook you. Can't have him get to much of that hillbilly blood in him. He might wake up and start saying, 'all'a ya'all ya'll.'"

"He'll be okay. What's the plan for getting out of here?"

They all looked at CB.

"I'll let you know when I have one. But for now, once the storm passes, I want Scout to see how high he needs to go to get a good signal. We can call for evac once we know where we are."

Scouts computer came alive.

"What the hell? I'm getting signal. He's cut into my satellite again."

The familiar voice came over the speaker.

"Bring him to these coordinates. Be there by 0530 hours."

"Hey, hey, dude. How'd you hack into my satellite?" Scout asked.

"Sorry, but it's a state secret."

"How about we have a beer and you show me yours and I'll show you mine?"

"How's our friend?"

"Holding his own. We have a doc taking care of him. He'll be alright."

"Put the tablet up to his ear. I have a message for him."

Scout touched Cobalt's hand. "Man, someone wants to talk to you."

At the words *"Dlya Svyatoho Mykhayla,"* Cobalt whispered, *"Tak. Mykhayla."*

"He heard you, buddy. We'll be on top at 0530. Send in the Greyhound. Out."

****

"I guess we'd better get a few hours sleep. I'll take the first watch," Scout offered. "Can't sleep anyway. I'll be trying to figure out how I got hacked."

At 0345, CB heated water for coffee over what remained of the coals. The aroma woke the rest. His team spent an uneventful night snoring and drying out. Cobalt received another dose of pain meds before being transported.

"We need to head out in fifteen." Scout said, "I can't see any obstacle to the summit. How's the patient?"

"I'm fine," was Cobalt's response. "If you drop me, you die."

"Don't complain about the ride, bro, unless you can drive your own."

"Just keep your shit together and get me up on the hill for evac...ya'll."

"You were listening all night, you faker. I should jackhammer your other ribs," Zero threatened.

"Bro, since you're getting feisty, I'm going to knock you back down with some jungle juice." Diego said. "It's gonna be a tough ride. Nighty night."

Doc gave the go ahead. The team adjusted their packs and headed out.

****

The top of the mountain was windswept barren rocks. It reminded Zero of a small moonscape.

"What happened here, CB?"

"Mountaintop removal mining. They take coal that's near the surface. Supposed to restore the area, but there's a lot of discussion about it. Sure looks like hell, doesn't it? In a hundred thousand years, Nature might put it back, but for now, looks ugly like a blind date. Deacon's County didn't have that much coal to begin with, so it was a waste of time. Should have left it the way it was."

"0525, gentlemen, we're right on time. I wonder where our ride is?"

"From the west." Scout pointed to a helicopter descending to their position.

"Well, I'll be. That's a Black Hawk. Best taxi in the business." Diego tapped Cobalt on the shoulder which elicited a groan. "Sorry, dude. I forgot that's your sore arm."

When the chopper was a meter off the ground, three men dressed in black and carrying weapons hopped out. Diego and Zero brought the stretcher to the edge of the bay door when the aircraft landed. Two men pulled the stretcher aboard as CB and Scout pushed their end in the chopper. With all parties accounted for, the pilot took off.

"Thanks for the lift, guys. I'm Zero, this is Diego, Scout, and CB. We call this sleeping beauty, Cobalt."

The men wearing black face masks said nothing. One of them handed Diego another bag of fluids. A second one then opened a medical bag, conducted a combat physical, and proceeded to inspect Cobalt's dressings, nodding at the GSW. He removed the leg splint and Cobalt's boot. He then applied an air gel ankle brace. The doc in black took Cobalt's vitals, and gave Diego a thumbs up.

The chopper pilot set the craft down in the parking lot of the church on Davis Ridge. Once the extra men and the stretcher were off loaded, the helicopter disappeared into the rays of the morning sun.

It was a few moments later they heard the sound of sirens coming up the hillside.

"That's Sheriff Harris ready to gather us up and take us home. You got your computer back online, Scout?" CB said.

"Yes, sir I do. But, by the way, who were those masked men?"

<hr>

SATURDAY

<hr>

Andy Glassman arrives at the clinic before daybreak. He sees the unmarked black helicopter fly over the valley at a high rate of speed. Special Agent Coop is in one of the porch chairs holding a bloody thumb in the air.

****

Mike Green sips his first cup of coffee after the early rain. The air is fresh and clean. He trips over the muddy wet dog bleeding on his porch; the coffee mug lands in the begonia pot decorating his walk. The animal is lighter than he expects when he carries it to his truck. Its head rests on his thigh. Mike drives down the mountain to Dr. Glassman's.

****

Sheriff Bill and John Seven Star maneuver the curves and washed out shoulders of the road. The old Suburban accommodates the stretcher comfortably. Diego needs room to attend to Cobalt. This close to the clinic, he doesn't dare give Cobalt more morphine. The others are cramped and silent in their personal prayers.

****

Cleveland Coop sits stoically on the exam table while Andy pushes the barb of the fishing hook through Coop's thumb. The physician then cuts off the hook. He pulls the shaft of the hook backwards and out of the entry wound it made when Coop grabbed the fish. The fish got away. Coop did not. Dr. Glassman gives Coop two injections: a tetanus booster and antibiotics.

"Better your thumb than your butt."

Uball Gant applies the dressing and tapes it in place. "Do you want sick leave for this?"

The men laugh.

****

Magdelyn sits in the waiting room with Tater and Amelia Lemon. It's time for Bentley to have his bandages and stitches removed. She asks Tater if Dr. Glassman will give Bentley a kiss on his boo-boos. She sees Mike Green carry a limp dog. Scooting off her chair, she rests her forehead against the window. "Tater, look," she says. "I hope it ain't dead."

****

Agnes and Fishbone Crawford enter the clinic. Agnes needs an inhaler. Fishbone holds the door so the big men with Sheriff Harris and Mr. Seven Star can get the man on the stretcher in the building.

****

Tootsie watches the parking lot. She sees Luke Perkins and his friends dressed like they were playing Army in the woods. Mike carries a filthy cur dog into the clinic. The assistant knows she will not be leaving the clinic at noon. Tootsie hates Saturdays.

.

HEALING

Dr. Glassman watched both sides of his clinic fill with clients.

"Tootsie, put Mike and his dog into Exam 6. I'll take Luke and company into the OR. That room should be big enough to accommodate the woodsmen."

"Mrs. Cunningham and kitty cat, please come in this room, Exam 3."

"Agnes and Fishbone, have a seat in the lobby."

Andy stopped in the corridor between the two lobbies. To the right was Mrs. Cunningham and her monster cat, Moonie, then Maggie with Bentley for dressing changes. He'd gotten Mike Green and his dog hustled past Moonie before the cat turned into a saber toothed tiger. To the left was Luke Perkins and friends looking like they stayed out in the woods until one of them got more than he bargained for. Glassman would discreetly talk to Agnes about the injury to her face. Coop was staying for thirty minutes after the shots to check for reactions.

"This is where I need to be." He put on a blue scrub shirt and went into the OR.

****

"Okay, gentlemen, give me some information." Andy began an examination of Cobalt.

"We were separated in the woods and our friend got lost and fell down the hillside," Zero said. "We had to stay in the woods until the sheriff could bring us in."

"Doesn't have anything to do with the unmarked helicopter flying over my clinic at day break? Besides, whoever took care of this man did a nice job. Which one of you would that be?"

"Me, sir."

"You're the combat medic I heard about?"

"Yes, sir. There's a GSW under the dressing at his waist."

"You plug him?"

"Yes, sir."

"Let's get x-rays before we disturb the dressing. Tootsie," he called.

"Right behind you, Dr. Glassman."

"Set up x-ray for this patient. You and...?" He looked for a name.

"Diego."

"Hook him up to the monitor. When did he have pain meds last?"

"Early this morning," Diego stated.

"How many bags of fluids has he had?"

"This is his third since yesterday, sir. He's had one pint of whole blood. No expanders."

"Has he peed? Any bleeding?" Andy poked Cobalt's lower abdomen.

"Hasn't been fully conscious, sir. I kept him light."

"Cath him." He called his assistant. "Tootsie, get Diego a catheterization set up. I want blood work. Standard, nothing fancy."

"You," he pointed to Scout, "cut off his clothes." He tossed a patient gown.

"Diego, Tootsie will show you my x-ray setup. Take pictures of everything you think we need. Fluids are in the cabinet behind you. I'll be right back."

Dr. Glassman looked at Luke's face. "I take it you fell down the same hill?"

"Yes."

"You're Luke Perkins, Maggie's brother?"

"Yes."

"You work at the Library of Congress?"

"Yes." Luke looked at the others.

"I advise you to read up on hiking safety. Ice bags are in the small freezer at the back. Help yourself, Luke."

****

Glassman grabbed an albuterol inhaler off the supply shelf and went into the waiting room. "Agnes, how are you?"

"Doing better, Dr. Glassman. Doing better. Me and Fishbone are living in town for a while."

"That's good. Are you having any pain?"

"No, not really. I get plenty of ice."

"It's nice to have you in the village, Agnes. I'll see you on Monday. Can you come in then?"

"Yes. Can I clean your office for the inhaler?"

"That'll be fine, Agnes. We'll call it even. Take care of your mother, young man."

"Yes, sir." Fishbone looked through the hallway and saw Tater. "Be right back Mom." He hopped off the chair and darted into the second lobby.

"Excuse me, Agnes," Dr. Glassman said. "Things are busy this morning."

"Thanks, doctor. I'll wait for my son on the porch."
****

"Didn't know you got another dog, Mike." Dr. Glassman washed his hands in the sink.

"I didn't. It got me. Found it on the porch this morning."

"Let me see." Dr. Glassman adjusted the stethoscope headset and placed the chest piece against the animal's lungs.

"Well, it's still alive, but I don't know how. Looks like he's been shot. There's the entry wound but I don't see an exit. Change places with me, Mike. I want to see if it came out one of its rear legs. It's got a strange coat, doesn't it."

Mike absentmindedly stroked the dog's ear, running his fingers from the base of the pinna to the tip, trying to will the dog to live.

Andy felt along the dog's back, touching each vertebrae, up to its neck. He pulled back an eyelid, surprised to see strange blue eyes.

"I think you've got a husky of sorts. Probably a wolf hybrid or something. Folks breed everything under the sun. See the blue eye? That's a gene mutation. You see that in sled dogs."

"Do you think it will live?" Mike smoothed the fur on the dog's head.

"Hard to say, Mike. He's wet and dirty."

"Dogs don't die of wet and dirty."

"Sorry. What I meant was he's in tough shape. Blood loss because of being shot and I don't know what else. I'll need to take some x-rays to see where that bullet is. That is, unless you want me to put him down."

Mike swallowed hard. He participated in far too many deaths in his lifetime. He met Dr. Glassman's eyes.

"No, do what you can, Doc. I'll take responsibility for him. Maybe when you fix him up, I can find who owns him or maybe he'll stay with me and not run away to be with the kids down the mountain."

The vet smiled. "Yes, Tater brought Mr. Green's Dog in for his shots. I'll do my best, Mike. Just stay with him until I get caught up on the other side."

Andy Glassman walked out of the room not so sure he could save Mike's dog.
****

"Tootsie, did you and Diego get the x-rays done?"

"Yes. Up on the viewer. I'll be in with Mrs. Cunningham's cat."

"Okay, I want x-rays on Mike's animal next. Diego can help with that, too. We'll be looking for a bullet someplace, maybe along the spine, hidden along bone. Also abdomen views. What's up with the cat?"

"She's here for a nail trim."

"Moonie?" He patted her on the shoulder. "I know that cat." Dr. Glassman made a sour face. "Wear Kevlar gloves, okay?"

****

Dr. Glassman washed his hands and changed his scrub shirt to attend to Cobalt.

He walked into the OR room as Diego left to help Tootsie. He could smell the military leaking from their pores. If one was military, they're all military.

"You guys out hunting in the area?" he asked.

"Something like that," Zero replied.

Andy began his second examination of Cobalt, noting that his breathing was slow and regular, skin color was normal in the areas that were not bruised, and his fingernails, toenails, and lips were normal color. Cobalt's pupils reacted equally to the small flashlight.

"Well, he's definitely beat up a bit." Andy noticed the glance between the other men as he brought the images up on the computer screen.

"Three ribs broken on the right chest. There isn't any displacement. Looks like they snapped back into position. By the look of those hands, he's been in a fight...skin is peeled back, maybe a knuckle is broken. Elbow is bruised but nothing fractured and held together the way God intended.

"A spiral fracture of the distal end of the right fibula. That will hurt like a bitch, but he'll get over it quickly. Not a weight bearing bone so I won't cast it. I'll have the results of his blood work in short order and we'll see where we stand on that."

Dr. Glassman brought up the next view of Cobalt's head.

"Nothing is showing up on the head and neck views. I don't see evidence of any brain bleeding. But that's out of my area. We need to get him to the VA where they have better equipment and a neurologist to look at his noggin."

"No. No VA. At least not until he wakes up. We can't make that decision for him." Diego stood at the doorway.

"Let's get real, gentlemen. Your business is your business, but if this guy is government property, he needs to be at Johnson VA Medical in Clarksburg. They've got the experience and a hell of a lot better equipment than I have."

Scout folded his arms across his chest. "Trust me on this, Doc. Don't let him wake up in the VA."

"Okay, if you say so. But, if anything shows up that I don't like, I'm calling a chopper and he goes. Deal?"

"Deal. I'll cover for you, Doc."

"I'm going to admit him and keep him for a few days at the clinic. Other than what I've said," he said staring at Zero and Scout, "he doesn't seem too bad. Luke, ask Gracie about sending meals. Make sure she knows he's a big guy."

****

"So, Mr. Green, I'm delighted we meet again." Diego wandered down the hallway and into the exam room.

Mike looked up at the sound of the familiar voice. *"Suka sin.* If it isn't the *ved'mak.* You work here now, witcher?"

Diego laughed. "Something told me you'd be glad to see me. How the hell are you?"

"I'm fine, *ved'mak.* Just fine."

"Dr. Glassman sent me in to help out with your dog. Relax, man, your secret's safe with me. I mean, who would have thought we'd meet again, eh? In the interest of goodwill, help me get your dog on the cart and down the hall. We can take him in for x-rays."

"In the interest of goodwill, I'll help to make sure you don't kill my dog, witcher."

Diego and Mike didn't speak until Diego moaned about the films.

"Hum, I think Doc's machine is screwed up. Look here...er, Mike. They're all black but for these two tiny white dots or, like in the second set, they're all white and again, we've got two tiny black dots in the same place."

"What does that mean?" Mike stroked the dog's back.

"It means I'm not messing with this machine. If it's broken, I didn't do it. Let's get back to the exam room and start the IV."

Mike was silent as they returned to the room. Diego turned on the clippers to cut the dog's hair.

"So, Mike, how do you like it here in the good old USA?"

"I like much better I'm no longer Mikhail Ivanovich Verkhovensky, but I am Mike Green, especially to you, witcher."

"Easy, easy. Got it, dude. No hard feelings, man. I was just trying to alleviate your pain."

"Da, koldon right into next vorld."

Diego looked at the dog's leg. The hair hadn't been cut. "How'd that happen?"

"Vat?" Mike corrected himself. "What?"

"I just shaved this dog's leg and the hair's back."

"Maybe it didn't cut? Maybe it's a dull blade?"

"Here. Look. The clippers go through the hair and after I make the pass, the hair is like it was."

****

Fishbone sat in the plastic chair next to Tater in the westside lobby of the clinic. "What's up, Tater? Is Mr. Green's Dog alright?"

"Yep, he is. Maggie's got to have Dr. Glassman take the stitches out of her dog's leg."

"That the one the coyote tore up?"

"Yep. Nathan shot it. My Dad's gonna have the hide tanned."

"Didn't have rabies, did it?"

"Nope."

"Where's Maggie and her dog?"

"In that room. Miss Lemon's in there, too."

"What's Miss Lemon doing in there? Where's your Mom and Dad?"

"They're having a date in Waybird. Luke is supposed to be watching us but he told us to stay with Miss Lemon until he got business done."

The boys bounced their legs back and forth while they sat and waited.

"What's Mr. Green doing in here?"

"Maggie said he brought a dog."

"Tater, let's go see what he's got."

"Okay, but go around the hall so no one sees."

They paused at the Dutch door to avoid Tootsie, then scurried down the hallway. Mr. Green saw them look into the room.

"Come in. Look what showed up on my front porch all dirty and hurt. See," he said peeling back the eyelid, "it's a husky of some sort. Has blue eyes."

Tater and Fishbone knew who Mr. Green had but all they said was, "Hope your dog gets better," and left.

****

They ducked into the men's room and locked the door.

"Oh, good hell, that's a snow dog, Fish. What're we gonna do?"

"Tater, it can't stay here."

"We gotta get it to the woods with its friends. And we got to do it fast. Mr. Coop is nosing around."

"He the one who you told your story to?"

"Yep. And, the twins told me Mr. Coop don't just collect stories, but he cuts things up in little pieces for under a microscope."

"Good hell *no*!"

"Good hell *yes*!"

"You think he'd cut up the snow dog?"

"Probably. I bet him and Mr. Gant would get some kind of science award for it."

"We gotta help it escape."

"And we gotta do it quick."

"*Carpe diem.*"

"What's that mean, Fish?"

"Latin. Aunt Gem taught me it. Means seize the day. Means is do what you gotta do when it needs to be done and don't be a afraid. We gotta figure out the escape and then do it."

"Okay, but I think it's *carpe doggem*."

****

"Scout, bro." Cobalt's throat was dry. His words came out like a frog croaking after a drought.

"Want some water, man?"

Cobalt nodded. After a few sips, he looked around. "Where am I? VA?"

"No," Zero whispered. "Still with Luke. It's a Doc's office that does people and dogs."

"Which side am I on?" Cobalt felt his crotch.

Zero laughed. "You're good, bro."

"It was an interesting rescue. Too bad you slept through most of it." Luke said. "Our helpers did a lot to get us off the mountain."

Cobalt raised his head. "God, Luke, who beat your ass?"

"We can talk later, bro."

"Cobalt, sore subject." Zero winked.

"Yeah, I can tell by looking at his face. I thought I taught you better in hand-to-hand."

"We can drop this," Luke said.

"Yeah, bro, but not as hard as you got dropped on your face." Cobalt tried not to laugh. He held his sore chest with a sore arm and moaned.

Scout bent over so he couldn't be overheard outside of the room. "I want to meet your friend, the one who talks like a movie star and hacks into my freaking satellite."

"The satellite you stole from the Army?" Cobalt took another sip of water.

"Army, Navy, CIA, does it matter? For the time being, it's mine and your buddy hacked me. I need to know how."

Cobalt smiled. "His name is Alex and he likes Leadslingers."

"Okay, he's a bro. But he owes me a case. I don't take hacking lightly."

Glassman popped back into the exam room. He put his stethoscope to Cobalt's heart.

"Is he going to be alright?" It was Zero who spoke what they were all thinking.

"Yeah, I think he will. He's hydrating nicely, and the x-rays and lab work don't look all that exciting. I changed my mind and I'm going to cast that leg. Maybe weld a section of pig iron to slow you down."

Cobalt was suddenly alert. "Oh, no, I'm fine. Just let me sit up."

"You'll lay down or I'll drug you." Dr. Glassman warned.

"You worked at Reed?" Scout was smiling.

"Yes. For a while."

"It shows." Even Cobalt smiled.

When Tootsie entered the room, Andy asked, "What's up?"

"Your twenty grand x-ray machine is on the fritz. And what smells in here?" Tootsie sniffed the air.

On cue, the men smell their armpits and down the front of their shirts.

"I think it's us, ma'am," Zero admitted. "We'd better go."

"Guys, get me something to eat." Cobalt rubbed his head and smiled his sweetest at Tootsie.

"Yes, go stink up the diner while I try to get this mess cleaned up. Out of here all of you, except you, Doc. You need to check out that machine."

Luke smiled. "I see you've found someone to keep you in line."

"And to think I pay her to boss me around." Doctor Glassman winked as he made way for the Rangers and Luke to leave the exam room.

****

"Looks like Cobalt is in good hands. Luke, you never said you had a Walter Reed doc working here." Zero checked his image in the window of Hammond's Hardware store.

"I heard about him from Sam and Spencer. He was their doc when they got hurt."

"That would be the Marines we met at the cookout?" Zero said.

"Yeah. Glassman saved Sam's leg when everyone else wanted to cut it off. Spencer was pretty banged up, too. I don't know all the particulars, but they just about got blown off a mountain."

The Rangers nodded. They knew the dynamics.

Scout grabbed Luke's arm. "Hey, pull up, slick. See that green truck in front of the diner?"

"So, the boys are back in town," Zero nodded toward the figures sitting beside the south window of the restaurant. "Our babysitters from the 'Stan. And to quote the littlest bear, 'they're sitting in my booth.'"

"I'll give a bottle of Leadslingers to the man who can get a sensor on their truck," Scout said. "The gauntlet is thrown."

"You both are too dirty and ugly to be seen, I'll pick up the glove," Luke advised. "It's a CIA thing."

Scout searched his pockets for the extra electronics. "Here, take two. They're small."

Luke looked down both sides of the street for anything that would cover his walk in the open. He punched in a number on his phone.

"Hey, Gracie, this is Luke. Do me a favor? Pull down the shade on that row of booths at the front? Thanks. I owe you."

"Wait a minute, you called the owner of the diner for camouflage? I thought you'd use your spy skills and sneak across the road, plant the sensors, and belly crawl back like a snake." Zero feigned exasperation.

"You gotta work smarter, not harder." Luke tapped the side of his temple.

"I'm impressed." Scout grinned.

"Excuse me, gentlemen," Luke said. "Duty calls."

They waited in the dimness of the alley until Smith and Jones left the diner. Only when the truck disappeared, did Luke, Scout, and Zero cross the street. Gracie sat them at a secluded table in the banquet room.

"I suppose if I ask what ya'll's up to, I won't get the truth, so I won't ask. But, I will ask you boys to clean up a bit before you sit up front with the payin' guests."

"I've got money, Gracie," Luke said as he pulled folding money from his cargo pocket.

"No, put it away. Sheriff Bill told me a little about what all ya'll did up there. I'd kiss each one of you, but ya'll are a little ripe. Order what you want. Dodger is cookin' up a storm today."

"Remember, not a word, Gracie."

"I know, Luke, I know. Ya'll just eat up. I'll have a bag to go for your missing man when you're ready."

****

"Damn it, Tootsie. What's up with this machine?"

"I don't have a degree in why machines worth twenty grand go haywire six months after they're paid for. Not my area. And don't say 'damn it, Tootsie' when you actually mean 'damn it, IBM or damnit, Riyence, or...'"

"I get it. Sorry."

"Forgiven. Now, what's wrong with your machine? Never saw it take pictures like this. Worked okay on the big guy in the OR, but it stopped working when I set it up for Mike's dog."

"I don't know. Let me fiddle with the software. Did we get the latest updates?"

"Dr. Glassman, what did I just say?"

"You're not an IT technician."

"I'm going to check my patients, two and four legs, while you fix this. And don't forget Maggie Perkins is here for stitch removal and dressing changes. She'll be looking for you."

Tootsie left Dr. Glassman cussing at the machine.

****

"Gant, what are you doing? Slow down, son. You're getting too excited. You don't have a search warrant to be taking things out of that man's truck."

"Coop, this could be the break I've been looking for. You saw him bring that dog in. Help me find hair in the front seat. Look for drops of fluid, blood, urine, anything we can collect and examine. If I match hair from this dog with the samples you sent weeks ago, we're sitting on a monumental discovery. I could get a promotion for this. So could you."

"I don't want a promotion. I'm retiring soon. Gant, we still have to follow protocol. Getting overly confident isn't a reason to break the policy and conduct an unlawful search."

Ubell paused in this examination for samples. "Yeah, Coop, in all your years, don't tell me you didn't let the paperwork follow?"

"No, I didn't do things that way."

"Well, you're old school and I'm new school and this is the way it's been going for some years."

"Gant, don't ruin a career over an illegal search. Remember whose side you're on. We play by the rules."

"Do you want to sit on the greatest discovery the world has known?"

"And that is?"

"Evidence of first contact. We 've discovered an alien species on Earth."

****

"Look, Fish. Coop's going through Mr. Green's truck."

"Bet they're looking for specie mens."

"If they don't find them, they'll cut up the snow dog."

"Tater, I thinks now's the time we *carpe doggem.*"

"But how?"

"Just like Master Spies, that's how. We just need a dirt version."

The boys walked down the hallway from the east side of the clinic to the animal west side. They paused to see Mr. Cobalt sleeping as Tootsie checked his IV. They tiptoed past the room where Dr. Glassman was busy removing the bandages from Maggie's stuffed dog. Then they came to the room where Mr. Green was sitting, staring at the dog on the cart.

"How's he doing?" Fishbone asked.

"I don't know. Maybe I'll know something in a little while."

"Mr. Green, there's a man in your truck."

"You boys watch him and I'll be right back."

"Sure, Mr. Green. We'd be glad to."

As soon as Mike left the room, Tater and Fishbone covered the injured dog with a sheet from the shelf. When the hall was clear, they pushed the cart down the delivery ramp, out the back fire door, and across the employee parking lot toward the woods.

****

"Excuse me, but what are you doing?" Mike was indignant to find Ubell searching his truck while Coop stood by.

"Mike, Ubell thought..."

"Where'd you get the dog, sir?"

"Gant..."

"I said where'd you get the dog?"

"You know you're talking to a deputized law official of this county, Mr. Gant?"

"That's fine, then you understand issues of national security."

"You got a warrant?" Mike was losing himself to Mikhail.

Coop stepped between them. "No, we don't, and if we need one I'd get it to you first, Mr. Green. I'm sorry for the intrusion. It won't happen again."

"Coop," Ubell shouted, "it's getting away." He pointed to the cart being pushed toward the woods.

****

"Damn it to hell." Dr. Glassman returned to his x-ray equipment.

"Another fun day at the clinic, Doc?" Diego asked from the doorway, sipping from a mug. "Hope you don't mind. Miss Tootsie offered me a cup."

"No, that's fine. I'm almost ready to call the company. It's still under warranty. I don't know why it suddenly went on the fritz. It worked fine on Cobalt."

"So you found the bullet?"

"Bullet? There's no bullet in him."

"I treated a gunshot wound on him. Left side, just above the beltline."

"That man wasn't shot. The dog was shot."

Diego grabbed Andy's arm. "Bro, I said I dressed a GSW on him. You saw the dressing. I know what I'm talking about."

"Hey, man, it's okay." Andy had seen that look before, but it was on another soldier in a different land. Andy gently removed Diego's hand from his arm. "Diego, it's cool. Here, let me show you."

Dr. Glassman flipped the switch on the viewer. "Here's his chest, AP and lateral. Upper and lower abdomen. Pelvic area. Show me a bullet."

Diego saw nothing but textbook anatomy and bones.

"Come with me."

Diego followed Dr. Glassman down the hall to where Cobalt was sleeping. The doctor held up the blanket and the edge of the patient gown.

"No bullet wound because there's no bullet."

Diego touched Cobalt's skin. "It was right here. I used Celox and plugged the wound. The doc on the chopper checked it. I saw it. What the hell?" He searched Glassman's face.

"I don't know what to say. When I checked him again, the tape and gauze were there but there was nothing under it. I removed the bandage. I believe you but I also believe my own eyes."

"You've got them mixed up then."

"We've taken two sets of x-rays today, Diego, and you were there for both of them. Here, look what came out with the dog." Dr. Glassman moved the mouse and clicked on "Green, Mike. GSW dog."

"See? There isn't any comparison. The machine stopped working after Cobalt. The dog's pictures are either totally overexposed or totally underexposed. The machine is screwed up or the software."

"Stop, Doc. Look. Can you enlarge the two dots, here and here, then on the other one, here and here."

"What are you looking for?"

"Just wait. Enlarge more. More. Max it out, Doc."

After a few moments, Diego got what he wanted.

"There's noting wrong with your machine. Here's one bullet, and here's the other. The mushroom one has to be the one that caused the wound on Cobalt. And this one, still has the shape it had when it was chambered. It's Zero's bullet. He shot it."

"What the hell?"

"You got some strong juju going on in your little town, Doc. Let's go see the dog."

****

"Hey, you kids. Stop!" Ubell started screaming. "This is federal business. Stop!" The image of his Nobel Prize in Science was fading just as fast as the kids were running while they shouted "*carpe doggem.*"

They pushed the cart towards the woods as fast as their legs would allow. Gant didn't notice the blue mist forming, a faint aura emanating from the trees.

"Gant, that's no way to handle those kids." Coop, with Mike Green following, jogged across the pavement.

Agnes was startled as Dr. Glassman and Tootsie exited the front door, letting it slam behind them. Amelia Lemon rushed from the clinic, calling Tater to come back.

Tootsie touched Agnes on the arm as Agnes rose to get her son. "Stay here. We have no business in this. The boys are safe." They watched from the steps.

"Amelia, don't." Tootsie said.

"Faster, Fish. They're coming. *Carpe doggem, carpe doggem.*"

"Can't go any faster, Tater. It's too bumpy."

Diego leapt over the porch railing and sprinted toward the boys as he shouted, "Guys, it's okay. Hold up."

****

The wheel hit a small pothole. Cart, kids, and dog spilled to the ground.

"We killed him, Tater. We killed him."

"Look, Fish. They're coming for him. We just gotta wake him up."

Tater scrambled to the dog's head. He shook it's shoulder. Then using his thumb and index finger, he parted the animal's eyelid, placing his own eye just inches from the dog.

"Hey, you gotta wake up before Coop comes to take your specie mens. Wake up. Fishbone and me saved you. You just gotta wake up. Hurry, wake up."

Tater watched the wave appear, just as it did in the church. All the adults who were chasing him were frozen. Only him and Fishbone were able to move.

"You gotta go. You can't stay here."

"Dog," Fishbone pleaded, "*carpe doggem. Please.*"

A blue fog was radiating from between the pine trees. It surrounded the two boys and the dog on the ground. It twirled around, narrowing as it rose to a peak above the threesome, then falling and widening out, swirling around, deepening and finally coming to rest over the now white dog.

It moved its hind legs, then struggled to its front. It stood and shook itself from nose to tail. The mist hovered on the ground.

"You gotta go now," Tater said.

"He's right, dog. You did all you needed to do so, it's time to go leave. They're waitin' on you. See? Just over there." Fishbone pointed to a huge pine tree.

The white wolf-dog sniffed their hair, then ran its tongue along their cheeks and faces.

The boys watched the animal walk to its pack. The mist deepened in color from blue to violet to purple, then melted into the darkness of the shadows among the trees.

"Tater, your hair's all sparkly."

"Your's too, Fish."

Diego broke free first and ran to the boys. "You kids okay? It didn't hurt you anywhere?"

"We're okay, Mr. Diego," Tater said. "Just a little sparkly is all." The boys giggled.

A light breeze dissipated the foggy mist. On the black asphalt, two spent bullets glinted in the sunlight.

****

"Maggie?" Amelia called. "She was right here a minute ago."

"She's here somewhere. Probably back looking at the kittens," Tootsie said. "Come with me, Amelia. We'll find her."

Dr. Glassman waved to the women when they came away from the cat boarding area.

"I found her. She's on this side."

Dr. Glassman held the door. Amelia saw Maggie sleeping in the crook of Cobalt's arm with Bentley tucked around the Ranger's neck.

Making Plans

Diego pulled out a chair at the table and sat with a weariness he hadn't felt before.

"Man, you look like you just saw a ghost," someone murmured.

Luke touched his shoulder. "Hey, you're among friends. Spill your guts."

"Come to Daddy," Scout joked. "I can make the blind see, and the deaf hear." They all snickered but Diego.

He slowly raised his head and looked at each one in turn, his stare dissolving their humor.

Using his fork, Scout tapped the place setting in front of Diego. "Hey, what is it?"

"I'm not sure. I'm just not sure. Order me Leadslingers."

Luke shook his head. "It's ten a.m. and you're not starting now." He waved at Barbara. "Coffee all around, please."

"I don't know what I saw, but Mike's wounded dog went back to the wild, Cobalt does not have a gunshot wound, and Dr. Glassman offered me a job."

Barbara brought coffee and water to the table. "Okay, fellas, what can I get you?"

"A good stiff drink would help. For medicinal purposes only. Trust me, I'm a doctor." Diego sat back in his chair.

Luke said, "We'll have the special, all around, Barbara. One check."

"Okay. Be right back," she said.

A few minutes later, Barbara returned with a fifth of Leadslingers Napalm Cinnamon Whiskey. She placed it in the center of the table.

"From our climate controlled wine cellar."

"What's this, angel from Heaven above?" Scout held the bottle gently in his arms. "How'd you know, my pet?"

"A little bird told Gracie so she ordered some. You boys get one shot in your coffee, and only one shot. It's too early for any nonsense but ya'll look like you been rode hard and put up wet." She took the bottle, with a little struggle, from Scout.

"Get the mugs up here. Come on, don't be shy. All you get is one."

Barbara poured one shot exactly. When she was away waiting tables, they helped themselves to a second and third. On her way to the kitchen, she removed the bottle. Raising one eyebrow, she noted the fill line. When she brought their food, none of the men made eye contact with her; their sin hung in the air like dead smoke from a campfire on a windless night.

"I'm telling you guys," Diego whispered across the table, "you all saw me plug that wound. Now it's gone. Not a mark on Cobalt. Gone. Period." He paused. "Your brother and his friend stole the dog and got it out the back. They ended up dumping the cart, dog, and themselves, and poof! It was gone back in the woods and the little boys were giggling. What do you know about this white wolf slash snow dog stuff, Luke? You know something because I can see it on your swollen face. I'd like an explanation so I know I don't have to check into the VA psych ward."

"Some folks believe in them and others think it's all drunk hillbilly delusions from too much distilled corn mash. What I've been told is that it goes back to the Civil War."

"It's not a delusion to us. We saw it up there with Cobalt." Scout tucked his napkin in the front of his shirt as Barbara served the plates.

"You spoke to it, Luke. We all heard you." Zero stuffed a large spoonful of baked beans into his mouth. "Gawd, this 'tuff is gud."

Luke looked around the room and lowered his voice. "They saved me once. I was out hunting for rabbits, dropped my rifle between two rocks. My arms weren't long enough to retrieve it. I didn't know I was being hunted until I rolled on my back in exasperation. I saw the cougar on the stones above me. When it leapt, I got up to run, and it snagged me on my back, but it was caught by one of the snow dogs. I was that close to being dinner for some cubs. When I reached down between the rocks, it was like my rifle jumped into my hand. There was nothing to shoot. It was gone.

"The three dogs sat at the edge of the woods, staring at me with their crazy blue eyes. I was frozen.

"Then my Dad was calling me and everything came back into focus. He was squeezing me and shouting to never go hunting by myself again, wanting to see my back. He was crying he was so scared.

"Dad and I watched the blue cloud recede into the woods. He made me promise to never tell anyone outside of him and Mom."

"So when I shot it, it didn't die?" Zero poked at his mashed potatoes.

"No, it found its way to Mike's place. He thought it was just a stray dog and brought it to Dr. Glassman's. We arrived with Cobalt about the same time."

"So what is it, Luke? What do people think those things are?" Scout wiped his face with this hands. He was tired. "Ghosts? Jin? Spirits from God?"

"I don't know, but I think the quieter we are about whatever they are, the better off the Hollar is in the long run. We all saw it happen. We saw the dog laying next to Cobalt. Zero, you shot it. I know those things are real and now you all do, too. However, there seems to be something else involved. I think there are other planes of existence and these wolfish dogs can travel between them. Just don't tell a psychologist that. The locals accept things happen and get on with life."

Luke stopped his narrative to eat the roast beef on his plate. "I miss food like this. Can't get it in D.C."

The men were silent as they ate.

Diego shivered. "I wish she'd bring back that bottle. The medicinal effect is wearing off."

"Fat chance. Barbara won't. Once she cuts you off, you're cut off." Luke examined his arms. "I think we all need to get cleaned up and get some sleep. Maybe we can meet later?"

Scout nodded. "I just want to add that Nathan and Tobias are spectacular kids. I know men who don't have that mental toughness."

"Agreed. Luke, they did an amazing job up in the caves," Diego said as he mopped the last of the meat juice off his plate with a wedge of buttered bread.

"I'm still figuring out what to tell Mom and Dad."

"Luke, whatever you say, your Dad will handle it well, I'm sure. But mothers are different. Don't mean to throw shade, but," Zero laughed, "she might not take too kindly to her boys being in a firefight at twelve."

"I'm more interested in how they raise such strong offspring." Scout spoke as he checked out the pie case from across the room.

"Dad made them do things to challenge them. He says it builds the mental tenacity men need to have. Always said his job is raising men, not boys.

"I made my mom cry once when I was about their age and I got set right. Dad said, 'A mother will take her kid's shit time after time but a dad's job is to teach his kids when the shit stops. And it stops now, son. You're mine and I'd die for you, but she's my wife, so know your place.'"

Luke broke out laughing, "He said...he said if I made his wife cry one more time, I could live in the woods with the other ignorant animals. To him, Mom came first." Luke was laughing so hard, the tears were forming in his eyes. "My dad said us boys were the result of a night of passion and he was stuck with what he got so he had to make the best of it."

"Your dad said that?" Diego started to laugh with the rest of the men at the table.

"Hell, yes. He was always telling us we were second to her. Once he said if we didn't behave, he'd call the Department of Natural Resources and have us returned to the wild."

"That's really good parenting, Luke." Zero wiped tears from his eyes. "Your dad's a trip."

"He's an active parent for sure."

"Something worked because I don't know any twelve year old's that are that mature." Scout pointed at the pecan pie Barbara held up for him. He gave her a thumbs up.

"They're not ruined by the internet or social media. Mom won't have them obsessed by it."

"Well," Scout said, "she's got a point. Are they familiar with computers? Tobias was really interested in my equipment."

"Yes, we have a computer at home. Internet is spotty and they've lost interest in it. They can always go to Birdie Spry's. She's got a hookup at her place."

"Who's that?" Diego asked.

"One of our senior citizens. She was born and raised here. Birdie dabbles in plant medicine."

Zero and Diego exchanged glances but said nothing.

Barbara came over to clear the dishes. "Hey, does anyone else want pie?"

"Not me," Zero sighed. "I am full up to the gills. But another coffee won't hurt, ma'am."

"Coming up. Be right back." She took both arms full of stacked plates back to the kitchen. On her return, she gave Scout a big slice of pie with ice cream on the side.

"Luke, what are we going to do about Smith and Jones?"

"Where are they now?" Luke asked.

Scout checked his small tablet. "I've got them at the motel in Waybird City."

"Good. Keep an eye on them. I think they're trying to figure out their next move."

Diego started tapping his foot as soon as he put his cup down. "I'm going over to check on Cobalt. I'll meet you two at the bed and breakfast. You going home, Luke?"

"Yeah. I need to see how the twins are making out. They'll need to talk about what happened."

"Good man. Get some sleep. It's been an interesting visit to your little hamlet in the mountains, Luke. Something to tell my grandkids."

"Zero, you better get married first."

"Don't worry, I'm an honorable guy. I know how to wine and dine a woman. Make her feel special. I've done it a hundred times."

"And you don't have the right one yet? Out of a hundred?"

"I'm picky. Just gotta find the one who makes me feel special. That's a two way street."

"Make sure you invite us to the wedding," Luke said. "We'll want to see those fireworks."

****

The cheap motel was uncomfortably confining.

"Well? Come up with a plan? We need to do something. I'm getting stir crazy after two weeks hiding out." Smith folded clothes still warm from the laundromat.

"I can't get through to anyone. I'm sure there are a few bags of cash in one or more of those caves. Here, look what I picked up when we were there."

"A fifty? That's all?"

"Where this came from, there's more. We've lost product, but we can always get more of that, too. They'll never know what happened. We swoop in, swoop out."

"Sounds like a plan. Get a couple blondes or redheads. Boss says they go for more money in the Middle East."

"I suppose but we have to make contacts and hook up with an established organization."

"You really think Boss has money stashed up there?"

"I'm sure of it. A dude who has five thousand dollar shoes has cash everywhere."

"There was a lot of firepower that went into that ambush. What, maybe fifteen dead? Three vehicles down. I'd like to know who's trying to move in on the action."

"We won't know for sure until we connect with Boss."

"What if he's dead?"

"Man, they come and they go. You know that."

"The crew's all dead and who knows where Boss is now. He trusted Clarence, Skull, and Allen a lot more than was healthy. And the fat one, what'd they call him?"

"Jiggy."

"Yeah, it fit him good. I bet if we do a little recon we'll find a duffle bag stashed in a cave. Maybe we start our own organization?"

"Possible. We'll need help from the cartels. Go get something to eat and I'll call. Get two pizzas and soda. And bread and dipping sauce. Make them extra large with everything but no anchovies. I hate those little salty bastards."

"Anything else?"

"See what they have for dessert. Maybe we'll make a little trip to the caves. Thing's should have cooled off by now."

"You don't think we'll meet up with any of the competition?"

"They'll be long gone. We can still use the setup Boss had. Get a crew lined up, routes, and a clientele. Tapping into the Arab trade in the Mediterranean will get us all the money we need."

"Have you checked the weapons?"

"No. Bring them in after dark and we'll take inventory and clean everything. Get used to being here until I can make arrangements. We'll shop around, go to a movie. You still like bowling?"

"Yeah. Maybe go to a park and get some fresh air. Just two guys on vacation. Fishing is supposed to be good."

"Go get something to eat. I'm starving."

"Extra large, no anchovies."

"Yeah, I hate those salty little bastards."

****

Luke and his barbarians met at Gracie's Place.

"Scout, got anything?" Luke forked the last of the raw spinach from his salad bowl, keeping his voice low.

"One of them went to a hunting store for twenty minutes. After that, he took pizza back to the motel. They've been really quiet."

Scout held his glass steady while Barbara topped off his ice tea."

"Sure you don't want a fresh glass, sugar?"

"No, ma'am, Barbara. I'm fine."

"It's not a problem to get you fresh and dump out what's gotten warm in your glass."

"No, thank you. I'm good." Scout flashed one of his best boyish grins.

Barbara took the extra dishes back to the kitchen while she mumbled about stale tea.

"Makes me wonder why they're staying around here." Diego kept his voice low.

"There has to be something," Luke said. "They know by now the organization is broken up. There has to be something they're waiting on or for."

"You're forgetting one thing," Cobalt said. He adjusted his casted leg on the extra chair.

"What's that?" Luke asked. He looked at the empty tables around them. Satisfied he could speak frankly, he asked Cobalt again. "What would keep them here? They surveyed the area, saw the dead, the burned out cars, and they left. There's nothing for them here."

"It's not what you think is here for them, it's what they think. They'll stay until they have confirmed there is nothing."

"And nothing is?" Zero took a wooden toothpick from a tiny glass sitting on the table.

"Money. They can always get more victims or join another organization, but they need money to do that. If they're going to go independent, they'll need money for that, too. As long as they think there's the possibility of obtaining lost revenue, they'll be here. And as long as they're here, everyone in the Hollar is in danger. Especially the women and children. You saw the condition of those kids."

Cobalt made a face when he squirmed in the chair. "I think it's time for my medicine."

From under the tablecloth, Diego brought the half empty bottle of Lead-slingers.

"Here, bro, your cup. Diego Doc can sooth your anxiety."

Cobalt passed his mug, looking around for Barbara or any other person who might rat him out to Dr. Glassman.

"You taking pain killers?" Luke held his mug up for a shot.

"Nope. Just over the counter. But this is better."

"Here, fill me up. I had a close call with Barbara taking my glass. I need my nerves steadied again." Scout stole a couple of ice cubes from Luke's glass with his long handled iced tea spoon. "Just a few, bro."

Once the bottle was safely tucked away under the table, he said, "So what's the plan?"

"We wait." Luke gazed out the window of the diner at the new playground and picnic tables across the street.

"Okay. We wait." Zero sat back in his chair. "When they make the move, according to Scout's sensors and your magic decoder ring, we take them out on one of the winding roads that snake around the area without being seen. Not a great idea, Luke, but doable." Zero put his ball cap on backwards.

"Zero, man, you're inside. No cover inside. Where is your military bearing?" Cobalt grinned. "You been here too long. Starting to act like a civilian."

"What do we do while we wait? Us four still have plenty of leave to burn up and no place to go."

Luke smiled. "Don't worry. There's plenty of work to be done around here."

The truck broke the motion detector beam at the end of his driveway.

"*Suka sin!*" Mike scurried to the bedroom monitor and zoomed the camera view on the driver. "Ah, my little CB."

Stopping in the bathroom to refresh his breath with mouthwash, Mike made a few attempts at smoothing his hair with the brush. Looking in the mirror he said, "Still handsome."

He checked the living room area for incriminating evidence of his electronic surveillance. Satisfied he'd put everything away, he stepped out on the porch to await his visitor.

Luke got out of his father's truck and walked up the manicured pathway. He noticed the grass was cut, the flowerbed weeded, and the vegetable garden was immaculate.

"I thought we agreed there would be no contact."

"That's a thing of the past. My barbarians know you're here, but they have no idea the details of the agreement."

"That's nice. What's interesting is I haven't seen anything about the information I gave you. I thought for sure it would be on six o'clock news."

"Really?"

Mike started to grin. "You haven't even turned it in. Ahhghh. It's no matter. Old information, out of date. I will have to update it for you." He released a low growly laugh from his throat. "You're such a bad CIA case officer. Toss it and I will give you new for the big dance, *da*?"

"It's safe until I need to look at it."

"Ahhh, Luke Chaw Bacon." Mike threw his head back and laughed from deep in his belly. "What will your Deputy Director think about his apprentice?

"He doesn't think much of me now. I'm not here to talk about Afghanistan."

Wiping the tears from his eyes, Mike invited Luke into the cabin.

"What do you want, eh? Soda? Tea? I can make you a cup of my wonderful Russian coffee. That is if you think you are man enough, *plemyannik*."

"I'll take a shot of the Zyr I left for you."

"Sorry. Too soon in the day for vodka. You'll take a diet Dr. Pepper."

"That'll do. With ice."

"Sure. Now," handing Luke a glass of the brown fizzy, "what do you want?"

"I need your help. I need a favor."

"I'm listening."

"Remember the two men attached to my squad in Afghanistan?"

"*Da*. I told you to watch out for them. *Cherit.*"

"Well, they've found their way here."

"I know."

"You know? How?"

"The outfitter, Wink Decker. He took them on a hog hunt weeks ago. Garl McFee went along with dogs. I overheard…well, eavesdropped. It did not go well."

"My dad told me that McFee and his hounds retired from hunting for some reason."

"It was them. I'll tell you what I heard but I wouldn't ask Decker or McFee. Dogs were traumatized by it."

Luke glanced out the window. "How'd you know I was here?"

"Come," Mike said. He opened the bedroom door from the hallway.

"Whoa. Where'd you get all this?" Luke saw wall to wall monitors, screens, and enough equipment to make Scout jealous.

"I bought bits and pieces in Waybird, then some in Charleston. Some online. Some of it came from electronic conventions. As you suggested, I did not have the heavy stuff delivered to protect Edgar Stanton's back and keep Livisia out of my business. I remain a good citizen."

"Who are you hooked up to?" Luke walked around the room examining the drives, screens, mics, and power boosters.

In his thick Russian accent, Mike said, "No peeking. Is secret."

Luke laughed. "I've heard that before."

"So why do you think the *chort* were here? What's connection with Afghanistan and this mountain paradise?"

"I think in some way they were working with Cobalt's old company commander and a smuggling operation in the US. The shoot out the other day in the mountain, well, the kids were rescued from the caves. We took out the operation."

"So it was you conducting the boom booms. I figured that for some reason."

"I thought you would know all about it with all the stuff you've got here."

"Come, Chaw Bacon. Let's talk in other room."

****

Luke leaned back in his chair and sipped the soda. He didn't want to tell Mike everything but he wanted an indication of what Mike knew.

"I'm still an outsider. Sheriff Harris made me a temporary deputy so I pick up information here and there, but the locals don't feel comfortable enough to gossip with me yet. When your brother and Fishbone come to spy on me, I get some information. Only cost me sodas and a bag of potato chips."

"Tater sells himself out cheap I see."

"About three dollars and some change."

"What'd they tell you about the dog you brought into Dr. Glassman's?"

"I haven't seen them since then. I did see the blue fog once when I was bringing the boys back down the mountain. They made me stop and not drive through it but they wouldn't tell me what it was. I figured at the time it was some made up kid mystery."

"Do you think it's a made up kid mystery?"

"Not at all. The animal I took in was near death. I could see it had been shot, and I thought maybe it could be saved. It was real. I carried it. I could smell its odor. Its head was on my leg. But, I will tell you this, little CB, it was not of this earth. I think it saved your friend. An animal with those kinds of connections to the next life, well, nothing like that needs to be around me. My ticket to Hell already purchased."

"No matter, you're involved. You've been drawn into the narrative of those snow dogs, but that's not why I came. We know no one is safe as long as Smith and Jones are here. I've got an idea they'll try to pick up where the last crew left off. Continue to use this area to hide women and children, set up new currier routes, and lay low from the law. The mountains can hide a lot of what goes on."

"Okay, Chaw Bacon. What do you need?"

"First, I have some equipment stashed here, and then I'll need a ride to Waybird City."

****

Mike followed Luke down the steps into the fieldstone basement. On the south wall, Luke tapped a jutting rock back even with the others. A smaller stone popped out on his left. Luke pushed it and a door swung open to a set of stairs leading to a small underground room.

"Ah, very clever. And all this time I thought you might be a little stupid," Mike said. "But, I'm a grown man and can admit I was wrong. Not so stupid, are we, *plemyannik.*

"I just might surprise you." Luke pulled on an overhead string attached to a ceiling bulb. He tugged on a black duffle bag and selected a briefcase off one of the shelves. "I've got everything. I need to borrow your bathroom for a few minutes."

Back in the kitchen, Luke said, "You're welcome to explore my special closet if you want to. You know how to open it."

"Thanks, but Lubyanka cured me from liking small dark places."

"I'll be out in about twenty."

Mike busied himself making a couple of ham sandwiches with mayo, mustard, and pickle on bread. He warmed last night's borscht.

"Luke."

"What?"

"I've made you a sandwich. Aunt Gem keeps me in bread and cinnamon rolls. That alone is worth coming to America. Got homemade butter from Wink Decker's woman. She feels sorry for me living up here without a wife."

"I thought you were going to get a plump hill woman when you got here." Luke called back.

"Most of them around here are too skinny. Couldn't keep up with a virile man like myself."

Luke spoke up from behind the bathroom door, "You might see a couple you like when we get you to Waybird. They've got a lot of fast food places. I hear the lady population has become inflated."

"Don't worry about me. Birdie Spry invited me to take her to the fair over in Waybird. She's going to introduce me to a couple of her nieces. Says there may be one or two that would suit me."

Luke stepped out of the bathroom, not as Luke Perkins or Chaw Bacon but as Anna Smit, sixty year old cleaning lady of the Take-A-Rest Motel.

"Ahh, if I didn't know it was you, I would swear...come here. Let me see up close." Mike examined the hairline, eyes, and face of Anna. "Amazing. What is it?"

"Foam latex and silicone. I've got a couple of them the Agency fitted me with. I never know when it is better to be someone else. Everything looks okay?" Luke turned around.

"Yeah, but your slip is showing."

"It's supposed to. Distracts their eyes from my face."

"Good idea. I like the fat legs."

"Latex padded stockings. There's a couple of varicose veins for realism. But I have to say they can get hot in the summer if you wear them for long."

Mike bent to pick up the hem of Luke's dress. "Let me see just how real everything is."

Luke slapped his hand away. "Don't make me hurt you."

"Here, take sandwich and mug soup."

"It's soup mug."

"Finish the rest of your soda. You'll have to direct me to motel in Waybird."

Mike looked Anna up and down again. "Ah, if I didn't know better I'd ask you out on a date."

"Sorry, I'm spoken for." Luke took a bite of the sandwich. "We'd better get if we're going to pull this off."

"Just don't spill food in my truck. I'll make you clean it...Anna Smit."
****

There were three housekeeping carts lined up on the promenade of num-bered doors. According to Scout's report, the women sometimes took a ninety minute lunch when the owner was away. Today, the owner's Cadillac was nowhere to be seen.

Mike watched Luke amble along the shaded motel veranda. He knocked on door number eleven.

"Housekeeping, gentlemen." The voice modulator around his neck, cov-ered by a high collar, made his words sound like an elderly woman. He knocked again. Suddenly the door was opened by one of the men Luke recognized from Afghanistan.

"Need your room cleaned, mister?" Anna Smit asked as she turned, taking towels, sheets, and pillowcases from the housekeeping cart.

"Yeah. You can pick up the trash...there's some pizza boxes, but leave the beer cans for turn in."

A voice from within the room said, "Hell, let the old gal take the beer cans. She can turn them in for her tip." The other man laughed.

"Thank you kindly, gentlemen. Thank you kindly." Anna kept her head down but her eyes were busy scanning the room. "I'll have ya'll nice clean sheets and a sweet smelling bathroom."

One of them looked at the name tag. "You do a good job and we'll leave you a really good tip, Anna Smit."

"Just give it to her. Let's get something to eat."

"Here, honey." He handed Anna a one hundred dollar bill.

"Oh, oh...oh my, my. That's more than I make in three days here at the motel. Oh, my."

"Take your time."
****

In the dimness of the room, Anna looked for phones, laptops, any kind of electronics she could place a tag, in or on. She found one phone in the bathroom and placed a rice kernel sized tracker beside the battery.

She placed others underneath the collars of shirts, inside the seams of jackets and managed to place them along the waistband of their boxers. She added several of the tacky seeds to the inside zipper of their shaving kits. She found a small bag of cash and removed bills from top and bottom of the bundle. Two drinking glasses and pop cans she bagged for fingerprints.

Satisfied, Anna sprayed the bathroom with bleach water, wiped down the sink and shower stall doors. As she tore the sheets from the beds, she heard a feminine voice singing outside the door. A small woman with a pile of towels on her arm was surprised to see Anna in the room.

"Hello." Anna grabbed the name tag off her collar.

"What are you doing here? I don't know you work here."

"State sanitation inspection. And you are doing an amazing job. Here's extra for your work." Anna placed her index finger across her lips as she pressed money into the lady's hand.

Anna walked out, shutting the door behind her. She walked around the back of the motel as she removed the wig, latex mask, and pulled off the dress. Stuffing everything in a plastic bag she grabbed from the housekeeping cart, Anna became Luke.

Ducking between two trucks, Luke scanned the parking lot. Mike was leaned back in the driver's seat with his ball cap pulled over his eyes as if sleeping. The area looked clear. Luke casually walked to Mike's truck and got in.

"We need to leave."

"Sure," Mike said. "But take off the fat legs. Not sexy."

Luke peeled off the leg stockings and stuffed them into the plastic bag.

"Done what you needed?"

"Yeah. I have items for prints and maybe find out something about the cash."

"I've been reading up on my adopted homeland," Mike said as he pulled out of the parking lot and onto the street. "As a CIA case officer, you don't have the authority to conduct a mission on US soil."

Grinning, Luke responded, "What mission?"

****

Scout entered code on his laptop.

"Oh, Daddy, that feels so good" came the response from the satellite miles above his position.

"For crap sakes, Scout. Change the voice on the damn thing. I'm starting to think you're some kind of freak." Diego slid a fire roasted hotdog off the stick and onto the bun.

"You're jealous. I can tell. If you've never had a 500kg girlfriend the size of a school bus, you've never known love, Diego." Scout bit his lip.

"Any girl that size would kill me for sure. Hey, pass the mustard and catsup."

"You insult my Daddy, you can get it yourself," the satellite replied.

"Scout, for the love of all things holy, change that voice. You're creeping me out."

"Diego's got a point," Zero added. "Make it like a drill instructor, or a lumberjack. Better yet, shut it up. Anyone want another beer?"

Luke dumped an armload of firewood. "It does sound strange, Scout."

"Okay, okay. I get it. You're all jealous as hell of my talents, so for that, we go dark."

Cobalt adjusted his leg in the chair Zero provided.

"When do you get the cast off?" Diego tossed him a pillow.

"Glassman says tomorrow. Wasn't much of a fracture to begin with."

There were many unasked questions hanging in the air: how did the bullet come out of him and into the dog? What made him heal like that? Who were his friends who could hack into Scout's satellite and override it? They thought, but did not ask. He's a Ranger of the 80th and that's all that mattered.

"If Glassman doesn't take it off, I will. I need to start working out. Sitting around makes my muscles ache. Hey, Luke, get me some logs to lift."

"My dad's weight set is in the barn. I'm sure he wouldn't mind if you used it." Luke put three hotdogs in the rack, closed the handles and started the roasting process. "Who likes well done?"

"If you mean charred beyond recognition, I'll take two," Cobalt said. "With onion, relish, and all of it."

"Anything going on with our friends?" Luke was curious if Smith and Jones had broken their inactivity.

"Not yet," Scout replied. "but I expect they will. They don't sit tight for long. They can't. They survive on adrenaline and the thrill of power."

"Are all the sensors Luke placed responding?" Diego finished one hotdog and began roasting a second one

"The two Luke placed on the vehicle are dead. Maybe they fell off."

"What? Scout," Zero admonished, "you can't keep getting that cheap stuff from China."

"Not my fault. You know the government buys from the lowest bidder."

"True, bro, but for your own personal use, you should buy from the Israelis. Mossad knows how to make their shit."

"Yes, and they know how to blow shit up. That being said, we are good on my end. If they dump the phone, I can still track them with their clothing. A really smart CIA ghost stuffed a few in their underwear."

"But we're screwed if they go commando," Cobalt laughed.

"I've got it covered. Shirts, blue jeans, shaving kit. We can track them."

A silence descended upon the men as they ate and stared into the orange and red flames, the occasional pop from steam boiling under the bark, and a few hot ashes bursting forth into the sky.

"Luke." Scout was the first to speak. "What about Mike? Can we trust him?"

"Yeah. I'm sure. I read a dossier on him. Basically, he did everything he told me about in Moscow. Was an interrogator in addition to running a network. He was working over a female who was suspected of being an infiltrator and..."

"In Russia, that's anyone who breathes oxygen and walks." Diego said.

"...when they took the hood off, it was his sister."

The Rangers shook their heads at the horror of what must have been the scene.

Luke continued. "It was a test of his loyalty. They promised she would be safe, then had him kill her with his own hands."

Luke passed a steaming hotdog in a bun to Zero. "Thanks, bro."

"He spent some time in Lubyanka prison. When he got out, he was a changed man. He was off the grid in Siberia and everyone lost track of him. He showed up in St. Petersburg at some point. After making contacts, he got back in the game but not with the same enthusiasm. According to the investigation, he became subversive and counterproductive to the Russian cause. His handler, Dimitri Abramov, had been on our payroll for a while and helped facilitate Mike's defection.

"Getting back to your question, he gave me information that has national security ramifications."

"Did the Agency give you an award for it?" Zero was on his fourth hotdog.

"No. What I turned in was a dry cleaner's bookkeeping records."

"Oh, you're a dirty dog, Luke. I'm surprised they haven't brought you up on charges." Diego handed Cobalt a charred, heavily condimented sandwich.

"I'll worry about that later. Suffice to say, he's ours, like it or not. I think he's an asset." Luke passed beers to the group.

"Is the plan still a go?" Cobalt asked. "I'm getting that old itch again."

"Still on. Mike's familiar with Smith and Jones, maybe not them personally, but he knows the type. Whatever he thought about them in Afghanistan, has been confirmed by what he knows about them now. This is no joke. They are dangerous. Mike agrees they have to be erased."

"That kind of filth doesn't just go away." Cobalt threw a bag of marshmallows at Scout. "Hey, look alive. Fire these up."

The sound of Maggie Perkins' voice pierced the night air. "Coblew! Coblew!"

The little girl ran to the fire pit in her footed pajamas, then scrambled into Cobalt's lap. "You all better?"

"Here's my girl," the Ranger said. "Yes, all better."

Elsie brought a thermos of coffee and a bag of potato chips. She was followed by Nathan and Tobias, each bearing a bowl of cold salads. Tater passed paper plates and plasticware to the men around the fire.

"Just in case someone would prefer coffee over beer." Elsie smiled as she set the thermos on the butt end of a log. "What do ya'll have planned for this week? Anything exciting?" She made a small plate for Maggie and handed it to Cobalt.

"Nothing really, Mom. Thought we would go to Agnes Crawford's place and help the Morris brothers with the reconstruction of her house."

"We're pretty good fixing bathrooms," Zero added.

"That's nice. Dad is local this week. He's bringing some of the equipment home to fix the road to the church. I think a backhoe to run the water line to the barn for Maggie's pony."

"I'm getting a pony, Coblew. It's exciting."

"Yes, I know." Cobalt moved her from his casted leg to the other in one smooth movement without upsetting her plate of potato salad and cut up hotdog.

"You can ride with me when your leg is fixed."

"I'd like that, Miss Perkins."

"Guess what I do tomorrow, Coblew?"

"What's that?"

"I go to Amerilia..."

"Amelia," Elsie corrected.

"..to make cookies. I make you some."

"Luke, will you take her into the tea room? Amelia wants to babysit Maggie for the morning. The twins will be going to Clemmon's to help bale hay. It will just be me and Tater here. Maybe we can get the garden weeded, make some bread or biscuits. Have some mom and son time."

"Sure."

****

Elsie had the twins gather the dishes, bowls, and pick up the trash. She left the men sitting around the fire, smoking cigars, while she put Maggie to bed.

After Elsie was out of earshot, Zero said, "I take it you and your brothers haven't talked to your mom and dad about the gathering?"

"Well," Luke hesitated. "We're waiting for the appropriate time. They know about Maggie but not the rest of it."

"What'd you say about your face?"

"Just that we were boxing and..."

"You got your ass beat."

****

When Luke arrived at Crawford's, his team was working alongside the Morris brothers. The thirty yard waste bin in the driveway released drywall dust like a waft in the wind. Waybird City home store boxes lined the walkway. Agnes would have new cabinets, sink, stove, and refrigerator, paid by an anonymous benefactor.

"Luke," shouted Deputy Johnson, "grab that red toolbox and bring it in, will you?"

"Sure. Didn't recognize you out of uniform. Who's minding the shop?"

"Sheriff Bill. The rest of us are here. Deputy Hodding's good with wiring so he's updated the electric box. If Agnes ever gets air conditioning, she'll have the juice to make it work. Your buddies are hammering drywall and have started taping and spreading mud."

The inside of the house was noisy. Between hand vacuums sucking drywall dust and the buzz of the circle saw cutting two by fours, Luke could barely hear Zero speak when he came out of the back bedroom.

"Hey, Luke. Here. See what we've done to the boy's bedroom. Bay window, built in desk, computer stand, recessed closet for shoes, clothes, storage. Diego is in the lady's bedroom helping Robby Morris hang drywall on the ceiling. I'm having a good time."

"Not blowing anything up?"

"Nope."

Luke nodded. "Where's Scout?"

"Up on the top of the hill. Too much dust for his computer. He's...um...looking around at things."

"Got it. Point me in his direction."

"Better yet, here's a walkie-talkie."

****

Luke located Scout on an outcropping of stone, legs stretched out, reading his screen.

"Mind if I join you?" Luke asked.

"No, and as a matter of fact I was just going to call you. We've got some movement."

"What's up? Are our boys getting bored?"

"Yeah, I think so. They went to breakfast, then to a sports and hunting store. Can't tell you what they bought, but they were in there for a while."

"Can't you get a visual?"

"Not now. Too much cloud coverage over there. And I think someone at Langley or Huntsville is making noise about my satellite. I may have been discovered."

"You? Communications genius? Busted?"

"I'm not sure, but I'm being tickled here and there."

Luke smiled. "I know someone who can help if you get thrown out of the sky."

"Really? I have thought about the day I have to give it back. Who?"

"Mike. I've been to his cabin. He's got enough stuff jammed in the spare bedroom he could run NASA."

"Again I say, really? I'll have to renew an old friendship just in case I need him."

"It would be a good idea. There's more to him than you think."

"I suppose it's possible." Scout tapped a stick on the rock beside him. "Luke, I'm glad I get the chance to talk to you alone, get your take on something. I'm not going to renew my contract. I'm a free agent."

"Now it's my turn to say really."

When I peek in on my mom's house, I see there's a lot to be repaired. Maybe I should be there more for her and Leigh."

"You're not the kind to just up and retire. Got your twenty in?"

"No, but I can fill out my military time with National Guard. Maybe get a couple of short active tours here and there. See if there's room for me in Space Force as a consultant."

"I wouldn't put it on your resume that you stole one of their satellites."

"Yeah. Might limit my employment chances. But, on the other hand..."

"You're welcome in my playground."

"CIA? I'll have to think about that one. I don't know how nice their toys are after the Space Force took over. I heard there were fights over who got what." Scout looked to the blue sky.

"Well, yes and no, but..."

"Something tells me I don't want to know what comes after the 'but.'"

Luke leaned back and absorbed the sun. "Should I presume this has something to do with a Ranger who wants a date with a beautiful Space Force colleague?"

"Kinda like that. I'd have that ESP of yours checked. You're getting a little too precise for my comfort."

"Just let me know if she has a sister. We could double."

"Maybe...maybe not...but maybe."

"What about the other guys?"

"I can't speak for them so you'll have to ask them directly. Zero has more time in so I think he'll go for straight twenty. Can't see Diego leaving soon, but I know the boy has nightmares."

"We all do," Luke said.

"As far as Cobalt? I think he's on the "Lend-Lease" program. I thought he had connections outside the Army, but when I saw that chopper come in for the rescue, I was sure of it. He's got a better offer than the 80th Regiment. He's a strange dude, for sure. I get a feeling that he'll be out somewhere doing his thing. Cobalt's always been pretty tight lipped. That being said, your little sister could get him to walk on his hair."

"She likes the coloring book on his arm."

Scout noticed his friend was staring at a gathering of wildflowers. "What're you thinking?"

"You said they went to a sporting and hunting store?"

"Yeah." Scout could almost see the wheels turning in Luke's head. "You okay, bro?"

"Scout, what if they found the seed sensors?"

"Doesn't matter if they found one or if one stopped working. You have plenty of others."

"If they found one, they could presume there would be more. What if they went to the hunting store to buy new clothes?"

"Relax. First, I don't think they're that smart. Second, my granular sensors are so small, unless they've got microscopic vision, all they will see is a rice kernel. You have to know what to look for with those things *and* you have to have the equipment it takes to connect to them. They'll need a phone with them and you put one of my seeds in it?"

"Yes."

"I doubt they'll get burner phones. I've still got thermal imaging and Barney Googling eyes. Let's not worry about it until we know it has happened."

"I guess. I get these gut feelings I can't ignore."

"So what are your guts telling you at the moment?"

"That it isn't over."

"What? Get that out of your head. They brought their business here. They put in the order and, in a manner of speaking, we make the delivery. There's two more to clean up, then we're good to go. We'll be drinking Leadslingers at Shorty's before you know it."

"Yeah. You're right."

"Dude, stop worrying. You've got the four of us at your six. Chill, bro."

Luke smiled and laid back against the rock, letting the sun soak into his skin. As warm as he was, he still couldn't shake the cold feeling of impending doom. The restlessness returned. He left to help with the drywall work hoping it would distract his mind and calm his gnawing doubt.

****

"Did New York call you back?"

"Yeah. We're good. They're sending two men. A welcoming committee. We'll get up to the caves first and look for any cash Clarence left behind. You know I'm gonna kill that pig when I see him again."

"Don't forget Jiggy."

"Boss has to be dead by now. A bear or something got him. I'm sure of it."

"How long until the new crew gets here?"

"About three or four days. Do you think you can find your way back up to the caves?"

"I don't know. All these winding roads look alike."

"We can stay out of sight at the hunting cabin at Decker's. The old man will know the area. Want another pizza?"

"No. Let's go to that Chinese place. Food must be good because the parking lot is full all the time. We can sort out our equipment when we get back."

"Sounds like a plan. Got the outfitter's number?"

"Somewhere. I'll look for it after we eat. I'm hungry."

Elsie Perkins

He asks to play one game of hide and seek before they eat lunch.

How can she say no to the child who wears the same face as her husband at that age? Six is such a magical time for the boy.

Yes she says. Who will go first?

Me, me, me he says. I found a new place to hide.

Okay. I'll stay here and count out loud to one hundred.

No peeking, Mom.

I won't.

She sits at the pine table, covering her eyes.

One...two...three...*maybe only count to fifty...one hundred is too big of a number...four...five...six...*

I was seven when Howard gave me my first kiss in second grade...

Eight...nine...ten...

Our wedding was at Birdie's...all her beds were in bloom...Aunt Gem made a flower crown for my veil...matching buds for the boutonnieres and corsages...

Fifteen...sixteen...seventeen...eighteen...

Howard was sick that first winter...the only one in the Hollar who never got mumps as a kid but he sure got them as an adult...Running Deer took such good care of him...

Thirty-one...thirty-two...thirty-three...

First Luke, then two miscarraiges...the twins were a real surprise...took a rest and then Tater and just when I thought I was done, here comes Magdelyn...

Forty-six...forty-seven...forty–eight...

She felt his warm hands, one her forehead and one on her chin, but it wasn't her husband. She had but a second to feel the danger. Her last thoughts were of Howard and her flower crown.

****

His excitement propels him into the woods, one foot after the other, to the new hiding place he found by the rotted log. He knows she will not find him easily. The best part of the game comes when he jumps out and surprises her. She always laughs and tickles his ribs.

He hesitates, confused, where was he supposed to hide?

It is cold among the trees. He no longer knows the way he came or where home is from here. Tired and dirty he sits by a tree and remembers not to wander.

He wishes she was here to find him.

Truck Hunting

"Luke. Over."

"Go for Luke. Over."

"Zero, tell him I need him up here. Out."

Coming out of the utility room he was drywalling, Luke looked like a Christmas elf sprinkled with powdered sugar.

"What's up?"

"Scout wants you."

Standing on the porch, Luke started to brush himself off. "Tell him I'll be right there."

"Be still." Zero started the shop vac and sucked off as much of the powder as he could. "Gotta keep the chief looking good."

Luke laughed as he jogged up the trail to Scout's position, while Zero laughed at the drywall dust blowing off Luke as he ran.

****

"What ya got?"

"Trouble," Scout replied. "I managed to pick up the conversation from Smith and Jones to an outside party. They made contact with someone in New York. Sounds like they intend to fire up the business model and pick up where Cobalt's old company commander left off. Here, listen to this."

Luke put the small receiver to his ear. He sneezed and used an old red bandana to blow his nose. "Now there'll be four to terminate."

"Yes. I'd bet on it. Maybe a couple more. These beasts tend to travel in a herd."

Luke coughed, spit, and sneezed again. "How much time are you talking about?"

"Three, maybe four days."

"That'll work."

"Maybe not. Our boys from the 'Stan are on the move again. Looks like they are headed toward the Hollar."

"Okay. Keep me informed. It will take them a little while to get here with some of the roads washed out. Just keep an eye on them."

"Copy that. A little trouble keeping the signal. These mountains keep blocking me and my girl. Anything happens, I'll call."

****

"You didn't have to kill her."

"So what? You think if I said please, she'd give it to me? Get the truck. There won't be sensors on that one. I'd like to know who's trying to track us. Lucky you got us lost and we stumbled on this place."

"You don't suppose the Feds or state boys are on to us?"

"Doubt it. The law likes to swoop in. Makes for good press. Someone knows we're around but they're being cagey about it."

"Where's the keys?"

"Probably on the driver's visor. That's where all these hillbillies keep them. If you think you can find your way to the caves, let's get out of here before her kid comes back."

"Shouldn't we look for him?"

"Hell no. There's plenty around here to build up inventory. Leave him. He's lunch for the bears."

****

Scout ran down the hill. He slowed not to alarm those still working on the Crawford home.

"Zero, Diego, grab Luke. We need to get to his house. They found the sensors on the truck and abandoned it on the road. Everything was down and I lost them. I got eyes on them driving away from Luke's. His mom is at the table in the yard. She's not moving."

Diego whispers, "For how long?"

Scout glanced at his watch. "I was off for maybe an hour."

"That's not good. Where's Cobalt?"

"At the clinic getting his cast off." Scout closed his laptop. "I'll call him to get to Luke's immediately. We've got to get over there now."

Diego and Scout sat in the Excursion. "I guess it's all coming to a head, isn't it, dude."

"I'm not hoping much for Mrs. Perkins. They killed that woman. I can feel it in my bones."

"No mercy."

"No mercy."

They broke the news to Luke as they raced to the farm.

****

Cobalt received Scout's message in his ear piece.

"Gotta go, Doc."

"But I'm not done removing the cast."

"Here, I'll help." Cobalt grabbed the edges of the seam Andy had just cut. With one jerk, he broke the rest of the cast down to his ankle, then smashed his foot on the floor breaking the rest of it off.

"Feels fine. Good job, Doc." He walked out the door without a limp.

****

"Men, take an early lunch," Howard called over the radio. "The gravel truck is late again and there's no sense sweating to death in the sun. It can wait on us."

He took his hard hat off, wiping his brow and face. Howard opened his wallet, checking his pay voucher was still there. The picture of him and Elsie on their wedding day fell out on the ground. He picked it up and kissed it.

"Howard." His name crackled over the walkie-talkie from the traffic man a mile north of his position.

"Yeah, Charlie."

"There's two guys just passed me and it looks like to me they're in your truck. You got that dented tailgate and the hunting club logo on the back window?"

"Yeah. Sounds like my truck but I don't know who'd be driving it."

"Should be coming your way."

"Manny."

"Go, Howard."

"Bring your front loader around and block off that lane until I can see what's going on with my truck."

"Got it."

Manny inches the massive earth mover forward allowing cars through until he saw Howard's truck come over the hill. He steps hard on the accelerator and black diesel exhaust spews out of its upright pipes.

"Two of them, Howard. Big beefy dudes...holy shit, gun, gun, gun."

Howard heard the bullets ricochet off the steel of the front loader.

"Get down, Manny. Everyone take cover," he shouted into the radio.

Howard squatted behind an empty dump truck, then managed to get to his car. He grabbed his rifle and returned to the bed of the dump. Using it as cover, he rose and fired three rounds into his stolen pickup, breaking the rear window before the driver spun around Manny and his rig.

"Dispatch, Dispatch. This is Howard Perkins on the 219 repair crew. Call Sheriff Harris. We've been shot at and someone stole my truck. Get someone up to my place as fast as you can."

The radio check confirmed that all his men were alive but shaken by the exchange.

"Manny, keep in touch with dispatch and you can report to the law when they get here."

"Where you going, Howard?"

"I'm going after my truck."

RESTORING BALANCE

"Howard. Take your boys into the house."

"I can't, Bill."

"The funeral director from Waybird will be here soon."

Howard composed himself. "You're right. Thank Deputy Hodding for bringing the twins back from Clemmon's. There's a lot of phone calls to make." Howard touched Elsie's hair and kissed her cheek, not phased by her dead stare, thinking only of her as he last saw her.

"You've got good sons, Howard. Lean on them. Lean on the Hollar. We're all family." Sheriff Bill nodded at Coop to begin collecting evidence.

Tobias squeezed his father's shoulder. "Sheriff Bill's right, Dad." The boy began crying as he walked his father to the house.

"Luke," Howard said, "Where's Tater? I left him here with Mom."

"I thought he was with Nathan."

"No, no, no," Howard choked.

Luke turned to his friends. "My brother..."

"We'll get him, Luke," Zero said.

Cobalt was at the back of the vehicle sorting out gear. He was joined by the others.

"Here, let's each take an ENVG-B. I mean, he's a kid. He couldn't have gotten far. We'll get him in minutes," Scout added.

Diego disagreed. "I don't know. They say lost people can travel for miles from where they started."

"I asked Sheriff about getting one of Hector's dogs but they're all out on searches. It would be a good idea and save time to have one of his bloodhounds along." Zero checked his sidearm and put an extra magazine in his cargo pocket.

"Where's little Maggie? Does she know?" Diego asked.

"No. She's in with the lady who owns the tea shop," Scout said.

"Amelia Lemon." Sheriff Harris came from the other side of the trailer. "Maggie is okay. No need to put her into this until Howard and the boys get a grip on what has happened. Coop says Elsie didn't suffer. Broken neck."

"I can't imagine how you explain to a little girl that her life will never be the same." Scout stated what they all were thinking.

"You can't. You just got to be there each time she crumbles. Kids don't grieve the same as adults. It will be just as painful for her on her first day of kindergarten as it will be on Christmas when she is nine." Bill wiped his eyes.

"Ready to go, gentlemen?" Diego asked.

Cobalt checked the batteries on his tactical flashlight. He flashed on the leaves in the trees, startling a bird or two.

"Yeah," Scout said. "Someone's come up with an idea. I know that look."

"Come on." Cobalt led the team behind the house and along the path leading to the partially finished barn. He opened a stall door.

"Guys, the forgotten member of our team, Mr. Green's Dog." The big man knelt down and ruffled the dog's fur. "We need your help. Let's go find Tater."

With Mr. Green's Dog leading, they entered the woods.

From inside the house, Howard choked back his sobs. "Luke, what about Tater?"

"They'll find him, Dad. Don't worry. It's what they do."
****

Cobalt kept his light focused on the dog. He was positive Mr. Green's Dog would take them to the boy. After a twenty minute hike, the beam of the tactical light caught the dog's white spots wiggling at the base of the tree. He heard the boy call the dog by name.

"Hey. I've got him over here."

"Mr. Cobalt?"

"Tater. It's me."

"I'm cold, Mr. Cobalt."

Diego did a quick eval of the child. He wrapped the boy in a heat blanket. "This will warm you right up. You didn't fall or get hurt?"

"Nope. Just playing hide and seek with my mom. This blanket is orange. My Dad wears orange when he hunts."

Zero handed Diego a cup of energy drink.

"Tater," the medic said, "drink a couple of sips for me? There you go. Couple more sips. I see you got a few bug bites but looking good." He nodded to Cobalt who lifted Tater in his arms.

"Where's my mom? She was supposed to find me."

"Your dad is home, Tater." Cobalt whispered. "He'll explain. Let's just get you back."

The only sound they heard was the jingle of the beagle's collar tags as it followed them back to the sadness in the house.

****

The four Rangers and Luke watched Cleveland Coop collect trace evidence around and on the body of Elsie Perkins. When the funeral director arrived, the barbarians tenderly put Elsie in a body bag and placed her on the gurney at the back of the hearse.

"Take your father and the boys and go someplace," Cobalt said.

"I'm going with you."

"No," Diego said. "This is on us. You're too raw and could be a hazard. Hate to put it to you like that, bro, but the four of us are on the hunt and nothing good will come of it. You know how we are. Get your family away from here."

"He's right, bro. This is our game now. You stay clean of it." Zero climbed into the back seat of the big black truck. He would not comment further. It was a done deal.

Diego gave Luke a hug. "Go with your dad, bro. We'll take care of this."

They watched the taillights of the vehicle disappear down the drive as the Perkins men left home.

****

"I guess I need to deputize you all. I'd rather have you legal."

"This is personal now, Sheriff," Cobalt explained. "You can do what you want because this is your jurisdiction. It's your call. However, for us, the rules have changed. A deputy's star isn't part of the equation, Bill. It complicates things."

"Sheriff, with all due respect," Diego said, "we need to handle this our way."

****

Cobalt spread a map out on the hood of the Excursion. "Where did Howard find his truck after they ditched it?"

"Here," Bill pointed. "Howard told the deputy who picked him up there was blood on the front seat so he was sure he hit one of them. I had Deputy Johnson respond to the site and take photos. Ubell Gant rode along so he got blood samples, fingerprints, and whatever trace he could get to send in for ID."

"There won't be anything on those men, Sheriff. Trust me." Cobalt folded the map. "Scout. What do you have?"

"Tracing them along this road. They're on foot." Scout sat in the back of the truck with Zero. "Lost them," he said.

"But, not for long," came a familiar male voice into his earpiece. "Enter this code."

He did as instructed and his screen was awash in azure blue light. "What the hell? Who are you?"

"Your satellite is back in the control of the agency you appropriated it from and you are now a guest on mine."

Scout grinned. "Cobalt, my brother in crime is calling on line one."

"Alex."

"Davyd. Hope this helps. How are you feeling?"

"Little sore but a good work out at the gym will take care of it."

"Glad to hear it. Will be in touch."

"Yes."

"Cobalt, who the hell is that? We won't tell. You know us, bro."

"Zero, don't beg. It's unbecoming." Cobalt laughed. He reached over and patted Zero on the face. "When this is over, we'll go up on one of the mountains, build a fire, and throw back a couple of beers. I'll tell you everything, but then, I'll have to kill you."

"Seriously, dude?" Zero asked.

"About killing you?"

"Oh, good hell no. I'm not worried about that, I just want to know about you before you do it."

****

"Mr. Decker?"

"Yes. This is Wink Decker."

"You were the guide for a friend of mine and me on a hog hunt a while ago."

Wink concentrated on keeping his voice steady and his words unencumbered. He still had nightmares about that hunt. "Yes, I was."

"I wonder if the same cabin is available? We're back in the area and would like to rent it. We're going to…um…photograph some of the nature trails in the area."

"It's available. Do you want to hunt?"

"No, no Mr. Decker. This is just a relaxing vacation out in the wild."

"I'll have my wife make sure it's ready. When will you be needing it?"

"Maybe tomorrow night, or the next if that's not an inconvenience. We'll be in late. Would it be too much to ask for the kitchen to be stocked? Nothing special, just soups, meat, bread."

"I can do that, but it'll be extra."

"Not a problem. Happy to pay it."

"Key will be under the flower pot. Thank you for your business."

"Thank you, Mr. Decker."

Wink hung up the phone. "Hazel, honey, I'm going into town to pick up some supplies. I rented Cabin 5 for a few days."

"Yes, dear. I'll go make sure the heat is on and everything's ready."

Wink kissed Hazel on the cheek. "Be home before dark."

"Yes, dear."

****

In ten minutes, Wink was calling through Garl McFee's screen door.

"Door's open. Coffee's on."

Garl held a mug of coffee in each hand. He nodded to a worn rocking chair for Wink to sit. Behind Garl came the crippled catch dog, Lights Out. She limped over to Wink and sat at his feet for a head scratch.

"She accommodatin' to being a house dog?"

"Yeah. She's sleeps on my bed. Back to playing with the other dogs and they know'd she ain't right so they don't rough house with her." Garl sipped his coffee. He looked at the photo of his grandfather with the family hunting dogs on the wall behind Wink.

"They're coming back, Garl, and I need your help."

"I ain't going out hunting, Wink."

"I'm not asking that, Garl. You have to admit things have been out of balance since that…" Wink was afraid to say the word, but it was all he could think of, "…last h-hunt. I've talked to Cliffer Jennings and Running Deer. They both attest to strange things goin' on. Sam White Owl and Spencer told me there just ain't nothin' to hunt. When has there been nothing to hunt around here? When, Garl? We're at odds with Nature. I think it goes right back to that day. Now, we got a chance to correct things if you'll trust me. That's all I ask."

The cabin was quiet except for Lights Out panting in the dry heat of the wood stove.

"We can put things right?"

"I think so, Garl. I think we have to. It's owed."

****

"Zero, they've carjacked a station wagon and are driving toward the highway at a high rate of speed."

"You got eyes?"

"Yeah. Wait…wait. Looks like they blew the motor."

"What can you expect when you steal a fifty year old station wagon from some old bubba in the hills?" Diego laughed.

"Well," Scout said, "Lucky for them they broke down at Fat Bob's Auto Mart. They'll do some shopping."

"What's our ETA to Fat Bob's, Scout?" Cobalt accelerated, passing a wagon loaded with straw on the straightaway.

"About twenty minutes. They're running around the lot opening doors looking for a car with keys in it. Okay, they found one. Looks like they're in a…just a sec," Scout's new link displayed the silhouette and data about the car. "It's a…1968 Plymouth Barracuda. What's a pony car?"

Cobalt laughed. "It was a two-door car that came in and went out before you were born. Ford hit the market with the Mustang GT. Then followed the Pontiac Trans Am, Chevy Camero, and I think the Dodge Challenger was a pony car. My cousin was into muscle cars and had one at one time."

"Why would they steal one of those?" Diego asked.

"Old car would be easy to hotwire or they found the keys in the vehicle," Cobalt replied. "I'm getting thirsty."

Diego adjusted his seatbelt. "Anyone want to share what the plan is?"

"Pass me one of those colas, bro."

"Cobalt, here." Diego passed cans around the SUV.

"The plan," Zero said, "is to chase them down. I personally prefer a small charge placed in each one of their legs."

"We just get them is all I care about." Cobalt finished his drink and tossed the can out the window.

"Dude," Zero admonished. "That's littering. Turn around and get that can."

"Bro, do you know how many little bugs can live their whole life in a can? I'm doing them a favor and saving countless bug lives."

"Dude, it's littering. They've got dirt to live in."

"But, *bro,* they're not safe in dirt like they are in the can."

"*Bro*, the dirt is their natural environment!"

Scout cut in. "Ladies, stop. I got a call from Sheriff Billy. On speaker, Sheriff."

"I'm going to ask you to stand down for the time being. Can you swing around and head to my office? I need to talk to all of you."

"No can do, Sheriff. We're on their tail. I thought we explained that back at Luke's place." Cobalt didn't want to give up the chase.

"They're in a 1968 Plymouth Barracuda that they stole from Fat Bob's by the service drive. Just got off the phone with him. I know where they're headed. That's why I need to see all of you."

"Roger that, Sheriff. Out." Cobalt said in the front seat. "Set a course for the sheriff's office, Mr. Chekov."

"Make it happen, capt'n."

"And we're stopping for that can so Zero doesn't have bug nightmares."

****

"Man, we've got to get someplace so I can get this wound cleaned."

"We'll be at the motel in a few minutes. You just got grazed."

"An armed road crew. Does everyone in this godforsaken place have a gun?"

"I wouldn't doubt it. This was supposed to be a backwoods layover and not a armored battery of pecker headed hillbillies. We'll get to Decker's place tomorrow. We can lay low for a few days then change cars."

"What about the guys coming from New York and the money?"

"Just let me think, will ya? We got time."

****

Diego pulled back the lacy curtain in Cabin 7. The team came up the back trails as directed by Wink the night before. They set up to watch the occupants of Cabin 5. It took two days before there was action.

He glanced over his shoulder at Cobalt and Zero sitting at the table cleaning weapons. Scout was in the back bedroom threading an antenna wire up along the inside of the chimney. After the Barracuda men left, he would extend the antenna up the trunk of the oak tree and into the top branches. It would be the only way he could receive a signal this side of the mountain.

"Everything all set?" Zero asked when Scout came back into the kitchen area.

"Will be. I'll connect with Cobalt's mystery man tonight so I can keep eyes on you tomorrow or whenever this hops off."

There was a soft tap at the back door. Each Ranger drew a sidearm— three more soft taps.

"Gentlemen, I believe Mr. Wink and entourage have arrived," announced Cobalt. He opened the rear door. Wink, Garl, and Lights Out stood waiting politely for the nod indicating they could enter.

Diego made the introductions and the men shook hands.

"Mr. Decker…"

"Wink. Ya'll can just call me Wink. And I think Garl would prefer his first name rather than Mr. McFee."

Garl nodded and touched his cap. "This here is Lights Out. She has an interest in this, too."

The dog hobbled over to Zero, leaning against him for an ear rub.

****

Scout welcomed the two men. "Come and sit. I'll explain what I have for you before we go.

"You both will get a phone. That's just for looks in case they want to take it from you. However, this earpiece is what I'll use to talk to you. Looks like an old fashion hearing aid. Any one will look at those and not suspect you are linked to a wireless unit. I'll be controlling the communications. This little speck on each earpiece is a microscopic camera. It aligns with your eyesight. Each way you turn your head, I can see what you see.

"The secret is to look at what you would normally. Don't try to direct the camera because your head movements will look artificial to anyone watching you. I'm going to connect with my laptop and run a few tests. If you hear a little buzz, that's me."

Cobalt held up a bottle of Leadslingers, nodding at Wink and Garl.

"No, thanks. If Hazel smelled that on me, I'd be a dead man."

Garl shook his head no, then touched his earpiece. "That's a bit loud."

"Sorry. Let's test again. You just keep talking until I get my levels. Better yet, I'll go out and check on distance." He grabbed his black jacket and went out the back door.

"Sheriff Harris speaks highly of you. He's got a lot of faith in this plan of yours." Diego went to the window as he spoke.

Garl and Wink looked at each other then back at Diego.

"He didn't say what it was, just that you had a plan and we were to be back up for you."

"Don't worry, Mr. Diego," Garl said. "It'll work out. There's been upheaval in the area. Wink and me can attest to that. Ya'll just do what Sheriff Bill says, and it'll all shake out the way it's supposed to."

"I'm sure it will." Diego smiled.

Wink said, "Yep. I can hear you, Scout. Can you hear me? Okay. Garl, he wants to test yours. Say something."

"The rain in Spain lies mainly on the plane."

Wink whispered to Cobalt, "Garl always did like musicals and Audrey Hepburn."

Scout stepped back into the cabin smiling. "We're good to go."

Cobalt laid the map out on the table. "Where do you want us?"
****

"Boss and his crew screwed this up. We had nothing to do with it. Franklin and Clarence was the connection. They stash product in the caves, make the money transfers, then north to Canada."

"Where are this Franklin and Clarence now?"

"Sir, we have no idea."

Smith and Jones sat across from the Albanians. They finished their story. Mr. Dervishi, a swarthy man with old acne scars on both cheeks, sat back in the chair. He looked at his colleague, Mr. Marku. Dervishi was not impressed.

"So where's the money and where's the product?"

"Mr. Dervishi, Mr. Marku, we're telling you Wells took off with all of it before Boss got here. There was an ambush. Everyone else is dead."

Mr. Marku raised his bushy black eyebrows and talked with a thick mixed accent. "So's hows you gonna make it right? Everybody gots a boss. Mr. Dervishi and me both gots a boss, so's what do you want we should take back to our boss as hows the two of yous gonna make this right? I mean, we're all businessmen. When a business takes a hit, someone has to make compensation or take a hit."

"Sirs, we can, and will gladly, make this right with Mr. Ramadani. We're giving you the guarantee that if you trust us, it will pay big profits later. We have international contacts for product, and quality product for your inventory."

"And what might that guarantee be?" Mr. Dervishi took a gold cigarette case out of his left breast pocket. A matching cigarette lighter flashed at the end of his Davidoff Supreme; he blew the smoke up toward the light in the ceiling.

"You have our word."

Dervishi jumped from his chair. "I'll have your tongues torn out of your throats if you cross me. You both got that? I know who your 'international contacts' are because I made them. So cut the crap. You have twenty four hours to come up with product and money. *A e kuptoni?*"

Smith and Jones were silent as they heard the wheels of the BMW kick up gravel speeding down the road.

****

In Cabin 7, Scout recorded the conversation. "It's gonna hop off soon. He gave them less than twenty-four."

"Okay. Call Wink and Garl to standby. As soon as we hear from Wink, we'll take our positions." Cobalt marked their areas on the map spread on the table.

Diego sliced several apples with surgeon-like strokes, displaying them on a paper plate. He popped the lid off the caramel dip container.

"Snack time, boys. Don't know when we'll eat next. Do you have any idea what the mountain men have planned?"

"No, I don't," replied Cobalt. "What I do know is Sheriff Billy said to trust them. So, that's what we'll do. Take our positions and if needed improvise, adapt, and overcome."

"I'm sure glad it will be a typical day." Scout dipped two apple slices into the brown gooey goodness.

"You know that stuff isn't good for the waistline?" Diego leaned against the kitchen sink in the dimly lit room.

"Don't you worry about my waistline or my caloric intake, Army boy."

Diego stepped away from the window. "Guys, the black car just left. Barracuda is still there."

Scout adjusted his laptop and licked the sweetness from his fingers before touching the keyboard. "Wink called. He's to pick them up and take them hiking. They asked about where to find interesting caves."

"Time?" Cobalt asked.

"They want to leave before sunrise."

"Okay, we know the drill," Cobalt said. "I'm thinking they'll kill Wink at the caves or just a little before."

"Roger that," Diego stated. "We can blow a few z's then head out at 0300 hours. It'll give us enough time to get into position."

"Gentlemen." Zero poured four healthy shots of Leadslingers. They held the cups high.

"A farewell toast to Mrs. Perkins. Fair winds and following seas to the Lady of Deacon's Hollar." They tapped the table with their cups, then finished the drink in one swallow.

****

"Good morning. Nice day for a hike."

"We appreciate helping us out, Mr. Decker."

"There's coffee in the thermos on the back seat."

Wink was sure they weren't going to hike but it made no difference. The plans were made and the dye was cast.

The pink sky of an early morning rose just over the tops of the mountain as the mist, warmed by the sun's rays, fell in droplets on the foliage. What bothered Wink was not the wetness of the morning, but the quietness. None of the early morning birds were singing.

After twenty minutes of driving, Wink said, "Damn it all to hell. My radiator's cooked." The three of them stood in the road and watched the steam pour from the front when Wink popped the hood.

"How are we going to get to the caves?" Jones began to sweat in the coolness of the dawn.

"Oh, dang that ain't nothing. Just up on the side of the hill over there is a friend of mine. Hunter Snipes. He'll have a phone to call Bowtie for a wrecker. He can also give you a lift the rest of the way to the caves. Should be mighty fine hiking by the time you get there." From the front of the truck, they watched steam dissipate in the light morning air.

"Okay, old man. Opportunity knocks but once." Smith grabbed Wink's pistol out of the holster.

"What? Hey, you don't have to…"

"Listen, stupid hillbillie. If you didn't have a piece of crap truck, maybe you and your friend over the hill would live. But now I'll kill you both. First the woman and now you. Is everyone here a hayseed redneck?"

"What? What'd ya'll say?" Wink tapped on his hearing aid.

"I said that bitch at the picnic table was first, now you, then Hunter Snips."

"Snipes. His name is Snipes."

"Whatever."

"Please, mister, please, I'm begging for my life."

"Where are the caves from here?"

"Don't shoot me, please. Just walk down to that little run and…and up the hill past Snipes place, like I said. The caves are about a mile up that way."

"Thanks." He shot Wink in the chest, the force spinning the outrigger around, dropping him on his face in the gravel.

"Did you have to kill him, Smith? He knew the way out of here."

"I suppose we should have asked the hag for the keys to her truck? Maybe have her fix a lunch for you and her kid?" Waving the gun at the prone figure he said, "He was at the end of his life cycle anyway. Grab the guns and let's get out of here."

A low hanging branch covered the sign for Crow Foot Fork.

****

"Shots fired. Shots fired." Scout spoke into his mic. "Decker. McFee. Over."

"Scout. You got a visual? Over." Zero radioed in.

"Decker's truck isn't anywhere near us. He's about 1500 meters east of our position. Over."

"There was only one shot. One of them has to be alive. Mike Oscar." Diego said.

The com was silent as they broke from their positions and descended to the road. Their grim faces set with the knowledge that another man was dead or dying who didn't deserve it.

The Rangers paused when they heard the crunch of boots on road stone and Garl's voice over the wireless: "You just gonna lay there or are you gonna have coffee?"

"Coffee sounds good, Garl. Give me a hand up. I just been shot."

Wink tapped his ear piece. "You boys can come out now and be quiet about it. There's coffee enough."

It wasn't long before the Rangers covered the ground and appeared from the brush. Garl handed out coffee in paper cups and added cream and sugar as needed.

"Where were you shot? I don't see blood or coffee pouring out any holes," Diego said.

"He shot me in the chest, but us mountain men don't kill easy."

"What's up with this, Wink? We were ready." Zero wiped the sweat from his face with his boonie.

"Follow me, boys."

The six men reached the outcropping of limestone and waited for the sun to filter through the trees lighting the valley below. They each had binoculars, although Wink said his eyesight was good enough. Lights Out positioned herself alongside Garl. She leaned against him, her stub of a front leg on his thigh as he sat.

"Look," Wink said.

Smith and Jones were struggling to make their way through the brush and brambles. Several times on their way down to the fork, they fell, tumbling a few feet, before righting. The further down into the fork they traveled, the fainter their swearing at the turn of events.

****

The boar slept under leaves and rutted grasses he tossed over himself the night before. The rest of the herd was quiet, piglets nursing on their sows.

A scent traveled down the side of the hill reaching his snout before he saw the interlopers. A memory cell triggered the alert. He snorted at the pictures of carnage appearing in his mind.

He started a series of low volume grunts. Other mounds of leaves and grasses started moving. The sounder was waking up, ready for fight or flight. For the massive feral boar, wearing the scar of a previous hunt, there would be no flight.

The men came to the trickle of a creek. They stopped to scoop the cold water into their mouths. Uncovered now, the boar was standing in the shadows. He clicked his tusks as a warning; his loud grunt echoed around the trees. Smith and Jones looked across the water into the pig's eyes. One more click of his tusks, the herd charged.

"Shoot it! Shoot it!"

"I am. Nothing's happening. Shoot it!"

The gargantuan boar waved his tusks and sliced through Smith's Achilles tendons. The herd of porcine fell upon him—mauling him, tearing at fresh human flesh. The boar focused on his next target. Jones was able to make it to a tree but the boar's stroke cut his femoral artery as the human tried to climb.

Jones clung to a branch, still firing at the pigs; bright red blood pumped from his leg. He dropped to the ground, weak but still able to cry. The nursing sows turned their attention to him, chewing on his thighs and working their way up to his beltline.

From their position above, the Rangers, Wink and Garl, watched the two men below repeatedly fire into the charging herd, then failing, become part of the food chain in the wild.

"Blanks," Wink said. Lights Out wagged her stubby tail.

"Should I put them out of their misery?" Zero asked.

"No," Wink replied. "They deserve this. Let the boar have his due." He turned and walked back to the road.

****

"Well, that's the last of it." Wink dumped the cold remnants of his coffee on the ground.

"It was interesting how you cut us out of the action, Mr. Decker," Zero stated flatly.

"I had Garl as back up. I made sure Garl had back up, too."

"What do you mean, back up to the back up?" Zero asked.

"Take those Army issue binoculars and focus on that clump of white trees across the valley."

Scout was the first to see Sam White Owl and his mother sitting by the birch. "What could she do from there?"

"Look up."

"Holy sh..What are those, Wink?"

"Golden Eagles and crows. Had Garl and me failed, Running Deer's birds would have made sure the balance was restored."

Garl picked up Lights Out and placed her on the front seat of Wink's truck. She started licking the steering wheel and then the back window.

"Give me a lift?" he asked. "My truck's just down a ways."

Cobalt saw there was a trickle of steam coming from the radiator. "Looks like you're still smoking, Wink."

"That's nothing. Should be cooled off by now." He removed the radiator cap with an old rag from his hip pocket. "Yeah, she's cooled off enough. Hand me that jug of fluid, Garl. Behind the seat." Wink unscrewed the cap and poured as he explained.

"You see, I had to have a reason to stop right here. In order to do that, I took just enough antifreeze out of the radiator so it would overheat in this area. Gave them a reason to get out of the truck and walk down the fork."

Wink stopped pouring and peered into the radiator neck. "That about enough, Garl?"

Garl took his turn peeking. "Maybe a tad more, Wink."

The outfitter continued to pour a little more and then capped the radiator.

"When they were here before, they was entirely different characters. More animal, savage like if you know'd what I mean. Maybe hopped up on drugs, but this time, one-eighty degree flip. There was something motivating them to be nice. Zebra can't change his stripes. You know'd what I mean?

"Other day I saw them come out of Gracie's diner. I have to admit it scared me a little. Time comes to man up. I lost my nerve last they was here but I was bound I wasn't going to lose it again. That's when I comenst to planning in case they called me.

"The fact that they wanted to hike and explore caves told me all I needed to know. That kind ain't nature lovers. I knew'd I'd have the opportunity to make things right. I had to get them down into the fork, then let nature take its course.

"They were what made Lights Out loose her leg. What was owed, has been paid."

****

Scout drove to the cabin. He glanced in the rear view mirror and saw Cobalt brooding, a dark look on his face.

"What's the matter, big guy? You're looking a little depressed."

"I was just thinking, ten years Ranger time, probably a couple million the government has invested in me. I've been around the world, in firefights, battled my way out of more tight situations than I care to think about. I come to a backwater village in West Virginia, while on vacation mind you, only to get bested by a couple of twelve year old kids and two old men with a three legged dog. Time to hang it up, gentlemen. I'm beginning to think my shit is weak."

The Church Basement

From the monitor, Mike watched Aunt Gem walk up his driveway. The death of Mrs. Perkins cast a painful shadow on the valley.

He went to the living room to meet her before she could knock on the door.

"Gem, I was just on my way to pick you up. You didn't have to walk all the way up here."

"I needed it. Being outside clears my head. Besides, I've been baking for three days, ever since I heard…well, you know, about Elsie." The name came across her lips almost like the whisper of a prayer.

Mike gave her a gentle hug. "I know. It's sad for everyone."

"We'll I guess we'd better get going. We can stop by my place and get over to the church with food in time to set everything up. Birdie and me will stay while everyone goes to the cemetery. Things'll be ready when they get back to eat."

"Oh, before I forget." She handed him a set of keys.

"What's this?"

"I thought it would be a good idea to check on the place if maybe I'm gone sometimes. Just in case."

"Yes. Okay. I just need to gather my jacket."

Without a word, Gem turned and walked toward Mike's truck. She didn't hear the buzzing of his equipment in the back room.

"Just a second, Gem. I'll be right there." He crossed the room and opened the door to his communications center. He hit the on button of his monitor. What came into view was the black BMW with New York plates parked at Cunningham's Bed and Breakfast.

"Welcome to the Hollar," he mumbled before switching off the screen.

****

Luke watched his friends walk down the church basement steps. The four of them wore dark suits purchased from the men's store in Waybird. Their shoes were highly polished and they all wore a high and tight cut from the barber shop.

"Let me introduce you to some of the folks. This is Cliffer and Florence Jennings."

"Mr. and Mrs. Jennings, we're happy to meet you."

"Sorry it is under these circumstances, boys. You know Luke from D.C.?"

"Yes, sir," Scout replied.

"So nice to meet you, gentlemen." Florence kissed Cliffer on the cheek. "If ya'll excuse me, I'm going to help Gracie and the ladies set things out."

"Guys, that's Aunt Gem behind the table. And in the kitchen, the lady with her hair in a bun, is Birdie Spry."

Diego nudged Zero and nodded. Luke noticed but didn't say anything.

"You all met John, Running Deer, Sam, and Spencer at the cook out, and this is Dodger Lemon. He's the head chef at Gracie's. He made the hot food for today."

Without thinking, the Diego extended his hand first. Looking at a button on Luke's shirt, Dodger reached out and gave each man down the line a firm handshake.

"We're glad to meet you, Mr. Lemon," Diego said. Dodger waved as he walked away.

"Luke, don't worry about us. Go on and help your dad."
****

Mike Green looked up to see Scout and Cobalt pull out chairs across the table as Zero and Diego took chairs on either side of him.

"So glad to see you again, Mike." Diego put his arm around Mike's shoulders and gave a squeeze.

"Get your arm off me, witcher *ved'mak*, or I shoot you in the face."

"Oh, Mikey. Don't be so cold. I know you're happy to see us." Scout adjusted his chair and smiled.

Zero put his arm around Mike and kissed him on the ear. "I know you still love us, Mikey."

"You I shoot in the face twice," he hissed. "And you, *glaza smerti*," he said to Cobalt, "I shoot in the face three times. Go look someone else with radioactive eyes."

"And me?" Scout asked.

"I won't shoot. You, I like."

"Mike," Scout whispered. "It's all taken care of."

"You got them?"

"Well, sort of. I'll tell you later, but our buddies from the 'Stan were an early breakfast so to speak."

"You mean 'had' early breakfast?"

"No, I mean 'were' an early breakfast." Scout looked away snickering.

Gracie stopped by the table to deposit a basket of dinner rolls and a dish of butter. "Nice to see you socializing, Mike."

Mike patted Diego on the head. "Yes, like old friends."

****

Waiting in line for the buffet, Zero whispered to Mike, "I heard you tell Luke there were two down and two more to go."

"What? You have radio telescope for ears? Actually," Mike replied while looking at the dessert table Birdie Spry laid out, "there are three. But you kids don't worry about it. This will take a real man to finish."

****

Scout and Cobalt stayed at the table. "Something tells me we had better tag along and look after old boy if he is on to something." Cobalt suggested.

"Already on it, bro. Zero got two on his truck and Diego planted two others on his shirt."

"What if he washes his shirt?"

"Are you kidding? You saw him when we picked him up in the 'Stan. He's at least a three-day shirt guy."

"Agreed."

"I have an idea the black BMW plays a role in Mikey's evasiveness. Doesn't look like he's done much physical fitness while he's been here, so maybe we can help him out. Hate for him to strain his trigger finger shooting someone in the face."

****

Howard returned from the church yard after the last guests were gone.

"I'm so sorry," Mike said to Howard and hugged him.

"Thanks, Mike." Changing the subject was a safe move for Howard. "Every time I come home, Tater tells me how he's been to your place. He says you're helping him and Fishbone get their master spy buttons."

"And certificates, Howard. It isn't official without the certificate." They all smiled.

"And thanks for keeping an eye on them."

"My pleasure, Howard. They're good boys."

Mr. Perkins thanked Luke's friends after which he said, "Please excuse me, I'm going to pick up my daughter before she becomes a nuisance to Amelia." Howard steadied himself with the railing when he went up the stairs.

It was Luke who spoke first. "Thanks for everything, guys. It's been a tough few days."

"Brothers take care of brothers. You know that, Luke."

"I know." He wiped his eyes and cleared his throat before he could look at his friends. "Mike told me there were two more."

"Yes," Scout said. "In a black BMW. I've got recordings of the conversation between them and with the late Smith and Jones. With Jose Garza's crew out of the way, it looks like the ones from New York, Dervishi and Marku, were going to take over. I gather they plan to use the surrounding area for hiding and transporting the children."

"I wonder how Mike knows them," Luke said.

"Maybe we can arrange a reunion? Those two old geezers cheated us out of paybacks," Zero added.

"What old geezers?" Luke was surprised.

"Wink and Garl plotted an ambush this morning. I was impressed," Cobalt said. "Anything left to eat?"

"No. Gem and her posse of old ladies cleaned the place up. Church mouse couldn't find a crum. Let's go to Amelia's tea room," Luke suggested. "I'd like to know what I missed."

"Bro, I don't want tea and cookies. I want some man food." Cobalt rubbed his stomach.

"She's got a room in the back just for the locals. Dr. Glassman, Sheriff Bill, and some of the chosen go there on Saturday nights for dinner and poker. Amelia cooks steaks and fries for them. And yes, before you ask, she's got Leadslingers Napalm. Gracie told her what you like for refreshments." Luke started to smile for the first time in three days.

Diego threw his arms over the shoulders of Zero on one side and Luke on the other. "Poker, you say? Onward, boys, I'm feeling lucky tonight!"

RETRIBUTION

"Watch out," shouted Dervishi.

Marku slammed on the brakes of the BMW. A figure appeared in the glow of the high beams.

"What the hell is that?"

Marku's hands were shaking as he brought the window down. "Hey, get out of the road, *handikapat.*"

Dervishi got out of the car.

"You wanna a new *budallage* on your ass? Get out of the road."

"Boys, don't you recognize me, *vëllezërit?* From old days?"

"Mikhail? Is that you?"

"Yes, is me, *dobro pozhalovat.* I hear you in neighborhood. I want see you, maybe talk over old times. Please, on low beams. Is hurting my eyes."

Dervishi started stammering. "Mikhail, old f-f-friend. W-we can let b-by-gones be bygones, eh? *Dakord?*"

"No, I don't agree. Marku, step out of car, please." Mikhail Ivanovich Verkhovensky waved his weapon at the men.

"Can you imagine my surprise when I see you in New York City? And Mr. Ramadani? How is he? Well, I hope."

"He is well, Mikhail. Have you seen Father Lev Nikolayvich?"

"Yes, yes I did. But he left go back to Russia. Too hot in US."

Mikhail moved just out of the head lights and into the shadows at the shoulder of the road where the chance of his being shot was reduced.

"Ramadani will be disappointed you hold a gun on us."

"But what if he don't know, eh? Is okay. Eh? *Da?*"

Devishi took several deep breaths. "Mikhail, I think we can reach agreement. Times have changed. We all grow older and wiser. Maybe we can break bread, drink *raki,* come to an agreement. There is much money to be made, Mikhail. We can be associates. Business is business. We be brothers, yes?"

"Nyet. Nyet. Last business not so good for me. For my sister."

"We didn't know. How could we know, Mikhail?" Marku waved his right arm and tried to draw his gun with his left.

The distraction didn't work. Mikhail pulled the trigger of his Glock. Marku was dead before he hit the ground.

"Just you and me, Mikhail. We can split 50-50. I know Ramadani will welcome you."

"You delivered my sister to me." Mikhail's emotions were ice. "You delivered her for killing."

"And you killed her. You killed your own sister. If you would have pulled the hood off you would have seen. You're guilty, too, Mikhail."

Dervishi heard movement in the brush; he lowered the knife from his arm holster into his hand.

"But that is past. I didn't know she was your sister, Mikhail. I didn't know. Ramadani did, but I didn't. Of everything I've told you, this one thing is the truth. Maybe the only truth."

Dervishi felt a whoosh of air around his head and ducked. He spun, stabbed widely, slashing back and forth in the dark.

Mikhail was too close, taking the blade tip to his liver. He was bleeding bright red but he knew the dark organ blood would follow. He had to move quickly before he couldn't move at all. He fired.

The bullet enters Dervishi's pelvis, shattering his bladder and blowing through his sacrococcygeal joint. Dervishi falls to the ground in agony.

Mikhail deftly cuts the wrist tendons of the moaning Dervishi. Mikhail gasps for air, his hand instinctively moving to his side. Dark liver blood now, death to follow.

Mikhail tries placing a small gray block of C-4 under the car but it is too painful to bend.

"What the hell, *suka.*" He tosses it in the car.

Climbing up the hill takes its toll on Mikhail. The rise in elevation above his ambush makes him weaker and weaker as he claws his way up and away from the road.

Mikhail presses a small button, triggering the arming device on the explosive.

"Do svidaniya, blayd suki."

With the car in flames, Mikhail Ivanovich Verkhovensky collapses on the ground.

****

The sound of the cruiser's siren pierced the quiet of the bed and breakfast. It's red and blue lights flashed against the walls. Scout rolled out of the bed, promising to never drink again. The wha-wha of the siren bounced around his brain, exploding behind his eyes. Cobalt stepped out of the bathroom, still brushing his teeth.

"Sleeping Beauty, fire up your computer and find out where Sheriff Billy is going in such a hurry. And, see where Mikey landed last night after he left Amelia's."

"I think I'm gonna puke."

"Suck it down. Get the eye in the sky going, then you can puke."

"I should have bunked with Diego."

"Diego would have cut you off on the second bottle. I am your true friend because I let you drink to your heart's content." He crossed the room and patted Scout on the head. "Who's your Daddy?"

Scout's punch missed Cobalt's knee. "Now, now, let's not get crabby or I'll call the boys next door."

Zero burst in the room.

"Bros, we need to do some recon. Mikey must have held a barbeque last night without us. Sheriff Bill is on his way to a burned out car. Scout, dude, you look like hell." Zero patted Scout's head and dodged a wide swing from the communications sergeant.

"Sheesh, he's cranky like a little girl. Here, bro. Take my coffee."

Scout sat at the desk and slurped the coffee. "I've got Mike's truck on the ridge above the car and there's a heat signal about sixty-five meters directly below it. I'd say Mikey had a night out."

"Mount up. We need to get to Mike before Sheriff Billy starts looking around the woods."

****

"You'll have a sharp turn just over this rise, Zero. Hairpin to the left, then 400 meters and hairpin to the right. There's another sharp turn to the left. Mike's truck should be just over the second rise above where the sheriff is."

Diego checked his medical bag. "Anyone know his blood type?"

"No," Cobalt said. "I never got that personal with him."

"Here," Scout pointed, "his truck. We'll have to go on foot."

"Where's Sheriff Harris?"

"Still down the hillside on the other part of the road. Sound will carry so we need to Charlie Cobra through the weeds."

Zero saw it first, the pale blue mist hanging in the air around the base of the pine tree. "He's over there. He has to be. Same as Cobalt."

The men paused, not sure how to advance without Luke's advice.

"You go, Cobalt, I think it likes you."

"How do you know that?"

"It took a bullet out of you that's how."

"Yeah, but maybe it's hungry this time."

They heard a moan coming from the mist.

"Hell with it. Let's go," Cobalt instructed. The mist receded on their advance, revealing Mike Green between the thick exposed roots of the massive pine tree.

Diego saw the wound first. He unzipped his RATS pack and grabbed bandages without looking.

Zero disappeared down the slope, backtracking Mike's route from the night before. It lead directly to the burned out car.

"Mikey. Wake up, man. Someone put a hole in your liver." Diego handed Scout a thick pad of bandage, then slapped Mike's face.

"Ah, devil *vad'mak*. Come kill me."

"He's got a massive clot over the wound," Diego observed. "Must have some great Russian platelets in his blood. I don't want to dislodge that when we move him, so I'm going to bandage him tight. Scout, put the pad here and hold it. Let's make him an Israeli citizen with this bandage." Diego swiftly applied the dressing. "Hope you like falafel, Mikey."

"Get him as ready as you can, Doc," Cobalt said, "before Sheriff Billy finds a blood trail and makes his way here."

"He won't," Zero whispered.

Cobalt rolled Mike toward his knees as Diego wrapped a tight dressing over the blood clot and around Mike's torso. Zero placed the assembled semi-rigid stretcher under the unconscious man. The four Rangers carried Mike up the hill as gently as they could. They slid the stretcher into the back of the Excursion.

"Where to, Doc?"

"Get him to Glassman's place. I don't know how long this clot will hold. Andy is the best one to look at it. Let me get an IV line started. Zero, grab a bag of fluids from my RATS."

"When you're ready," Cobalt said, "I'm going to give you a little push so the sheriff doesn't hear the truck start."

"What about Mike's truck? We have to come up with a story."

"You guys head to the clinic. I'll drive Mike's truck. We were out hiking and he fell off a cliff. Tree branch stabbed him. Sounds good?"

"Not really," Scout said, "but it'll have to fly."

****

Mike opened his eyes to see Cobalt reading a book at his bedside.

"Russians are noisy. Even your eyelids are loud, so I know you're awake."

"*Suka*. Leave me before I shoot you in face."

"I can't, bro. My turn to watch you."

"I not your bro. Leave, *suka*."

Cobalt held out his arm.

"What that is?"

"It's the gauze Glassman used when he transfused my blood into you, *bro*."

"Death in Lubyanka be better."

"Fat chance. Now," Cobalt put his book down, "what were you doing out there and who were those two chard bodies Sheriff Billy found in the car?"

"What car?"

"The burned car."

"Know nothing burn car, *suka. Blayt*."

"I think you do."

"*Nyet.* Smoking accident. Go away. Sleep now."

****

"How's our boy?" Luke looked in at Mike and Cobalt.

"Stubborn as ever. Don't let anyone in to see him. His American accent slips when he's under stress. He called me *suka* again."

"Must be a term of endearment."

"No, it's not. Trust me on that."

"How did he take the information you and him are now related?" Luke smiled.

"Not as well as expected. I'm family now, so he'll have to stop threatening to shoot me in the face."

"Get any information?"

"He mumbled a name. Ramadani. And a present for you in Lubyanka."

Deacon's Hollar

"Bill, get out of the office."

"Donald, there's paperwork to get caught up on...and..."

"I've got it all under control. Coop and a friend of Luke's will be here in a few minutes."

"For what?"

"For you to take them fishing for brook trout. Spencer and Sam'll be waiting at the public access with Ubell. Gracie packed a lunch and she said I was to kick you out or she will. Besides," Deputy Johnson continued, "you can't get paid unless you're in uniform. That's your rule, Bill."

The honk of a vehicle sounded from the parking lot.

"I told you. They're waiting. You teach Zero he doesn't need grenades to fish."

****

"How about we go for an early dinner? Maybe catch a movie?"

Janice Streeter looked up to see Luke leaning over her desk. "I'd love to but the Deputy has so much going on right now and I'm up to my ears in status reports and personnel..."

"Mad because I didn't bring the nesting dolls from Moscow?"

"Of course not. You'll make another trip. I'll take the rain check for the dolls." She returned his smile. "I want to tell you how sorry I was to hear about your mom."

Luke gazed at the sun pouring in the office window. It would be the excuse he needed if she saw tears in his eyes. "Thank you. I appreciated the flowers you sent. My mom loved spring flowers."

"I suppose your friends back home are a big help."

"Yes, they are."

From the deputy's office, they heard the Director roar like a lion.

"Janice, we're going," Luke insisted. He came around her desk, reached into the drawer and retrieved her purse.

"Wha...what?" Janice stammered.

"We're going *now*." Luke gripped her elbow with more strength than he intended and steered Janice out of the office.

"Luke, the elevators are back there."

"Service elevator. Trust me."

As Luke and Janice drove away, a caravan of US Marshals' vehicles surrounded the front and back of the building.

"You have something you want to tell me, Luke?"

"Over drinks and a steak?"

"Sounds fair enough."

****

Mr. Ramadani buzzed for his limo. The Russians were not happy about the lost men, product, or the exposure, but things might work out for the best with the Nordic blondes filling the order of Dubai. He was free to see his mistress; he needed Angelina to put him in a better mood.

The limo was at the curb. A security guard hopped out of the back and held the door.

"Where is the regular man?"

"I'm sorry the agency didn't notify you about the change, sir."

"They'll hear about this. Take me to my apartment, 212 Fifth Ave."

"Yes, sir."

Ramadani looked up and saw a stranger return his gaze in the rearview mirror. "You're not my driver."

"Just today, sir. Sit back and enjoy the ride," Scout responded.

Diego jabbed the Albanian mob leader in the leg with a syringe. Ramadani didn't put up much of a fight before he succumbed to the drugs.

"How is he?"

After checking Ramadani's pulse Diego said, "He's fine. Luke told INTERPOL it'd be about an hour."

"Should be. Traffic's light."

"We can keep the limo until Tuesday. Wanna go to Boston and visit my dad? He'll be impressed."

****

Alice Cobb places glass quart jars on the cement footings where the headstones will sit. She fluffs the flowers, moving the tall ones in the center and the smaller ones around the edges. At Aunt Mae's grave, she digs out the old earth from the urn and replaces it with new potting soil. Hector steadies a flat of periwinkle, petunias, and ornamental grasses on his knee, squatting beside her.

"Will this be enough for all of them?"

"I think so. When the headstones and little urns arrive, I'll get new ones for the babies."

"Maybe let's put some over on Elsie's grave?"

"That would be nice, Uncle Hector."

"Do you think Mae would approve burying the little ones on the family plot?"

"Yes. It's the right thing to do. They'll be taken care of here."

"Well, for at least as long as I'm around, sweetie. You get your education and get up out of here. Find some guy who'll be head over heels in love with you."

"Uncle Hector, I'm not leaving."

"Well, if that's the case, you can bring your boyfriend around but not if he wears the same size shirt I do or if he don't like dogs. Period."

****

Gracie hit the enter on her laptop. Peeking through one eye at the total, she let out a sigh of relief. "Profits are up third month in a row." She bowed her head and said a silent prayer. She noticed a work application under the receipts. The handwriting was steady and precise, the work history included experience she needed, and above all, the application was honest. She dialed Sykes Grocery.

"Ambrie, Gracie here. Our prayers have been answered. I've got Ivan Becker's job application in front of me. He's back. Bill will be so pleased."

****

John Seven Star drives Aunt Gem to the Perkins farm. He watches her carry her satchel to the house.

Howard greets her on the front porch.

Howard she says.

Aunt Gem he says.

We have children to raise.

Yes, Gem, we do. He waves to John as he holds the door for Gem.

John adjusts the side mirror before he leaves the drive. His foster daughter sits quietly beside him.

****

Birdie Spry closes her eyes and listens to the songs of the birds. They bring such joy to her heart with their chatter. She takes a sip of hot mint tea as she rocks on the porch. The bucket is still attached to her tractor. Her chickens scratch and dig at the fresh earth, eating bugs and grubs from the two new flower beds. "Don't you girls dig too far down. We don't want anything to show." She throws back her head and cackles.

****

Welcome back. Haven't seen you for a while.

The client with black hair and violet eyes sits in the chair handing the artist a photo.

This, here. The client points to a place on his chest.

He sets his inks in order then pulls on his gloves. Pretty little thing. What's her name?

Her name? Viking Princess.

****

"Mr. Garza. I'm going to release you to your own recognizance based on the information you provided the Sheriff on another case. So, Mr. Garza, you do get the benefit of the deal. However, you are to stay within the county. If you need to leave, you must have permission from the court. Do you understand?"

"Yes, your Honorship. I'll stay right here until I hear from the court."

"Good. You can collect your things from the deputy. I have ordered the red car be given back to you as it is registered to you but, the truck without VIN numbers will stay impounded. I repeat that you are not to leave the county."

"Yes, sir."

When Jose started the car, he had half a tank of gas. He felt for the envelope trapped in the springs of the passenger seat. The money was still there. He was sure it was enough to get to Miami.

As he drove onto the entrance ramp of the 219, Jose jerked on the steering wheel to avoid hitting the white dogs. He lost control. The car bounced up and then turned over, propelling Jose under the wheels of a semi trailer loaded with steel headed to Iowa.

****

Amelia welcomes Cliffer Jennings into her tea room. Ah, you have company today, Cliffer.

Florence is shopping for my little buddy. We're fostering until things get settled. He likes the name Stevie. He doesn't talk yet but we know when he's happy. He'll clap his little hands and wiggle his toes.

Okay, Cliffer and Stevie, follow me. I've a special booth for the gentlemen.

She delivers milk and a sugar cookie to Stevie. He smiles, claps his hands, and wiggles his toes.

****

Agnes Crawford hesitantly taps on Running Deer's front door.

Hello, Agnes. Come in. What can I do for you?

Agnes shows Running Deer the contents of a small bag. She tells Running Deer that Jackson Latcher wants to take her and Fishbone to the fair in Waybird. She's forgotten what the little jars of makeup are for. The women spend the afternoon drinking herbal teas and making notes for Agnes to follow.

****

Esin stands between Tobias and Nathan in the children's choir on Sunday morning. Mr. Cobb and Alice will take her to the airport for her flight on Tuesday to California. Through her new Afghan parents she will become a US citizen. Fish and Tater turn to smile at her, their Master Spy buttons pinned to their robe collars.

****

On the screen of his computer, Mike Green watches the news flash from *WVKNTV-9*:

"This is Aleta Butters reporting from Washington, D.C. Just shortly after four p.m. yesterday, the Channel 9 team learned an unnamed deputy director of the CIA was arrested and charged with human trafficking. At the same time, US Marshals raided several offices on Capital Hill, the Department of the Treasury, the DOJ, and offices on Wall Street. Confidential sources told this reporter there will be more arrests in the coming days.

"This is just in. Breaking news.

"I'm getting information that similar arrests are being conducted in Paris, Athens, Budapest, and Kyiv. I will keep you updated as factual information is provided. This is Aleta Butters reporting from Washington for WVKNTV-9."

"So, Chaw Bacon, *Spacibo*."

Mike changes the dressing. The wound is much smaller and no longer seeping. The buzzing of his phone starts as he places the last length of paper tape on his skin.

"What?" he says.

"It's done, Mike."

"Yes, is done, Chaw Bacon. You at restaurant? I hear sounds."

"Yes. I'm taking a friend to breakfast."

"Is pretty?"

"Yes."

"Then marry and have lots of babies."

"I just might do that. Mike, I want to thank you for the Katya files. We couldn't have done this without you."

"Katya files. Is what you call?"

"Yes. She was your sister, right?"

"Yes. Deserved better. But can not change past. Now get off phone. Go kiss pretty girl." He hangs up.

Mike removes the drape from the canvas. A beautiful face stares back at him. Her image overwhelms him with memories of playing in the sun by the water, dancing in the waves.

"I'm sorry, Katya. But now we find peace. *Da*."

Resources

Special thanks to:

Aristotle. *Nicomachean Ethics.*

The Barma's Last Dance. Memoir of Barbara G. Van Niman

Bloodhounds: Rip, Dotty, Penni, and a cast of thousands.

The Battle for West Virginia: A Case for Triple Treason.

https://wvforgottenfolklore.com/2019/11/26/

G.H.O.S.T Certified Program.

https://www.gcsomichigan.com/ghostcertified

Goldman, George. Hog Hunting in Louisiana.

Phone conversation notes for research of hunting wild boar with dogs. 1/24/21.

Hemingway, Ernst.

On the Blue Water. First Sports Reader. Esquire. April 1936.

International Centre for Missing and Exploited Children. +1 703-837-6313

Internet open sources for military equipment, character development, and general stuff I never knew about.

Leadslingers Napalm Cinnamon Whiskey.

https://leadslingerswhiskey.com/

National Center for Missing and Exploited Children. 1-800-THE LOST (1-800-843-5678)

National Sexual Assault Hotline 1-800-656-HOPE (4673)

O.U.T. Operation Underground Trafficking.

https://www.ourrescue.org?

PerSys Medical. Israeli Bandage references.

https://persysmedical.com/products/hemorrhage-control/

RATS PACK (Rapid Access Trauma System)

https://www.mysteryranch.com/rats-pack

Sergie Labakow

Moscow, for assistance with language, customs, and the development of Mikhail Ivanovich.

Shakespeare, William.

The Tradgey of Richard III. The Hamlyn Publishing Group Limited. 1970

Snow Dogs: The Tuna, The Irris, The Berger

Tammy M. Lons, DVM.

Medical clarification and terminology.

Big Pie.

That guy in Odesa, Ukraine who helped with translations and refuses to read my books.

Washington Elementary School teachers who taught me how to write my name, and Mrs. Lori who taught me to love writing.

West Virginia Department of Natural Resources. W. Va R. §58-52-3

Note: It is illegal to use dogs to hunt hogs in West Virginia. This is, after all, a work of fiction.

Cover image licensed under iStock.com